Legacy

Sometimes good intentions aren't enough

Jim Napier

"If you like Dalgleish, you'll love Inspector Colin McDermott, an unflappable, stoic Brit with a warm heart and a professional's eye. Napier's London is 21st-century cosmopolitan, while his St. Gregory's College is an amiable throwback to the cloistered world of eccentric—and perhaps deadly—academics. Rich, textured, atmospheric writing with sensitively rendered three-dimensional characters that keep you turning the pages. The writing is first rate."

Eric Brown, author of the Arthur Ellis Award finalist *Almost Criminal*

● ● ●

"Very well written, the English setting and the characters utterly believable. Colin McDermott is a most attractive character, the kind of man you always want to know."

Maureen Jennings, award-winning author of *The Murdoch Mysteries* and originator of *Bomb Girls*, both filmed for television

● ● ●

"Addictive reading. The story draws you in and keeps you hooked till the ending you never saw coming. Set in the dysfunctional halls of British academia, Napier nails it with a great story [and] wonderfully compelling characters that stay with you long after the book is finished."

Peter Kirby, winner of the Arthur Ellis Award for Best Novel of 2016 for *Open Season*

● ● ●

A COLIN MCDERMOTT MYSTERY

Theresa,
I hope you enjoy reading it as much as I did writing it!

Legacy

Sometimes good intentions aren't enough

Best,

Jim Napier

Jim Napier

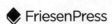 FriesenPress

Suite 300 - 990 Fort St
Victoria, BC, V8V 3K2
Canada

www.friesenpress.com

ISBN
978-1-4602-9975-3 (Hardcover)
978-1-4602-9976-0 (Paperback)
978-1-4602-9977-7 (eBook)

1. FICTION, CRIME

Distributed to the trade by The Ingram Book Company

Dedication

For the women in my life, Kathryn and Meredith,
and Roya, who made it happen;
and for Sam and Jill, the future.

"Every new beginning comes from some other beginning's end."
—Seneca

"Be careful what you wish for."
—Unknown

Prologue

A t the base of a cliff overlooking the North Sea a young girl with curly flaxen hair strolled with an older woman on the coarse shingle. The day was unusually fair save for a bit of wind, and overhead the gulls circled endlessly, creating a raucous din and keeping an eye out for anything resembling food. While the woman walked at a steady pace, watching her footing on the uneven rocks, her young charge ran ahead of her, darting to either side as something caught her eye. Heedless of the stones beneath her feet, occasionally the youngster would fall, sometimes scraping her knees; but she always got up laughing, already looking around for the next object to catch her attention.

The salt air prompted the elderly woman to think about lunch—they'd already been walking for nearly two hours—when she heard her granddaughter cry out excitedly: she'd found something unexpected. She ran back, brandishing what seemed from a distance to be a battleaxe. As she got closer it appeared to be a bone, large by the standards of flotsam and jetsam that usually littered the beach. The girl held it up to the woman's face, proud of her find.

'Look at this, Nana! Have you ever seen such a large bone?'

Her grandmother was forced to admit she had not. The object was perhaps two feet long by several inches wide, though at one end it broadened out into a slightly rounded and much thinner, almost knife-edged shape. Perhaps a shoulder bone, she thought, but not from a human. Far too large for that, and it was an off-white, pinkish colour, not yet bleached by the sun.

'What do you think it is?'

The woman considered the question. 'I'm sure I don't know, Sally. I don't think it's from a large fish, or even a seal. Maybe it belongs to a whale, although I think it would have to be a very young one.'

'A whale?' The girl was nearly beside herself with excitement. They'd walked on the beach many times before, but she'd never encountered anything so exciting as this. 'Can we take it somewhere to find out for certain?'

'Why not?' She smiled, realizing the discovery would make her granddaughter's day, and possibly her entire visit.

They turned back with their newfound treasure, and before long they were picking their way along the footpath that led back toward Whitby. When they breeched the hill they looked down on the twin arms of the harbor quay, which sheltered a small, sandy beach and the inlet to the river Esk, which provided access for what nowadays were mostly lobster and crab boats and small pleasure craft. The town had moved on from its maritime roots some decades ago: the economy now rested on several industries year-round, and tourism during the summer months. Fishing was still a part of it, but growing less important with every year.

They left the footpath for the paved walkway next to the river, and before long they saw a fisherman sorting his gear after returning to the port. They stopped and showed him the bone, but he'd had no idea what it was, and to Sally's dismay, seemed uninterested as well. He suggested they visit the local maritime museum nearby. This they did, but the curator there was a part-time volunteer, and was of little help. The girl was crestfallen. Her gran suggested she return home with it and take it to school one day. As she walked away toward the door the curator smiled. 'She's a bright one, isn't she? And so curious. A lovely child.'

That was how it always was. Everyone who saw her remarked on how happy she always seemed. So joyous, so full of life, and so open to the world around her.

WHEN SHE WAS FIFTEEN her gran had died suddenly. A stroke, they'd said. It hadn't helped that it was on Sally's birthday.

After finishing primary school Sally's grandmother had paid for her to attend a prestigious boarding school where her talents could be given full flight. At first it had gone well, the teachers, the resources, and the activities available slaking her thirst for knowledge. But in the year following her gran's death Sally's marks had slipped dramatically, and she was on the cusp of leaving school altogether. There was nothing for her there. Not any longer.

Now she stood silently on the cliffs above the sea, taking it all in. There was a chill wind, and except for a stray dog exploring the surf, she had the scene all to herself. *So many memories,* she realised. *And yet, not nearly enough.* Her eyes glistened. She had become a different person, more melancholy, more troubled. The shrill call of a gull in the sky above shook her from her thoughts and she glanced at her watch, unaware till then that she'd been standing there for the best part of an hour. Slowly she turned and picked her way along the footpath toward town, knowing that this might be the last time she saw this place. But she knew the memories would remain with her always.

The good ones and the bad ones.

ONE

T he city was packed with young people determined to extract a last bit of pleasure before returning to the tedium of another year of studies. At a bus queue midway along High Holborn, among the usual assortment of tourists, shoppers and office workers on their lunch breaks a trio of Japanese girls giggled nervously in response to a group of young Italians nearby who were openly flirting with them. A few older people watched with amusement.

At the corner a young, well-dressed young woman turned confidently into the street. She glanced back at traffic, squinting in the bright sunlight to identify a bus approaching in the distance. A number seventeen. Not going her way. Looking the other way she noticed the sidewalk was blocked with scaffolding and construction fencing; she would have to go around it. She stepped off the kerb between two parked lorries and waited for the bus to pass. She was already engrossed in her thoughts again as it approached, so that she was totally unprepared for what followed.

As the bus drew nearer she suddenly stumbled and went sprawling into the street, followed by horrified screams as the heavy vehicle passed over her body, not once, but twice, the driver struggling to bring it to a halt. The crowd surged forward, looking to see if there was anything they could do, but there could be little doubt: the woman was dead.

A few days earlier

JANE SHORT GLANCED ANXIOUSLY at the clock on the kitchen wall. Nearly ten to eight; in fifteen minutes—twenty at most—she would have to leave for work. She called to her son. She knew from long experience that if she didn't prod him Simon would merely grab a piece of toast, or skip breakfast altogether. Jane was a firm believer in starting the day on a full breakfast.

At the end of the narrow hallway, in the larger of the two bedrooms, Simon listened to his mother making noises in the kitchen and decided that the lesser of the evils was to get out of bed. He swung his feet from underneath the covers and winced as they encountered the chill of the floor. Despite (or perhaps because of) the fact that their flat had been erected in the seventies it was poorly insulated and let in the damp. Simon rummaged amongst the sheets at the bottom of his bed and produced a pair of socks, which he pulled on more from habit than conscious intent. He surveyed the room looking for clothes, letting his eyes decide for him, then reached for a pair of jeans that looked reasonably clean, and pulled them on over the y-fronts he had slept in. He was still not yet fully awake, and he rubbed his eyes with the palms of his hands, yawning as he did so. He fumbled on the nightstand for his glasses, and gave them a perfunctory wipe on his pillowcase. Glancing out the window between two grey tower blocks he saw a small sliver of a sky that was equally grey and comfortless, and a large shopping precinct in the distance. Simon rummaged through a drawer for a tee shirt, selecting one in black with the caption *Charlie Chaplin is alive and well and living in Argentina.* Above it was a likeness of the little tramp from the back, wearing a sombrero. He pulled it over his head and looked for something heavier to wear over it, and picked up a crumpled grey hoodie from the floor, where it had fallen off the doorknob. He ran his fingers through his slightly greasy hair and stuck his feet into a pair of trainers that had originally been white, but had long since taken on an indefinite shade of grunge; then, without lacing them up, he made his way down the dark hallway and into the kitchen.

His mother looked up from the cooker. 'Morning, dear. I didn't hear you come in last night. Were you very late?'

It was a lie, and he knew it; part of a ritual they went through almost daily. She had known when he had come home, probably to the minute. She had lain awake for hours waiting, and when he finally had returned she had been too tired to ask him where he had been or what he had been doing, simply grateful that he had returned. Instead, she had looked at the clock by her bedside, noted the time, and promised herself to enquire casually the next morning, as she was doing now.

Simon opened the fridge and extracted an open carton of milk from which he drank directly. 'No, not late.'

That, too, had been a lie. He knew that it had been well after midnight when he'd returned home, a consequence of having miscalculated how much change he had on him, and, finding himself short for the underground fare, having to walk part of the way. It didn't matter that it was a lie, because he didn't expect her to believe him, no more than his mother expected him to tell her the truth.

'How about a nice egg, dear, and some brown toast? There's some juice left as well.'

Simon raised the plastic milk jug to his mouth a second time and drained its contents. 'This'll do, thanks. I'm off into town. They're showing some classics at the Film Institute.'

His mother put on a patient face. 'That's nice, dear. But shouldn't you be getting ready for the start of term? What is it—two days away?'

'Don't always be on at me!' he snarled, then put a brake on his belliger-ence. 'Anyway, I need some dosh. Got a twenty?'

She looked at him guiltily. 'I haven't had a chance to get to a cash machine, dear. I can let you have a ten.' She reached for her purse and extracted a single note.

'Can't get far on that,' he said, taking the money anyway. 'Got to run.' He set the milk jug on the counter and closed the door behind him.

TWENTY MINUTES LATER Simon boarded the District Line at Chiswick Park, heading for the Embankment. The carriage was already half full when he got on, and by the time it had passed through Stamford Brook it was jammed with office workers and shoppers planning to make a day of it in London. At the next station a trio of scruffy, unshaven youths boarded, sporting numerous tattoos, studs, and attitude, elbowing their way through the already-crowded car before positioning themselves near Simon, where they proceeded to focus on two girls who were clearly flustered at their attention, and an elderly man, who was not. When they tired of this one of them noticed Simon and, sensing his vulnerability, singled him out.

Simon had never been particularly fond of his given name. At school, when the other boys learned he was not very good at his sums, he became known as Simple Simon; and later, when adolescence brought with it a severe case of acne, that had changed to Spotty Simon. Never robust, his response was to turn inward, shutting out what he didn't want to see or hear. Now, at nineteen, and still bearing the blemishes of acne, Simon Short was still Spotty to those who knew him from his younger days. He had few interests and no close friends; when he was not studying film history at St. Gregory's College, London, he was playing computer games or surfing fantasy websites on his computer. Occasionally he would summon up the courage to ask a young woman out for a drink or to the cinema; but Simon had few social skills, and even those who took pity on him seldom accepted twice. He endured the taunts of the youths, hotly aware that everyone's eyes were on him, and bristling that he was powerless to do anything about it. When they got off before his stop he drew a sigh of relief.

At the Embankment the crowd fanned out, and Simon moved with them. In two days' time he would transfer directly to the Northern Line, which would take him to Goodge Street, almost to the door of St. Gregory's. But today, still seething at his bullying at the hands of the yobboes, Simon walked toward Charing Cross and entered the newsstand at the station, where he looked over the stock of recent magazines to the obvious disdain of the sales clerk. He soon tired of this and took the stairs toward Trafalgar Square. On a Saturday, even at nine in the morning, it was already jammed with tourists, so Simon doubled back to St. Martin's Church, where a handful of enterprising vendors had begun setting up stalls to display their wares. Simon wandered amongst them, smiling at the stallkeepers and chatting up the younger female ones, until the sky opened up and he was forced to seek shelter. Not one for religion, Simon bypassed the main entrance to the church and instead made for the side entrance to the crypt, which he knew concealed a café where he would be left alone. He spent some change on some tea and biscuits, and waited out the rain.

When the downpour had eased off Simon took the tube to the South Bank, spending the remainder of the morning and most of the afternoon watching vintage films from the silent era. Most he'd seen before, but it didn't matter; Simon was in his own little world, and for a brief time, he was happy. That evening his mother came home to find that Simon had hoovered the carpets and straightened things up. She fixed them each a pair of pork cutlets, complete with roast potatoes and snap beans, and they ate their meal in a companionable silence. It had been, by their standards, a mostly good day.

TWO

In the staid atmosphere of Bloomsbury as the holidays ended the population of the area shifted from tourists and academic researchers in sports jackets and corduroy trousers to undergraduates wearing tee shirts over jeans, and carrying rucksacks stuffed with mobile phones, laptops and electronic tablets. St. Gregory's College was taking on new life as once more students flooded the hallways and stairwells and moved their belongings into their new rooms.

St. Gregory's was the most junior college of the University of London, being established in the early nineteen-sixties in anticipation of the coming baby boom. It was the result of a generous bequest by one of the nation's industrial magnates who had prospered as a result of the Second World War, and who, being without family, sought to enshrine his achievements in a manner that could be suitably admired by a grateful public. As a gesture, it was grand indeed. The developer, Sir Gregory Pickersgill — for he had subsequently been knighted for his largesse —had managed to acquire a parcel of land uncommonly large by London standards. This had enabled him to give relatively free rein to his architects, fettered only by the Greater London Council, who in a temporary fit of sanity proved to be receptive to new—or rather, to old—ideas.

The result was a design worthy of the scale of the project: a new, self-contained college in the heart of London. Resisting the concrete-and-steel functionality that characterised Pickersgill's commercial projects, St. Gregory's was designed in the Oxbridge manner, and constructed of light grey stonework in a Neo-Gothic style that glowed pink in the sunset. It was composed of two quadrangles, the second of which consisted of a large grassy area that was lightly landscaped, and during clement weather it was indeed an oasis of relative calm and quiet in the midst of London, whose pastoral attraction was only slightly marred by the imposing larger-than-life bronze statue of Sir Gregory that had been installed, at his insistence, in the centre. The benefactor had initially proposed that this newest addition to British higher education be named Pickersgill College, but his plans were thwarted when, to his considerable annoyance, it was learned that an obscure school of mining technology in North Wales had usurped that privilege some decades earlier. The choice of his canonical namesake had proved to be an agreeable compromise, with its suggestion, however oblique, that Sir Gregory himself had been canonised. Among the devout there was some speculation that this might indeed be true, the developer having been called to his Maker shortly before the project was completed. The more cynical suggested that the developer had finally been held accountable by his Maker for the sin of Pride.

IT WAS THE DAY BEFORE classes commenced, and the Senior Common Room stirred to life as faculty members reluctantly returned to their duties. In the normal course of events the room was almost exclusively inhabited by men. In earlier years the Principal had contrived to swell the ranks of women faculty members to the impressive level of two; but of those only one remained.

This morning the only occupant of the SCR was in fact its sole female teaching member. For an academic she was well turned out, wearing a cream-coloured blouse and a flattering wool suit in muted shades of heather. Blessed with a presence the equal of any man, Clarissa Soames, M.A., Hertford Professor of Classics, although unmistakably feminine, seemed in fact right at home in the aggressively masculine atmosphere of the Senior Common Room.

Sitting at a reading table, looking over a copy of *The Observer* with her back to the large central window that was the focal point of the room, Clarissa glanced up as the door opened just a crack, and someone peered diffidently round its edge. After taking in the entire room, a frail, ferrety-looking man with thick spectacles ventured inside.

'Afternoon, G-J,' Clarissa greeted him. 'Have a good long vac? Went to Aberystwyth again, I take it, to see your sister?'

'Good afternoon, Professor Soames,' he returned cautiously, like a mouse looking for the trap. 'No, as a matter of fact I didn't visit my sister this year. She and her family went to the Algarve,' he sniffed, as if this were vaguely unpatriotic. 'So I went up to Leamington Spa—to take the waters.'

'Indeed, did you?' Griffith-Jones's hypochondria was a matter of some amusement amongst the Fellows. 'And did you find them agreeable?'

'I must confess I do feel somewhat refreshed. But then, one hardly knows whether to credit the summer holiday or the effects of the waters.'

Clarissa was already beginning to tire of this conversation. 'Perhaps it was both,' she ventured, and returned to her newspaper.

Griffith-Jones stood looking at her, blinking, for some moments, and sensing their conversation was at an end removed his coat and found a leather armchair, immersing himself in the latest issue of *The Review of Celtic Literature*. By such small rituals Griffith-Jones managed to convince himself he was staying abreast in his field of study.

Some moments later the silence was broken by the abrupt entrance of a tall, muscular man in his mid-forties, unseasonably dressed in baggy wool trousers and a cricket sweater, and exuding the faint odour of unwashed gym socks. As outgoing as Griffith-Jones was introverted, Hugh Fraser Campbell, Lecturer in Politics and History, was clearly a man of action.

'Morning, Soames.' He glanced around, noticed Griffith-Jones, and ignored him. 'Any tea about yet?'

'I should think you'll find some in the usual place.' She had little use for men of action in general, and none at all for Fraser Campbell.

'All spiffed up and ready to go another round?'

A complete idiot, she reflected, and returned to her paper.

Finding his meagre conversational efforts rebuffed, Campbell turned to the tea table and poured himself a cup. He was considering whether to turn his attention to Griffith-Jones when the door opened once again, and the Principal of St. Gregory's, Professor Norman Anscombe, entered the common room and looked around.

'Ah, good morning, Campbell. Just the man. Good to see you back,' he lied. 'I wonder if we might have a word in my study?'

'Of course, sir. A good summer, I trust?'

Anscombe ignored the question. 'I shan't require much of your time.' He held the door for Campbell, and the two left together, leaving Griffith-Jones engrossed in his reading and Soames wondering about the exchange she had just witnessed. The Principal seldom ventured beyond his office, owing to his belief that the Fellows should not generally be disturbed. The faculty returned the compliment by avoiding his presence whenever possible. This had proved to be a practicable arrangement all around, as the Principal's secretary, Mrs. Coates, was more than capable of overseeing the daily activities of the college.

More out of boredom than genuine curiosity, Clarissa Soames contemplated the scene that had just been played out before her. The Principal had made no secret of the fact that he planned to retire at the close of the coming term, and Soames suspected that Campbell hoped to replace him. She took comfort in her conviction that he would fail in the attempt. It wasn't that Soames coveted the post herself; she had absolutely no interest in moving to the dark and turgid waters of administrative life. But in her opinion Fraser Campbell was entirely wrong for the position. More to the point, she was fairly certain that Anscombe—whose recommendation would be crucial—shared her views. No, she decided, he must want to speak with Campbell for some other reason. That off her mind, she returned to her reading.

'COME IN.' Anscombe once again held the door for Campbell. 'All geared up for the new term, I trust?'

'Absolutely, sir.'

'Good, glad to hear it. In fact, just what I would expect, considering your tenure here at St. Gregory's.' Anscombe took his chair behind his desk, and motioned that Campbell should sit opposite. 'I understand you've applied to succeed me, Hugh.' It was the first time in a long while that the Principal had used his Christian name, and Campbell took it as a favourable sign.

'Yes, actually. Been in my present position for some years now. Thought it was time to move on. New challenges and all that. So I take it the Selection Committee has considered my application?'

Anscombe sighed inwardly. It wasn't going to be easy. 'Well, in a manner of speaking.' Actually they had given Anscombe the thankless task of suggesting to Campbell that he withdraw his application, so he wouldn't feel compelled to resign altogether if he were passed over for the post. 'I can certainly appreciate your aspirations. It doesn't seem so long ago that I was in your position. Of course there are several promising candidates for the post. It isn't going to be at all easy for the committee to make its selection.'

'So I should imagine, sir. Your recommendation is bound to carry a lot of weight, then.'

Anscombe sensed the trap and shrugged. 'Not all that much. You'd be surprised. Not like the old days. The committee has a mind of its own. There's even an external candidate—' Anscombe winced; he hadn't meant to reveal that. The existence of external applicants always made it awkward for internal candidates, and in this case the possibility of such an appointment was certain to be resisted by the faculty.

At this revelation Campbell's hand jerked involuntarily, spilling the contents of his cup on to the saucer. Oblivious to Anscombe's glare, Campbell's face revealed his dismay. 'Surely the Board must see that appointing an— *outsider*—would be a slap in the face to the Fellows.' His mind raced for rationalisations. 'A new chap won't know us, or our traditions. Valuable time will be lost getting used to...*things*. Might not even work out, in the end. Square peg, and all that. Valuable time will have been lost, and for what?'

The Principal stared at him sharply. 'Actually, there's some sentiment that an external appointment might be just the thing. We don't want to become moribund in our first half-century, do we?' The question was clearly rhetorical, but to his dismay Anscombe realised that Campbell was actually groping for a response. 'In any event,' he continued, 'you will appreciate that I cannot, at the moment, say more than that your application will be given every consideration. But whatever the outcome, er, Hugh, I want you to know that you are regarded as a valued member of St. Gregory's, and the Board would very much like you to remain so. Perhaps you should keep to yourself the matter of external candidates,' Anscombe added, not hopefully. 'After all, it's all very conjectural at this point.'

At that moment Campbell looked less like a valued member of a university college than like a wounded dog; and, as Anscombe was to reflect later, wounded dogs can be dangerous.

THREE

As the first day of classes at St. Gregory's began, students sought out their classrooms and chatted with one another, arranging and rearranging their notebooks nervously, and glancing around hopefully, searching for a familiar face. A few of the older students adopted an air of insouciance that they imagined made them appear more sophisticated. Their ages varied: many had only recently completed their A levels, or were returning to their studies for a second or third year; but there were also several middle-aged individuals who had been made redundant in the workplace, and were seeking to reinvent themselves for a changing world for which they were poorly prepared. A few were clearly past retirement, taking specific courses out of a genuine interest in the subject. Less common were students in their mid-to-late twenties.

Sheila Bannerman belonged to the latter group. At twenty-six she fitted easily enough into the ranks of the younger students. Yet even in the melee that marked the onset of term it did not take a careful eye to spot the small but significant differences that set her apart from others. Her clothes were more carefully chosen than most of her peers: in place of denim jeans and a jumper or shapeless hoodie she wore dark grey wool trousers and a satin blouse of a subdued lavender, complemented by an expensive scarf in tones of dark green and grey with small purple accents. Instead of scruffy trainers she wore expensive leather flats. Missing was the ubiquitous nylon rucksack;

in its place was an initialed leather handbag that matched her shoes, and was barely large enough to contain her wallet, basic cosmetics, a couple of pens, her mobile phone, and a small notepad. Her hair was well cut and carefully brushed, her makeup subdued, and her hands professionally manicured. Perhaps most telling of all, there was in her eyes a sense of determination and purpose that would not appear in her classmates for some years, if ever. With a maturity that belied her years Sheila had recently taken stock of where she had arrived in life. It had been precipitated by a casual look in the mirror at an unguarded moment. She hadn't liked what she had seen. It was the eyes. They always gave one away. The skin tone, the bone structure, the hair style, the make-up were fine. But her eyes had become hard, and if you looked closely, wary. She had seen it, and in a few years others would too. By then it would be too late.

Many young women would have been satisfied with her lot: a secure, if not particularly well-paying, job, mates who enjoyed going out for a drink and a laugh after work, a bit of money put by (actually quite a bit, if she were being honest with herself). But although she got on well enough with her friends, they all knew she really wasn't one of them. Her accent and her mannerisms gave her away. In the long run, then, it was a no-go: she needed to reinvent herself, return to a happier time. And that meant changing her entire life. Sheila pulled herself out of her thoughts and entered the classroom building, checking her notes for the number of the room.

Despite its architectural pretensions, St. Gregory's College had from the outset been influenced by American educational practises. The traditional tutorial system had been largely replaced by lectures, a decision that resulted in both large classes and significant savings in the salaries of the teaching staff. But after much debate the college had opted to provide each of its undergraduates with a broad intellectual curriculum worthy of Oxford and Cambridge, the successful assimilation of which would have challenged many a Renaissance thinker. Sheila reviewed her list of courses: *European History Since 1945*, *Greek Culture and Civilisation*, *English Romantic Poets*, *Ancient Western Philosophy*, and *Understanding Western Art*. It was in fact typical first year fare, designed not only to expose entering students to a wide range of issues and ideas, but also to separate the sheep from the goats. Sheila sighed.

It was going to be a long eight months. Still, she reasoned, it would mark a new beginning for her. A chance to start over, to reclaim her life.

Looking about, Sheila marvelled at the size of the lecture hall. It must hold close to two hundred people, she calculated. Not much chance of individual attention, then. She glanced at her watch: in three minutes the class was scheduled to begin. Spying a vacant seat at the back of the room, she threaded her way through a knot of chatting students and laid claim to it.

SIMON SHORT WAS ENGROSSED in a magazine about computer gaming as Sheila took the seat next to him. He did not look up immediately, but gradually became aware of the scent of her expensive perfume. When he did look up, his first thought was that she had to be a fashion model, so exquisite was her beauty, so immaculate her appearance. Her elegant profile, her shiny dark hair, and her pale clear skin reminded him of some of the classic movie actresses whose likenesses adorned his bedroom walls. He stared at her until, aware of his attention, she turned toward him and smiled. Taking that as a sign of encouragement he summoned up the courage to speak to her.

'Hi. I'm Simon. I don't remember seeing you before. Your first year?'

Sheila appraised him carefully. Her tone was civil, but deliberately cool, her accent carefully middle-class. 'Yes, actually. Are all the classes this large?'

Simon was reassured. Here was a subject about which he was knowledgeable. 'Not really. The lower-level classes are the largest, naturally. This is a required course—it's bound to be huge.'

'Of course. Stupid of me.' She opened her bag and, after rummaging a bit, extracted a pad and biro. Simon searched his mind for something to say, something witty or clever, but came up empty. His efforts were interrupted when, a few moments later, the professor entered the lecture hall, strode over to the podium, and the murmur gradually subsided. Sheila listened attentively as she and her classmates were informed in some detail on the requirements of university life. The rules for attendance were reviewed, followed by a brief geography lesson indicating the location of the library. Plagiarism, it was made abundantly clear, would not be tolerated, and any student found guilty of presenting the words of others as their own would be summarily sent down from the college.

During this soliloquy (for no questions were invited, and it was clear that it would be folly to interrupt) Sheila's attention focused on the lecturer with increasing interest. The face was familiar; of that she was sure. But who, and from where? Twice the speaker had glanced in her direction, and the second time Sheila thought she noticed a glimmer of recognition, but she couldn't be sure. It disturbed her, for she knew that she could not put the matter entirely out of her mind. Oh well, it would come to her with time.

By the time Sheila emerged from her third class of the day she had been exposed to a range of ideas considerably wider than she had experienced during of her previous twenty-six years. She had also made an intriguing personal discovery, having placed the face she had recently seen. As she finished her sandwich and tea at a nearby cafe she contemplated how best to make use of her knowledge. She looked up from her meditations to find Simon standing over her, his backpack of books slung over one shoulder. 'Hi again. Mind if I join you?'

Sheila eyed him warily, then decided he was harmless. In any case such encounters would be unavoidable, inasmuch as they were taking the same course. 'Why not?' she shrugged.

If Simon was offended he did not show it. 'Hope your classes were better than mine,' he ventured, setting his bag at his feet and looking over the menu. 'Dead boring, some of that stuff.' He motioned for a server and ordered a coffee. 'You from around these parts—London, I mean?'

'No. Cambridgeshire, actually.'

'Really? It must be nice there. I mean, I've heard so.' He hesitated, unsure of how to go on. 'I've an uncle near there, but we don't see much of him, not since my dad died. That's going on ten years now. I suppose I've not been back since I was nine or so. I remember because it was Spring and the fens were flooded. Fog everywhere.'

While Simon nattered on, Sheila stirred her tea absentmindedly. Finally she came to a decision. Glancing at her watch she said, 'Sorry, I've got to run—Simon, was it? I'll see you in class.' She was out the door before Simon could wonder what he had—or hadn't—said to cause her to leave. She crossed the street to a stationery store, where she purchased a small packet of inexpensive envelopes, and continued on to Bloomsbury Square, which was nearly deserted. After checking to see that she was alone she sat down and, taking a page from her pad, carefully composed a brief note. Having satisfied herself that her message was clear and to the point, Sheila folded it carefully and placed it in one of the newly purchased envelopes. Then she rose and walked in the direction of St. Gregory's College.

AT APPROXIMATELY THE SAME TIME, having concluded his midday meal, Miles Burton-Strachey emerged from his Georgian townhouse at the foot of Regent's Park. He walked to Euston Road and proceeded at a leisurely pace toward St. Gregory's College. It was very agreeable, he reflected, to live well away from his colleagues and to be able to take full advantage of the altogether more pleasant surroundings that his wife's inheritance had provided. Convenient, too that Harley Street, with its battery of eminent physicians to whom his wife regularly submitted herself for a variety of largely imaginary complaints, should be mere streets away. It was indeed fortunate that they should be comfortably provided for, for Hillary would have been most unhappy at having to submit to the vagaries and delays of the National Health Service, or the indignity of having to shop at Tesco's or travel about in an aging Ford Metro, rather than their gleaming dark-green Jag; for truth be told, Professor Burton-Strachey, Wycombe Professor of History, shared his wife's fondness for the finer things of life.

Yet Miles was a troubled man. Only a few years earlier, frustrated by the complexities of the investment market, Hillary had left their financial affairs entirely in his hands. Her incessant shopping forays in Regent Street and Knightsbridge, together with her interminable social activities on behalf of various charitable causes, added to a litany of minor medical complaints, had left her little time for anything else, including Miles.

In the beginning Miles had been pleased with the arrangement. He had poured over his wife's portfolio of stocks and bonds, had followed daily *The Economist* and *The Financial Times*, and over a period of years had converted most of her holdings from a stodgy, even moribund collection of assets, which were nonetheless almost unassailably secure, into what he had perceived was a much more aggressive portfolio of 'growth' ventures. Unfortunately they had lacked the stability of their previous holdings, and a whimsical fate, combined with the machinations of a financial world he only dimly understood, had in recent years reduced Miles' (or more accurately his wife's) investments to a fraction of their former worth.

Panic-stricken, Miles had moved to sell the shakiest of these issues, and found to his dismay that there were few interested buyers. Eventually he had turned most of them over, and reinvested what remained in the same pedestrian securities that formerly he had found so unimaginative—but which seemed to exhibit a remarkable stability, with the additional appeal of paying regular, if somewhat conservative, dividends.

Miles knew, however, that he was far from home free. The loss of capital that he had sustained meant that their dividend income would be sharply reduced. That income, he knew, together with his salary, paid for their lifestyle, as well as for his wife's frequent visits to her Harley Street specialists. Moreover, in an effort to conceal his malfeasance from his wife, Miles had actually signed her name—'forged' was a word he could not bring himself to use—to several transfer certificates. All perfectly innocent, done in good faith, he assured himself. But if that were to come to light—well, the domestic implications simply did not bear thinking about.

So as he turned from Gower Street into St. Gregory's, Miles Burton-Strachey mind was occupied by his personal problems, and it was more a mark of desperation than of mental acumen that before long he hit upon a solution. The Principal, he knew, was about to retire. His successor would assume not only a tidy salary, but also residential quarters within the college sufficient for entertaining, as well as a budget to cover such expenses. Were he to be appointed to replace the Principal, his financial problems would be resolved. Although Miles knew that it must be close to being decided, it was not yet too late to apply. The unease which for the past several days had plagued Miles Burton-Strachey's waking hours began to dissipate, and the minutiæ of planning how best to proceed began to dominate his thoughts.

FOUR O'CLOCK CAME, and with it for all practical purposes the end of the first day of term at St. Gregory's. It had been a fine day, one of the agreeable surprises that London occasionally bestows upon its unsuspecting inhabitants, and Miles Burton-Strachey decided to walk the dozen or so streets from St. Gregory's to his home. In threatening weather it was his habit to go by taxi, but more recently he had eschewed even such modest luxuries.

He knew, however, that such small economies could hardly hope to forestall a financial disaster of major proportions. Still, he had submitted his letter of application for the Principalship, and Anscombe had, he told himself, actually looked pleased.

Returning home, Burton-Strachey called out to his wife as he closed the front door. Receiving no answer to his summons, he glanced at the hallway table and saw a note. Unfolding it, he took in the firm handwriting:

> *At an antique auction in Chelsea.*
> *Charity event. Home late. Your dinner*
> *is in the microwave. H.*

Miles frowned. Spending more money, no doubt. There might not even be enough in their chequing account to cover it. He glanced at the clock in the hallway and then called his broker to arrange the sale of some minor securities. This was followed by another call to the bank, to inform the manager that a transfer from his broker would be coming, and that meanwhile the bank should cover any cheques that might come in. The manager had been most accommodating. The Burton-Stracheys were valued customers, he assured him; he was only too happy to oblige.

THAT EVENING, as Simon opened the door to their flat, he smelled supper being prepared. He kicked off his running shoes and dropped his jean jacket on the back of the chair nearest the door. 'Lo, mum,' he called out. 'How's tricks?'

His mother appeared in the kitchen doorway, a wooden spoon in her hand, grease on her apron. 'Really, Simon. You know I don't like you to talk like that. It's so *common*.'

Simon glared at her. 'We *are* common, mum. Look around you. Does this look like the bloody Savoy?' He picked up the post from a small table next to the sofa and sorted through it, singling out an advert for a set of DVDs entitled *The Golden Age of Silents: Classic Movies of the 1920s*. 'What's for supper?' he asked.

'I got us a nice bit of fish, dear.' She smiled. 'How did school go today?'

Simon slumped down on the sofa, tearing open the envelope as he spoke. 'All right, I guess. Some of the courses they make us take you wouldn't believe. Got nothing to do with anything. Met a nice-looking bird in one of them, though.'

His mother ignored the colloquialism. 'Really? You must tell me all about her!'

'Not much to tell,' he replied. 'We had coffee together after class.'

Jane Short was pleased. It had been months since he'd spoken about a young woman. Privately she acknowledged that Simon was, well, *different* than other boys, but the right young woman, she told herself, could make all the difference. Things hadn't really been the same since that incident with the police three years ago. So unfair. If only Robert were still alive...

That thought was still with her several hours later, as she lay awake, the noise from the television in the other room keeping her from sleeping. *If only Robert were still alive.*

FOUR

Owing to the London housing scene, St. Gregory's had quickly proved unequal to the task of accommodating the swelling ranks of undergraduates within its walls. The majority of students were obliged to find private lodging in the area, mostly bunching up three or four or more to a flat, the sexual permutations depending on the proclivities of the students and the tolerance of the landlord. Some remained at home with their parents and commuted daily; many of the foreign students found the nearby Overseas Students' Residence more to their liking.

The Teaching Fellows, however, were a different matter. When the college was being designed it was thought that having a residential faculty would make them more accessible to students and create amongst the Fellows a sense of collegiality. As a result, for the most part the teaching staff at St. Gregory's lived *in situ*. Miles Burton-Strachey was one of the few exceptions.

The Fellows were also provided with college post boxes, overseen by Mr. Bateman, an elderly Lancastrian whose taciturn manner did little to reveal his private opinions concerning the scholars, layabouts, martinets and misfits whose postal activities he superintended. The Porter's Lodge was located at the College gate, and it was the custom each morning for the Fellows to stop by and check their boxes before commencing their daily tasks.

It was close on nine o'clock when Fraser Campbell entered the Porter's Lodge. 'Morning, Bateman,' he ventured. 'Anything for me today?'

'Yessir, Mr. Campbell,' the porter replied. 'Parcel of books. Too big for your box. Here somewhere.' He disappeared behind the counter that separated their two worlds and returned in a few moments, a large cardboard carton in hand.

Campbell tore open the packing slip, glanced at it briefly, and delved into the parcel. It was an assortment of forthcoming texts in his field, sent to him for his opinion and for possible adoption in his courses. Campbell regarded this as one of the more lucrative perks of his profession. They, the publishers, were seeking his opinion! He conscientiously returned the evaluation cards, although it was a measure of his reputation that his considered judgments were often read by a junior clerk and then binned. The more impressive of the lot would receive a place on Campbell's study shelves, where they would remain largely unused, for he seldom changed texts, an exercise that would require updating lecture notes and exam questions. The rest, after inking out the offensive stamp 'Complimentary Copy—Not for Resale' he would take to one of the many nearby used-book shops. Even allowing for his modest investment in time and energy, over the course of years Fraser Campbell had turned a tidy profit.

He was packing the books up again when Miles Burton-Strachey entered the Porter's Office. The two were not particularly good friends, but, like most of the Fellows of St. Gregory's, they managed to maintain a thin veneer of civility between them.

'Morning B-S, uh, Miles,' he appended. The unfortunate locution had, he knew, been adopted by Burton-Strachey's students, to describe his classroom approach when confronted with a difficult question.

'Morning, Fraser,' Miles returned genially. He seemed chipper, and not at all put out by Campbell's momentary lapse. Reaching into his box and extracting a magazine and two or three envelopes, he was even whistling softly. *Seems rather pleased with himself,* Campbell speculated. Miles shuffled his letters briefly, then selected one and opened it.

The contrast in mood was striking. As he read the letter, he stopped whistling, and became quite pale. For a moment Campbell thought he was actually going to faint.

'I say, are you all right?'

Burton-Strachey ignored him for a moment. 'What? Oh, yes. Just a little wobbly. Skipped breakfast this morning. Probably a mistake. A cup of tea will set me right.' He turned and scurried out, leaving Fraser Campbell standing there dumbfounded. It wasn't like the man to pass up a meal, he knew. In fact the rest of the faculty were usually hard pressed to keep up with him, as he fancied himself something of a gourmand. Still, Campbell reflected, he might have risen late and had to rush things to make his morning class. He picked up his parcel and made for his study, ignoring both Bateman, who had missed little of what had just occurred, and Clarissa Soames, who had witnessed the scene from the doorway.

IT WAS TURNING OUT to be a glorious morning, and leaving her last class of the morning Sheila Bannerman strode confidently into the quad at St. Gregory's, her mind a million miles away. Suddenly the young man she had seen the other day was, quite literally, blocking her way. She recoiled instinctively from the prominent acne scars that disfigured his face. 'Hello again,' he said, oblivious to her reaction. 'I thought I might see you here. There's time for a coffee before class. Are you up for it?'

In his enthusiasm Simon had raised his voice, and other students, Sheila noticed, were staring. 'I'm afraid not, Simon. I've got some things to take care of before class, actually.'

'Then what about after class? I can duck old Anscombe's lecture on the Presocratics. We could make an afternoon of it. There's a silent film series on. Today they're showing the 1925 version of *The Wizard of Oz* and Murnau's interpretation of *Faust*. They're great fun, really. Or—'

Sheila saw with dismay that they were fast attracting a small crowd. Some of the students were exchanging glances and sniggering amongst themselves; one or two looked at her enquiringly, wondering whether they should step in. The last thing Sheila wanted was a public scene. She decided to nip it in the bud. 'Look, Simon, you're a nice guy, really, but I don't really want any—distractions—in my life right now. We're only classmates, right? Let's leave it that way.' And with that she turned and elbowed her way through the small knot of onlookers without looking back.

For a moment Simon stood there, stunned by her reaction to his overtures. He had been rebuffed before, but never so publicly, nor with so much humiliation. He felt the eyes of the other students burning through him. He turned and stalked out of the quad, down the street and into the park at Russell Square, where he collapsed onto the grass, his face flushed with anger, furious with Sheila and with himself.

A few minutes later Miles Burton-Strachey made his way up Montague Street, past Russell Square, on his way back to the college. Ignoring the zebra crossing at the corner he stepped out into the middle of the street. There was a great squealing of tyres, followed by the cursing of an irate taxi driver. A few heads turned, attracted by the commotion. Miles apologised perfunctorily, then scurried on his way. On a bench in Russell Square, Fraser Campbell put down his newspaper and stared after him, a trace of amusement in his eyes.

WHILE CAMPBELL WAS REFLECTING on what he had just seen, a few blocks away Norman Anscombe was interrupted by a knock at his office door. He glanced up from the files in front of him.

The door opened and a tall, youngish man with a thin, aquiline nose and long, sun-bleached locks appeared. He was dressed casually in cream-coloured linen trousers and a dark burgundy silk shirt, open at the collar; over his shoulders was draped a cashmere sweater in pale pink. The man had an envious tan that suggested more time spent on beaches and tennis courts than in the dark recesses of university libraries. Anscombe's face hardened. 'Oh it's you, Asquith. Then you've finally arrived? Classes began yesterday, you know.' He bestowed a look usually reserved for truculent undergraduates.

Asquith was unabashed. 'Yes—sorry about that. My research took rather longer than expected to complete, and I had a horrid time getting a lift from Grasmere to Kendal. Then the train to London was absolutely *beastly!*' Neither his expression nor his tone indicated the slightest trace of sincerity.

'Well, you're here now, I suppose. You'd best consult Mrs. Coates about your teaching schedule. You don't want to miss any *additional* classes.' Asquith seemed to take it all in stride, and left the room as casually as he had arrived.

Anscombe reflected on the cravenness of his colleagues in the profession. Two years ago, when Asquith had joined the teaching staff, Anscombe had—or so he thought—thoroughly vetted the man. Indeed, Jeremy Asquith had come highly recommended: full marks for his reliability and his serious, scholarly attitude. In retrospect it was clear that Asquith's glowing recommendations had been less the result of an objective appraisal than of a keen desire to be rid of the man. Anscombe briefly considered the possibility of extracting payment in kind, and then returned to his work.

FIVE

In his flat not far from Little Venice, Colin McDermott lingered over the aromas of strong coffee and burnt toast, when a voice from the other room interrupted his thoughts.

'You won't forget the dinner for Daddy tonight, will you?'

McDermott winced. Even after a relationship of some eighteen months it still annoyed him that a grown professional woman would refer to her father as 'Daddy.' He wondered maliciously whether it might be a case of arrested emotional development. 'No, I haven't forgotten. Your parents' place at eight, right?'

She turned from the sink, where she was clearing the breakfast dishes. 'Actually, half seven would be better. I know Daddy always likes a chance to chat with you. You do like him, don't you?'

'What's not to like?' McDermott forced the words out. He resented such obvious manoeuvring, and considered, not for the first time, the merits of their relationship.

By many people's standards, McDermott knew, he ought to have been well pleased. Victoria Chambers was an attractive and accomplished woman who routinely turned heads wherever she went. In her late teens and early twenties she had excelled at Somerville College, Oxford; now, a dozen years on, she was a successful barrister in the prestigious law firm presided over by her father. Her family also dominated much of the social life of Surrey, but determined to establish her own identity Victoria had established a comfortable house of her own in Hampstead Heath.

'Well? Half past? You'll be there?' The question brought McDermott back from his wool-gathering.

'Oh. Of course,' he said, not liking himself very much at the moment. Should I bring a bottle of plonk?'

'Dolt,' she replied good-naturedly. Her father's wine cellar, McDermott knew, was a matter of some pride, a quality it seemed the family was not short on.

As Victoria left for work McDermott glanced out of the sitting room window and, noticing the darkening sky, reached for his Mac. By the time he eased his front door shut a gentle rain was descending, forming small puddles and tiny streams in the street.

Since the death of his wife nine years earlier, McDermott had three passions in his life beyond his work. The first was his daughter Megan, now eighteen and experiencing her first year at Oxford. The second was a vintage Morgan Plus Four, acquired fortuitously when he had been a university student over thirty years earlier. Finally, and somewhat improbably, he had a modest but impressive collection of antique maps.

Most psychologists would have understood McDermott's attachment to his daughter while dismissing the Morgan as a clichéd attempt to hold on to his youth. Certainly the car held many pleasant memories of his university days; but a full account of McDermott's attraction for his aging motorcar would have had to include some reference to its grace of line and quality of craftsmanship, the use of leather and wood silent testimony to the elegance of a bygone era. In quiet moments it gave him a sense of permanence, a sense that, whatever the capricious swings of modern taste and fashion, some things remain worthy in their own right, and deserving of admiration.

To some extent that same regard for objects of quality also explained McDermott's interest in antique maps. Most of his casual friends were unaware of his collection. The few who did know passed it off as an investment, explainable by the swiftly rising value of collectibles on the world market. Since the Saudis and Japanese (and more recently members of the Russian Mafia) had taken an interest in Western art, the prices of fine works had soared well beyond the reach of most collectors. In fact, however, his friends did McDermott a disservice, for he had a keen interest in seventeenth-century cartography, and, having written several monographs, was regarded in academic circles as something of a minor authority on the subject.

The rain showed no sign of stopping, and McDermott decided to leave his car in a nearby lock up and walked to the nearest tube station, catching the Bakerloo Line just in time. He made his way to Charing Cross, and emerging onto the street, walked the few streets to Agar Street and the handsome building in Portland Stone that housed the Charing Cross station of the Metropolitan Police.

FIFTEEN MINUTES LATER McDermott was sitting at his desk reviewing the overnight reports when the telephone interrupted his thoughts.

'McDermott,' he acknowledged.

'Morning, McDermott,' a husky voice replied on the other end. 'Sid here. I've got something I think calls for your special talents. If you're free, I'd like to pay you a visit.'

Sidney Pitt was a good friend whose intelligence and dedication to his work had led to a number of promotions, culminating in his present rank of Chief Superintendent of the Traffic Division for the whole of London. Although protocol dictated that McDermott should make the trip to New Scotland Yard, he knew that Pitt, by nature a man of action, welcomed any excuse to get out of his office. 'Come on over, then. The exercise will do you good, and the intellectual atmosphere will be a change of pace.' After ringing off he picked up the phone again. 'Lay on a couple of mugs of tea, will you, Marsh? Chief Superintendent Pitt is on his way over. Sounds as though he may have something for us.'

Before long Sidney Pitt had arrived. McDermott's office was not obsessively tidy: his desk and the bookcases behind it were littered with stacks of case files and divisional memoranda. The furniture was Civil Service Spartan. The only exceptions were two framed and glassed prints of his own choosing: one a brooding but energetic seascape by Turner, the other an equally charged Kandinsky abstraction. Their juxtaposition took some visitors by surprise. An appreciation of art, however, was not at the moment amongst Sidney Pitt's interests. After sampling the hot tea and exchanging the usual pleasantries he came to the point.

'We had a traffic fatality in High Holborn yesterday, shortly after Noon. A double-decker ran down a young woman—mid twenties I'd say—crossing in the middle of the block. She died instantly, according to the ambulance boys. No question of it being the driver's fault. One minute the road was clear, the next she was right in his path. Driver didn't even have time to sound his horn. Poor bugger had to be treated for shock.'

'Hard luck,' McDermott's sympathised. 'It's not a nice way to go, particularly for a young person. Her family must have taken it hard.'

'That's just it,' Pitt explained. 'We can't locate her family. In fact, we can't ID the victim. She had nothing, nothing at all, beyond a couple of quid in change and a tenner stuffed into one pocket. No wallet, nor handbag. No one who witnessed the accident knew her, and you know the area—mostly offices and shops. Must be thousands of people pass by there in a day. No point in doing a house-to-house, then. We've nought to go on.'

McDermott straightened in his chair, wondering why Pitt had brought him the case. 'A bit early days to try Missing Persons,' he reflected. 'I know it sounds a bit callous, but perhaps you should simply wait a bit longer.'

Pitt straightened in his chair, and his expression grew stern. 'Look here: I've got two young 'uns at home. Off to university soon enough, and I'd sure as hell want to know if anything happened to either of them!'

McDermott leaned forward. 'Of course you would, Sid. So would I, come to that. But a front page photo of a mortuary corpse in the tabloids, under the banner *DO YOU KNOW THIS PERSON?*' isn't the best way to break it to her family, is it?' He went on. 'I'm curious why you brought it to us: is there any reason to think it might be anything more than a straightforward traffic fatality?'

'Well, one old dear suggested the victim might have been pushed. Said she seemed to just "jump out" as the bus approached. Driver said the same thing.'

'Not much to go on,' McDermott reflected. 'She might simply have been in a hurry, and stumbled, or even have been a suicide.'

Pitt's expression was caustic. 'In front of a bus? There must be easier ways to go. Stranger things have happened, I'll grant you,' he conceded. 'However, there's one other thing. As I said, the victim had no ID on her, but several witnesses thought she'd been carrying a small handbag. We searched the immediate area and couldn't find it. We even checked all the alleys, bins, and drains for a radius of three streets, on the chance that some enterprising young felon saw his chance in the confusion and copped it.'

'Wouldn't be the first time,' McDermott agreed. 'Still, you'd think that any self-respecting thief would rifle the contents and get rid of the bag itself at the first opportunity. Anything else?'

The Chief Superintendent played his trump card. 'One other thing. I've been in touch with the lab this morning. The victim's clothes were all brand spanking new. Trousers, blouse, scarf, shoes, even her knickers—all right off the rack. And not too shabby either,' he added. 'The scarf is from Liberty's. Very pricey, I'd wager.' McDermott nodded, and Pitt continued. 'Now, why do you suppose a young lady of means would venture into the East End— because that's the only place the buses run from that stop—alone, and with almost no money—maybe even no ID—on her person?'

'To visit a boyfriend? Do a bit of slumming?' But McDermott had to concede that it was an interesting question. Pitt had piqued his curiosity. 'Officially there's no evidence of a crime here, much less a homicide,' McDermott pointed out. 'Anyway, DCI Loach is senior. Shouldn't you be speaking with him?'

Sidney Pitt grunted. 'The man's a twat. You know that. And I hear he might be in the running for Galbraith's job.'

'He does have his detractors,' McDermott admitted. Loach and he shared a mutual dislike for each other. If he became Galbraith's successor in a coming shuffle it would mean that McDermott would be reporting to him. Not a pleasant thought. 'Well, I'll have to clear it with the Super.'

Pitt grinned. 'No need, lad. You don't think I'd waste your valuable time if I hadn't already done that? Galbraith says it's all yours.'

McDermott grimaced. 'Cheeky bugger!'

SIX

A s Pitt left, McDermott considered their conversation. Not much to go on, really. No hard evidence of any crime; the most he had was a possible petty theft. He glanced over at his Pending tray. Not much on his plate; he could spare a day or two for someone to look into matters and see if they could put a name to the face. He thought back to the time, over ten years ago, when his wife had been the victim of the bus bombing at Tavistock Square. McDermott had been one of the first CID officers on the scene, and it had been he who had recognised some of the victims' effects as belonging to his wife. Their daughter Megan had been seven at the time. A difficult age for a girl to lose her mother; not that any age was better. He'd meant it, then, when he told Pitt that if he were the father of the dead woman he would want to know. He buzzed the outer office once more, and Marsh entered the room. 'If Ridley is in the duty room I'd like to see him.' His eye caught the personnel file in his In tray. 'Oh, and tell DC Quinn to stand by, please.'

Albert George Ridley was one of the last surviving relics of an endangered species: the post war bobby on the beat. In his late fifties, he was tall and heavy set with brown eyes and a ruddy complexion, and what little hair remained was combed straight back and slicked down. Whether he stood or sat he maintained a strict military posture, the result of twenty years' service with a light infantry regiment based in Yorkshire; but an old leg wound meant that he walked with a rolling gait. A man not easily given to change, years of living in London had done little to erase from Ridley's speech the broad brogue of the Dales, which became more pronounced whenever he became excited or angry. In the manner of his day he had received only a limited education. That he had not progressed beyond Detective Sergeant during his time at the Met spoke more of his ambitions than his abilities. George Ridley had found his niche, and it was working the street. And he was highly conscientious: once he got hold of a case he would worry it until he'd solved it, like a dog with a bone.

McDermott's reflections were interrupted by a knock at the door. Ridley entered without waiting for a further invitation. 'Mornin', Guv. You wanted to see me?'

'Morning, George. How's the Mallord case coming?'

'About tied up,' he beamed. 'Sussed him when I first laid eyes on him,' he added with some pride. 'Paperwork's almost ready for CPS. With a bit o' luck he should be in a nice warm cell 'afore day's out.'

'Nice work.' McDermott knew that although several officers had a hand in the case, it was largely due to Ridley that an arrest was imminent. 'How are Dora and the kids?'

Ridley shot him a look that would wilt fresh lettuce. 'Now then, when you ask me that you've always got summat up your sleeve.'

'You're on to me, George.' he admitted. 'As a matter of fact I've got something from Traffic. Death of a young woman. Yesterday. No ID. Hit by a bus. We need to put a name to her so we can notify the family.'

Ridley frowned. 'Sounds like job for Uniform Branch. They havin' a manpower shortage, or have we been demoted?'

'It seems they've hit a bit of a dead end, George—no pun intended. They need your considerable deductive powers to solve this one.'

'Oh, aye? Well, I'll get right on it, then. Shall I draw some help?'

It was now or never, McDermott decided. 'That won't be necessary, George. We have a new DC coming on board. Someone for you to take under your wing—benefit from your considerable experience.' He buzzed the outer office. 'Send Quinn in, please.'

McDermott watched the Sergeant struggle with his composure as their new colleague entered the room. 'Good morning, Quinn, and welcome aboard. We can always use some new blood. I don't think you've met DS Ridley.'

Wilhemina Quinn was in her early thirties, of medium height, slender, with sandy-coloured hair cut to shoulder length and intelligent blue eyes above a thin, generous mouth that smiled easily. She turned and in a carefully measured voice that indicated a university education said 'No, sir, I haven't had the pleasure. How do you do, Sergeant. I'm looking forward to the opportunity of working with you.'

Ridley looked fleetingly at McDermott, with an expression that would have done a despondent beagle proud. 'Pleased, Ah'm sure,' he mumbled. He did not appear to have anything further to add at that moment, and it fell to McDermott to pick up the conversation.

'I was just about to go over your background with the Sergeant, if you don't mind. A good solid record. Degree in Social Work, coupled with two years as a Disability Employment Advisor. That must have given you a good knowledge of people. Graduated from the Midlands Police College near the top of your class. After three years as a PC with the Met you did the course at Hendon and joined the CID at Bromley. I understand that since then you have been instrumental in solving a number of difficult cases. Tell me, why did you request a transfer here?'

She paused before answering. 'To be frank, sir, I didn't ask for this posting, at least not specifically. But I want to become better at my job, and I was told that I could learn a great deal here.'

McDermott permitted himself a small smile. 'You can't believe everything you hear. But George has been with us a good long time—longer than I've been, actually. I've found that he has something to teach all of us.' He turned toward the Sergeant, who by now had regained some of his aplomb. 'George, will you show Quinn where to park her things, and then call Traffic to get the specifics on that case we discussed? I'm sure she can help. Let me know if you need any additional staff.'

Ridley glared at McDermott on the way out.

ARMED WITH THE DETAILS of the incident from Traffic Division and a forensic photo of the victim, Ridley and Quinn made their way toward Regent Street.

Their first stop was Liberty's, where the sales manager identified the silk scarf as indeed one of their own. That, however, seemed to be the extent of his helpfulness. Lacking the sales receipt, with the volume of business they did daily, he suggested, the clerk who sold it couldn't be identified. And without more information—the date of sale perhaps?—the store copy of the sales receipt could not possibly be located. Ridley pointed out that the man's indifference was impeding an official police investigation, and Quinn added, more helpfully, that the scarf in question had most probably been purchased recently. Finally the manager was persuaded to detail someone on his staff to check sales records for the previous fortnight. A computer search of the sales code on the scarf turned up twenty nine sales for that particular article during the date range in question. Almost all had been paid for by credit card or the customer was known to them and quickly eliminated. Nearly an hour later the relevant sales slip was located, and the floor clerk identified. That, however, proved to be a dead end. The scarf had been purchased ten days ago. The bill had been paid in cash and the clerk had no recollection of either the particular transaction or the customer. Moreover, store CCTV for had been erased three days previously. Undeterred, the pair worked their way through the crowd of shoppers and back into the fierce sunlight of Regent Street.

'What now, Sergeant?' Quinn asked.

Ridley looked up and down the street, and wiped some imaginary sweat off his brow. 'Name's George, seeing as how we're workin' together. Time for a pint and a nosh, I reckon. We'll just beat the lunchtime crowd. I know a decent local nearby.' With Quinn in tow he walked down Regent Street, turned into Foubert's Place, and proceeded toward Carnaby Street, stopping at a corner pub. Moments later the harsh sunlight and smell of petrol had been exchanged for a more agreeable darkness and the heady aromas of best bitter and pork pie.

As Ridley had predicted, the lunch time crowd had not yet materialised, but the pub was crowded with tourists, and with practised ease he snagged a table vacated only a moment before, narrowly beating a party of Americans who gave him a withering look.

'Here we are,' he stated with patent obviousness. 'What's your pleasure— half a lager or a shandy?'

'A pint of bitter, thanks, with a packet of crisps. But the next shout's mine.'

Ridley raised an eyebrow. 'Too right.'

Over lunch they contemplated what to do next. 'That scarf were our best bet, I reckon,' the Sergeant admitted, tearing into his ploughman's. He opened the packet of crisps and thrust it across the table to Quinn. 'Rest of 'er stuff were more normal like—nice enough, but the devil to trace. Must be 'undreds 'o shops in London as stock that sort o' goods. Shame we don't have a handbag.'

'You know, I've been thinking about that, George,' Quinn said, taking a single crisp.

'What do you mean?'

'Well, she didn't have any ID, but her clothes tell us quite a bit about her. You probably noticed that she chose them very carefully.'

'Can't say I did.' Ridley's wife was given to putting on whatever happened to be at hand in the morning, and her taste ran mostly to house dresses with large flowery patterns that, given her short stature and bulky frame, only succeeded in making her look even more frumpy. Consequently the latest in *haute couture* was seldom at the forefront of George Ridley's mind.

Quinn picked up the thread of her thoughts. 'It's almost as if she had dressed for the first day on a new job. Nothing flashy, but everything calculated to make a good impression. Know what I mean?'

'Oh, aye?' He lifted his glass and drained the contents.

'Well, suppose she had recently bought that ensemble as a single, coordinated outfit. We know she didn't buy the rest of it at Liberty's. Their label is in just about everything they sell, and quite frankly, although her blouse and trousers are of good quality, they're not in the same league.'

Ridley knew when he was out of his depth. 'Go on.'

'So fashionwise, the scarf was the crowning touch. She put out good money for one item, which was undeniably of first quality, to accent the rest of her outfit.'

'How's that help?'

Quinn leaned over her glass as she warmed to her theory. 'You recall the pale lavender blouse she was wearing? Not an easy shade to match. Most women don't buy a blouse, and then a week or two later in another shop say 'that's just the scarf to go with that outfit I recently bought.' If you're just a little off, you'll have a horrid clash of colours. If I'm right, our young lady shopped for all her outerwear—at least the major items—at one time, to be sure she achieved the total look she was after.'

The light was dawning. 'You think we can retrace her steps? I thought you said rest of her things were less upmarket,' George protested. 'So where do we go from here?'

'Well, if I'm right, no further down Regent Street. The rest of the shops there are just too pricey. No, I think we should go up, toward Oxford Circus, if necessary do Oxford Street itself.'

Ridley's face fell. Oxford Street was the largest single area devoted to women's fashions in the middle price range in the whole of London. On the rare occasions when his wife had dragged him along on shopping expeditions he hadn't particularly enjoyed it. He didn't think he would now. He examined the empty glass before him. 'Thirsty work.' Quinn took the hint and stood him another round.

BY THE TIME MCDERMOTT ARRIVED HOME it was shortly after ten. Judging by the lack of lights on the street his neighbours had decided to call it an early night as well. After dropping his jacket on the coat rack near the door McDermott poured himself a drink. Victoria had not been pleased by his leaving so early, he knew, but truth be told there were times when he found their relationship more than a little daunting. That evening had been one of those times. He suspected her parents thought he liked her for the wrong reasons. Come to that, was he certain that he liked her for the right reasons?

It had been nearly ten years since Anna had died, and here he was, he realised, still feeling guilty about dating other women. McDermott recalled the first time after her death that he caught himself quietly humming as he did the washing up; he had stopped abruptly, ashamed and feeling guilty about enjoying even that small pleasure in the wake of her death. Later that evening he had looked in on their daughter Megan as she slept, tracing on her face the grief that had marked the several months that had passed since she had lost her mother. Since then McDermott had dated a few women, but found them all wanting. Or perhaps it was him. Was he destined to become one of those pathetic old gits who lived out their waning years alone, with only sympathetic neighbours and casual friends for company? He shuddered. *Not bloody likely, mate.* Putting it out of his mind for the moment,

McDermott checked his answering machine for messages and, finding none, went upstairs to bed.

SEVEN

The next morning when McDermott entered the canteen at the Charing Cross station he found George Ridley pouring himself a cup of coffee from a large chrome urn.

'Mornin', Guv. Fancy some tonsil varnish?'

'Not that stuff, George. Should be a felony even to dump it in the Thames.' He noticed Willie Quinn sitting at a table near the window. 'How's the new bloke coming along?'

'Bloody riot, you are,' Ridley muttered under his breath. 'Been with you best part o' ten years, and you stick me with a wopsie!'

McDermott scowled. 'Get with the times, George. Besides, WPCs don't exist any more; she's a fully fledged Detective Constable—and according to her file a good one at that. Any headway on that Traffic fatality yet?'

Ridley looked pleased with himself. 'Matter o' fact, we did. Quinn reckoned lass might a' bought all her kit at one go. Turns out she did, or just about. We were able to trace her from Liberty's up to Debenham's, where she got most 'er togs, and then along Oxford Street to a shoe shop in Great Portland.'

'I don't suppose she paid for any of her purchases with a bank card or cheque?' McDermott asked hopefully.

'Now, then, it don't take much to satisfy you, do it? But a clerk in the shoe store was taken with her—got a foot fetish, if you ask me,' Ridley sniffed. 'He chatted 'er up a bit—asked her if she lived in the area—you know the kind of thing. Said she didn't live that far, but doubted they'd see that much of each other. Fair pissed in his whisky, I shouldn't wonder.'

'So your next move is to show a mortuary photo of her around and see if anyone can put a name or address to her?'

He grimaced. 'We're on it first thing today, Guv. Starting at Oxford Circus we're working north, between Baker Street and Tott'am Court Road. With any luck we should have a result by tomorrow this time.'

McDermott pondered his Sergeant's plan. 'That's a large area, and it's already been'—he looked at his watch—'forty four hours since the accident. You'd better draw some help from Uniform Branch. I'll arrange it. Incident room in thirty minutes.'

As McDermott headed downstairs he reflected on their conversation. He had been in touch with Missing Persons, and come up empty, although they had promised to keep him advised of any queries regarding anyone resembling the victim's description. Almost two full days had elapsed since an attractive young woman, apparently not without means, had been crushed under the wheels of a London Transport bus, and no one had come forward to file a Misper report. Not impossible, particularly with all the tourists about; but certainly unusual. In his experience people who were not reported missing usually fell into one of two categories: those whom nobody cared about any longer, and those who deliberately sought to lose themselves. This was no teenage runaway, nor a vagrant sleeping rough in a doorway or a Tube station, nor a tourist on her own. It went against the odds that someone of her age, appearance, and apparent resources wouldn't be missed.

RIDLEY RANG THROUGH WITH THE NEWS that afternoon. A Mrs. Twigg, who ran a bedsit in Carburton Street, had tentatively identified the victim. He was on his way with her to the mortuary to get a positive ID. McDermott asked him to bring her to his office if the identification was confirmed.

Before long McDermott's door opened and Ridley and Quinn ushered a stout woman in. 'This is Mrs. Twigg,' he said, pulling out a chair for her. 'Inspector McDermott, missus.'

Mrs. Twigg was nothing like her name. She must have weighed all of eighteen stone, he judged. In her late sixties, she was dressed in a large, paisley-patterned dress that did little to conceal her considerable size. Her expression managed to combine mild distress with undisguised curiousity at her surroundings.

'How do you do, Mrs. Twigg.' He gestured toward an empty chair, and then took his own. 'I know this must be a bit of a shock for you. I gather that you've been able to help us identify the young woman who was—who died two days ago.' It was stated as a fact, with just the hint of a question at the end.

'Oh, yessir,' the woman replied. 'I wondered when she didn't return the other night, but you know how young girls are these days. I didn't want to seem a nosy parker.'

'Perfectly understandable,' he assured her. 'Now perhaps you can assist us in notifying her relatives. What was her name?'

'Sheila Bannerman, sir. She'd only been with me a few days. Said she'd been accepted at the University of London. It's just a few streets from my place,' she beamed proudly. 'Always popular with the students.'

That explained it, thought McDermott. If she'd recently come to London to go to university she probably wouldn't have been in daily touch with her family. They might not have become concerned until the weekend, at least. Perhaps not even then. If she was from outside London, the unwelcome task of informing her family would fall upon someone else, he reflected gratefully.

'And you have her home address?

'Yessir. Remember it perfectly. Nothing wrong with my memory,' she said proudly. 'Elm Cottage, Newsham Road, Cambridge.'

McDermott thought about what he'd just been told. If she was from Cambridge, why had she come down to London to attend university? Not enough A levels, perhaps, or a matter of finances? Or perhaps she simply wanted to leave the nest, go to university without her parents looking over her shoulder. McDermott was considering how many plausible explanations must exist when George Ridley caught his eye.

'You'd best have a look at this, Guv.' The Sergeant handed him a scrap of paper torn from his notebook. On it was written, in his almost illegible scrawl,

Accdg. Camb. Constab. no such address.

McDermott frowned, then looked up at the landlady. 'Did Miss Bannerman indicate which college of the University of London she was attending?'

'She may have done,' the elderly woman conceded, frowning. 'But if she did, I took no notice. It don't mean much to me, you see, not having much schooling myself.' She looked faintly embarrassed.

McDermott sighed. Another obstacle, but not a formidable one. 'In cases of this kind we have to proceed carefully, Mrs. Twigg, as I'm sure you'll appreciate. Sergeant Ridley and DC Quinn will need to have a look at Miss Bannerman's rooms'

Mrs. Twigg stirred uncomfortably, her fingers playing with her wedding band. 'Well, I'm not sure—'

McDermott cut her off. 'You understand that we have to be quite certain about the victim's identity. It wouldn't do for us to inform the wrong family that their daughter had just been killed. I'm sure you can see that.'

She relented, as McDermott knew she would. Rising from his desk, he turned to Quinn. 'Perhaps Mrs. Twigg would like a cuppa before you and George take her home. Thank you for your cooperation. You've been a great help to us.'

When they had left the room, McDermott fixed his eyes on Ridley. 'I'm less and less happy with this case, George. Nothing about it is what it seems to be. As soon as she's ready take her home and give the girl's digs a good going over. I want anything that might suggest an identity or an address: cleaning tags, receipts, Oyster card, rail pass, student ID card, letters, anything. Is there any chance the old girl might simply have got the address wrong?' he asked, not very hopefully.

'No chance at all, I reckon,' the Sergeant replied. 'Street doesn't exist—nor anything like it. Reckon as how she didn't want anyone checkin' up on her.'

'Very well,' McDermott conceded. 'It's not the first time we've run into someone who wasn't what she seemed. We'll puzzle it out.'

But McDermott wondered what dark secret could make someone jettison their identity, and undertake the formidable task of constructing an entirely new persona. Was she running away from an abusive husband? A jealous exboyfriend? Simply a mountain of debts? Or was she running towards, rather than away from, something? The attractions of living in a big city?

That wouldn't explain why she'd felt it necessary to take on a new identity, though. Realising that more information was needed, McDermott turned his attention to other matters and waited for Ridley's report.

LIKE MANY OTHER LONDON DWELLINGS, Seventeen Carburton Street had succumbed to the pressure of ever-increasing property prices. What once had been an attractive pair of spacious flats over a shared entryway and parking garage had been converted into a number of tiny bedsits, most sharing a bathroom. A corner of each functioned as a kitchen. Ridley doubted that the conversion had been done with the knowledge and approval of the planning authority; he shuddered as his glance extended to the wiring, which was easily twenty years old and seemed even to his eyes dangerously outmoded and amateurishly done.

'Here we are. All the mod cons. My husband Alfred did most of the work when we made it over,' Mrs. Twigg offered, apparently oblivious to the implications of her admission. 'Just before he died,' she added gloomily.

It fell to Quinn to bring the discussion back to matters at hand. 'Tell us again what you know about Miss Bannerman. How did she learn that you had rooms?'

'She just showed up on my doorstep one day—that would be about three weeks ago, maybe a little less. Said she saw my card in a newsagent's window. I always put it up about a month before the university starts. The young people say they find it ever so handy here, being so close to their classes.'

'And did she move in right away?'

'Not so's you'd notice. Gave me a deposit—insisted on paying cash, though I told her I'd be pleased to take a cheque—and it was a day—no, I tell a lie—two days after that she moved in some clothes. Not much, either, poor thing. I was about to feel sorry for her until she returned from a shopping trip with all new togs—very swish they was, too.' Mrs. Twigg managed to convey the fact that she had no longer felt sorry for her lodger.

'Did she say she'd just come down from Cambridge, or that she'd been in London awhile?'

The landlady shook her head. 'She didn't say one way or t'other, though now as you mention it she had no problem finding her way around. Just set off down the street on foot one day, she did. Said she had a few things to do and she'd be back in a day or two. That's why I asked for a deposit up front. You'd be surprised how many folks say they want a room, and ask me not to rent it to anyone else, and then just disappear, leaving me high and dry. What with the prices of things these days,' she puffed, ascending the stairs, 'losing a month's rent is the difference between making do and having to do without.'

Leading them up to the top floor, Mrs. Twigg paused to catch her breath, then unlocked the last door in the hallway and entered the room. The window was closed tight and the curtains were drawn. Although it was a cool day, the heat had been turned down and the room had a musty air. Pushing the curtains back to admit the daylight, she glanced about briefly and turned to Ridley and Quinn. 'This is—was—her room. Very quiet she was. No men friends—in fact no visitors at all. Expect she wasn't here long enough to make new friends, though she was pretty enough. What about her things? I mean, I'll need to rent the room again, seeing as she won't be using it, won't I?'

Quinn moved toward the door, all but guiding the landlady by the arm. 'The sooner we can trace her, the sooner you'll be able to move her things out, Mrs. Twigg. Though at that point you should box them up for her family, who will doubtless want to have them. Thank you for your help. We won't be long, I expect. You will be downstairs, I take it, if we have any further questions?'

The landlady took the hint and left them to their work.

As soon as she had gone, they surveyed the room. It was unpretentious, going on Spartan. To the right of the hallway door, they saw, was a tiny bathroom. In the corner nearby was a single bed and bedside table that had seen better days. Next to it stood a wardrobe and dresser, both finished in a handsome dark wood but also showing signs of age. The wardrobe contained assorted tops and slacks which vied for space with a small collection of hand-bags and shoes, all of good quality, and mostly new. A search of the handbags only revealed an open roll of breath mints, a few coins, and some tissues. The top of the dresser was equally uninformative: several shades of lip gloss, eye liner, and blush, all tasteful, and three pair of sunglasses, one with metallic frames, one in black, and one in tortoiseshell. In front of the window was a small plain desk, scarred and worn, and next to that a bookcase, almost bare, save for a few books that were obviously texts.

The other end of the room served as the kitchen-dining area. One corner was occupied by an elderly refrigerator under a tiny laminate countertop with a single set of drawers alongside. The fridge revealed little: a small plate of half-eaten pate, some cheese, and surprisingly, a bottle of expensive wine. On the countertop a toaster vied for space with a tiny microwave and a double electric ring, on which rested a kettle. To the left of the counter was what, at some earlier point in time, had been a white porcelain sink, with a pair of taps that would have benefitted from a good cleaning. Painted shelves contained perhaps a dozen mismatched plates and cups and glasses, and two wine glasses, both clear of prints and dusty. The remainder of that end of the room consisted of a small kitchen table and a single chair, its mate having been moved to do service at the desk.

A worn linoleum floor stretched the length of the room, interrupted only by a small square of carpet next to the bed. The entire space was illuminated by a single fitting placed squarely in the middle of the ceiling, another over the sink, and a desk lamp that did double duty as a light next to the bed. There was no television—not surprising for someone of her age— but neither was there a laptop or tablet, and, tellingly, no mobile. What struck Quinn most was not the furnishings, but the barren, totally impersonal quality of the room: nowhere was there a photograph, a souvenir, a stuffed animal, anything that would reveal even the smallest facet of the dead woman's personality.

Quinn spoke first. 'It's not exactly home, is it, George?'

'I've seen worse,' Ridley allowed. 'Best get down to it, then. I'll start with the desk.'

The pair of them spent the next hour combing the space with professional expertise. Had it been a crime scene or suspicious death they would have called in Forensics to give the room a thorough vetting, but in the absence of anything sinister, they set about checking the scene themselves.

Quinn searched the tiny bathroom, hoping for a bottle of prescription medication, or perhaps a packet of birth control pills, that would give her some lead by which to trace the woman, but to no avail: the top of the dresser was no better, containing only a few cosmetics and toiletries. She went through the drawers and noticed that much of the victim's wardrobe was similar in style and price to what she had been wearing the day that she died. The colours of her clothing harmonised so they could be combined in various ways. A small teakwood box surrendered a few bits of inexpensive jewelry. They gave an impression of innocuous but informed good taste. Nothing was flashy or out of place, or of exceptional value, the quality was apparent. All in all, the clothing was certainly out of character with the room, Quinn reflected. Having gone over the young woman's most personal apparel, she was as unenlightened about the real Sheila Bannerman as when they first taken on the case.

For his part, Ridley was having little success. The single drawer in the desk had proved to be virtually empty, yielding only a couple of small blank notebooks, a few biros, a packet of unsharpened pencils, a roll of sellotape, and a package of plain white envelopes. He turned, not very hopefully, to the texts in the bookcase. After checking for a name or address inside the front cover, he held each upside down, and shook it. So far he had come up empty.

The Sergeant was on his fourth book, somewhat intimidatingly titled *Modern European History: the Ottoman Empire to the Collapse of the Soviet Union*, when something fluttered out from between the pages and onto the floor. George bent over to pick it up. He examined it for a moment, and then whistled softly.

Willie Quinn put down the dark green silk blouse she had been admiring and looked up. 'Strike gold, George?'

'More like platinum, I reckon,' he replied. 'Cash machine receipt for East End branch o' HSBC, last entry dated three weeks back. Shows balance near 20,000 pounds!'

'Doesn't sound like your run-of-the-mill impoverished university student—or the bank balance of someone living in digs like these.'

'Another thing,' Ridley observed. 'Name o' depositor. It's not Sheila Bannerman. It's in the name o' Sally Beck.'

EIGHT

When **Ridley and Quinn** returned to the station they found McDermott had some news of his own.

'I've just been on to the path lab,' he revealed. 'Seems our victim wasn't considered a priority item since the cause of death was so evident. However, they turned up some interesting results. It seems our middleclass, manicured young woman wasn't quite what she seemed. According to the lab she had been more than a little sexually active. Not to put too fine a point on it, she seems to have been on the game.'

Quinn, who had been removing her jacket, paused. 'That would explain why she has absolutely no social media presence. How many young people do you know that aren't on Twitter, or even Facebook?'

The Sergeant knew no one on any website, but he didn't say so. 'Explains cashpoint receipt as well, I reckon.'

'What receipt?' McDermott queried. Ridley filled him in.

McDermott shifted uneasily in his chair. 'That leaves us with quite a few loose ends. Who was she, really? Where did she come from? What was she doing at the University—if in fact she was? And is it likely that a streetwise person would fall into the path of a crosstown bus?'

The three spent the next ten minutes mapping out their next moves. McDermott would check the new name and her fingerprints against the Met's databases, and send a copy of the dead woman's photo, together with her known alias, to the Cambridgeshire constabulary, on the off chance that someone there might recognise her. He would have a notice put in the dailies, without a photo, asking anyone with information concerning the accident to come forward; and he would also confer further with Pathology to determine what else of interest they might have turned up. Ridley would meet with the branch manager of the HSBC to determine when the account had been opened, what transactions had taken place, and most importantly, what address had been given. Quinn would contact the various colleges of London University, to establish whether they had any record of a Sheila Bannerman or a Sally Beck.

Quinn looked up from her notes. 'sir, if you're right about her being a sex worker, then she'd have had to have a mobile, right? I'll check with various service providers to see what we can turn up.'

'Good idea, Willie. But I'm betting it was either in another name altogether, or she used a pay-as-you-go phone. She seems to have known what she was about—'

The civilian aide interrupted McDermott with the news that an inquest on the dead woman had been scheduled for the following morning.

After making a couple of telephone calls to set things in motion, McDermott made his way to the Mortuary at St. Bartholomew's Hospital. It wasn't a domain that he frequented, relying instead on reports sent by email. But for all its prosaic elements this was shaping up as no ordinary case, and he had another, more personal reason for making the trip. He emerged from the lift and walked down the long, antiseptically-white corridor. The sickening odour of formalyn lingered in the background. Halfway down the hallway he turned and passed through frosted double glass doors. An attractive, auburn-haired woman wearing a white laboratory coat over a faune-coloured skirt was seated at a desk in one corner. A nameplate on the front edge of the desk read *Dr. D. Fielding, Forensic Pathologist.* She looked up as he approached. He noticed, for the first time, a yellowed sign over a sink in the corner: *Wash Your Bloody Hands Before Leaving.*

'Hello, Daph. Cute sign. Your idea?'

'Here ages before me, I'm afraid. This is a treat, Colin. We don't often see your face down here.'

'Can't imagine why.' He sniffed the air conspicuously.

She laughed. 'Point taken. I guess it's not everyone's cuppa. Here about your Miss X, I expect?'

'That's right. The inquest is set for 10 o'clock tomorrow, and we haven't yet confirmed her identity.'

'Can't help you there, I'm afraid. Not my patch, as you lads say. But you got my message, I assume. It seems your young lady wasn't all that much of a lady after all: clear evidence of extensive sexual activity. She was almost certainly a paid sex worker.'

'So I gather. Actually, I'm here to see if you have anything else for me. We're short of hard facts at the moment. A lot of girls on the game are into drugs. Was she a user?'

'Surprisingly, no. There were no needle marks anywhere on the body, and that includes the scalp, even between the toes. Also, her toxicology was negative. She didn't wander into the path of the bus because she was stoned.'

McDermott wondered whether he had anything solid that would justify a full investigation. 'Could she have been *pushed*?'

Daphne considered the question. 'It's possible. That's all I can say. Thankfully the wheels missed her head. There is subcutaneous tissue and bone damage to her head, one shoulder, arms, hips and thighs, but those injuries were a result of her initial impact with the bus. The underlying musculature was extensively traumatised. There were also multiple contusions and abrasions on her hands, elbows, shoulders and head, as a result of her impact with the roadway. Bits in the cuts. Lots of cosmetic damage, in short, but nothing the funeral home won't be able to deal with.'

'Cause of Death?'

'Well, it was almost instantaneous, and due to massive chest injuries and the resulting internal haemorrhaging sustained when the vehicle passed over her.'

McDermott shuddered inwardly. Somehow hearing the details aloud was always more grotesque than reading about them in some report.

'Is it a suspicious death?' she asked.

'Not from what we have at this point. What will you say if you're asked at the inquest tomorrow?'

'I'd have to say I have no reason to believe it was anything but an accident, Colin. Sorry.'

He smiled. 'Don't be. If it was murder the perpetrator may be watching the papers to see whether he got away with it. I'd like to put him off his guard.'

'If it was murder, how do you know it was a man?' she smirked. 'I'll do what I can. If something turns up I'll let you know.'

'Thanks, Daphne. Not a pretty way to go. If she was murdered I promise I'll have the bugger that did it for breakfast.'

'Charming. Speaking of promises, the last time you were down here—that would be at least three weeks ago, when I gave you a hand with the Webster case—you said you were up for a night on the town. Does that still apply?"

'Right. Of course. What have you got in mind?'

'It just so happens that I have two tickets for a rock concert in a couple of week's time. Interested?'

McDermott regarded her warily. Rock concerts were not his first—or, come to that, his second or third—choice. 'I've got another idea, Daphne. There's a concert at the Albert Hall this Saturday. Debussy and Ravel. I have season tickets. My treat. What do you say?'

She looked at him, amused. 'Why not? One of us has to be open-minded, I suppose.'

McDermott glanced at his watch, avoiding her mocking smile. He wondered how Ridley and Quinn were getting on, and whether there had been any replies to his email queries to Cambridgeshire . After making his goodbyes he headed back to his office.

WHILE MCDERMOTT WAS MAKING HIS WAY back to the Charing Cross Station a respected member of St. Gregory's College was leafing through the daily newspapers in the Senior Common Room. In itself this was not unusual. What was, perhaps, remarkable was the close attention being devoted to the task. The reader skimmed page after page, as if searching for something specific. Finally the reader paused, lingering over a brief notice:

INQUEST SET FOR BUS VICTIM

An inquest has been scheduled for tomorrow at 10 AM in the
Coroner's Court, Golden Lane, into the death of a young woman

who was killed by a London Transport bus on High Holborn east of Southampton Row at approximately 1 PM on Tuesday last.

The woman is described as in her early to mid-twenties, of average build, with medium length brown hair. She was wearing dark grey woolen trousers and a silk blouse, lavender in colour, with a paisley scarf.

Police are having difficulty identifying the victim, and anyone having information is urged to contact the nearest police station or New Scotland Yard.

After reading it carefully, and then reading it once more, the paper was carefully refolded, and quietly replaced on the reading table with the other periodicals. A moment later the Senior Common Room was empty.

NINE

Norman Anscombe sat at his desk and considered the files before him. It wasn't going to be easy. The Board had received a total of seven applications to succeed him. Weeding out those who were clearly non-starters left four serious candidates. Three of these were internal, Fellows of the College. None of them, in his judgment, was really suitable. That posed a problem, for Anscombe was committed to achieving an easy and orderly transition. His own appointment, he recalled, had been as an external candidate, following a sudden and fatal coronary suffered by his predecessor. There had been months of recriminations and petty jealousies over the Board's failure to appoint from within. In the wake of such hostility and bickering, many worthwhile reforms he had envisaged had to be modified or abandoned altogether. Anscombe was determined not to let history repeat itself.

A fourth application was from a member of the Board, a banker of some standing. In Anscombe's view the man was a philistine; his appointment would be certain to cause a furore amongst the Fellows. Yet to ask the Regents to reject one of their own, Anscombe knew, also would be difficult. Pity that the really capable faculty were uninterested in replacing him as Principal. What was it Plato had said? *The only reason good men consent to govern is the fear of being ruled by worse men.* That, Anscombe reflected, might be the key to persuading the one person he knew who would command the respect of the faculty and the support of the Board as well. He consulted his calendar. Today was Wednesday; he would have to work quickly. The Selection Committee was scheduled to meet in two day's time. If they could come to an agreement and the Chancellor could be persuaded to hold an extraordinary meeting of the Board the following afternoon, the deed would be done; for Anscombe wanted to be in a position to announce his successor at the Principal's Dinner scheduled for Saturday evening. He consulted the schedule of classes. Free this afternoon, he noted with satisfaction. An omen, he decided, and picked up his telephone.

WHILE ANSCOMBE WAS DOING HIS BEST to influence the fates of succeeding generations of students, Ridley and Quinn sat in McDermott's office reviewing with him their progress in what he was coming to regard as The Sally Beck Homicide. It was late afternoon, and, after fortifying themselves with fresh coffee, McDermott led off the proceedings.

'I've been down to the mortuary,' he said, carefully sipping the steaming liquid. 'It's not conclusive, but it's a possibility that our young woman may have been deliberately killed. Either of you have anything that would tend to confirm or deny that?'

McDermott looked at George, who obliged. 'Well, I spoke to branch manager where she had her an account. At first he weren't keen on letting me have any gen. Usual prattle about confidential records and court orders. But once I told him she were dead, and said his delicate sensibilities might obstruct an official police investigation, he came across right enough. When I showed mortuary photo to tellers, they identified her as Sally Beck all right. Seems she had savings account under that name, and it's sizeable: current balance is £17,800.'

McDermott placed his fingers together, and leaned forward, putting his elbows on his desk. 'Not exactly your average impoverished student, then. But what did you find out about the history of the account? When and where was it opened, and how often and in what amounts did money flow in and out of it?'

Ridley looked hard done by. 'I were just comin' to that, Guv. Seems she opened it at that branch about six months ago. Up till three weeks ago it were all deposits, nearly always by cashpoint. Most every Monday for past six months, regular as clockwork, between seven hundred and seven hundred and fifty quid. Always in cash, and always around midday. No withdrawals till recentlike, when she took out three thousand quid.'

McDermott considered the new information. 'So there's your twenty thousand pounds, all deposited in the past six months—in cash—and it's largely untouched, so she must have had another source of support. It's possible she was married, or still lived at home with her family, though that would have been awkward if she worked the streets. What do we have for an address?'

'That's where the interesting bit comes in, Chief. We know she hadn't got 'round to closing her account and opening 'nother in her new name. Seems she hadn't found time to change address, neither,' he added ungrammatically. 'Number 3 Gravel Lane, just east of Liverpool Street Station—*and* two streets north of route of number 8 bus, which passes down High Holburn, where she were killed.'

McDermott allowed himself a smile. 'Looks like we're finally making headway. Good work, George.' He glanced at his watch. 'Tonight might be a good time to get down there and ferret out her friends. If she was on the game, that'll be the time to catch them.'

'I'm way ahead of you, Guv,' Ridley smiled, clearly enjoying himself. 'I've got a mate in local nick nearby. He knows area like back o' his hand. I'm headed down there just after supper.'

'You've done a good day's work, George.' He turned to Quinn. 'What did you find out about our mysterious young woman's academic ambitions?'

She had no need to consult her notes. 'Good and bad results, sir. On the bad side there's no record with any of the London service providers of a mobile under either name we have for her. Looks like you were right about her using a disposable phone.'

McDermott frowned. 'What's the good news, then?'

'It seems that under the name of Sheila Bannerman our young woman applied for admission to St. Gregory's College of the University of London three months ago. She gave her age as twenty-four. That meant she was considered a mature candidate and was not required to submit any A Level certificates. Only a letter from a former employer stating she'd been working for him for the past five years.'

'Clever, that. I suppose the letter was forged?'

'Not much doubt about it, sir. I checked. She—or a friend—pinched some stationery from an office temp firm. No one there had heard of her before.'

'A bit risky, wasn't that?'

'Not really, sir. I checked with the Registrar there. A few months before the beginning of term it's like a zoo there, what with getting out the previous term's marks and processing new applicants. Apparently they're primarily interested in whether mature candidates have the necessary fees. Gave me a lot of high-sounding rubbish about their 'mission' being to democratise education.'

McDermott passed a knowing glance at Ridley, who was savouring the moment. 'Place must have changed since my day.'

Quinn flushed a crimson red. 'Sorry, sir, I had no idea! I'm sure that in your day—I mean—'

'That's all right, Willie.' McDermott laughed, clearly enjoying himself. 'You weren't to know. Go on. What else did you find out?'

Quinn continued, this time considerably more subdued. 'Well, sir, she gave them the runaround about her address. Said she was in the process of moving, and would give them her new address. She also had a student ID photo taken. I have a copy here.' She passed it over to McDermott, along with the mortuary photo. 'Not much doubt it's the same person.'

'Nice work. Were you able to find out anything else?'

'Nothing about her friends, if that's what you mean. It seems that with the job market being what it is the college has been flooded with close to three hundred new first-year students this term, and of course no one could say whether she'd made any friends. I did, however, get a copy of her list of classes if we want to pursue that angle. Also a copy of her receipt for partial payment of fees. It seems she paid £1550 toward her tuition at the beginning of term, just a few days ago. In new bank notes,' she added.

'Squares with her bank records, Guv,' interjected Ridley. 'Between school fees, new togs, and deposit to landlady I reckon we've accounted for most all her spendin' in past month. Seems to rule out possibility that her bag went missing 'cause it had a deal of cash.'

McDermott was thoughtful. 'Yes, I don't think this case is about money—at least not what was on her person.' He looked at his watch. It was nearly six. 'Time to call it a day,' he drained his cup. 'Except for you, George. Let me know tonight what you learn from Gravel Lane. The inquest is at 10 tomorrow, and I'd like to know what I'm going to tell the Coroner.'

AS IT HAPPENED, McDermott did not have long to wait. As he was watching the late news his telephone rang. McDermott reached for the phone, upsetting a glass and spilling the remains of a stale beer over a small occasional table as he did so. 'Damn! Yes, hello?' he answered testily.

'That you, Guv? Sorry to bother you at home like, but you wanted to know about Gravel Lane.'

'Of course, George. What did you find out?'

'Well, my mate and I went to flat in Gravel Lane, but place were locked up tighter than a nun's knickers. We got name of 'er flat mate from a neighbour, though. Must've hit half a dozen pubs 'afore we found her. Name o' Beryl Potter. Didn't want to say much at first, till I showed her mortuary photo. Very cut up, she were. After that she opened up. Knew our young woman as Sally Beck, all right. Shared digs for past year, up till recentlike. Seems she—Sally, that is—worked days sewing job lots at textile factory three streets away, and disappeared on weekends.'

'Looking more and more as if she was working the streets,' McDermott reasoned. 'She certainly wouldn't be able to put away that kind of money in the rag trade. Anything else?'

'Yessir,' Ridley replied. 'I asked this Beryl bint what she could tell me about her mate. She played it close to vest. Said Sally told 'er she were staying weekends with boyfriend and decided to move in with him. I asked if Beck girl had left anything behind. Seems there were a couple of boxes of clothes she'd left behind to pick up later. I got Beryl woman to open up flat and we had a right good look. In a pair o' denims I found a letter.' Ridley paused again.

McDermott's ears pricked up. 'Spit it out, man. I know when you're holding out.'

Even over the telephone, George's satisfaction was palpable. 'It were addressed to a Miss Sally Beck, Guv, from a Mrs. E. Beck, with a return address in Clap'am.

TEN

McDermott arrived at the Charing Cross police station the next morning to find a message on his desk: *DSupt. Galbraith would like to see you ASAP.* He frowned, even though he'd been expecting this. Passing through the outer office he took the stairs to the next floor.

Derek Galbraith headed the station CID, and was responsible for the Major Crimes Unit—supervising DCI Loach and McDermott and a staff of some two dozen other CID officers. A tall, heavy-set man with wavy brown hair and matching eyes that could be searching or kindly as the need arose, he was generally supportive, and would run interference for the officers in his division, while allowing them a wide latitude for action. But McDermott knew the Super expected to be kept abreast of each investigation, and lacking anything substantive, McDermott had not yet brought him up to speed on this case. He said his hulloes to the civilian assistant and was immediately ushered into Galbraith's office, where Galbraith was having his morning coffee and reading the overnight incident reports.

'Good morning,' he said, not looking up. All business, then.

'Morning, sir.' Usually they were on a first-name basis, but McDermott was testing the waters.

'What's on your plate this morning, Colin?' *The temperature was warming,* he thought to himself.

McDermott suspected that he already knew the answer. 'Just an inquest, in an hour's time. The young woman killed in High Holborn Tuesday last.'

'Umm. Oh yes. John Pitt put us on to that, as I recall. Tell me again: why are we interested in it?'

McDermott dropped into a nearby chair and moved it slightly toward the desk. 'It's not clear yet. At first glance it seemed to be a routine traffic accident. But as you know, when Traffic couldn't put a name to her, Pitt asked us to look into it. So far we've discovered she used an alias, and according to Pathology she was on the game. It raises the possibility that she might have been pushed.'

'I see. What are your plans for the inquest?'

'At this point, containment. I'm simply going to ask for an open verdict and an adjournment pending further enquiries.'

'How many people do you have on this?'

'Just two at the moment: Ridley and Quinn—the new DC you sent me—remember?'

'Oh, yes. A quick study, as I recall. How's she working out? Any difficulties with George?'

McDermott seized on the change of topic. 'Not really. You know George. He made some noises about working with a woman, but he's coming around. She seems intelligent enough—knows how to take the initiative without seeming to be pushy. Diplomatic.'

'Had lots of practice, I dare say.' Galbraith leaned back in his chair. 'Not the most flexible of persons, our George. I trust he won't make it too difficult for Quinn. A bright young woman, an up-and-comer, I should think.' He paused. 'How many years until George retires?'

'Five, if memory serves. But he's a good officer. Just last week—'

Galbraith waved him aside. 'Yes, yes, I know. He's done us proud in the past. But not to put too fine a point on it, he's beyond Old School: he's a bit of an anarchronism, which doesn't always reflect well on the Met image.' Galbraith shifted some papers on his desk. 'I don't have to tell you about the current belt-tightening measures from above. Ridley came to the Job late, and as one of the most senior Sergeants in this division he's at the top of his pay scale. If he took early retirement we could replace him with two officers—or use the money elsewhere. Perhaps we can find him something internal to fill out his days.'

McDermott struggled to control himself. 'George's work is his life, *sir*, and he can hold his own against most of the youngsters who will be taking his place soon enough. It would be a great loss to put him out to pasture before his time.' He stood up and strode toward the door.

Galbraith stared at him. Confrontations were not the Superintendent's style, and although he could overrule him easily enough, Galbraith liked to pick his battles. 'Very well, we'll table it for the moment. But it's on your head.' His expression sharpened. 'You might have heard that Sam Bradford is retiring as Chief Super in a few months' time. That means a vacancy upstairs, and I intend to apply for it. If I am successful my desk here will be up for grabs, and I needn't tell you that there will be a certain amount of interest in it. You're a good officer, McDermott, with real potential for the senior ranks. I'd hate to see you passed over simply because of misplaced loyalty.'

McDermott took a breath and gathered himself. 'No one has ever had cause to doubt my loyalty, nor my judgment. The day I conclude that George Ridley is past it, I will personally ask for his resignation. But not before,' he added pointedly. After a moment's silence he added, 'If there's nothing more, sir.'

Galbraith was caught off guard. He hadn't expected McDermott to fight him on this. As McDermott left the room, the Superintendent pondered his reaction. Perhaps Loach was the right person to succeed him after all.

THE CORONER'S COURT was located in the Barbican Centre, some distance from the Charing Cross station, and it was nearly ten o'clock when McDermott pulled into the car park and made his way though a side entrance and along the busy corridors to the appropriate hearing room. As he entered he noticed Daphne Fielding sitting in the front row, next to DCS Pitt. Alongside Pitt was a young PC who McDermott supposed had been first on the scene. At his side was a middle-aged man wearing the grey uniform of London Transport. A second man in a dark grey suit sat next to them; McDermott supposed he was either the driver's supervisor or a representative for the driver's union.

Two men dressed in crisp white uniforms, clearly ambulance attendants, sat in the second row. Next to them, Ridley and Quinn flanked a blonde woman in her early twenties who looked vacantly about. That would be the roommate, he supposed. Nearby, an elderly woman whispered to a young man. Witnesses at the bus stop? Several young men dressed in blue jeans and casual shirts in vibrant colours sat behind them, jabbering and gesturing animatedly, and at the other end of the row three Japanese girls dressed in dark skirts and crisp white blouses sat sedately, murmuring to one another in hushed tones. At the front of the room, flanking one side of the Coroner's table, were seated several individuals of both genders and varying ages: McDermott knew they constituted the jury that would render a verdict as instructed by the coroner.

There were a number of other people in the room: some no doubt were there for cases that would arise later in the morning; others were merely there out of morbid curiosity, like birds of prey circling carrion. At least the girl's parents would be spared this spectacle. He made his way toward the front of the chamber, nodded to Ridley and Quinn, and spoke to Pitt.

'Good Morning, Chief Superintendent. This is a surprise. Here to watch us in action, are you?'

Pitt looked up. 'Don't flatter yourself. I want to make sure the driver isn't hung out to dry on this one. It all depends on the luck of the draw: whether you get a coroner who's on a crusade, or one simply trying to do his job. Whoever said justice is blind—'

But Pitt didn't get a chance to finish his sentence, for at that moment a door at the front of the chamber opened and an usher appeared. He stood by the open doorway and in a tone of voice calculated to bring all conversation to a full and complete stop, instructed them to all rise, and informed them that the Central Coroner's Court for the City of London was now in session. They were told that the coroner would be his worship, Sir Humphrey Caldicott, which was followed closely by the appearance of a tall, elderly and rather thin man in a dark suit, who walked briskly to his place, sat down, and for several moments shuffled some papers as the onlookers gradually quieted themselves. Then he looked up, instructing the usher to please read the first case.

The court clerk dutifully picked up a paper on the table before him. 'Your Worship, we have before us the case of a woman fatally injured in a collision with a London Transport bus in High Holborn Street on three

October last, shortly before one o'clock in the afternoon. All persons having information regarding this case are informed that they are required to come forth as directed and give testimony under oath.' He consulted his list. 'Present to testify in this case is Detective Inspector Colin McDermott of the Metropolitan Police.'

The Coroner's eyebrows rose slightly. CID's involvement in what appeared to be a routine traffic accident signified to a man of his experience that this would be no ordinary inquest. Proceeding carefully, he turned to the jury. 'Ladies and Gentlemen, the first purpose of this hearing is to make a preliminary enquiry into the identity of the victim. The second objective will be to determine insofar as possible the precise cause of her death, to decide whether it involves any act of criminal intent or negligence, and if so, to fix responsibility for that act if it is possible to do so. Should you choose to so find, you should be aware that such a verdict may form the basis for criminal charges being laid by the Crown. In the event that it is not possible to fix responsibility at this time, you may return an open verdict, which will allow the case to be reopened at a later date.' He turned his attention to the usher. 'Call the Inspector to the witness box, please.'

McDermott rose and moved past the others in the front row, entered the witness box, and took his oath.

'State your name, occupation and rank, please,' the coroner instructed him.

'Colin McDermott, Detective Inspector, London Metropolitan Police.'

The coroner examined the file before him. 'Inspector, according to these records you have yet to positively identify the deceased. Is that correct?'

'I regret to say that it is, sir Humphrey.'

The coroner's eyebrows, which had settled into place, rose once again. 'Indeed? And why is that?'

McDermott leaned in slightly toward the microphone. 'Because the victim had no identification on her person, and since then no one has come forward to report anyone missing who answered to her description. It may be that her family, if she has any, is as yet unaware that she's missing.'

The coroner appeared to be studying the matter. 'I see. Terrible the way young people go about these days without the slightest regard for their own families. Really quite deplorable. What are you doing to ameliorate this situation, Inspector?'

McDermott paused, knowing that he was coming close to misleading the court. 'Well, sir, we've located a young woman who is in court today—whom we believe may have formerly shared a flat with the victim. She has tentatively identified the victim, but as you are aware, not being a relative, her identification is not considered definitive. Moreover, she has no knowledge of the family, and the name by which she knew the victim does not correspond with any known missing persons. We are examining the victim's personal belongings further in the hope that we can locate a member of the family who can confirm her identification.'

The coroner leaned toward McDermott. 'Have you considered using the newspaper and television media to publicise the particulars of this case?'

'Yes sir, we have. And we haven't ruled that option out. But at this point we are concerned to avoid unduly traumatising the victim's family if we can avoid it. However, we have not ruled out using such means if we are otherwise unsuccessful in the near future.'

Sir Humphrey was mollified. 'Quite so. Your concern is quite in order. I shall expect to be notified when the body is identified. For the purposes of this enquiry, then, we shall refer to the victim as Miss X. Thank you for your testimony. You may stand down.'

McDermott resumed his seat in the front row, and prepared to listen to other witnesses.

Next the Coroner called on Daphne Fielding. She confirmed that death had been caused by massive internal bleeding when the deceased passed under the wheels of the bus. There was no evidence that the young woman had been intoxicated, or under the influence of any form of illicit drug, nor was there any evidence of prescription medication in her system. When asked how it was, then, that she could have fallen into the street, Daphne replied that the evidence was inconclusive: perhaps the victim had stumbled, or had been preoccupied and had simply failed to see the oncoming bus in time. She glanced at McDermott, whose expression remained unchanged.

The driver was the next to be summoned to the witness box. He gave his name, address, and occupation, and in answer to a question indicated that he had been a driver with London Transport for seventeen years. No, he had not been involved in a fatal accident before. Traffic had been relatively light at the time of the accident. Yes, he had been driving at a normal speed, slowing, in fact, as he approached the stop. No, he could not account for the accident: one moment the street had been clear, the next moment the victim was directly in front of the bus. There had been no time for him to avoid striking her. He had applied the brakes immediately; indeed, several passengers had suffered minor injuries as a result.

The ambulance attendants confirmed that the young woman was dead on their arrival, and noted that several passengers, along with the driver, had been treated for shock.

Their testimony was followed by that of the elderly lady, who had to be helped to the witness box by her middle-aged son. She confirmed that the young woman had appeared in the street quite suddenly, and without being asked offered her opinion that it would have been quite impossible for the driver to avoid hitting her. When the coroner inquired about her eyesight she became somewhat indignant, and asserted that although she had worn spectacles for some years, her corrected vision was quite adequate to the task of getting around London and had not failed her yet.

The coroner next attempted to question several Italian youths who had queued at the bus stop. Unfortunately it transpired that they had a limited grasp of English, and since the Coroner's Italian was nonexistent, an interpreter was sent for; but the boys were of little help, their attention prior to the incident being fixed wholly upon a group of Japanese girls nearby.

The evidence of the Japanese tourists proved similarly fruitless. Though their English was excellent, they testified that they had not seen the young woman enter the street, admitting somewhat sheepishly that they had been distracted by the antics of the Italian boys nearby.

Less than two hours later the small knot of officers emerged from the darkness of the courtroom into the full sun of London. The inquest, McDermott reflected, had gone extremely well from his point of view. He had persuaded the Coroner that, in the absence of testimony by a relative, the identification of the victim should remain on hold for the moment. Daphne, for her part, had contrived to describe in full clinical detail the immediate cause of death, while leaving open the unstated possibility that the victim might have been pushed. Pitt was pleased that absolutely no blame had been assigned to the driver. Although the Coroner's expression suggested that McDermott had not been entirely candid, on the whole he seemed prepared to let the police have their way: the body had been released for burial pending identification by next of kin, and an Open Verdict as to the cause of death had been returned, leaving the possibility of criminal charges being laid at a later date.

As the group made their way out of the crowded courtroom they ignored the many onlookers who had been sitting quietly at the rear of the chamber. One person in particular had listened most attentively, and would have agreed with McDermott's assessment that the inquest had gone well, though for quite a different reason; for absolutely no mention had been made of the fact that the dead woman had been a student at St. Gregory's College.

MEANWHILE, IN A MODEST COUNCIL FLAT in Clapham, a small, elderly woman checked the morning post: a bill from the Electricity Board, an advertising flyer from a chemist's shop, an appeal for donations from a national charity, and a printed leaflet from the local MP, informing his constituents of his considerable efforts on their behalf. Silently she gave a thought to her daughter. It was unlike Sally not to write or telephone for—what had it been now—the best part of a week? The last time she called, hadn't she said that she would have some news for them soon? Well, she would certainly turn up this weekend. The woman wiped the care from her face and returned to the kitchen. It was time for Bert's morning tea.

ELEVEN

Following lunch McDermott met with George Ridley and Willie Quinn to review their progress. The envelope found in the flat had given them the breakthrough they'd needed. It had taken only a brief check with British Telecom to confirm that an Albert Beck and his wife Edna lived in Clapham, at number three, Twenty-seven Hope Street. He wasn't keen on breaking the news to the girl's parents, but as yet he lacked a positive identification of the body by a relative or close friend of some standing, and he hoped they could shed some light on the victim's life. McDermott ordered a car; although he didn't relish having to give them the bad news, he took some comfort from the fact that that that he had apparently run the elusive young woman to earth.

As they drove to the Beck's McDermott mapped out their strategy. These were in all likelihood the girl's parents, or at the least, close relatives. Since no MisPers Report had been filed for a Sally Beck—he'd checked—they probably had no reason to think that anything had happened to her. Her death would come out of the blue, then. He stressed the need for care and tact: the mother might need some assistance—father too, come to that. The two officers nodded.

As he turned into Hope Street McDermott surveyed the neighbourhood. Seldom, he reflected, had a place been so ill named. Builder's yards, trucking firms, warehouses and automotive repair shops seemed to dominate the run-down area. A public house on the corner vied for attention with a newsagent's shop across the street. Further down the street were a launderette and a lunch counter, with an off-licence sandwiched between them. Then came a line of brick council houses, converted into flats by the look of it—two dwellings to a floor, two floors high. Identical, mostly pre-War, they had somehow escaped the destruction during the bombings suffered by those in the heart of London or closer to the docks. Here and there were tiny accents of colour: a yellow door, a piece of blue trim, a window box filled with geraniums—token efforts by the inhabitants to bring some small measure of attractiveness to their dwellings. For the most part their attempts seemed unsuccessful. They pulled up in front of number Twenty-seven.

'Not very impressive, is it, sir?' Quinn ventured. McDermott didn't reply. He was thinking of the misery that was about to descend upon the unsuspecting couple.

The Becks' flat was on the second floor. To get to it they had to edge past a stroller blocking the stairs. On reaching the landing the prattle of a daytime television show competed with a domestic squabble taking place in the flat across the hall. They made their way to number three and McDermott knocked at the door. After a few moments a small, frail woman in a patterned pinafore appeared, and looked from one to the other of them.

McDermott's first thought was that they'd made a mistake. The woman in front of them was at least in her middle sixties. Elderly for having a daughter in her twenties. But not impossible.

'Mrs. Beck? Edna Beck?' he enquired.

'Aye.' There was a hint of wariness in the woman's eyes, as if she suspected them of flogging encyclopedias. McDermott put it out of his mind: In the internet age encyclopedia salesmen had gone the way of the dodo.

'We're from the police,' he said, producing his warrant card. 'My name is McDermott, and this is Detective Sergeant Ridley and DC Quinn. I wonder if we might step inside and have a word?'

The woman's eyes widened with apprehension. She turned her head toward the sitting room behind her. 'Dad,' she called, 'can you come to door? It's the police.'

After a moment a stout and equally elderly man appeared. He was unshaven, and his stubble had gone mostly white. This contrasted with his teeth—at least those that remained—which were stained a permanent yellow. He was wearing a grey and white plaid shirt and baggy trousers of an indeterminate shade, which were held up by a pair of black braces. If she was in her middle sixties, he must be in his early seventies at least. 'Aye? Summat you want?' he asked.

McDermott began again. 'Mr. Beck, is it? We're from the police. We'd like to speak with you, if we may.' When the man seemed reluctant he added, 'It's about your daughter.'

'Sally, you say? You'd best come in, then.' *So they were her parents after all.*

The man held the door ajar and showed them into the small sitting room where his wife was standing, clasping and unclasping her hands self-consciously. McDermott tried to decide whether their obvious unease stemmed from suspicion or merely from concern.

Once inside, McDermott looked around. The room, doubtless the largest in the modest flat, was cramped by too many pieces of furniture, dating from an era when rooms had been more spacious. The walls were hung with a flowered paper that had long ago faded from the sunlight, and were decorated with two unremarkable sepia-toned landscape photos and a small religious print on the facing wall. Against the third wall, facing the window, was a worn sideboard cluttered with photographs in a variety of inexpensive frames. The carpet was worn along one end, which led toward what McDermott guessed was the sole bedroom. The overstuffed sofa and single matching armchair had once been an attractive shade of dusty rose, but years of exposure to the sun had faded the material to an anæmic pink. There was a faint murmur of traffic in the street below.

McDermott took the armchair offered him, and the Becks sat on the edge of the sofa. Ridley and Quinn remained standing near the doorway of the tiny room.

McDermott looked at the elderly lady. 'You said your daughter is named Sally?'

Mrs. Beck nodded her assent.

'Can you tell me where she is now?'

Mrs. Beck looked to her husband to speak for them. 'She's at work, I reckon.' Then his eyes narrowed somewhat. 'Why do you ask?'

McDermott looked around the room, and spotted the sideboard covered with cheaply framed photographs, most of the same person. One showed a pigtailed girl of perhaps four or five at the seaside, with a much older woman; another, riding a pony at a summer fair, taken when she was perhaps nine; a third, taken at Christmas time, showed her in her early teens. He selected one that seemed to be most recent. It was a school photo, solemn, and seemingly taken in her mid teens.

'Is this Sally?' he asked.

Again Mrs. Beck glanced at her husband. She was growing more apprehensive, McDermott thought. 'Aye. That's right. Taken just 'afore she left school, it were. What's this all about, then?'

McDermott reached into his pocket, and pulled out the student ID Quinn had obtained from St. Gregory's. 'Is this what she looks like now?' He passed it over to the couple.

The man took it in his large, beefy hands, and they stared at it for only a moment. 'Aye, that's our Sally, right enough,' the man replied warily. 'Where'd you get this?'

McDermott could put it off no longer. 'I'm very sorry to have to tell you this,' he began, 'but I'm afraid your daughter has been involved in a road traffic accident. It involved a bus. There was nothing anyone could do for her. She didn't suffer.'

'Oh dear God, no. Never!' the woman exclaimed. She had gone deathly pale in a matter of seconds.

McDermott glanced at Quinn, who took the woman's arm. 'Let's go into the kitchen, Mrs. Beck. We could all do with a nice hot cup of tea.' Keeping her busy, she knew, was one way for the woman to come to terms with her grief.

Mrs. Beck temporarily taken care of, McDermott turned his attentions to her husband. He had aged visibly in the past few moments. 'I'm sure this must come as a great shock to you, Mr. Beck. Was she your only daughter?'

'Only child,' the man replied, staring dully at the photograph. 'We had her late in life—never no chance for 'nother.' He began to sob inaudibly, only the heaving of his chest giving silent expression to his grief. 'Are you sure it's her?' he asked, grasping at a straw.

McDermott commiserated. 'I'm afraid there's little room for doubt. I'm sorry, Mr. Beck. We'll try to make this as brief as possible. As her nearest relatives, however, I'm afraid you'll have to identify her for the record.'

The man looked at him pathetically. There were tears welling up in the corners of his eyes. 'Do both o' us 'ave t go? It'll just about kill the missus.'

McDermott felt sorry for the man, sorry for himself that this was part of his job. 'No, of course not. If there is someone nearby—a neighbour perhaps—that could stay with your wife...'

He shook his head. 'No close friends since we moved here. All young crowd. We don't go out much, 'cept to do the shopping. Sally—she were about all we had.' His voice trailed away as he turned to stare out the window, not wishing McDermott to see the tears welling up in his eyes.

Twenty minutes and a pot of tea later McDermott had extracted what little information he could from the couple. They were unaware that Sally had quit her job as a factory seamstress and applied for university. Mrs. Beck revealed that Sally had hinted at having some news for them only the week before, promising to tell them all about it when she saw them next. They hadn't heard from her after that. Their grief at their daughter's death was, McDermott thought, somewhat assuaged by the sense of pride they felt in her having been accepted at university. There was no escaping, though, the bittersweet aspect of their situation. Her hopes, their pride, had been suddenly and tragically ended. He wondered how they would fill their remaining years.

Quinn spoke with a young mother next door, who agreed to stay with Mrs. Beck until her husband returned. Then the four of them returned to central London.

An hour later Albert Beck had confirmed that the body in the mortuary was indeed the remains of his only child. The tears had gone by then, replaced by a stolid expression that revealed little of the grief that would remain in the weeks and months and years to come. He signed an affidavit confirming the identity of the body, which would be forwarded to the Coroner's Court so the body could be released for burial; then a car was arranged to take him home. As he left McDermott reflected on what they had learned.

'They're not aware of their daughter's sexual activities, that's for certain. She was the apple of their eye. He told me they didn't know she had applied to go to university. It brought some pride to the poor bugger, I'll tell you that. I'll tell you something else,' he said, his expression becoming grim. 'They hadn't much to look forward to, the Becks. A modest flat, a small pension to get by on, no close friends—just the one child to take comfort from in their old age. And now that she's gone, they've not even that. If she was murdered, I want the bugger that did it.'

TWELVE

S **idney Westgate sat at his study desk** and considered his application for the Principal's post. The internal competition did not worry him greatly. It hadn't taken much guile to ferret out of Campbell that he had applied for the post; the man simply had no tact at all. Surely anyone—even the Board—would realise that Campbell's appointment was simply not on. But to Westgate's certain knowledge—Anscombe had said as much—there were at least two other candidates, and that worried him. One was internal, the other was not. The latter, he decided, he could do little about. Lacking even a name, the man was simply a wild card. The remaining internal applicant, however, was another matter. If he could discover who it was, he could perhaps talk to the man, discourage him. He might even find out his strategy, and appropriate the most useful features of it for himself.

MEANWHILE, NORTH OF THE COLLEGE, an immaculately-polished midnight blue BMW 7 series slid out of a side street just north of Hampstead Heath and merged into the traffic on Spaniard's Road. As Victoria Chambers made her way toward the Inns of Court she thought back to the previous evening, and the haste with which McDermott had made his good byes following dinner. Daddy had been disappointed. He liked her latest beau—wasn't it obvious? She suspected that it was her family that put McDermott off, but she was damned if she was going to apologise for her social position—or her family's money, come to that. On a double yellow just before a curve she passed a van that was going too slowly and nipped back in, narrowly missing an oncoming car. Without missing a beat she resumed her thoughts. It wouldn't do to call him so soon. The thought aggravated her further. Wasn't she the injured party? She'd let him stew for another day, wondering if she would call. Not too long, though. After all, there was the concert at Albert Hall coming up.

THREE HOURS LATER McDermott and his team had returned to Charing Cross and had broken for lunch. The midday crowd was thinning out, and George Ridley had settled comfortably in the snug of a pub located conveniently near the station. Over half an hour passed as they lingered over their drinks and sandwiches, and the glances of a group of people standing nearby were beginning to turn into glares. Ridley took a last pull on his pint and said, 'So where do we go from 'ere, Guv?'

McDermott lifted his own glass and stared meditatively into its amber-coloured contents. 'Well, let's review what we know: an East-End tart decides to chuck the sordid life and aspires to Higher Things. So far as we know she has no unresolved grudges, nor ties to her former life. She gets herself accepted at university, moves to a respectable neighbourhood, and inside of a week she's road kill filed under London Transport, Accidents Involving.'

'Excuse me, sir, that's a bit harsh, isn't it?' Quinn objected.

'You're right, of course,' McDermott admitted. 'I'm still in a funk over this case. It just doesn't gel. If it was murder, it's unlikely it was someone from her old neighbourhood. If you're not part of the university crowd you don't follow someone around for half a day without being noticed—or pick them up without knowing their schedule, and our young lady seems to have kept her cards to herself. So if it was murder it must have been someone from her new surroundings. And yet by all accounts she hadn't been there long enough to know anyone—let alone long enough to give someone a reason to top her.'

'Excuse me, sir,' Quinn interjected quietly, struggling to hold together the remains of a large cheese and tomato bap.

'Yes? If you've any ideas, Willie—'

The officer stirred uneasily in her seat. 'It's just that you—we—seem to be assuming that these were two mutually exclusive worlds she moved in. Is it possible that they somehow intersected—for example, that in some way her past caught up with her in her new life, and by suddenly appearing at St. Gregory's she somehow posed a threat to someone there?'

McDermott considered her words. 'You might be on to something there.'

'Oh, aye. What?' a voice gruffly interrupted. Ridley, it was clear, had not yet seen the light.

McDermott was already warming to Quinn's theory. 'It's simple, George.' The academic world is a cloistered existence, and its members will forgive— or overlook—many sins: sloth, lack of imagination, stealing another person's ideas, even the occasional discreet dalliance with an undergraduate or a colleague's spouse. What it won't condone is sordid sex, commercial sex—at least not if it comes to light. There's even a special phrase they have—'Moral Turpitude' I think it's called—and it's grounds for instant dismissal. If someone at St. G's used the services of a sex worker and our Miss Beck—as a former professional—was involved, and someone learned about it, well, more than a reputation would be involved: someone's very livelihood would be on the line.'

The older man was scandalised. 'Here now, you're sayin' one o' them professers might'a been shaggin'—words failed him—'a common *tart?*'

McDermott laughed. 'You surprise me, George. Do you think that academics are any different from the rest of us below the belt? Anyway, at the moment it's the only explanation we have that makes sense. It wouldn't be an ordinary student, would it? Not when they can get into all the knickers they want for nothing.' He glanced sideways at Quinn, who rewarded him with an icy glare.

Ridley was clearly reluctant to jettison his view of an ordered, familiar, and above all English world in which people in certain circles were clearly different from those in others. 'Well then, where do we go from 'ere?'

McDermott drained his glass and reached for his coat. 'To St. Gregory's, of course. Willie, do you still have that list of the courses that Sally Beck was taking? As George here would say, let's put a ferret down a hole and see what comes out the other end.' He reached for his mobile and speed dialed his office. 'Marsh? Call Uniform Branch and tell them I'd like a driver and marked car standing by. We'll be there in two ticks. Right.' As he pocketed the phone he said, 'Time to make an entrance.'

IN THE HALLOWED CLOSE OF ST. GREGORY'S FORECOURT the presence of a police car with its garish markings sounded a discordant note, one that could not be easily overlooked. Even as the trio were ushered into the Principal's Office window blinds were being discreetly drawn aside, and curiosity clouded the faces of several members of faculty as they speculated on the cause of this unseemly intrusion into their private domain.

Reminding McDermott of Cerberus zealously guarding the gates of Hell, the Principal's Secretary admitted them to Anscombe's study.

McDermott entered the room with Ridley and Quinn following closely behind. The spacious, panelled chamber with its crowded bookshelves and thick carpet suggested both tradition and authority, which was precisely the message its occupant intended to convey. It stirred up a vague recollection of an incident, many years ago, when McDermott had been summoned to the same room following a rather exuberant demonstration following a football match.

'How do you do?' asked the Principal, rising to meet them. 'I'm Norman Anscombe. 'To what do we owe the pleasure of your visit?'

McDermott took in the man with a single glance. Mid sixties, he guessed. Short, full chested, and basically fit. Blue eyes, whose sharpness was not entirely masked by the thick spectacles he wore. Balding, but with a tan that spoke of time spent in warmer climes, or perhaps on the golf course. Yes, that would be consistent with the man's position and accent. Not much on his desk. McDermott wondered who was the efficient one—the Principal or his secretary.

'Good day, Principal. I'm Detective Inspector McDermott of the Metropolitan Police, and these are my colleagues, Detective Sergeant Ridley and DC Quinn. I apologise for disturbing you on such short notice, but we're engaged in an investigation involving one of your students and we think you—or more accurately one of the Teaching Fellows—may be able to help us with our enquiries.'

Anscombe's eyebrows rose, but he maintained the social graces. 'Please make yourselves comfortable. ' He motioned them to a pair of leather upholstered wing chairs facing his desk. McDermott took the chair closest to the window. Ridley looked at Quinn, and, deciding that rank prevailed over gender, settled into the remaining chair. The Principal turned to his secretary.

'Mrs. Coates, would you be so kind as to bring us another chair?' Resuming his place at the desk Anscombe clasped his hands in front of him and focused his full attention on McDermott. 'Now then, how can I help you?' he smiled. 'Some of our undergraduates been up to some early term highjinks, I gather?'

'Nothing quite so trifling, I'm afraid,' McDermott replied. 'We don't usually detail three officers from CID to investigate school pranks.'

Anscombe spread his hands of the desk before him. 'Of course you don't. Just my rather poor attempt at humour, I'm afraid.' He smiled deprecatingly, as the secretary entered with a small, uncomfortable-looking straight-backed chair in hand. Quinn thanked her and sat down next to Ridley.

'It seems that one of your students was hit by a bus and killed two days ago. We have rather little information on her, I'm afraid. It is possible that certain members of the faculty may be able to help us fill in the blanks.'

Anscombe looked pained. 'How terrible! I will do what I can, of course.' He paused, looking quizzically at McDermott. 'Forgive me, Inspector, but is it customary for someone of your position to concern himself directly with a traffic accident?'

McDermott's voice was casual, but his eyes focused intently on the Principal. 'I didn't say it was an accident. There is some reason to believe she may have been murdered.'

There was a brief silence. As Anscombe took in the implications of McDermott's remark he stared at him with an astonishment that was either genuine or revealed exceptional guile. At this point McDermott was prepared to believe either.

'I see. What is the name of this student, Inspector?'

McDermott decided not to play all of his cards at once. If she had been murdered it was possible that the perpetrator knew the victim by her other name, and that might come out in the course of conversation. 'Sheila Bannerman,' he said.

Anscombe showed no reaction, but scribbled the name on a notepad. 'Indeed. And you think someone here—one of the Fellows—may have been involved? I really cannot credit that.'

McDermott looked at the man unflinchingly. 'I didn't say that a member of the faculty was involved, only that they might be able to assist us in our investigation. I'm sure that you are as anxious as we are to clear this matter up.'

But it was evident that Anscombe did not share McDermott's enthusiasm for getting to the bottom of things. One could almost see the wheels turning as the man considered the implications of the situation. Was it the reputation of the College or self-interest that motivated him? Again, McDermott couldn't be certain.

When the Principal spoke again, it was in the first person plural voice reserved for nurses, royalty, and bureaucrats the world over. 'Of course we shall do what we can,' he assured them. 'What do you require?'

'Not a great deal, actually.' McDermott pulled a list from his coat pocket and handed it across the desk. 'First, we would like the names of the students in each of these courses.'

'Nothing could be easier, Inspector. What else can we do for you?'

'I would also like to speak to her tutors, this afternoon if it is possible.'

Anscombe examined the list. 'Of course. As it happens this afternoon is free of classes—for various committee meetings associated with the start of term, you see.' He smiled benignly. 'I see that my name is here. I suppose you would like to begin with me?'

'If you can spare the time.'

But after asking his secretary to contact the faculty on McDermott's list and have them assemble in the Senior Common Room in fifteen minutes, Anscombe proved to be less than helpful. Consulting his records he confirmed that, indeed, a Sheila Bannerman had been enrolled in his course on Greek Philosophy. But it was early days, the Principal explained. He had not known her personally; he could not as yet put a face to her name—or to many others, for that matter. 'I'm afraid you may find that is the case with several of the Fellows,' he admitted. 'What with class sizes—we have more than three hundred new young people *in statu pupillari*—' Again he spread his palms on the desk before him.

'I understand,' McDermott replied. 'Still, we can but try.'

'Of course. Oh, there is just one thing.'

'Yes?'

The Principal was clearly attempting to be as circumspect as possible. 'You will not be aware of it, but this is my final year at St. Gregory's. The Board of Regents is in the midst of selecting my successor. There are several external candidates who are socially prominent. I need hardly add that any adverse publicity for the College at this time could prove most unfortunate.'

McDermott decided to inject some realism into their discussion. 'You would prefer to keep the College's name out of the papers. Of course, I understand, though I cannot make any promises. The investigation will take us where it takes us. However, Principal, you must realise that many of your students are likely to be active on social media – Facebook and the like. If she was known to them it's almost certainly going to be public information in a matter of days, if not sooner.'

As Anscombe sighed aubibly, McDermott reflected on what he had just been told, and realised that he'd just been handed a possible motive for murder.

THIRTEEN

By the time they entered the Senior Common Room most of Sally Beck's teachers had already assembled. Many of the faces were unfamiliar to McDermott, although he had recognised one from his own days at St. Gregory's. Most were seated in lounge chairs around the room, and looked up with varying degrees of curiosity as Anscombe and his entourage entered. Clearly, being summoned to a meeting with the Principal was not an everyday occurrence.

Just as Anscombe was about to begin the door opened and a tall, sandy haired man burst in. 'I say, am I late? Sorry all.'

Anscombe's glare was withering. 'Come in, Campbell, I was just about to begin.' He turned his gaze to the others. 'Thank you all for coming. My apologies for calling you together on such short notice, but the circumstances'—he looked at McDermott, then back again—'are rather exceptional. It seems one of your students—one of our students, that is—has been killed. Possibly murdered, in fact. This is Detective Inspector McDermott, and, ah, two of his officers. They have asked for our assistance, and while I am not hopeful that we can shed any light on this regrettable matter, I have given them my assurances that we will do what we can. Does anyone have any questions before we begin?'

The question was clearly rhetorical, and for a moment it remained so. Then a voice emanated from the back of the room. 'Am I to understand that one of us is suspected of having committed this crime, Principal?'

Anscombe looked to McDermott, who responded. 'Certainly not, sir. At this stage of our enquiry we are merely trying to get a better overall picture of the victim and her time here—fill in some blanks, as it were.'

The Principal stepped in. 'Dr. Westgate, I myself have just finished being interviewed, and I can confirm that the questions they are asking are general in nature, and the whole process should be very brief. I know you will be as anxious as I am to resolve this...situation. After all, a significant number of our students are from outside London—outside Britain, even—and their parents must be assured that St. Gregory's is a suitable and safe place to send their children.'

'For pity's sake, Anscombe, our students are not children,' Westgate replied. 'Most of them are of voting age, and when they're not rutting like goats they're either taking drugs or demonstrating in support of legalising them. We cannot be held responsible for their machinations and perversions, even when they have tragic consequences.'

Anscombe flushed a deep red. Clearly he was not used to being publicly challenged, particularly with outsiders present.

McDermott took up the cause, raising his voice just perceptively. 'Perhaps I should say—Dr. Westgate, is it?—that at this point there's no reason to believe that this is some undergraduate affair gone awry. In any event, we can speak with you all formally, one at a time if you wish. I assumed that you would prefer to make our visit here as brief as possible.'

The man glared. Several others looked uncomfortable, but it was clear that he had won the day.

'Shall we begin, then? Constable, will you take notes?' Quinn took a chair at a nearby reading table and produced her notebook.

McDermott looked around the room. 'The young woman's name was Sheila Bannerman. She was enrolled in courses taught by each of you.' McDermott described her briefly, including the clothes she had been wearing when she was killed, and circulated her student photograph. 'We would like to know if she is familiar to any of you, and whether you can identify any classmates with whom she may have struck up a friendship.'

McDermott studied their faces as the photo made its way around the room. One or two showed some glimmer of recognition, but most received it with the bland insouciance of a sphinx.

It was a woman in the middle of the room who spoke first.

'Inspector, you must realise that in the past few days we have each been exposed to perhaps two hundred faces, most of which we have not seen before. The undergraduate courses, especially the first year subjects, tend to be handled in large lecture halls. It is surprising that we recognise them by the end of term.'

McDermott decided that it was time to stir the pot. 'I appreciate the difficulties involved, professor. However, we have some reason to believe that Miss Bannerman may have been killed by someone from St. Gregory's. Thus, we will be asking each of you to account for your movements on Tuesday last, between noon and one thirty.'

The effect was electric. Westgate looked up. 'Then we *are* suspected in this affair.' I am appalled that you would think any of us capable of murder. I resent such an allegation, and I'll have nothing to do with it!'

McDermott was prepared for this response, in fact had expected it. 'I assume that precisely because you *are* all upstanding members of the community you will recognise the importance of setting an example for the students. However, if you wish we can conduct our enquiries individually at the station.'

The threat had its effect. Westgate said nothing further, though dark glares emanated from him like shafts of lightning.

'Well I, for one, am delighted to be of assistance, Inspector.' McDermott turned his gaze toward the source of the plummy voice. The speaker seemed to be in his early thirties, wearing a rose coloured sports jacket over pale green trousers, a dark green shirt, open at the collar, and white canvas running shoes. McDermott half expected a full set of tail feathers to reveal themselves if the man turned his back to them.

'Excuse me, sir,' he replied. 'You are?'

'Oh, how stupid of me. Jeremy Asquith, Lecturer in Romance Languages and Literature. I am also—or rather I was intended to be—Miss Bannerman's faculty advisor.'

'I see. And when did you first meet her?'

Asquith adopted a pained expression. 'I regret to say I never did. I'm afraid I was somewhat tardy arriving for the start of term, as the Principal can attest.'

'Exactly how tardy, Mr. Asquith?'

'I arrived Tuesday afternoon, having come directly from Euston Station.'

McDermott glanced at Anscombe, whose expression confirmed the fact.

'Thank you, sir. The timing would seem to place you out of the running for the moment, though we will need confirmation of your movements. DC Quinn will take the particulars when we've concluded here. Anyone else?'

'I can tell you where I was,' volunteered a high-pitched voice from the back of the room. Its owner was unimpressive. A small, slightly built man with thick spectacles and a mousy countenance sat almost engulfed by a thickly upholstered wing chair. McDermott thought he had never seen anyone look less like a murderer. Still, he recalled Crippen.

'Yes? Your name, sir?'

'Ewart Griffith-Jones. Professor of English—and *Celtic*—Literature.'

'Thank you.' McDermott glanced at Wilhemina Quinn, who was writing rapidly. 'What can you tell us?'

'Well, the time you describe corresponds to our luncheon hour here. Morning classes end at eleven fifty. At twelve o'clock I was on my way to a health food outlet in Southampton Row, to pick up a supply of organic vitamins. Quite superior to the synthetic variety, you understand. You see, much of the vitamin content gets lost in—'

'Excuse me, sir. What did you do next?' McDermott said, determined to ignore the professor's side trips.

Griffith-Jones looked offended. Apparently he was unused to being interrupted in mid flight. 'I made my purchase and returned to my rooms, where I prepared and ate a light lunch until approximately twenty past one, when I returned to the classroom wing for afternoon lectures.

'I see. And what time would you say it was when you left the shop?'

Griffith-Jones considered the matter. 'Well, it must have taken ten minutes or so to get there, and another five minutes there—no, I remember there was this awful woman in front of me, badgering the shop assistant about a special order that hadn't come in—she must have taken ten minutes at least—and then another ten minutes to return here. I suppose I was back by twelve thirty or so, and ate in my rooms, as I say, until quarter past one or so.'

'Did you eat alone?'

Griffith-Jones looked as if no alternative arrangement had ever crossed his mind. 'Of course.'

'So in fact, no one can confirm that you were in your rooms?' McDermott probed gently.

There was a prolonged silence. 'No, I suppose not,' Griffith-Jones conceded. He looked extremely uncomfortable.

Elsewhere in the room someone stirred, clearing her throat. McDermott turned his attention in her direction. 'Yes? Professor—'

'Soames, Reader in Classical Languages and Literature.'

McDermott recognised the voice as that of the woman who had spoken earlier. 'Are you able to help us?' he inquired hopefully.

'That may be rather too strong a word, Inspector. I was about to say that I believe I recognise the face—the young lady had enrolled in my course on Greek Civilisation. I doubt I saw her more than once. To my knowledge she made no close acquaintances. At least in my course she seemed not to talk to anyone.'

'I see. Well, even negative information is sometimes helpful. Can you tell me where you were on the day in question?'

'Certainly, though I expect it will be of little use. Last Tuesday I snacked in my rooms, and worked on some lecture notes.'

Riveting, thought McDermott. Aloud he asked, 'Can anyone confirm that, professor? For instance, did you have your lunch delivered?'

'I'm afraid not. All I had was biscuits and tea, which I prepared myself. Oh, I recall that I did telephone the library to verify that some books had been placed aside for my students. Will that help?'

'Every little bit is useful, thank you. What time would that have been?'

She paused. 'I should think it was shortly after twelve. I remember because the circulation librarian was on her lunch hour, and would not return until one o'clock. Quite annoying, really.' She seemed to think that the non-teaching staff should forego such mundane trivialities as daily sustenance until their duties were ended for the day.

McDermott glanced again at Quinn, who confirmed that she was getting all this down. 'Thank you for your assistance, Professor Soames. Has anyone else something to contribute?' He surveyed the room, straining to make out those individuals who had yet to speak. In the back, next to the outspoken Doctor Westgate, another man was seated. He was of average height, in his late forties or early fifties, with an expansive waistline and thinning hair. He wore steel-rimmed spectacles, and was, to McDermott's eye, expensively dressed. 'May I have your name, sir?' McDermott asked.

'I am Miles Burton-Strachey, and I hold the Wycombe Chair of History,' the man replied.

McDermott turned to Quinn. 'Got that down, Constable?' he asked, deadpan. Her efforts to stifle a smirk were not wholly effective.

'Thank you, sir. Were you acquainted with Miss Bannerman?'

'Unfortunately, no. I gather she was taking a course from me, but I'm afraid I couldn't tell you which one.'

'I see. And did you take your lunch at the college as well?'

'Certainly not. If you ever have the misfortune to eat here, Inspector, you will find that generally the food is generally appalling. I lunched, as is my custom, at home.'

'And where would that be, sir?'

'Number eight, Park Crescent, Regent's Park,' Burton-Strachey replied, with evident satisfaction.

McDermott suppressed his surprise. A pricey area. Well beyond the reach of a typical academic's salary. Then there were the clothes. He made a mental note to look into Burton-Strachey's finances.

'That would be about—' he calculated—'three quarters of a mile from here. May I ask how you got there.'

'I walked, of course.' The look was contemptuous. 'In good weather I always walk. Now to anticipate your next question I left the College at the conclusion of my last class of the morning, at precisely eleven fifty. It takes me almost exactly fifteen minutes each way. I spent the balance of the time lunching with my wife. We had a *potage* of cauliflower with Stilton, grilled sole amandine, and a rather interesting Chardonnay. I returned to the College in time for my afternoon lecture, which began at half past one.'

'Thank you, sir. You've been very helpful.'

But one person in the room knew differently. Surely that account could not have been correct. What time was it when he had seen Burton-Strachey coming from the other direction, up Montague Street, heading for the college? It couldn't have been later than one o'clock. Still, his manner had been convincing in the extreme. He decided to keep that bit of information to himself for the moment.

McDermott let his eyes wander around the room, looking for anyone who had not yet spoken. 'Who has yet to give us a statement?'

From somewhere toward the rear of the large room a baritone voice responded avuncularly, 'That would be me, I think. Colin, isn't it? I thought I recognised you. What has it been—nearly twenty years, I believe?'

FOURTEEN

A **murmur went round** the room. Ridley, who had been standing by
the door, maintained the blandest of expressions, but Quinn looked
up from her note-taking. Anscombe was clearly intrigued, as indeed were
the other Teaching Fellows. McDermott turned slightly, and stared intently,
in the gloom of the SCR, at his questioner. 'Good afternoon, Professor
Boothroyd. It has been rather a long time.'

J. K. S. Boothroyd taught Art History. Amongst the Fellows of St.
Gregory's he was unquestionably its most widely respected member. His keen
grey eyes and silver hair, largely unchanged since McDermott's day, were
matched by a soft-spoken voice and an unfailingly gracious nature. A gifted
scholar who communicated to his students his passion for art, he was nonetheless often more influential in their personal, rather than their academic,
lives, by the example he set of patient dedication in his work and taking a
genuine interest in each of his students. Persuading Boots to join the faculty,
Anscombe had reflected more than once, was one of his predecessor's most
propitious achievements.

While Anscombe was thinking this, McDermott was searching for
a way to maintain control of the meeting at hand. 'It's a great pleasure to
see you again, sir—though under more pleasant circumstances would have
been preferable.'

Boothroyd was unperturbed. 'Nonsense, my dear boy. You're just doing your job, after all. I was about to give you—what is it—my 'alibi'? He seemed to regard the situation with his characteristically quiet humour. 'I'm afraid I cannot add anything to what my colleagues have already told you about your young lady. At this point in the term she was but one of many, I fear. As far as my movements are concerned, I, too, was at home, with Alyce having lunch. Not much of an alibi, I suppose. When you finish here you really must join us for a drink. Alyce would quite enjoy seeing you after all this time.'

McDermott was torn between acknowledging Boothroyd's obviously sincere overtures and attempting to maintain some semblance of authority to what, after all, was an official police investigation. The other Fellows were by now watching the proceedings with undisguised fascination. Soames was staring at him intently, in a manner reminiscent of a teacher confronted by a congenitally dull student who has suddenly made an uncharacteristically acute observation. Even Westgate's previously caustic expression had been replaced by one of quiet amusement; he was clearly intrigued by the scene being played out before him.

'I look forward to it, Professor Boothroyd. For the moment, however, I'm afraid we must resume our enquiries.'

McDermott canvassed the room. Only two persons remained who had not as yet accounted for their actions. He focused on the younger of the two.

McDermott levelled his gaze at the sandy-haired man who had been late arriving at the common room. 'Mr. Cameron, I believe?'

'Campbell,' the man corrected him. 'Fraser Campbell. I'm afraid it's more empty innings, Inspector. I recognise the name, but that's about all. Always have been bad with faces. Sorry.' He grinned inanely.

'That's all right, sir. Your movements?'

'Ah. That's a different matter. I can tell you exactly where I was, practically the entire time. Trouble is, no one can confirm it.' He cast a sideways glance at Burton-Strachey.

When no further comment was forthcoming, McDermott asked patiently, 'And where was that?'

'I was in Russell Square the whole time, Inspector. Eating a sandwich and reading the *Daily Telegraph*.'

The motif of the unsubstantiated alibi was beginning to wear a bit thin. *And yet, why not?* he realised. It made as much—or as little—sense as the other explanations he'd heard that afternoon.

But another person in that room considered what had just been said, and was troubled. If Campbell was telling the truth—and there was no reason to believe otherwise—he posed a possible threat. *Something might have to be done.*

Oblivious to these thoughts, McDermott lifted his gaze to the back of the room. 'Very well. Thank you for your contribution.' He turned to the remaining person in the room. 'Dr. Westgate. We have already taken up too much of your time, I'm afraid. Can you tell us what you were doing on the day in question?'

But Westgate had lost none of his truculence. 'Certainly not.' he replied. 'I will not be badgered like a common criminal. My movements are my own business. If you wish to lay charges, get on with it. From the tone of your questions I gather you are hardly in a position to do so. Good day!'

And with that Sidney Westgate strode from the room.

Returning to his office, Norman Anscombe considered the afternoon's developments. Almost two decades of conscientious, if not inspired, work on his part could not be jeopardised by the petty misadventures of some feckless undergraduate. Another student, he reasoned, would be the most likely explanation, and one on which the police would almost certainly focus. He permitted himself a modest smile.

FOLLOWING HIS EXCHANGE WITH BOOTHROYD, Ridley and Quinn had shown an almost malevolent interest in McDermott's undergraduate days at St. Gregory's, and over their good-humoured protests he had sent them back to the station. Before long he found himself mounting a set of stone steps to face a large dark blue door, the top half of which was given over to a bevelled glass oval. He pressed the bell, and almost immediately Boothroyd opened the door and beamed. 'Good of you to come, dear boy. It's been donkey's years. You remember Alyce, of course!'

McDermott moved past a crowded umbrella stand and into the foyer, removing his coat as he did so. 'Of course. How are you, Mrs. Boothroyd? It's good to see you again after such a long time.'

Almost four decades of entertaining undergraduates and colleagues had made Alyce Boothroyd's social skills very much the equal of her husband's. 'Far too long, Colin. I was delighted when Boots telephoned and said you'd be dropping by.' She motioned him into the sitting room.

It was almost exactly as McDermott had remembered it from nearly two decades earlier. Deep blue walls were set off by gleaming white wainscoting; a pale blue sofa in a muted lattice-weave pattern faced the fireplace, flanked on either side by two high-backed leather chairs; in the centre was an oak colonial-period campaign chest with brass fittings which served as a coffee table. The furniture was comfortably worn, and one of the chairs was rather threadbare on one corner, apparently from cat clawing, as a tortoise-shelled cat lay curled up in it, blissfully ignoring the humans in its midst. An eggshell carpet echoed the wood trim; the hearth was composed of tiles that were the same deep hue as the walls; the overmantel held dozens of small photographs of different and apparently unrelated individuals, all seemingly in their early twenties; presumably reminders of generations of students whom the Boothroyds had befriended. On either side of the fireplace, from floor to ceiling, and extending the length of the long wall, white shelves were crammed with books of every conceivable size; an ottoman in one corner was similarly piled high with books, magazines and scholarly journals. Next to it, a large oak writing table overflowing with papers and more journals overlooked a large window fronting on to the street below. Despite, or perhaps because of its age, the house was well constructed, and only the faintest whisper of the traffic beyond reached the room.

McDermott tickled the cat's ear before sitting down. The animal responded by raising his head, opening one eye, giving him a cursory look, and then settling down again, determined to ignore such presumptuous overtures.

'Surely that's not the same cat you had when I was here last?' McDermott asked.

Boothroyd chuckled. 'No, no, dear boy. Let's see — that would have been Calpurnia, I think. We had to have her put down, poor thing. Urinary tract, you know. Consequence of having them neutered. This one — Napoleon, he's called — has been with us for, let's see, almost twelve years now. We decided to call him Napoleon because of his rather imperial bearing.'

'Then all cats should be called Napoleon — at least all those I've met,' McDermott replied.

'Quite so,' Boothroyd chuckled again. 'Do make yourself comfortable,' he said, pointing to the sofa. 'Alyce, do we have anything for our visitor?'

'I've made some tea, darling.' She motioned McDermott to a comfortable armchair. 'Earl Grey, I think you preferred. And do have some Madeira cake. As I recall you were rather fond of it.'

McDermott marvelled at the woman's powers of recollection, then turned to regard her husband. Boothroyd had changed little: the lines in his face were more deeply etched, and his hair, already silver when McDermott knew him, and now only slightly thinner. But his eyes were still clear and bright and sharp, and the same strength of character shone through. McDermott struggled with the notion that his former mentor could be involved in murder.

McDermott spoke first. 'I apologise for losing touch over the years, sir. I'm afraid I haven't attended many of the Old Boys' Days.'

'Please, call me Boots. You and I are much too old for formalities—well, I am, anyway.' The man's eyes sparkled amiably. 'I know my memory isn't what it was, but it took some time for me to equate the dedicated student of art history in my classes all those years ago with the rather imposing figure of a police detective conducting a murder investigation this afternoon! Forgive me for asking, but how did you come to make such a curious transition?'

McDermott spent the next half hour recounting the events in his life since they had last met. On matriculation from St. Gregory's he'd been unable to find an opening in his field of study, and at first he'd taken on part-time work at the Courtauld Institute. But budget cutbacks loomed, and on the advice of a colleague on the Art Squad he'd applied to the Metropolitan Police for fast-tracking in the CID. To his surprise they'd accepted him, and following his training he'd been posted to West Yorkshire. But the Dales were not London, and shortly after being promoted to Detective Sergeant he asked for a transfer to London, where a few months after being posted to London he'd met his future wife. Within a few months they'd married, and the following year had a daughter, Megan. But McDermott's life had changed forever when she'd been killed in the London terrorist bombings of 2005—in Tavistock Square, near where they were now.

It was evident to the Boothroyds that his wife's death had devastated McDermott. In the months following her death McDermott had hardened, increasingly coming to define his life through his police work. His focus shifted to violent crime and its victims and McDermott asked to be posted to the Homicide and Serious Crime Command in London.

As he paused, Boothroyd expressed his admiration. 'You've done very well for yourself, Colin,'—McDermott noticed with relief that the 'dear boys' had ceased—'but then I always knew you would. After so many years in harness one comes to sense these things. It's clear that you find real satisfaction in your present job, and that's crucial, isn't it?'

McDermott saw an opportunity to get down to business. 'Which brings me back to the case at hand, I'm afraid. You said you were at home during the time that Sheila Bannerman was killed.'

'Just so. Alyce here can confirm that,' he said, patting her hand.

Not very helpful, though, McDermott realised. A spouse's testimony was notoriously suspect.

He tried another tack. 'I was somewhat surprised that your colleagues were not more helpful this afternoon.'

'You mustn't be too hard on them,' Boothroyd smiled. I'm afraid it's not like the old days. Become a bit of a circus, in fact. Both the Fellows – and for that matter the students – have changed. Instead of tutoring perhaps a dozen of the most promising, we now lecture to as many as two hundred of the decidedly average. And now we are reaping the results of our sins. The younger academics applying for posts reflect a watered-down curriculum. Some of them are hardly able to put together a literate journal article, never mind a major contribution to their field. Sometimes, you know, I wonder if public education doesn't follow the Second Law of Thermodynamics: there's a finite amount of knowledge; one can either concentrate a lot of it in the minds of a very few, or spread it around more widely, but with each person receiving only a token portion. Do you suppose there might be anything to that?'

McDermott laughed. 'You may be on to something there, but I'd be careful: it's the stuff counter-revolutions are made of.'

They spent another three-quarters of an hour together, chatting pleasantly about old acquaintances, until McDermott made his good byes. As he walked down the front steps, McDermott reflected on their conversation, and the fact that more than once it had wandered from the matter at hand. If this meandering had been intentional on Boothroyd's part, he had been clever about it. But he already had Boothroyd's alibi, such as it was. No worse, but also no better, than that of most of his colleagues.

Alyce Boothroyd handed her husband a fresh cup of tea, and sat back in her chair. 'It was nice to see Colin again, wasn't it? He seems to have matured nicely, don't you think?'

'Um,' Boothroyd muttered between sips. He put the cup down on the table and poked at the embers in the fireplace. 'Very nice, indeed. Something of a shocker, finding him working as a policeman. I'd never have guessed it. The art world's loss. Still, if he's happy...'

After so many years together, Alyce could read her husband like a book. 'Something's bothering you, dear. What is it?'

Boothroyd looked up from the fire and smiled. 'Never could put one over on you, could I?' He resumed stirring the coals. 'Fact is, Anscombe's been on to me just this morning about the Principalship. Seems he wants me to apply. I told him we'd think about it.'

She raised her eyebrows. 'But we¾that is, you¾had planned to retire in another two year's time.' She struggled to conceal her dismay. 'What do you want to do, dear?'

Boothroyd looked up at her and smiled. 'It would mean leaving here, of course; we'd have to live at the college. So many years,' he said, looking around him. 'And then there's the committee work, and the entertaining. We'd have a lot less time for ourselves.'

Alyce had her answer, and moved to make it easy for him. 'There's no denying you'd be good for the college, dear. Much better than—' she stopped herself, considering whether anyone was better suited to the task and coming up blank.

'It's merely a possibility,' he reminded her. 'I'm still not sure what I would say if it were offered me.'

'Yes you are,' she smiled. 'After all, it's an opportunity to make a difference, and put your own stamp on the college.' She caressed the back of his neck and tried to look pleased.

FIFTEEN

When McDermott returned to the station Ridley informed him that Galbraith had been asking after him. If he was looking for a quick resolution of the case he was an incurable optimist. McDermott was quickly coming round to the view that nothing about this case was going to be simple. He wanted an update, though, so McDermott paid a visit to his office.

As he settled into a chair, Galbraith said, 'I understand you visited a former professor this afternoon, alone.'

McDermott was taken off stride. 'Yes, sir. I thought that in view of our previous relationship he might be more forthcoming in an informal setting, one on one.'

'Christ, you know the drill. You have a personal history with the man. As senior investigating officer it's down to you to set a good example, especially with a new DC on the team. Interviewing the man at home—and with his wife present—for God's sake, it sends a bad message.'

McDermott was unrepentant. 'Actually, it wasn't an interview, sir. We already had his explanation of where he was at the tie of the victim's death. It was more in the nature of a personal catching-up. And if you recall, when the case first led back to St. Gregory's I said I wanted no part of it. It was you who said my personal knowledge of the place would be an asset.'

Galbraith glared at him and fidgeted with a file on his desk. "Be that as it may, I want another officer present when you meet with any person of interest with whom you have a personal connection. Is that understood?'

McDermott struggled to retain his composure. *Was Galbraith's promotion in jeopardy? Was he simply dotting his i's?* The fact was that, save one, all of McDermott's former teachers at St. Gregory's had moved, died, or retired. But he saw an opening he could exploit. 'I'm not sure I can promise that, sir. We have a small team on this case as it is, and Ridley and Quinn are busy pursuing several lines of enquiry. Unless, of course, you can give us additional personnel.'

'You know as well as I do that I can't spare any additional staff at this point.'

Staff, thought McDermott. It was clear where the man's priorities lay. He threw Galbraith a bone. 'If anything develops pointing to anyone I've had prior personal contact with, I'll be sure to have another officer present when I question him.'

'Very well. But keep me informed.' He waved one hand dismissively.

Returning to his office McDermott was still seething from his exchange with Galbraith. *Sanctimonious bastard. Only looking to his promotion.* He found a telephone message from Victoria waiting for him on his desk. It was not quite five thirty. No doubt she had left her chambers by now and, along with several million other daytime Londoners, was attempting to escape from the city core as quickly as possible. He folded the note and put it in his shirt pocket, then he summoned Ridley and Quinn.

From the smirks on their faces as they entered it was clear that they were still relishing McDermott's encounter with his former tutor. He was determined to deny them that pleasure, nor to put them in the picture on his exchange with Galbraith, and instead got directly to business.

'Right. Not one of our more productive interview sessions. Still, if we're on the right track it may flush something out of the woods. Impressions?'

'Of who, Guv?'

'Take your pick,' McDermott responded.

'Well,' Ridley began, 'There's Anscombe himself. Very smooth, I'd say. Makes all the right noises 'bout wanting to help, but when it comes down to it, he weren't doin' us no favours.'

'That's hardly surprising,' interjected Quinn. 'It's his college, after all. A scandal at this point—even one in which he was not directly involved—could tarnish his reputation, perhaps overshadow years of work.'

'I think you're right, Willie.' McDermott agreed. 'And that's precisely why it might be an excellent motive for murder if he was involved—or if one of the Fellows who is a candidate to succeed him is involved.' He scribbled a note on the pad before him: *Who else amongst faculty has applied for Principal's post?* 'Other thoughts? George?'

'Well, I didn't much fancy that Westgate feller,' the Sergeant admitted.

'Nor did I, come to that,' agreed McDermott. 'Still, you can understand the man. People in his position aren't used to being questioned by the police. If arrogance were a crime, the entire House of Lords would be in the nick.' he grinned. Changing tacks, he asked, 'Can we exclude anyone at this point?'

Quinn spoke up. 'I think we can pretty well dismiss Campbell from our list of suspects, sir.'

'I agree. The man is a git. I don't think he has the guile—not to mention the wit—to be a murderer. Still, we should run a routine check on them all, just in case.' He looked at Quinn, who nodded. 'The others?'

It was Ridley who spoke next. 'That perfesser Soames. Took me as sharp. Doesn't miss much, I'd wager. If anything funny's goin' on, it'd be hard to get it by 'er.'

'Good point,' agreed McDermott, and made a note to have a private word with Clarissa Soames.

The Sergeant continued. 'What about that feller Jeremy Askew? Somethin' not right there. Spruced up like a tart at a tombola. A poof, I shouldn't wonder.'

McDermott smiled. 'Possibly, but not a crime for some years now, George. Any other impressions at this point?'

Once again Ridley broke the silence. 'The history feller—what were his name? Oh, aye. Burton-Strachey. Bit of a nob, you ask me.'

'There's certainly the matter of his finances,' McDermott agreed. 'He lives in a posh area, our professor. If he were up to sexual hijinks, he certainly could afford the services of a professional. George, you seem to be having a run of luck lately with things financial. Get on to his bank manager. See if there have been any withdrawals—in cash—which might correspond with the dates and amounts of deposits made by Sally Beck. And while you're at it, nose around. Ask the neighbours about his relations with his wife. Do they quarrel, take separate holidays—that sort of thing.'

'Right, Guv. Anything else?'

Quinn spoke up. 'I'm still disturbed by the fact that we haven't found any phone records for the victim. If she was a sex worker it's virtually impossible that she'd have done without a mobile, or even more than one.'

McDermott paused. 'You're right, of course. Check with the service providers in the Greater London area. Look for either name. Maybe we'll come up lucky.'

Quinn groaned. Something else on her plate. Still, she had no one to blame but herself.

Something clicked, and McDermott sat up. 'Say, weren't Sheila Bannerman's new digs somewhere near Burton-Strachey's?' He rose and walked over to the wall and consulted a London street map. 'Yes, I thought so. It's thin, I'll admit, but it would have been convenient for them if he was having it on with the girl—' His thoughts were interrupted by the door opening and the I'm-all-business face of DCI Sam Loach. 'There you are, McDermott. Could we have a word?' Without waiting for a reply, he withdrew to the hallway.

McDermott sighed. 'This shouldn't take long.' He left the room and found the man pacing outside the door. In Loach's case, never a good sign.

'What can I do for you, Loach?' He left off the man's rank deliberately. There was no love lost between them.

'Look, I don't like asking you this, but a case I'm working has taken a new direction, and I need your man Ridley—strictly on a temporary basis, you understand.'

McDermott's response was automatic, but gave him pleasure nonetheless. 'I'm sorry, he's needed here at the moment.'

Loach wasn't used to being turned down, especially by a subordinate officer. 'My understanding is that you're working a simple MisPers case. How urgent can that be?'

'I'm afraid you've been misinformed. It began as a question of the victim's identity, but it's looking more and more like a murder enquiry. As the most experienced officer on the case, George is needed.' Then, as almost an afterthought, McDermott threw him a bone. 'What about Taylor? I believe he's processing staffing analyses for the Super at the moment.' As a bone, it was a very old bone indeed, and well picked over. "Tinker" Taylor—he'd earned his nickname by constantly peering over the shoulders of his colleagues, making suggestions that invariably turned out to be time wasters—was a DC in his late thirties, and unless McDermott missed his guess, would retire as one.

'You're kidding,' Loach sniffed. 'The man's a berk—a complete waste of time.'

Hello, pot calling kettle, McDermott thought to himself. 'Well, perhaps Galbraith will have other suggestions. Sorry I can't be of help.'

Loach gave him a dark look and stomped off down the hallway.

After a moment McDermott returned to his desk. Their expressions told him they were curious about Loach's interruption.

McDermott smiled. 'Nothing serious. The DCI just wanted to borrow George here to work a case.'

George's face fell, and McDermott moved to reassure him. 'Don't worry, George, I told him I couldn't spare you.' Then he turned back to the case at hand. 'Right, where were we?'

There was an awkward and protracted silence. Finally Quinn asked quietly. 'We hadn't got round to Professor Boothroyd, sir.'

McDermott shuffled the papers in front of him, then his eyes met Quinn's. 'Right. No one is beyond suspicion in this case, Willie. If there's something queer there, I want to know it. Let's put that one on your plate. Now, as for the routine work...'

'Sir?'

'The class lists.' McDermott picked up a sheaf of paper Anscombe had given him. 'Willie, you go over them for duplicates—students she shared more than one course with. If she recognised someone from another class she might have latched on to that person—or they to her. Start by interviewing those students. If you come up beggars you and George split the remaining names and interview the rest.' He handed the lists to her.

She winced. There were, she saw, between two and three hundred names, all told. Had she been on familiar ground she would not have hesitated in asking for assistance. As it was she shrank from admitting she wasn't equal to the task.

The silence was broken by McDermott's mobile. It had been set to vibrate, and was on his desk. Now it was making a buzzing noise and moving erratically toward the edge. He grabbed for it before it could fall to the floor, and seeing who it was, answered immediately. 'Meg, it's good to hear from you. Where are you? Nothing wrong, is there? No, dinner sounds great. I'll see you at home in'—he glanced at his watch—'forty minutes. Right. Bye for now.'

He looked up to see two curious faces. 'My daughter. Down from Oxford for the week end.' He looked at his notes. 'I think we're done here. Everyone has their assignments, right? Any questions?'

But Ridley and Quinn were anxious to leave as well, and within five minutes the incident room was just a distant memory.

SIXTEEN

Sidney Westgate poured himself a whisky and reflected on the singular events of the day. In retrospect, he had to admit, he had not acquitted himself particularly well. Bad form, challenging Anscombe in public—he needed his support in committee. Still, he reasoned, he had been goaded into it. Nonetheless he realised that apologies were in order. Reluctantly he picked up the telephone and dialed the Principal's extension.

IN HIS ROOMS, Fraser Campbell put down a book he had been reading half-heartedly, as he mulled over the events that had transpired in the SCR that afternoon. One thing was certain: Burton-Strachey had lied—to the police, no less—about his whereabouts on Tuesday last. Campbell had been over and over the matter in his mind, and there was no doubt about it: the man had been in Russell Square, which lay in the opposite direction from his house—at a time when he said he'd been nowhere near.

Campbell tried to form an image of Burton-Strachey as a murderer, and came up short. The man was a buffoon, thought Fraser, who had a knack for projecting his own weaknesses on those around him. Well, that was all to the good. He'd overheard Burton-Strachey confide to Westgate in the common room that he'd applied for the Principal's position. The revelation had brought agony to Campbell at the time: he was just the sort of polished, more urbane type that would appeal to the Board. And now, Campbell realised, he had the perfect way to take him out of the running. Campbell returned once more to the notion that Burton-Strachey was a murderer. The idea fascinated him. What could have been his motive? Sex, decided Campbell. Yes, that must be it. Wasn't that wife of his always seeing Harley Street specialists? She probably couldn't satisfy the poor bloke, and he had turned to other sources. The randy old bugger! So what had happened? Had the girl got herself pregnant? Pity that police inspector was so close with his information. Oh well, he knew what to do with what he had. He looked at his watch. It was four forty five. Campbell reached for his telephone.

TWENTY MINUTES LATER, anyone familiar with the denizens of St. Gregory's College would have been surprised by the sight of two of its Fellows, whose conversations did not normally extend beyond perfunctory greetings and indifferent inquiries into each other's health, sitting together over drinks and apparently engaged in earnest conversation in the corner of a nearby pub.

Burton-Strachey spoke first. He wasn't quite certain why Campbell had wanted to speak with him. Still less did he care for the man's attitude. But he could hardly afford to ignore the pointed references on the telephone to his candidacy for the Principal's position.

'Well, Campbell? What's all this about?' he asked.

But Campbell was clearly savouring his position, and in no hurry to lay his cards on the table. 'I couldn't help being surprised by something you said during our little get-together with the police in the SCR today.'

'Indeed. What was that?' The tone was offhand, but Burton-Strachey's eyes became wary.

'Well, you told the police that you went home for lunch on Tuesday last, and did not return until just before afternoon lectures.' Campbell smiled at him disingenuously.

Burton-Strachey's grip on his glass tightened fractionally. 'Indeed. What of it?'

'Not much really.' Campbell was enjoying their relative positions. So often in the past he had been the butt of Burton-Strachey's barbed wit. But all that would change now. 'It's just that, as I told that Inspector, I was in Russell Square during the noon hour. And I'd swear I saw you coming along

Montague Street at about one o'clock—one fifteen at the outside.' He smiled again and lifted his glass.

Burton-Strachey tried to brazen it out. 'Quite impossible. As I told that Inspector, I went home for lunch. You must have been mistaken.'

But Campbell was not to be put off so easily. 'I don't think so. If you think back, you'll recall that you tried to cross some distance from the Zebra Crossing. A taxi almost ran you down, in fact. I should think that the police could trace the driver and confirm it—if they'd a mind to,' he added slyly.

Burton-Strachey's heart sank. Certainly Campbell could cause him embarrassment; there was no doubt about that. 'What exactly is your point, Campbell?' he asked, his voice edged with anger.

'It's simple, really: I want you to withdraw as a candidate to succeed Anscombe.'

'You *what?*' Burton-Strachey could not restrain himself from raising his voice. Several heads turned, and the barmaid looked up from polishing glasses. He lowered his voice. 'You must be mad!'

'You heard me correctly. If this comes out your application won't be worth a brass farthing. You might as well cut your losses. Whatever you're hiding, it must be worse than not gaining the Principalship, especially now that you've lied to the police.'

Burton-Strachey strained to control himself. 'Listen, you little worm,' he hissed. 'If you know what's good for you, you'll stay well out of my affairs.'

Campbell could not restrain himself. 'An interesting choice of words, B-S,' he intoned deliberately. 'Is that what this is about, then?'

'I'm not joking. If you go messing about in things you don't understand, you'll live to regret it!'

Campbell was becoming uneasy. Things were not going as he planned. Surely the man should recognise his own long-term interests. 'Look,' he said, adopting a more conciliatory tone, 'I'm sure we can come to some agreement. Think it over. Sleep on it and I'll get back to you tomorrow.'

It was not what Burton-Strachey had envisioned, but then, few events in his life had turned out the way he had anticipated. He realised that Campbell was in a position to cause him a great deal of mischief. 'Very well, but if I were you I'd consider my actions carefully.'

And that, Burton-Strachey reflected, was just what he himself would do. His accession to the post of Principal was absolutely essential if he were to avert the financial disaster that loomed just around the corner. And nothing— certainly not a fool like Fraser Campbell—was going to stand in his way.

'I CAN'T TELL YOU how good it is to see you.' McDermott swept his daughter up in his arms and hugged her.

'You too, dad. Have I been away that long?' she asked, straightening her clothes and rearranging her hair as he put her down.

'No, of course not. It's just that it's been a depressing last few days, and hearing from you out of the blue was just the tonic. He looked at her sharply. 'Why are you in town, anyway? You haven't been sent down, have you?'

She laughed. 'Very funny. It is Friday, you know, and I thought we could spend some time together before studies really become a grind, and I can't get away at all. Speaking of tonic,' she added, 'I'll have a gin and, if you're offering.'

'I'd forgotten that you're running in more sophisticated circles now,' he said, approaching the drinks cabinet. 'Speaking of the staff of life, what about dinner? Where would you like to go?'

'Oh, no place special. I thought we might just have something here—that is, if you're free.'

'Never fear,' he replied. 'But as you say, we might not get another chance for some weeks, so let's make it a night out. My treat, Meg—what do you say?'

Megan smiled radiantly, and not for the first time McDermott was reminded of her mother.

MEGAN HAD CHANGED HER CLOTHES AND ARRANGED HER HAIR in a sophisti- cated style that made her look ten years older, and she and her father lingered over the remains of dinner at *The Gay Hussar* in Soho.

'I didn't know you liked peasant food, Meg,' McDermott said mischievously.

'*Ethnic* food, Dad! Actually, it's a recently acquired taste, if you must know. I met this boy in class last term—Karel Gabor—'Gabby' everyone calls him.'

'Carol?' McDermott queried with a straight face.

'K a r e l, you oaf. He's a marvellous cook.'

McDermott raised an eyebrow. 'Not breakfasts, I trust.'

Megan smiled indulgently. 'You wouldn't be prying, would you? Anyway, you know Renniston College. Nuns must lead a less cloistered existence.'

'Maybe that's the answer: a convent,' he grinned.

Their waiter, who had been lurking in the background, sensed an opening and approached their table. 'Is everything to your satisfaction, sir?'

'Absolutely scrumptious, really,' Megan answered for him. 'Do you suppose,' she asked coyly, 'that the chef could be persuaded to part with his recipe for the cherry soup *au froid*? I know there's something special in it, but I can't quite identify it.'

'I'll see what I can do, Miss,' the waiter replied. 'Would you care for any... afters?' The Anglicism clearly grated on his Hungarian sensibilities.

'What would you recommend?'

'We have an excellent coffee cake,' he replied. 'Cinnamon and walnuts with a sugar glaze. Very nice with an expresso.'

'Sounds scrumptious. I'll have it. Daddy?'

McDermott surveyed his waistline ruefully. 'I'll just have a plain coffee, thanks.'

The waiter smiled a bit smugly, McDermott thought, and retreated in the direction of the kitchen. Megan watched him go, then turned her attention to her father.

'Gabby will be astonished when I prepare a Hungarian meal for him.'

McDermott's warning system went off: this was beginning to sound serious. 'Why don't you offer him some nice British fare—say, Toad in the hole, or haggis?' he asked with a straight face.

She grimaced. 'He already thinks that the only thing the English can do is boil sprouts—and then too much.'

'Does he?' McDermott was developing a genuine dislike for the young man.

Forty minutes later they left the restaurant, oblivious to the well dressed elderly couple seated against the far wall, and who had been observing them for some time with discreet interest.

IN HIS STUDY Norman Anscombe was reflecting on the recondite pleasures his position offered. A rather specialised knowledge of early Greek philosophers had not opened many doors, but a patient industriousness, beginning with a series of articles in various learned journals, had culminated in an impressive five-volume *History of the Presocratic Philosophers*. This, in turn, had brought with it a series of offers unique to the academic world: there had been several guest lectures, two visiting professorships, and nearly two decades ago the offer of a permanently endowed Chair of Greek Philosophy and with it, the position of Registrar of St. Gregory's. Three years later, when the sudden demise of the Principal had created an unexpected opportunity, Anscombe had gamely offered to fill the breach.

The offer had been gratefully accepted by an inexperienced Board relieved to be rid of the matter, and Anscombe had been duly installed as Principal, the investiture resembling the Changing of the Guard, but with rather more ceremony. He soon discovered that he was eminently unsuited for the position, for although his visionary skills and academic standing were equal to the task, his rapport with his colleagues proved somewhat deficient. In a word, his colleagues largely ignored him. It had not taken Anscombe long to appreciate this fact, and to venture forth from the Principal's Study only long enough to teach his classes and take his meals. By training a scholar rather than a diplomat, he had nonetheless come to appreciate the necessity for honing his human relations skills. Indeed, so gradual had the transition been that Anscombe himself had not noticed just when it was that he had become what others wanted him to be.

Fortunately the handling of the day-to-day affairs of the college rested in his secretary's capable hands. Mrs. Coates kept track of his schedule and reminded him of upcoming social occasions and professional commitments—and in short functioned as the *eminence grise* of St. Gregory's, ensuring that crucial matters were dealt with, leaving the Principal the less onerous task of presiding over the college on ceremonial occasions.

Now as darkness approached Norman Anscombe sat in his study, reflecting on his good fortune and his own imminent departure. He was staring out of his window when the door opened and Mrs. Coates appeared. 'General Braithwaite is here, Principal. Shall I show him in?'

'By all means, Mrs. Coates.' The Principal turned his gaze from the gathering darkness and prepared to greet his guest. 'Evening, Brigadier. Good of you to come on such short notice.'

'Evening, Anscombe. Actually not much of an inconvenience. The wife is down for her fortnightly raid on Harrod's.' He laughed heartily at his own wit. Anscombe merely smiled.

The speaker was a tall, thin gentlemen in his early seventies. He possessed a rapidly thinning crop of white hair, combed straight back, and a closely-trimmed grey moustache. Although he was immaculately dressed in civilian clothes (an elegant charcoal grey bespoke suit, clearly cut on Saville Row), his military bearing was evident in both his posture and his speech.

'Do you think we can get this business cleared up tonight?' Braithwaite asked casually, lighting a cigar in total disregard of the health and safety laws regarding smoking in the workplace.

Having anticipated just this contingency the Principal moved a large ashtray in his direction. 'I don't see why not. I certainly hope so. It would be convenient if I could announce the appointment at the Principal's Dinner tomorrow evening. It's a matter of getting the Board to meet tomorrow—if we can come to an agreement tonight.'

The Brigadier settled comfortably into a leather armchair. 'Leave that to me. Hobbs will—' his thoughts were interrupted by the Principal's secretary at the door. 'Excuse me gentlemen, but Mr. Hobbs has arrived.'

Amos Hobbs did not wait for an invitation, but entered directly. 'Evenin', lads. You wouldn't be starting without me, now, would you?'

Anscombe coloured. The man was deliberately irritating. 'Certainly not, Hobbs. Thanks for coming. The Brigadier's only just arrived.'

'How do, Braithwaite. Fought any good wars lately?' It was a running joke, of which the Brigadier had long since tired.

The General regarded him with thinly concealed distaste. Amos Hobbs was a self-made man, and looked it. Big and burly, with arms like hams and hands like meat hooks, and a ruddy complexion that spoke of a lifetime in the outdoors. He was wearing a tweed sports jacket that had seen many winters, and his shirt was open at the collar, with no tie. His jacket was unbuttoned, and his ample waist hung over his belt. He prided himself on being a simple man with plain tastes, and it was reflected in every aspect of his being.

'Evening, Hobbs,' the General returned civilly, though not warmly. 'Anscombe here was just saying that he hopes we can tie matters up tonight, and have the new man ratified by the Board tomorrow.'

'Don't see why not. Never did see sense of committees. One bloke can decide things in half the time, provided he's got common sense. Any road, sooner we get to it, sooner we can have a drink, eh?' He pulled an armchair up to the desk.

The Principal looked at Braithwaite uneasily. 'Yes, uh, well, here are the files of the candidates to date. You've been present at their interviews, of course, and it's my view that they sort themselves out fairly neatly.' He picked up one of the manila folders. 'I've taken the liberty of placing the candidates into one of two categories—purely for purposes of discussion, of course.' Anscombe looked at Hobbs, who was watching him carefully and, he thought, with some skepticism. 'The first file represents those applicants whom I would term non-starters: they really ought not to have applied, but for one reason or another we are bound to consider them. In that category I would include—'he consulted a list before him—'two of the three external applicants, Mr. Asrajhi and, er, Mr. Bernstein, and one of the internal candidates, Mr. Campbell.'

'Sounds right enough to me,' ventured Hobbs. 'Don't want any wogs or Jews running place, do we?'

Anscombe blanched. 'In my judgment it's a matter of professional background. While each has their strengths, neither of the gentlemen has any administrative experience in an academic setting.' It was an argument the Principal hoped to use to his advantage later.

'Yes, all right. I think we're in agreement there, Anscombe,' the Brigadier spoke up. 'What about the internal applicants? You mentioned that Campbell chap.'

Anscombe paused to light his pipe. If the Brigadier could smoke, so could he. 'As we agreed at our previous meeting I've spoken with the man, and given him to understand that his application isn't likely to be successful. I hinted that it might be better all around if he simply withdrew.' He paused again, and scowled. 'It says something about the man that as yet he hasn't done so. Still, I don't believe he'll resign if he's not appointed.' *More's the pity*, he thought to himself.

'Oh, aye? And what about t'others?' This time it was Amos Hobbs speaking.

The Principal turned to the other folder on his desk, glancing surreptitiously at his watch as he did so. It was just after nine PM.

ACROSS THE QUAD a study lamp burned exceptionally late for a Friday evening, as Fraser Campbell sat at his desk and pondered the events of that day. It was not the custom of the Fellows to toil into the evenings, nor was it common for students to call upon their tutors so early in the term. So he was surprised to hear footsteps in the hallway outside, still more surprised when those footsteps stopped outside his door, and were followed by a gentle tapping. He looked up.

'Yes? Come in.'

SEVENTEEN

Norman Anscombe concluded his remarks and nodded sagaciously at the Brigadier. The next few moments, he knew, could in large measure determine the direction and fortunes of St. Gregory's College for a decade or more.

Braithwaite took his cue. 'I'm in complete agreement with you, Anscombe. Westgate's full of ideas—perhaps too full, if you ask me. The College has been doing well during the past several years. I'm not against change, but if you ask me, too many schools are pandering to the shifting winds of public opinion. What we want is someone who's going to maintain the course we've set, but make damn sure that the quality of the college doesn't suffer.'

'We're agreed, then.' Anscombe avoided looking in Hobbs' direction. 'Now as far as the remaining external candidate goes—I personally found him very, um, interesting. That is to say,' he added hurriedly, 'in certain respects he seems well qualified for the position. Sound financial skills, good track record. However, like the earlier candidates we must consider the fact that he is not an academic.'

Hobbs looked up from the files before him. 'That's as maybe, but I'll wager he's got a damn sight more horse sense than them toadies and toffee-noses.'

The Brigadier straightened in his chair. 'You always did have a way with words, Hobbs.'

'You know me for what I am,' he replied. 'Grew up on a pig farm, I did— *afore* I built brewery that ships 'alfway 'round world. Get to know a lot 'bout folk from watchin' pigs, you do.' The Brigadier's lip curled in a moue of distaste. 'Tell you summat. There's two kinds o' pigs: them as go to trough and fight for food—they grow big and fat—and wieners, them 'as get nosed out. Even if they live they never 'mount t' much. What this place wants'—Hobbs thumped the desk with a massive index finger for emphasis— 'is some fresh blood. By rights there should be a deal of changes round here. A new broom never did no harm.' Having fired off his salvo of mixed metaphors Hobbs sat back, challenging either man to return the fire.

Anscombe sighed inwardly. It was going to be a long night. 'Would anyone care for a whisky?' he asked in a bland voice.

One hour and forty very tense minutes later the door to the Principal's study opened and the three men emerged. Anyone not familiar with the individuals concerned would nonetheless have been able to discern a sense of satisfaction on the faces of two of the gentlemen, while the third appeared less than pleased.

'The Board is scheduled to meet tomorrow midday, Anscombe. I think I can say with assurance they will accept our recommendation.'

'I certainly hope so, Brigadier. I trust we are all in agreement?' Hearing nothing, he turned. 'Hobbs?'

'Oh, aye. 'Appy as a pig in muck.' There was no attempt to conceal the sarcasm.

Anscombe ignored his tone. 'Good. Then I will make the announcement at the Principal's Dinner tomorrow evening. You will both, of course, attend?'

Amos Hobbs looked at him sharply. 'Don't set a place for me. If you'll excuse me, I've got a job o' work t' do.'

THE BOOTHROYDS WERE JUST TURNING OUT THE LIGHTS in the sitting room when the telephone rang. Alyce looked at the clock on the mantle instinctively. It was nearly eleven pm.

Her husband glanced at her and picked up the receiver. 'Boothroyd here. Oh, yes, Principal. You don't say? I'm flattered. Of course we've discussed it. Actually, Alyce has been very supportive. Yes, I'm sure she will—kind of you to say so. I suppose the answer is yes, then. When will you be making the announcement? As soon as that? Yes, we'll look forward to it. It's settled, then. Yes, you also. Good night.'

He put down the telephone and turned to his wife. 'That was Anscombe. Seems I've got the nod.' He looked at her uneasily. 'You don't think we've done the wrong thing, do you?'

'Not a bit of it,' she said, genuinely pleased for him. 'You'll do wonderfully. Oh, dear. I suppose that means I should start collecting boxes!'

SATURDAY CAME, and McDermott rose at first reluctantly, then more readily, as he recalled Megan was home. He put a pot of coffee on, and had just finished the first page of the morning paper when she entered the kitchen.

'Well, you're up early for a week end.'

'Morning, cupcake,' McDermott replied absently. It was one of a panoply of nicknames he had given her, each of which revealed as much about his own state of mind as it did about her. This one, she knew, meant that he was preoccupied, perhaps even troubled.

'What's the matter?' She glanced at the headlines. 'A case got you feeling out of sorts?'

McDermott smiled. 'Nothing so abstract. But let's not talk shop. What's on your plate for today?'

'I thought I might run up to Dillon's.' she replied, pouring herself a cup of coffee. 'One of my professors put her own book on the reading list, and of course Blackwell's is out of stock. She's certain to ask questions about it during classes next week.'

'Indeed?' McDermott reflected on the ethics of assigning one's own book as a course text. The meagre gain in royalties, he decided, was a minor issue compared to the question of objectively examining a student on one's own theories. 'What then?'

'I thought I might drop in on Pam during the afternoon. It might be ages before we see each other again.'

Megan's friendship with Pamela Townsend dated from their childhoods, and McDermott was Pam's God father. He knew that Megan had been blindsided when, a couple of years earlier, Pam had revealed that she was attracted to other women. She had never made any overtures to Meg—who had told her father as much—but they had become more distant, unsure of how to relate to one another, each wanting to maintain their friendship intact. That Megan had not wholly accepted her on her own terms had, he knew, upset Pam, and the two young women had spent the intervening months working that out, through long weeks of silence punctuated by brief periods of intense rapport.

Sensing his daughter's unease, McDermott changed the subject. 'What's on for the evening, then?'

She brightened up. 'I thought we might have a nice, home cooked meal here. My treat this time. You must be tired of canteen food and takeaways.'

'That sounds—oh, just a moment. I almost forgot. I have, er, a date tonight, actually. A concert at the Albert Hall.'

Megan looked at him with undisguised interest. 'Anyone I know?'

'No. A colleague, in fact. She works for the Met at St. Bart's. A doctor. I've known her for some time.'

'A doctor? How fascinating! Is she one of those people who cuts up bodies and tells you what they had for breakfast?' She smiled maliciously.

McDermott frowned good naturedly. 'Don't be impertinent. Actually, she's very nice.'

'Oh dear. I suppose that means she's as ugly as sin. By the way, what about that barrister you were dating—Victoria Secret—or is she yours?' Megan was clearly enjoying herself.

'That's enough from you.' Then more kindly: 'I'm sorry I won't be here, though. How about Sunday in the park?'

'Sounds great.' Megan still treasured fond memories of many Sundays in Hyde Park with her parents, watching the riders along Rotten Row mingling with the joggers, taking a boat on the Serpentine, or just renting deck chairs and soaking up the sun. In the middle of that tranquil green space, sheltered from the sounds and smells of the traffic, it was possible to forget one was in the heart of a great city.

'Done, then.' McDermott moved toward the cooker. 'Now, how about a fry-up?' As he spoke, however, he was thinking. It had been several days since he had spoken with Victoria. He recalled the telephone message he had received the previous day; he really ought to return her call, he knew. He looked at his watch. A quarter to nine. A bit early for a Saturday morning.

By the time McDermott had finished the morning dishes he decided he was taking the coward's way out. He picked up his mobile and keyed in Victoria's number. After several rings a voice answered sleepily.

It was a man's voice.

McDermott put on his best matter-of-fact voice. 'Hello. Is Victoria Chambers there, please?'

'Hang on a mo. Vicky!' There was a brief silence punctuated by muffled noises, as if someone was trying to cover the receiver. McDermott thought he heard a reference to an 'older man' followed by 'Oh dear!' Presently the noises stopped, and Victoria came on the line.

'Yes, hello? Is that you, Daddy?'

McDermott could sense her anxiety and was not inclined to relieve it. 'Not quite. It's Colin. Sorry to, disturb you, but I got your message late yesterday, and then Megan came down from Oxford, and what with one thing and another I didn't get a chance to get back to you until now.' Then he gave in to his baser instincts: 'Hope I didn't spoil anything.'

'Not at all.' By now she was regaining her composure. 'Actually, I called yesterday to see whether we have anything on for this evening. Some time back you mentioned something about a concert.'

Bloody hell, thought McDermott. *Did I actually ask both of them out for the same night?* He looked at the season's schedule for the Albert Hall on the bulletin board next to the fridge. Mahler/Mendelssohn tonight, and Impressionist music in a week's time. Hobson's choice.

'Are you sure it was this week?' McDermott asked, trying to appear casual. 'I rather thought it was next week. They're doing Debussy and Ravel, you know. Megan's down for the long weekend, and I'm not likely to see her again for some time.'

'Of course. I must have got my dates wrong.' Her voice was so cool by now that McDermott imagined the line from Hampstead Heath must be covered with frost. 'A week today, then. Give me a call if something comes up.' The line went dead.

Not the most successful handling of that, McDermott reflected as he ended the call.

A FEW HOURS LATER MEGAN THREADED HER WAY amongst the hoards of other university students picking up their textbooks at Dillon's. She searched in vain for her instructor's book on the shelves under the subject heading, and was just about to ask for assistance, when she spotted it on a large table in the centre of the aisle. It was one of many beneath a large sign that read 'Out of Print—Remaindered for Clearance.' She picked up a copy and smiled.

IN THE PORTER'S LODGE Bateman was quietly enjoying a cup of tea. Weekends were leisurely in his line of work, not that he ever allowed himself to be hurried. If you let other people run your life they'd drive you to an early death, he reasoned, and however slowly he might move, Bateman was not yet ready for the grave.

He put down his copy of *The Daily Mirror*—none of those fancy papers read by the toffee-noses in the SCR for him—and from a hook on the wall removed his set of master keys for the college. It was a point of pride with Bateman that he had been entrusted with the security of the college. To his certain knowledge not even the Principal had a complete set of keys, so he did not begrudge the fact that along with the keys went the task of periodically circumnavigating the offices and grounds after hours and on week ends, to ensure that all was as it should be. He had, in fact, performed this task since the inception of St. Gregory's, and had he possessed a more voluble inclination, his account of college irregularities—which ran the gamut from undergraduates copulating in the library after hours to members of the faculty who had actually forgotten where their classes were—would have astonished and regaled a wide audience. As it was, his taciturn manner ensured that such revelations would never see the light of day. Only a small notebook that he carried with him recorded his findings: a light left on here, a window left unlocked there, perhaps some boxes positioned too near the furnace. The Principal had insisted on a written record of all anomalies: necessary for the insurance, he had said.

Bateman examined the dregs of his teapot, and decided to forego the pleasure. He switched off the light—Anscombe was a right bugger about that—put on his hat, and prepared to make his rounds.

EIGHTEEN

That evening, as was the custom at the end of the first week of each term, the Fellows of St. Gregory's College and their wives gathered in the Principal's Dining Room for the semiannual Principal's Dinner. In part this tradition had been established as an exchange of pleasantries, an objective that became more difficult to achieve as the term progressed and the faculty pursued their respective goals and individual schedules. As well, it gave all involved an opportunity to enjoy a sumptuous meal, followed by some tolerable port at the College's expense. Few begrudged the fact that the price of this epicurean event was to provide the Principal with a captive audience for the inevitable announcements that he deemed important, the substance of which most faculty often already knew. In this, his final year, Norman Anscombe was determined to set a proper mood at the outset, one that would ensure that he left the College in happy circumstances.

This year's dinner, therefore, promised to be of singular importance. The Chancellor of the college and Chairman of the Board of Regents, Brigadier General sir Geoffrey Braithwaite and his wife were present—the other member of the search committee, Amos Hobbs, having declined the Principal's invitation. Characteristically absent from the gathering at this point was MacAuley Trewilliger, M. Litt., who had retired to his rooms following lunch, and had not yet reappeared. That, Anscombe reflected, was not an entirely unwelcome turn of events: a reclusive bachelor known for his fondness for the grape, an intoxicated Trewilliger on this occasion did not sound the best possible note for the coming year. Still, the man was not in the best of health. Perhaps it was worth checking into.

Anscombe also noted that Fraser Campbell was absent. What was the man up to? He hoped that their little tête-á-tête earlier in the week was not going to have any public implications. That would be damned churlish of the man, he thought, concealing his irritation.

The College had taken on extra servers for the evening, and he summoned the nearest of these to his side. 'What's your name, girl?' he asked.

'Molly, sir,' she responded with a thick Irish accent. 'Molly Dumphrys.'

The Principal appraised her carefully. Not, perhaps, the brightest person in the world—nor, he concluded, the most experienced. 'Search out the Porter—that's Mr. Bateman—and ask him to check on Mr. Campbell and Mr. Trewilliger, and see what is detaining them. If the latter is—unwell' he. improvised, 'Bateman is not to insist on his presence, but should report that fact to me here.'

As the young woman left the room a feminine voice intruded upon Anscombe's reflections. 'Well, Principal. I suppose we shall learn this evening the name of your successor?'

Anscombe turned and encountered Clarissa Soames—who was well turned out in a stylish and expensive ensemble that set off a professional hairdo.

'Good evening, Clarissa. Yes, you may expect an announcement tonight— one which, if I may say so, the faculty will have cause to support enthusiastically.' he added.

'Indeed?' she replied. She assumed he was referring to his replacement, and was intrigued, since to the best of her knowledge none of the applicants was capable of running a dog kennel, let alone an institution of higher education. She waited for some moments, and when it was evident that no further information would be forthcoming, moved off in search of a dry sherry and some canapés.

Ten minutes later neither Fraser Campbell nor MacAuley Trewilliger had yet appeared, and those faculty who were present were plainly growing restive. The Brigadier cast a furtive look at Anscombe from across the room, and the Principal decided he could postpone things no longer. He tapped his wine goblet with his knife, until the general buzz of conversation was reduced to a subdued murmur as everyone took their chairs. Then, in carefully modulated tones, he began to speak.

'Good evening, ladies and gentlemen. Thank you for your attention.' The residual chatter gradually subsided. 'As you know it has been a tradition at St. Gregory's for some years now to commence each term with a dinner for the Fellows and their spouses, provided by the College. This year's dinner will be something of a special occasion, in that I am retiring at the conclusion of this academic year.' A few token expressions of disappointment were followed by gracious disclaimers by the Principal. 'We are privileged to have with us this evening our Chancellor, and the Chairman of our Board of Regents, Brigadier General sir Geoffrey Braithwaite, who will shortly be announcing the appointment of my successor, and I am sure you will all join me in welcoming sir Geoffrey and his wife to our little gathering.'

The Brigadier acknowledged the polite, if not exactly overwhelming, applause, and was about to continue when Molly Dumphrys burst into the room as white as a sheet, and in evident distress. 'He's dead! Holy Jesus, Mother of Mary! He's dead!'

THE EVENING WAS GOING SPLENDIDLY, McDermott thought. Daphne was ravishing—there was simply no other word for it—in a flowing emerald-green frock that matched her eyes, and the concert had led off with one of his favourite pieces, Mendelssohn's Third Symphony. From its measured opening to the dramatic finale, Mendelssohn's elegiac piece never failed to remind him of the misty mood of Scotland. It was the Interval now, and McDermott was just collecting a gin and tonic for Daphne, and a neat whisky for himself, when he heard a familiar voice.

'Colin. Fancy seeing you here.'

He put on his most bland face—the one he usually reserved for suspects caught in a lie —and turned toward the voice.

'Hello, Victoria. So you came after all. Are you enjoying the concert?'

'Never more,' she replied, in tones that would have sent chills up the spine of an axe murderer. She transferred her gaze to the woman at his elbow. 'And this must be your daughter.' Her expression indicated that she very much doubted it.

'Actually, this is Daphne Fielding—*Dr.* Fielding,' he explained. 'One of my colleagues. Daphne, Victoria Chambers.'

But Victoria was not about to surrender her advantage. 'How nice for you both. I must have got it wrong, Colin. I understood you were spending the evening with Megan, before she returned to university.'

McDermott realised he would have to take the offensive. He looked past Victoria in hopes of finding the owner of the male voice who'd answered the telephone that morning. Instead he saw Victoria's parents, glowering at him from the background.

'She decided to see an old school chum at the last minute,' he improvised. 'You know how kids are.'

'Actually, I don't. I'm told I was never one myself. We must be getting back to our seats. Good evening, Colin. *Nice* to have met you, Dr. Fielding.'

As she turned and strode away, McDermott heard her father say 'Definitely *not* the woman he was with last night, either!'

'Well, that was certainly interesting,' Daphne said, smirking.

'An old friend, actually. Known each other since—well, for a long time.'

'And you're still friends? What was all that about seeing your daughter this evening?'

'Don't start, Daphne. Obviously I wanted to be with you—I'm here, aren't I?'

She grinned. 'That's all right, Colin. Actually I enjoyed myself. It's not often I get to see a grown man behave like a little boy caught with his hand in the biscuit tin.' She took his arm just as the lights dimmed to signal the end of the intermission, and they retook their seats.

A few minutes later McDermott felt the vibration of his mobile, and, making his excuses, went to the lobby to take the call.

Even with the congestion that marks London on a weekend evening, it took McDermott less than twenty minutes to collect Daphne and make their way to St. Gregory's.

THEY MADE A CONSPICUOUS ENTRANCE, to say the least. The uniformed officer at the main gate at first barred their way, explaining that the area was for the time being closed to the general public. When McDermott flashed his warrant card the officer apologized profusely, casting an envious eye at the couple in their formal attire arriving in an elegant classic sports car. McDermott threaded his way between the winking blue lights of the police vehicles and parked next to the mortuary van.

Entering the building, he commandeered a constable at the door who took him to the Principal's Dining Room, where DS Ridley was presiding uneasily over the assembled intelligentsia of the college. All eyes, not least Ridley's, widened at the entrance of the Met police officer in black tie accompanied by an elegantly-coiffed woman in a stunning satin dress.

It was Westgate who encountered them first.

'Well, Inspector, it appears that civil servants must be exempt from the present round of government austerity measures, judging by your clothes.'

McDermott was in no mood for the man's feeble attempts at humour. 'As I am an alumnus of St. Gregory's, Westgate, I suppose you may derive some satisfaction from whatever small measure of success I may have achieved.' Daphne looked at him in astonishment, and Ridley's jaw dropped as he worked out the meaning of McDermott's riposte.

The Principal hurried over to breech the silence that followed. He took McDermott aside, and in hushed tones said 'This is frightful, Inspector, quite frightful! Nothing even remotely like it has happened in the entire history of St. Gregory's.' he added, apparently oblivious to the fact that the entire history of St. Gregory's consisted of fewer than three decades.

'Well, it has now,' McDermott observed dryly. He turned to his Sergeant. 'What have we got?'

George produced his notebook. It was, McDermott knew, as much for effect as anything else. Ridley would have the relevant details at his fingertips.

'Seems the teachers, er, the perfessers were havin' supper and the Principal noticed two of them—that would be Mr., er, Trewilliger and Mr. Campbell—had gone missin'. He sent someone to look for them, and they found Mr. Campbell at his desk. Some pills were found next to half bottle o' whisky, which were mostly empty. Pills were prescribed for'—this time he did consult his notes—'Mr. Griffith-Jones. Sleepin' pills, they were.' He looked up, pleased with his succinct summation of events. 'Oh, something else, Guv,' he added, reaching into his inside jacket pocket. 'On desk, under body, were this.'

McDermott took a plastic envelope from Ridley, from which he extracted a small piece of folded paper. He opened it, being careful to handle it by the edges. The paper had been torn from a notepad, he noticed. The handwriting was neat and carefully formed, as if the author had put some effort into it. But it was the contents that held the greatest interest:

Dear Professor,

It took me a while. You've changed your appearance, but I finally worked out where I knew you from. I think you recognised me too. We need to talk. You did a terrible thing, and now you must pay for it.

S. B.

McDermott studied the note for some seconds, then looked up. 'Who found the body?'

'Bateman did,' Anscombe said. 'That's our porter. I had asked one of the servers to have him check on one or two of the Fellows who had not yet appeared. A few minutes later she returned, screaming hysterically'—he cast a reproving glance at a young woman who was sitting in a corner, still sobbing, and being ministered to by another member of the kitchen staff. 'sir Geoffrey'—Anscombe indicated the tall elderly man next to him—'and I went along immediately to Campbell's rooms, where Bateman had sensibly remained. We confirmed that Campbell was indeed, ah, dead, and instructed Bateman to remain where he was, and not to touch anything. Then I telephoned the police from my study, and we returned to this room.'

A tall, elderly man standing nearby intervened. 'Inspector, is it? My name's Braithwaite. Brigadier, retired. I am the Chancellor of St. Gregory's.'

McDermott eyed him carefully. 'Yes, Brigadier?'

'I'm sure you can appreciate how awkward this is. We were just about to announce the appointment of Anscombe's successor. The public, parents, even potential benefactors, will be looking for signs of continuity, stability. A suicide amongst our faculty isn't exactly reassuring, is it? Does all this have to be made public?'

McDermott gave him a hard look. 'In other words, you know what's in this note?'

'I'm afraid I must take responsibility for that,' Anscombe confessed. 'You see, when Bateman first showed Campbell to me, I thought perhaps the man might have been unconscious, or in a coma—you know, a diabetic, something of the sort. I lifted his head and chest, to see if he was breathing. That's when I saw the note.'

'I see. And did you touch anything else?'

'Oh no. Immediately on confirming that he was dead I posted Bateman outside his rooms with instructions to let no one but the police inside. He was there when your men arrived.'

'Who else knows about the existence of this note or its contents?'

Anscombe glanced at the faculty and guests gathered at the other end of the room, and spoke softly. 'No one, Inspector. You have my word.'

'Very well, then.' He looked at Ridley. 'Let's get on with things. First I want to see the body, then speak with the police surgeon. I'd also like a word with the porter. Is Quinn here yet, by the way?'

Ridley leaned in. 'I put in call for her at same time I called you, Guv. She should be here any time now.'

As they moved toward the door, the Brigadier took hold of McDermott's arm. 'Look here, Inspector. Can you give me some idea of how long this is likely to take? Damned inconvenient, you know, sitting around here twiddling our thumbs.'

McDermott fixed him in his gaze. 'That will depend in large measure on what the police surgeon tells me about the circumstances of Campbell's death. I'm sorry if we've inconvenienced you, General. I know that in military terms the death of a single individual is not always a cause for great concern. The Metropolitan Police, however, are used to dealing with somewhat smaller numbers.' He removed the Brigadier's arm and escorted Daphne from the room.

'You'll hear about that!' Daphne said, as they accompanied Ridley through the door and down the dimly-lit hallway toward Campbell's rooms.

'Probably. I'm sorry, Daph. It's not been the most pleasant of evenings, has it? Are you sure you wouldn't rather call it a night? I'm liable to be here till the cock crows.'

'Are you kidding?' Her sincerity was unmistakable. 'I wouldn't miss this for the world. In my job by the time I get a corpse it's usually delivered in a body bag, trussed up like a Christmas turkey. It's much more interesting to be in on the whole dinner, so to speak.' She smiled mischievously. 'Besides, who knows? I may be able to contribute something to the police surgeon's analysis.'

'There's no accounting for taste,' McDermott said, following Ridley down the hallway.

They passed the constable on the door and looked into the dead man's chambers. Several armchairs were scattered around the room, facing a fireplace that was flanked on either side by dark bookshelves extending almost to the ceiling. Directly under the largest window in the room was a writing table with a single chair next to it. There was a small drinks cupboard against the wall facing the fireplace, and next to that a door leading, he imagined, to a bedroom and small bath. The books, he noticed, did not reflect the presence of a great scholar: a few introductory-level texts, obviously for use in his lectures, and a larger body of older, slightly dog-eared books, vied for space with a stack of examination booklets and a reading lamp that hovered over one wing chair. Canisters of tea and sugar stood next to an electric kettle. From what he saw McDermott did not suppose that anything in the way of an exchange of great ideas had taken place between the late tutor and his charges.

The police surgeon, who was leaning against the wall, looked up from his notes.

'Well, if it isn't DI McDermott. As I live and breathe. And spruced up like a fourpenny rabbit.' It was part of their usual banter.

'Hello, Foster. You haven't been struck off yet, then? The medical profession does look after its own. Do we need paper suits?'

'Only if you don't want to bollix the scene and get yelled at by your Super.'

McDermott sighed and retrieved two sets of disposable crime scene suits and shoe coverings from the officer on the door. After struggling into the clumsy gear he and Fielding entered the room.

'What have you got for me?'

'Fairly straightforward, I should say. Deceased was in his early or mid-forties, I should say. Died of a combination of sleeping pills and alcohol—or at least that's what's indicated at the moment,' he added cautiously. 'Have to wait for the PM to be sure.'

'Time of death?'

'You know the drill. Body temperature, rigour subsiding. About twenty-four hours, I should judge.'

Daphne intervened. 'Not longer?'

Foster surveyed the woman before him with evident scepticism. 'And who might you be?'

'Sorry. I forgot to introduce myself. I'm Daphne Fielding. Dr. Fielding. Home Office Pathologist at Bart's.'

Foster's eyebrows rose fractionally. Women pathologists were generally beyond his ken; pathologists who arrived looking like they'd stepped out of the pages of *Vogue* didn't bear thinking about. 'Christ, McDermott, you people do stick together, don't you?' He turned his attention to Daphne. 'Sorry, Doctor. What did you have in mind?'

'Just that it's rather warm in here, and when I first entered I thought I detected a faint odour of putrefaction. The high room temperature might account for the delay in body cooling.'

'It might also account for the early onset of putrefaction,' countered Foster. 'However, I take your point. As I said, it's a preliminary estimate.'

"In any case, it's clear that the deceased didn't die tonight, and most likely copped it between twenty-four and, say, thirty hours ago?' McDermott asked.

'Interesting you should put it that way, Inspector. At this point I couldn't be sure he didn't die even earlier.'

'I can,' McDermott replied. 'Thirty hours ago I was speaking with the late Mr. Campbell.'

As Foster left, the mortuary attendants removed the body and a young man had just finished photographing the scene as the forensic team moved in to complete their work. There were three of them now, two men and a woman. The men McDermott had worked with before; the young woman was new to him. All wore the standard-issue disposable gear: paper suits, caps and boots, and neophrene gloves. Brynes, the taller of the two men, was armed with a fingerprinting kit; his assistant carried a roll of adhesive tape and evidence bags for collecting fibre samples. McDermott was pleased to see they had been assigned to the case. There'd been an uproar when the forensic analysis of crime scenes had been privatised by the government in 2012, after enduring huge financial losses and criticism in the courts for substandard work. But the gap had been filled in short order by independent labs, and the many cries of doom and gloom seemed, so far, to have been misplaced. McDermott knew these technicians to be capable and dedicated professionals; more than once he'd relied on their meticulous work habits to secure a conviction.

Brynes raised his eyebrows when he entered, noticing McDermott's formal wear. 'Hello, sir. Take you away from a night on the town, did we?' He stole a glance at his assistant, who was trying, not altogether successfully, to suppress a grin. 'You look absolutely smashing, sir. Really.' the junior man added.

By now the gag had worn thin. 'You ought to be on the stage, you two. Now if you're finished your Flanders and Swann routine perhaps you can put in a decent night's work.'

'Yessir.' The smiles vanished, and McDermott pointed Daphne toward the door, with Ridley trailing behind.

As they returned to the hallway, Daphne could not contain her curiosity. 'You think it's murder, then?'

'I'm as sure as I can be at this point. Consider the facts: the suspicious death of a young woman—the one you did the post-mortem on the other day—is traced back to this College, and the Fellows are interviewed, with the strong implication that one of them was involved. Scarcely a day later one of them is found dead, with a note virtually tacked to his body, signed with her initials but which may or may not have been written by the woman, the contents of which strongly suggest she was threatening someone here.'

Daphne looked at him blankly. 'But surely the most obvious explanation is that he killed her. After the investigation led to his doorstep, he decided you were getting close, that it was only a matter of time, and he chose to take the easy way out. Surely that explains everything.'

'That's just the point, Daphne,' McDermott replied. 'It's all too tidy by half. If the man had half a loaf—and that's just about what I would grant him, based on our talk—he would have seen that we had nothing. It was a fishing expedition, and we came up beggars. We left here with no more useful information than when we'd arrived. Even if he did do it, Campbell had every reason to think he was safe. No, my guess is that he was killed for some other reason; and unless St. Gregory's is populated by a gaggle of homicidal maniacs, it's likely because he suspected—or knew—who the real killer was.'

When McDermott entered the dining room he found DC Quinn waiting. 'Sorry to be late, sir. My parents were up from Torquay, and I had my phone switched off. I only got the message when we returned from dinner.'

'No harm done, Constable. Sorry to take you away from your evening out.' He glanced down at his own clothes. 'Seems to be a lot of that going around. I gather George has filled you in. It's early days here. I'd like you to take statements from several people. Find out where they were yesterday afternoon, say from the time we left the common room—which would be shortly before four—until midnight. Start with Griffith-Jones. In addition I want to know about a prescription he has for sleeping pills: where he got them, where he keeps them, who knows he has them. It looks as if they might have been instrumental in Campbell's death. Then talk to Professor Boothroyd. He's clear for an hour or so—I left him at a little after five yesterday. I don't suppose you had a chance to check our merry little band for form?'

Quinn reddened. 'I was planning to get on it first thing Monday morning, sir.'

'That's all right. None of us were to know. George, you handle Burton-Strachey. Same thing. Alibi for late Friday afternoon and all evening. No doubt he'll tell you he spent it at Fortnum and Mason's, or some such rot. Be sure to get the names of anyone who can confirm it. If he's such an epicure, doubtless he's known to headwaiters all over London. Dig deep enough, you'll probably find he took his wife for a MacDonald's.' He allowed himself a smile. 'When you finish with him, you get the booby prize: Westgate. Don't let him intimidate you. Let him know he can answer here and now, or at the Met later.'

'Aye. And who are you takin', Guv?' Ridley asked, certain that he had got the worst of the bargain.

'For starters I want to talk to that porter—Bateman, was it? Then I'll have a chat with the Principal and the Brigadier.' McDermott looked around the room. His eye settled on Jeremy Asquith, who was sitting in an armchair, casually demolishing the last of the canapés. 'I'll also have a word with Professor Peacock.' McDermott turned to go, and then paused. 'I think I'll pick Soames's brain as well; if anyone was acting oddly this evening, my guess is she won't have missed it.'

NINETEEN

After **Ridley and Quinn left,** McDermott turned to Daphne. 'Well, you've seen the interesting bits.' He looked at his watch. 'It's getting late. We'll be at it for hours yet. Let me get a constable to drive you home.'

'It's not exactly kosher, is it, bringing your date along on a case? You certainly know how to show a girl a good time,' she teased. She picked up her wrap, gave him a peck on the cheek, and headed for the door, still smiling.

When McDermott returned to the dining hall the porter was in the kitchen, helping himself to a glass of college port. He looked up defensively as McDermott entered.

'A right shocker, that was. Need to steady my nerves.'

'Of course.' McDermott recognised that this was a man used to doing things his own way, and suspicious of newcomers. 'I'll join you, if I may.' He took a glass down from the shelf and filled it and sat down. 'You are Mr. Bateman, I take it. My name is McDermott. Metropolitan Police. I understand you found the body?'

Bateman stirred. 'Well, now, that's not strictly true, sir. The Principal sent a kitchen helper after me. Said I was to look for Mr. Trewilliger and Mr. Campbell, and if I found them I was to fetch them down to the Principal's Dining Room. 'Her and I went round to the lodgings, where we found Mr. Trewilliger. Only he were...indisposed.'

'In what way?'

'In 'is cups. Tight as an owl, 'e were. Not for the first time neither. He'd drink with the devil if no one else was handy.'

'I see. What did you do then?'

The man drained his glass, and reached for the bottle, then, apparently thinking better of it, left it untouched.

'We looked in at Mr. Campbell's rooms—his digs is just down the hall from Mr. Tree's. When I knocked I never got no answer, but I went ahead and unlocked the door. I turned on the light, and there he was for all the world to see.'

McDermott interrupted. 'You say you turned on the light. The rooms were in total darkness, then?'

'Aye, that's right.'

'What happened next?'

Bateman smiled. 'At first I thought he were passed out. The bottle, you see. Then when I got closer, and tried to wake him up, I seen he were dead. Gave me a bit of a turn, I don't mind telling you.'

'I see. And then?'

'Then?' Bateman looked at him sharply. 'Then all hell broke loose. The lass went bloomin' mad. Started screaming about him bein' dead, and takin' oaths. Silly cow.'

McDermott allowed the shadow of a smile to cross his face. Probably Bateman had been as shocked as the girl. 'You tried to calm her down then, I assume?'

'I never did no such thing. I knows me duty. I checked to make sure the poor bug—Mr. Campbell—was dead all right, then I sent the lass for the Principal. I didn't use the blower. Figured if the police had to be called he could be the one to do it. I stayed on the door and 'afore long he and that other mucky-muck—you know the one—showed up and had a look.'

'The Brigadier?' McDermott inquired.

'Aye, that's him, right enough.'

'And when they appeared, did you enter Mr. Campbell's rooms with them?'

'Oh, aye. The Principal bent down and sniffed at Mr. Campbell's face—very delicate he was. Then he pulled him up by the chest, so he was almost sitting in his chair, like. The General, he saw a piece of paper on the desk. They both looked at it. Then the Principal said nothing should be touched, and everything should be put back the way it was. The General, he put the note back, and the Principal put Mr. Campbell's head back on the desk, and we left the room. The Principal told me to stay on the door and not let anyone in, and not to say anything to anyone. Said he would be calling the police. I reckon he did straightaway, on account of no more than five minutes passed 'afore your lot was here.'

McDermott paused to consider what he had heard. He had no reason to doubt Bateman's account. Clearly the scene had been tampered with, but although Anscombe's actions had been stupid, McDermott was inclined to believe they hadn't been malicious. He made a mental note to warn Byrnes and Carruthers that there were probably lots of elimination prints about belonging to Anscombe and the Brigadier. More out of desperation than anything else he asked, 'One more thing. Has anything unusual happened here in the past few days? Especially anything involving Mr. Campbell?'

Bateman sat still for so long that McDermott wasn't sure he had heard the question. At last he spoke.

'Not in the normal way. Only the letter.'

'What letter?'

'T'other day—Tuesday morning it were—Perfessor Burton-Strachey came over white as a sheet, he did, just after gettin' a letter. Thought he were gonna keel over right then and there.'

'I see. How did that involve Mr. Campbell?'

'Easy enough, squire. He were right there, too. Saw the whole thing, he did. Asked 'im if he were all right. Offered to get 'im a cuppa tea.'

'Interesting. Tell me, what do you know about Professor Burton-Strachey?'

Bateman shot a glance at the door, as if to be sure they were alone. 'Mind you, not a lot. But I'll tell you something: for someone as lives in a fancy great house and drinks la-de-dah foreign wines, he don't part with brass easily, that man. Every Christmas all them other perfessors slips a little something in an envelope for me—for duty above and beyond during the year.' He paused as if he was having difficulty identifying such duties.

'Tight-fisted, is he? Close with his money?'

'Close? He wouldn't give you the skin off a rotten tater.' Bateman reached for the bottle again.

ON HIS WAY BACK TO THE DINING ROOM McDermott reflected on the improbability of someone committing suicide by taking pills and drinking in the dark. The Sally Beck Murder was becoming the St. Gregory's Murders, and he didn't like it at all.

When he returned Anscombe and the Brigadier were waiting for him. Ridley and Quinn were still talking to the others at the far end of the room. It was the Principal who spoke first.

'Ah, Inspector, there you are. Just about finished, I trust?'

'Just a few questions for you both, if you don't mind.' Anscombe looked crestfallen; the Brigadier seemed resigned.

McDermott began before they could protest. 'You mentioned that you are retiring at the end of the year, Principal. Can you tell me whether any of the Fellows have applied to succeed you?'

'Of course,' the Principal replied. 'In such situations it is normal practise to promote from within. Good for morale, as well as continuity.'

'And was Mr. Campbell a candidate?'

The Principal paused, weighing his words. 'He had, in fact, applied for the post.'

McDermott sensed the equivocation. 'But was he a candidate?'

Anscombe was guarded. 'I'm not sure I take your meaning.'

'Come now, Principal. Was he in the running, or had he been eliminated? And if so, was he aware of it? Were others?'

Anscombe glanced at the Brigadier, who nodded almost imperceptibly, and lowered his voice a notch. "As a matter of fact I spoke to him earlier in the week. The man was a bit apt to rush his fences, if you take my meaning. I gave him to understand that it would be in his best interest if he were to withdraw his application. He chose not to do so.'

'I see. Then apparently he considered himself still in the running, despite lacking your support?'

'I suppose so. The human mind is capable of some amazing convolutions,' the Principal conceded grudgingly. 'But I don't see the point of these questions, Inspector. If I understand the contents of that note correctly, Campbell was your man. Somehow he had been involved with the Bannerman girl in the past. She recognised him upon coming to St Gregory's and tried to blackmail him. He killed her, and when your investigation seemed to be leading back to him, committed suicide rather than be brought to account for his actions. I must say it all seems perfectly straightforward to me.'

McDermott considered his comments. Was it possible that the man was that simple? Academics, though intelligent in their own way, often lived in a rarefied world. Perhaps he really didn't grasp the alternatives.

'I'm certainly not ruling out that theory at the moment, but you understand we have to examine all the possibilities. Can you tell me where you were late yesterday afternoon and through the evening?'

Anscombe looked again at the Brigadier, then turned back to McDermott. 'As a matter of fact I can. I returned to my study immediately you left. Mrs. Coates can attest to that. I took my evening meal there, around six-thirty—the kitchen staff can no doubt verify that. I wanted to review my notes on the candidates prior to a meeting of the Selection Committee that evening. At approximately half past seven the Brigadier arrived, and a few minutes later the remaining member of the committee, Mr. Hobbs. We must have spent about two hours deliberating over our final choice. That would make it about half past nine, or thereabouts. Mr. Hobbs left and I called the successful candidate to inform him that his name would be put before the Board. The Brigadier and I spent perhaps another few minutes over our drinks discussing plans for the transition. Then he left and I retired for the night.'

'That's right,' Braithwaite added. 'I recall looking at my watch as I left. It was just going on ten-fifteen.

McDermott looked at Anscombe. 'Who else from within St. Gregory's had applied for the post?'

The Principal hesitated. 'I'm not certain I should reveal that information at this point. With all the, um, confusion, we never did get around to making a formal announcement. The other candidates might be quite upset if they were to learn through the back door, as it were, that they had been unsuccessful. You can appreciate that.'

'And I'm sure you understand, Principal, that I have an investigation to run here. Another candidate might have wanted Campbell out of his way, you see, in order to increase his own chances. People have been murdered for less.'

Anscombe went pale. Clearly the thought had not occurred to him. After some moments he acquiesced. 'Very well. There were three external candidates, but none of them proved to be acceptable. I telephoned them myself the preceding day, so you see they could not have been involved.'

'So it would appear. And the internal candidates?' McDermott persisted.

'Among the Fellows Westgate and Burton-Strachey applied, and just recently Professor Boothroyd agreed to let his name stand.'

McDermott felt the hairs on the back of his neck stand up. 'I see. And whom did the Selection Committee recommend to succeed you?'

The Principal looked about to assure himself no one else, save the Brigadier, was within hearing distance. Then he replied. 'Your former mentor, I believe: Professor Boothroyd.'

AFTER ARRANGING FOR THEIR WRITTEN STATEMENTS McDermott thanked Anscombe and the Brigadier for their cooperation and told them they were free to go. He surveyed the room. Griffith-Jones was seated in one corner, sipping a glass of sherry and looking very distressed. Quinn had informed him that his medication had been found in Campbell's study, and was probably implicated in the man's death. Quinn was nowhere in sight, nor was Boothroyd. Presumably she was questioning him at that moment. McDermott gave an involuntary shudder. Purely in terms of motive, Boots was clearly the odds-on favourite, yet McDermott could not bring himself to seriously consider the possibility. His own feelings for the man were clouding his judgment, he realised, and he was developing serious misgivings about how much longer he should remain on the case.

McDermott was momentarily distracted by the sight of Sidney Westgate, who was in the process of being questioned by Ridley, but who spared the time to look daggers at McDermott. In return, McDermott nodded ever so slightly, and smiled to himself. George would drag it out as long as he could.

Surveying the room, McDermott's eye was attracted to a flash of colour among a sea of sombre dinner jackets. Jeremy Asquith was flamboyantly dressed in salmon-coloured trousers and a boldly striped shirt of turquoise and white, open at the collar, and casually demolishing the last of a tray of nibbles. McDermott approached him. 'Enjoying the festivities?'

If he was expecting a reaction he was disappointed. The man dabbed at the corners of his mouth with a linen napkin, and extended a limp hand. He did not rise. 'I must say, you people know how to put on a show. The next time I really must invite my friends.'

Christ, thought McDermott. *Is the man ever off stage?* 'There's the small problem of a repeat performance, considering the star is dead.'

Asquith was contrite. 'Of course. I do apologise. I'm afraid my remark was not in the best of taste. Did the poor man have family?'

'Why do you want to know? Are you volunteering to break the news?' McDermott asked. That seemed to shake some sense into the man.

'I'm sorry. Of course it's a genuine tragedy. It's just that as I didn't really know the man— I mean, I hadn't had a chance to speak with him since my return....'

'But you were here when Campbell died,' McDermott said, taking a chair. 'Mind telling me what you were doing Friday afternoon and evening?'

Asquith sipped at his wine and regained his composure. 'Just what you might expect. Getting settled in, getting a bite to eat, surveying the landscape, as it were.'

'You ate alone?'

'As it happens I was entertaining some friends. Just a small informal gathering.'

'Colleagues, Mr. Asquith?'

'Students, actually. Fellow travellers in the great journey of life. Every interest and inclination, Inspector, if you take my meaning,' he smirked. Standing near enough to catch bits of the conversation, Anscombe looked resignedly at the ceiling.

McDermott persisted. 'Where was that, sir? In your rooms, I suppose?'

'As a matter of fact it was in Great Russell Street—at the Museum Tavern—just across from the BM. A *darling* barman there.' He rolled his eyes lasciviously.

'And when would that have been?'

'It must have been fivish—no, I tell a lie—closer to five-thirty when I arrived. But my friends abandoned me after an hour or so for a *soirée* they'd previously planned.' The man actually pouted.

'And you stayed behind?'

Asquith recovered his grin. 'Until closing, dear boy. I told you the barman there was *such* a darling!'

'Is he in a position to verify your movements?' McDermott instantly regretted his choice of words.

'In the words of Oscar Wilde, Inspector, I know him intimately, but not well. As for verifying my movements, I should think he was admirably qualified to do that.' Asquith rolled his eyes again. Nearby, the Principal looked as though a migraine had suddenly come on.

After taking the barman's name McDermott excused himself and moved toward the centre of the room. Clarissa Soames was sitting in a corner, much like Griffith-Jones, but with a singular difference: sipping a glass of wine, she was clearly in control of herself. He walked over and took a chair next to her.

'Hello again, Professor Soames. An attractive outfit, very becoming. I hope the events of this evening have not upset you too much?'

She looked at him with piercing eyes and an indulgent expression. 'I should not say upset, Inspector. Interested, certainly. My colleagues seem to exhibit an astonishing variety of reactions to Campbell's death, wouldn't you say?'

McDermott was momentarily taken aback by her *sang-froid*: evidently she was uninterested in giving even the appearance of compassion. 'Tell me, what was your opinion of Mr. Campbell?'

'I shouldn't have thought you'd have needed to ask. The man was a dolt. I am not a hypocrite. I disliked him in life; he is, if anything, the more agreeable in death.'

Straight answers; McDermott was warming to the woman. 'I appreciate your candour, and I am relying on it in what I am about to ask you. Can you think of any reason why someone might have wanted to kill him?'

Clarissa Soames permitted herself a small smile. 'You mean, could he have done something or known something that would have been quite literally a matter of life and death?' She put down her wine glass and regarded him sharply. 'Fraser Campbell's paramount virtue was that he always said what he thought; his overriding vice was that what he thought never amounted to much. No, Inspector, I cannot imagine Fraser Campbell as a threat to anyone at St. Gregory's—or anywhere else for that matter.'

McDermott shifted in his chair. 'Well, then, since you brought it up, I'd like to speak with you regarding some of your other colleagues.'

'You mean Westgate and Burton-Strachey, I take it?'

'As a matter of fact, I do. But how did you happen to settle on those particular individuals?'

Soames gathered her skirt around her and gave McDermott a disapproving stare. 'As one of your fictional predecessors remarked, it's elementary. Within a day of your visit, one of our number is found dead, an apparent suicide, I understand. The rather lengthy interviews being conducted'—she glanced around the room—'would suggest that you are not entirely satisfied with that account. Campbell was up for the Principal's post: everyone here knew that. It is possible, then, that his death was not self-inflicted, the motive being—in Darwinian terms—to eliminate the competition. Westgate and Burton-Strachey had also applied for the post. Ergo they must be considered amongst the primary suspects—if indeed Campbell did not commit suicide. To answer your question directly, I suppose that Westgate is capable of almost anything, if he's a mind to it. On the other hand, Burton-Strachey couldn't organise a jumble sale and get it right. If it *was* murder, I cannot believe that he's your man.'

McDermott was impressed. 'You should be working for the Met.' Then he brought his mind back to the case at hand. 'I take it, then, that you believe Fraser Campbell committed suicide. Can you tell me why?'

'It's the only explanation that makes sense. Campbell was easily the weakest candidate within the College—perhaps overall, for all I know. That, I am sure, is a view shared by everyone at St. Gregory's—certainly everyone in this room. Now, no rational person—and most of my colleagues do have their lucid moments—would undertake the grave risks involved in murder simply to eliminate a non-starter, would they?'

'Very perceptive, Miss Soames. I'm surprised you didn't apply for the post yourself.'

She seemed amused. 'Can you tell me why I would want to exchange a life of ideas, however truncated, in the classroom, for endless rounds of committee meetings and writing up reports for the Board or the Ministry? Administrative staff are like those poor unfortunates who pick up the trash. We can recognize their usefulness, even their indispensible services, without in the least wishing to emulate them.' She glanced at her watch. 'Now if you don't mind—'

McDermott cut her off. 'Actually I do have one or two other questions. You realise we must investigate all possibilities, Professor. Can you tell me where you were following our meeting yesterday, until midnight?'

Clarissa Soames assumed a martyred expression. 'Following our "meeting"—as you so delicately put it—I returned to my rooms for perhaps two hours or so, and looked over my lecture notes for the coming week. To the best of my knowledge no one saw me. Certainly no one stopped by. Then I went to Poon's near Leicester Square, for dinner. I dined alone, and went from there to the theatre, also alone. I returned to my rooms immediately after the show, but it being a nice night, I walked. It was perhaps midnight or a bit later when I arrived—I really cannot say.'

McDermott wondered how many times in his professional life he was destined to hear that sort of alibi. Was she the type of person to hold on to ticket stubs? He doubted it. The restaurant was another matter. She was distinctive; they would remember her.

'That's fine. Just one more thing, more out of personal interest than anything else: what was the name of the play you saw?'

She looked at him curiously. 'The play was *La Rue de Fleurus*—about the literary scene in Paris during the nineteen twenties. An interesting epoch, what with Hemingway and his chums. Unfortunately it was rather disappointing. It is playing at the Garrick. I predict a brief run.'

McDermott favoured her with a smile. 'Unfortunate. Did you pay for your ticket by cheque or credit card?'

'Neither. Theatre prices in London have become outrageous, I had a ticket given me by a friend who was unable to attend. A good thing, too; a waste of money, as it turned out.'

McDermott changed tack. 'You seem a very perceptive person. Surely you must have been given some thought to the recent turn of events here. What do you think lies at the bottom of it?'

Clarissa Soames shrugged. 'On the face of it, Inspector, it would appear that Fraser Campbell took his own life, due to some mental disturbance, or perhaps as a result of some personal crisis in his life. In short, it would seem to be one of those rare instances in which appearance accurately reflects reality.'

McDermott smiled. 'Perhaps it is. Just one more thing. Whose rooms are located nearest Mr. Campbell's?'

'On one side my own rooms are adjacent to his. MacAuley Trewilliger is on the other side. Your friend Boothroyd, although he does not live in college, has a study directly across the corridor.'

McDermott paused. 'And the others?'

'Doctor Westgate's rooms are just beyond mine. Across the corridor, Griffith-Jones' rooms are at the far end, then Professor Boothroyd, as I have said, has a study. Next, Burton-Strachey has a study, although he too lives outside college.'

'I see. And Professor Asquith?'

'*Mr.* Asquith has recently moved into rooms immediately opposite Westgate. Beyond that is the stairwell.' She widened her eyes. 'Surely you're not suggesting that Asquith is responsible for—'she searched for the right word—'dispatching Fraser Campbell?'

'Not at this point,' McDermott replied casually. 'I take it that you don't entirely approve of him?'

Soames sat upright in her chair. 'The man fancies himself Ganymede, Inspector, when in reality he is merely Narcissus, enchanted by his own self-image. In my experience anyone who is so obsessed with his appearance is unlikely to take seriously more substantial matters, such as scholarly excellence, or even duty.'

Not for the first time McDermott was impressed by her astuteness. 'What do you think of Asquith as a person? Do you believe that he's really as fey as he appears?'

She paused, considering the merits of the question. 'I regard him as simply a poor man's Oscar Wilde. I take it that you disagree.'

'I wonder if it's not an act—at least in part—put on for effect, designed to pander to the student's fascination with the idiosyncratic, and perhaps to cause consternation amongst his colleagues as well.'

Soames looked across the room, where the subject of their conversation was taking evident delight in washing down the last of the canapés with a glass of sherry. 'You may be right. I really hadn't given the matter much thought,' she added, implying that he was wasting her time and his own. 'Now, if you have no further questions, it's getting rather late.'

McDermott thanked her for her patience, and told the constable on the door that she was free to leave. Then he sought out Ridley and Quinn.

Wilhemina Quinn had just completed her enquiries, and George was patiently pursuing his questioning of Sidney Westgate, who by now was almost beside himself with indignation. The two officers joined the Sergeant and Westgate in one corner of the room.

'Really,' Westgate exclaimed as McDermott approached. 'This is unconscionable. I shall certainly register the most vigorous protest at my treatment this evening.' He glowered at Ridley. 'Your man here has detained me on the thinnest of pretexts, asking me inane questions, and repeating the same questions ten minutes later. How much longer are we to be expected to endure such incompetence?'

'My apologies, Professor Westgate,' McDermott replied, in a tone that suggested he was not at all contrite. 'I'm sure we will be finished shortly. Sergeant, do you have what you need?'

Ridley looked at him as if he'd just stepped in something foul. On McDermott's instructions he had suffered Westgate's arrogance for hours; now the man was being cut loose without so much as a by-your-leave. In as civilised a tone as he could manage under the circumstances, he replied, 'Aye, Guv. Mr. Westgate's been most helpful. Very cooperative, I should say. I've taken 'is statement in full.'

McDermott turned to face the man. 'Well, then, it would seem you are free to leave, Dr. Westgate. Thank you for your assistance. If we need anything more, we'll be in touch.'

'Will you, indeed?' Westgate retrieved his jacket from the chair next to him. McDermott winked at Quinn. 'Good evening to you all!'

After the last of the faculty and staff members had been dismissed, McDermott consulted his watch. It was now past midnight, and a sense of fatigue permeated the room. The coffee urn was empty. Empty wine bottles, dirty glasses and plates littered the room. McDermott spoke to the Scene of Crime Officer and arranged for the constable outside Campbell's rooms to be relieved in two hours' time. He urged Ridley and Quinn to get some sleep, and under no circumstances to appear at Charing Cross before noon, then he drove home to follow his own advice.

TWENTY

When McDermott awoke he recalled that it was Sunday and he had promised to spend the day with Megan in Hyde Park. It would have to be curtailed, he knew, one of a long series of compromises that went with the job. Megan would understand, but that did not blunt the fact that their time together would be limited. He started her favourite breakfast, and when it was almost ready, called upstairs. Five minutes later a tousled head emerging from a terry cloth bathrobe appeared at the kitchen door.

'Good morning, squirt. You're looking chipper. Ready for some soft-boiled eggs and soldiers?'

Meg looked at him thoughtfully. 'You've got to work today, don't you?'

'Not this morning. We've got hours together yet.'

'How was the concert? I didn't hear you come in. You *did* come back last night, didn't you?' she asked mischievously.

'As a matter of fact we had to call it quits early on. Developments in a case I'm working on.'

'Poor woman! Are you going to make it up to her?' Megan moved past him into the kitchen.

'To be truthful, I hadn't considered the idea. Do you think I should? More to the point, do you think a father should be taking advice on his social life from his daughter?'

'Not necessarily. Some fathers are more socially adept than others.' She scurried away from his scowl.

FORTY MINUTES LATER they were standing at the Speaker's Corner in Hyde Park, listening to several aspiring orators vying amicably for the attention of the small but attentive crowd. It was an ambiguous day, the sun and clouds battling each other for supremacy, accompanied by a chill wind. An elderly man with an artificial leg, dressed in a shabby suit decorated with several service ribbons, preached against the evils of the fighting in Syria. Nearby a middle-aged, balding man with a florid face inveighed passionately against the arrival of refugees of that conflict. Off to one side, an earnest young woman with ginger hair and an engaging lilt in her voice urged the unification of Ireland. Separated from these, on the inside edge of Speaker's Corner, an elderly lady stood quietly with a small box accepting donations. A small card affixed to the open lid read *Support the neutering of domestic pets*.

After observing the spectacle for several minutes McDermott and Megan turned away and walked toward the Serpentine. Meg broke the silence.

'Dad, you remember I said I was going to visit Pam?'

McDermott nodded.

'Well, I did, and she worries me.'

McDermott searched for the right words. 'Her sexual orientation?'

'Well, her parents reaction to it,' Megan replied. 'Her father is still giving her grief about it. He wants her to seek help—you know, counselling. She won't have it. Insists it's simply a matter of personal choice. Philip keeps going on about how her grandmother will take it.'

McDermott stooped over to pick up a pebble, and tossed it into the Serpentine, near some ducks that were foraging for food. They all swam toward the ripples, squawking in anticipation.

'Dad, that's cruel.'

'Life is cruel, sometimes.' It was a response, he knew, not an answer. 'What is Pam going to do?'

'That's just it: I don't know. Last night she seemed rather depressed. Said again that it was her choice—in fact, she insisted that choice wasn't really involved—that it was simply a matter of discovering where her attractions truly lay.'

'Are you sure she's not just experimenting?'

Meg stopped and turned toward him, grasping the sleeve of his coat. 'I'm serious, Dad. She seems to be on the verge of making herself ill.' There was no doubting the depth of her concern.

'What do you mean?'

Megan thought for a minute. 'Well, she's been complaining about cramps—you know, "women's things"—being worse than usual the past few months. I wonder if it isn't stress, caused by arguments within the family. Can't you have a word with her father?'

McDermott considered what she'd said. Meg's remarks might be nothing more than the musings of a friend, but better to err on the side of caution. 'Of course I'll do what I can. Tell you what: suppose I have a talk with Phillip— see if I can get him to go a bit easier on her.'

'Thanks.' She brightened up and kissed him on the cheek. 'I knew I could count on you.'

They spent the rest of the morning watching the waterfowl and the children. At noon they had a cup of tea and a sandwich in the park restaurant. Then McDermott made his excuses and left.

WHEN HE ENTERED THE INCIDENT ROOM McDermott found George Ridley going over his notes. To his surprise, Quinn was brewing a fresh pot of coffee.

'Hello, sir.' She looked at the pot in her hand sheepishly. 'I had to do it. George makes horrid coffee.'

McDermott grinned. 'You're telling me? Don't worry, we'll see it doesn't become a habit.' He walked to his desk, pulling off his jacket as he did so. 'Right. Since our weekend's been ruined, at least let's have something to show for it.' He sat down and pulled a large pad of paper toward him. 'Willie, give me the gen on Griffith-Jones: it was his medication, I take it?'

Quinn took a chair facing him. 'No question, I'm afraid. It seems the old boy's a bachelor, and something of a hypochondriac. His rooms look like a flipping chemist's shop: full of prescription drugs and patent tonics. Boxes of pills and medicine bottles all over the place. He had to think a bit, but when I showed him the bottle he recognised it immediately. Seconol—a prescription barbiturate dispensed in 100 milligram capsules, originally eight months ago, and renewed several times since. He couldn't recall how many capsules had been left, but the label was dated only a week past, so unless he was munching them like popcorn there must have been close to thirty capsules of the original forty left. According to toxicology that's more than enough to do someone in—especially if taken with alcohol over a short time.' Quinn paused expectantly, and McDermott was quick to pick it up.

'A good summary. Do as well on the witness stand and you just might make Sergeant one day,' he smiled. 'I don't suppose the old boy told you how his own personal medication found its way into Campbell's digs?'

'Actually, sir, that's not too difficult to figure out. It seems everyone knows the old man's a wuss. He keeps complaining about draughts, and turning up the heat. He also suffers from insomnia. Keeps all his pills by his bedside, where virtually anyone can get their hands on them. He didn't even miss the bottle—he had an older one he'd not quite finished—so we can't pin down when it was taken.'

'Or by whom,' McDermott said. 'He hasn't made it easy for us, has he? But if Campbell had wanted to end it all, is it likely he would have gone to the trouble of nicking something from a colleague? Why not simply go out and buy something himself? Must be a lot of things, if taken with alcohol...' He thought a moment. 'I don't suppose we have a PM on Campbell, since it's Sunday?'

Ridley coughed. 'That reminds me, Guv. Pathologist called this mornin'. Said to tell you she's working on it as we speak.'

'I suppose I'd best put in an appearance later, then. What else do we have on Griffith-Jones?'

'Not much, actually. No form, as you might expect. He rattled on for the best part of twenty minutes. Says he spent the evening in his rooms, part of the time on the telephone to a sister in Wales. At least that bit can be confirmed, though it's Sunday.'

McDermott toyed with his pencil in exasperation. 'Right, it can wait for now. Let's move on. You also interviewed Professor Boothroyd, I believe?'

'That's right, sir.' Quinn shot an apprehensive glance at Ridley, who was irritatingly neutral, watching to see how far she'd take it. 'He said that after you'd left, he spent the evening at home. Turned in shortly after The News at Ten. Insisted I confirm that with Mrs. Boothroyd. At his urging I called her immediately and she did back him up—for what it's worth. But alibi or not, I don't see him as having much of a motive, sir.'

Now it was McDermott's turn to look uncomfortable. 'I'm afraid he can't be dismissed, Willie. He was—is in fact—about to be named as Principal of St. Gregory's.' He leaned forward. 'On one reading of things that puts him out of the running: he must have known he had the appointment virtually locked up, so he hardly had a motive to kill Campbell—not that anyone would have considered the man a serious rival.'

'Unless he didn't know, sir—or unless there is a different motive altogether.' Quinn had both men's full attention.

'Go on, Constable. I'm interested.'

'Well, sir, perhaps Campbell wasn't murdered because he applied for the Principal's post, nor because he was involved with Sally Beck. But suppose he knew who was? He might have been killed to keep that quiet.'

'It's certainly a possibility, though I would have thought he was unable to keep a confidence.' McDermott fingered his pencil meditatively, turning it over and over. 'Certainly no one can be eliminated at this juncture. Let's keep it in mind. George, what do you have for us?'

Ridley was not to be hurried. In every thing that he did, he had his own way. It might not be the best way. It was seldom the quickest way. But it was his way.

'Well, I talked to them perfessers like you asked.' he began. 'Mr. Burton-Strachey were more upset than angry. Said he left common room right after you talked with him, and went straight back to office. Says he spent best part o' two hours—he couldn't pin it down—goin' over his lecture notes, and then went home to supper. His wife were out, he says, so he et alone. I've not 'ad time to check with neighbours to see if anyone saw him.'

McDermott fiddled absentmindedly with a pencil. Was this going to be a case where no one had an alibi? He realised he was getting ahead of himself: suicide hadn't definitely been ruled out. He looked at his watch. Only half past one. Odds were that Daphne didn't have enough to go on yet. He looked at Ridley, who was waiting for some signal to continue.

'Sorry, George. Go on.'

The Sergeant resumed his account. 'That Westgate bloke were 'nother matter. At first he gave me sweet bugger all. Told me he knew his rights.

That he weren't no bloke off the streets I could ride roughshod over. That he'd better things to do. I could either charge him or he'd be on his way. But I remembered what you said about takin' my time, Guv. Told him that I were just doin' my duty, and he could say nothin',' that were his right, but obstructin' official investigation were a serious offense, and he might want to think on how it'd go down with folk. That shut him up, right enough.'

'He could do with a little humility, that man. What did you get?'

Ridley sat back in his chair. He was coming to his point, the one he had, until now, guarded so jealously. 'Since he'd refused to answer questions Friday, I asked 'bout his alibi for Beck woman's death first off. Turns out he were in dining hall havin' lunch—though I don't know why he couldna' told us that in first place. As far as Campbell's death goes, he's nothin' like an alibi, Guv. Says he worked awhile in his office, and then went for walk. Didn't see no'un—leastways no'un he knew. Returned to his rooms after dark—he says 'round half seven—and fixed a bite t' eat. Watched the telly, Channel Four'—he made a face—'and went t' bed.'

McDermott sensed that his Sergeant was holding something back. 'Anything else, George?'

Ridley grinned. 'Just the one thing, Guv. I checked with Criminal Records when I got in this mornin'. It seems the good perfesser's got form.'

'Never! What was the charge?'

'Actual Bodily Harm,' Ridley replied. 'Westgate were nicked for assaultin' his wife eleven years back. Charges were dropped when she refused to testify. Three months later she left him. 'Hasn't been seen since,' he added ominously.

McDermott allowed both eyebrows to rise. 'Interesting. Puts rather a new light on things, doesn't it?'

Quinn was skeptical. 'You think it's significant, sir?'

'Well, it certainly adds some new wrinkles. It's not just that Westgate was arrested for violence—though that's interesting in its own right.'

Quinn looked up from the file Ridley had handed her. 'It would be intriguing to find out why the charge was dropped.'

'True. But you and I both know that unfortunately that's often the case. What I meant was that it raises some interesting questions about possible motives. For example, did Westgate's ABH stem from some affair? I know it's a long shot, but could the Beck girl somehow have been involved?' He stopped to consider matters. 'Eleven years ago. That would make her about fifteen. A dalliance with an underage schoolgirl, perhaps? The wife finds out and cuts up rough about it. They argue, and Westgate loses his rag. And then what? Three months later he takes the opportunity to get rid of his wife? Willie, look into Westgate's wife's disappearance. Pull up the file and find out who was on the case. Ask them for details, if they're still around—as well as their own gut feelings about the case. But don't question Westgate yet; if there's something there I don't want to put the wind up.' McDermott looked at his watch. 'Pathology has had a couple of hours to work on Campbell. Let's see what they've got.' He moved to pick up the telephone again, then thought better of it. 'I'll drop by the lab. Anyone keen to come along?' Ridley's look was answer enough, and although Quinn might have preferred to acquaint herself with another aspect of police work, after the previous evening she suspected that McDermott's motive for the visit might not be entirely professional, and passed.

TWENTY ONE

Emerging from the lift at St. Bartholomew's, McDermott covered the distance to the pathology lab and passed through the glass doors to find Daphne Fielding just returning from the mortuary room beyond, peeling off her rubber gloves.

'Hello, stranger,' she said, smiling.

'Hi, Daph. I should have thought that one of the benefits of being a pathologist is that bodies can wait until regular working hours.'

She laughed. 'It's not the cadavers who give me grief, it's you lot. I have another PM scheduled for nine AM tomorrow, and I knew you'd be on to me about this one, so Mr. Campbell is jumping the queue.'

'It's about the last thing he will jump,' McDermott observed dryly. 'No hard feelings about last night?'

She laughed again. 'Of course not. I meant it when I said I wouldn't have missed it for the world.' Her enthusiasm was obviously genuine. 'But next time *I* pick the entertainment. In fact, I have tickets for a concert, if you're interested. It's a rock group out of Glasgow. As a Celt yourself, I wouldn't have thought you'd pass it up.'

'Enough.' He raised his hands in mock surrender. 'I'd be delighted.' *At least odds are Victoria won't be there.*

Daphne Fielding sat down at her desk. After consulting several blue binders on a shelf above her desk and scribbling some brief notes, she looked up. 'The PS— Dr. Foster, was it?—seems to have been spot on. My best guess is that your Mr. Campbell died somewhere around half past ten or eleven, Friday night, from an overdose of barbiturates consumed no more than two or three hours earlier. That would put it at between seven and nine Friday evening. Incidentally, he seems to have had some unusual drinking habits.'

'How so?'

'Well, for starters, he seems to mix his libations. Specifically, tea and Scotch whisky.'

'Unusual, perhaps, but not unknown.'

Daphne handed him her handwritten notes. 'Dog bites man is not news, as they say in America. But man who takes drink *after* death—that's news.'

McDermott, who had been skimming her notes, looked up. 'You're telling me that the whisky was forced down his throat after he was dead?'

'Well, it's not quite as simple as that. I did find traces of alcohol in his bloodstream—enough to suggest that he'd had a drink or two several hours earlier. But the analysis of his stomach contents revealed mostly tea and some biscuits—and of course the barbiturates. Given his weight, and allowing for what had been absorbed, it was enough to put a Welsh pony out of its misery. He hadn't drunk the whisky we saw on the table— at least not in the last couple of hours preceding his death. But plenty of 'raw'—that is, undigested—whisky remained in his upper esophagus.'

'In other words he was drugged with tea, and then someone poured good Scotch down his gullet after he died to make it look as if he'd taken the drug himself with whisky. Murder, then.'

'It certainly looks that way. Although he wasn't clinically dead when someone did it, he was the next thing to it. What I can't fathom is why the drink itself is important. Why does it make any difference whether the man snuffed it with tea or a whisky chaser?'

'Why indeed?' he mused. 'Certainly not to conceal the taste. Whisky would have been much more effective. To accelerate the effect of the medication? It's common knowledge that alcohol compounds the effects of many drugs. Perhaps the murderer knew that, and was simply taking out some extra insurance. Or...' he paused.

'What?'

'Oh, probably nothing. I was just thinking that perhaps the type of drink was switched to throw us off the track, just in case the suicide theory didn't wash. It could have been to lead us away from someone—a teetotaller, for example—or toward someone who had a marked fondness for single malts.'

Daphne laughed. 'That certainly narrows it down.'

BY THE TIME MCDERMOTT HAD RETURNED TO THE STATION Ridley and Quinn were wrapping things up for the day. He brought them up to date.

Ridley was unimpressed. 'Way I see it, poison's poison. Why get our knickers in a twist over what Campbell washed it down with?'

'It's not that simple, George,' McDermott explained. 'We're dealing with a clever lad here— someone who thinks they've got us by the'—he glanced at Quinn—'got us over a barrel. Whoever's behind this is trying to be clever, and that's all to the good. They attempt to weave a fanciful construction out of sticky paper and cellotape and it inevitably collapses under its own weight. Let's begin by reviewing what we set out to do Friday and last night, and add to that any steps we want to take based on this new information. George?'

'Aye. Well, we still don't 'ave all the bumf on Burton-Strachey,' Ridley replied. 'You wanted me to check his alibi for Beck girl's death with his neighbours, and talk to his bank manager. As it's Sunday and late an' all, reckon Ah'll call on him first thing t'morrow.'

'Do it, George. We've had two deaths in a week connected with St. Gregory's. When he gets the news about Campbell Galbraith will be all over us.'

Quinn said, 'Shall I go ahead and interview the students, sir? I had planned to get on to that Monday morning.'

McDermott read her expression. 'I gather you don't think so, Willie.'

Quinn laid aside her notebook. 'Well, sir, I think it's unlikely that a student is at the bottom of this. The Beck woman might have been pushed into the path of the bus by one—in fact, it's the most likely explanation, barring a simple accident. But to assume that a student knew where Griffith-Jones kept his pills, and was able to get into his rooms and steal them? Then managed to get into Campbell's rooms and poison him under his very nose? I just don't see it.'

McDermott considered this. 'I agree, Willie. So what's your best guess?'

'I think you're right about Westgate, sir. The ABH does lend credence to the idea that he's capable of violence. And so far, he's a bit of a dark horse—no friends or acquaintances. That's consistent with the profile of a deviant. Perhaps that's the hold that Sally Beck had over him.'

'It's an interesting notion, isn't it? Get on to Social Services to see if we can turn something up on Westgate's ex. If she's alive and we can find her she can probably fill us in on some of the nastier bits of his personality.' He paused. 'Any thoughts on Jeremy Asquith?'

'We've only his word for it that he arrived Tuesday afternoon,' Quinn observed.

McDermott pondered the matter. 'I don't see Asquith taking anything seriously enough to commit murder. However, it won't hurt to check. Willie, you have enough on your plate. George, after you've finished with Burton-Strachey's bank manager tomorrow get on to the railways. See if that business Asquith mentioned about the train from Kendal being delayed checks out.'

As Quinn and Ridley left, McDermott sat back in his chair and reflected on the latest turns the case had taken. He rose and went to the window, opened the blinds and stared down at the traffic below. Being Sunday, it was mostly cars, he noticed. Few lorries and even fewer pedestrians were about, brazenly contending with the clammy wetness that coated the streets and sidewalks and hung in the air. He lifted his gaze. From his window he could see glimpses of the Thames, and beyond that, he imagined, Clapham in the distance. Most likely the Becks would be in church, praying for the soul of their daughter or seeking solace in the ministerial clichés of their vicar. He hoped they would find it. It occurred to McDermott that the funeral must be soon—perhaps as early as tomorrow—and that, given their daughter's secretive life, there might be few mourners. Funerals, he knew, were more for the living than the dead: a way of coming to terms with the fact that someone in their lives was gone forever, would never again ring them on the telephone or walk through the door or sit with them at the kitchen table. No one should have to go through that alone. He returned to his desk and phoned the outer office. 'Call the Becks, in Hope Street, Clapham. Find out when and where their daughter's funeral is. Then let me know.'

A few minutes later Marsh got back to him. 'Yes? Right. No, I'll take my own. Thanks.' He scribbled a note to George saying he would be in late Monday morning.

WHEN HE ARRIVED HOME that afternoon McDermott found a note wedged in his door:

> Hi. Dropped by on spec. Putting in extra hours again? At home this evening if you want to call. Are we still on for Saturday?

It wasn't signed, but the handwriting was Victoria's.

McDermott felt guilty about being caught out the previous night. He took his mobile from his jacket and speed-dialed her number. This time on the second ring she answered herself. 'Hello, Victoria.'

'Hi, Colin.' *No mention of Saturday night's fiasco.*

'I got your note. I'm rather glad you dropped by, actually. I thought we might—that is, I was wondering if you were interested in dinner sometime soon.' *A peace offering, then: testing the waters.*

'Why not? This evening?'

McDermott recalled that he'd promised Meg he'd speak with Pam's father. 'No good, I'm afraid. How about Monday?'

'Sorry. I'm appearing in court in Devon. No telling when I'll get back.'

'Tuesday, then?'

'Let me think. Yes: there's a play I've been wanting to see. Suppose you pick me up for that instead—my treat—and we can have dinner after. What do you say?'

'Good. Your place at around seven?'

'Better make it half six. You know what the traffic can be like.'

'Right,' McDermott said. 'Half six it is, Tuesday.' Hanging up he realised he hadn't even asked her the name of the play.

McDermott had two hours before his date with Victoria. He used it to visit Pam's parents. As he walked down the path of their terraced house he still had not decided exactly what he would say to persuade Pam's father to be more accepting of his daughter's lifestyle choice. He was reflecting on the best way to broach the subject when a pleasant woman in her mid-forties, taking a carrier bag to a nearby wheelie bin, emerged from the door.

'Colin. What a nice surprise. It's been far too long.'

'Hello, Dierdre.' He kissed her on the cheek. 'It has, hasn't it? Is Phillip about?'

'Of course. He's in the garden now, just putting his tools away. No one except him can go near his roses, you know.' She led him down the hallway and through the immaculate kitchen, calling out the rear window as she did so, 'Darling, guess who's dropped by?'

Phillip Townsend emerged from a potting shed, pulling a gardening glove off his right hand and extending it. 'Good to see you, Colin. You don't get out our way much.'

'Not as often as I'd like,' McDermott said, admiring the profusion of flowers in the modest garden. 'I see the roses are keeping you busy.'

'More than you know. If it's not one thing, it's another. First aphids, then not enough lime in the soil.' He looked at McDermott. 'But you've not come all this way to chat about flowers, have you? Come on inside and I'll fix us a drink.'

As they returned to the house, McDermott noticed that his friend was slightly favouring his left leg. During the first Gulf War a helicopter in which he had been riding had crashed in the desert his knee had been badly injured, which had precipitated his early retirement. Townsend had received a Military Cross for his efforts, but discovered that his combat skills were not much in demand in a civilian world. He'd taken the first job that came his way, as a security guard at a local warehouse, and parlayed that into a position as a plainclothes store detective. Twenty five years on he'd become head of security for a large IT firm in the City. The income from that, together with his service and disability pensions, kept the family comfortably, and permitted Phillip to indulge in what had become his personal pastime, which was breeding roses. McDermott asked if his knee was acting up.

'Only when it rains. Of course, that's not often in London, is it?' They both smiled.

Limping slightly, Phillip led the way into the lounge, where his wife was already setting a drinks tray down on the coffee table. 'In honour of the occasion, Colin,' she said, handing him a glass.

'Thanks.' He took the drink, and as they took theirs, added, 'To old friends.'

Dierdre Townsend winced. 'Could we make that *dear* friends?'

He laughed. 'No one would take you for old, Dierdre. In fact, not many would believe you two have a grown daughter. How is Pam keeping these days?'

Phillip Townsend's jaw hardened, and his wife stepped in to fill the breach. 'She's fine, Colin.' But her expression suggested otherwise.

McDermott noticed, but sat back on the sofa. 'Glad to hear it. Is she at home? Meg would never forgive me if I didn't say hello.'

Again it was Dierdre who spoke. 'Actually, she's out with a friend this evening.'

'You mean her dyke lover,' her husband snorted.

'Now dear,' she interjected, looking to McDermott anxiously, 'don't go upsetting yourself. We've never met her. She might be very nice. You know it won't do any good—'

'That's just it,' he shot back, 'Nothing does any damn good.' He turned to McDermott. 'I know it's fashionable to be tolerant of 'alternative lifestyles' these days, Colin, but it's a damn sight different when it's your own flesh and blood screwing her life up.' He took a long pull on his drink, and moved toward the tray to refill it. His wife looked at McDermott, her pleading eyes betraying her calm exterior.

'I'm sure it can't be easy for either of you,' he replied, 'but we can't go on making choices for our kids, can we? We can only raise them the best way we know how, and then let them go on to make their own lives as they see fit.' He was embarrassed by the clichés even as they tumbled from his lips. 'I'm sure that in the long run—'

'That what? We'll get used to it? Pam will change? I wish I could be certain of that. Perhaps if it was Megan—'

'Phillip!' Dierdre's voice was no longer pleading, but commanding. 'Colin is our friend. Do you want to drive him away too?'

There was an uneasy silence as Phillip Townsend stared at his glass. McDermott leaned forward, wanting to refill his glass but knowing that would only encourage Phillip to do the same. 'I don't know what I'd do, Phillip, if our positions were reversed. But what Pam needs more than anything else right now is to know that she can count on both of you for support. Surely you must see that the more you rail against her values, the more you'll drive her to define herself in opposition to your attitudes. You don't want to lose her forever, do you?'

Phillip Townsend stared at the pitcher of drinks, his eyes lost somewhere in the middle distance. 'Don't you think I've told myself the same thing? There's a long way between theory and practise. That's the worst part about being a parent: you have to learn from scratch. You start out by saying 'I'll never do that to my kids,' and before you know it you're saying 'How could I have done that?' The worst of it is you blame yourself for something that you mightn't have been able to do anything about.' He looked away.

Dierdre moved once more to ease the tension. 'How are you doing, Colin? Is there anyone...special...in your life at the moment? Are you still seeing that lady barrister?'

'As a matter of fact, we're getting together later this week, for a play and drinks.'

She sensed the hesitation in his voice. 'And are you looking forward to it?'

'I think so—yes.'

'Then good for you!' She smiled, and lifted her glass.

As he drove home McDermott wondered if his visit had done any good at all. Certainly the couple had been willing to discuss Pam's situation, but they had also shown signs of strain, both in what they said and what they hadn't. Outwardly, when he had left they had seemed the same as on dozens of earlier visits, both coming to the door, Philip admiring his motor, the both of them entreating him not to make it so long next time, and waving goodbye together as he drove off. But there had been a palpable tension all evening, as Dierdre looked to him for support whenever Phillip's bitterness threatened to break through the thin veneer of their conversation. McDermott knew he had said all the things he'd planned to say, but in the end he wasn't sure that talking would suffice.

What bothered him most was that he knew he didn't have any clear answers.

TWENTY TWO

Monday morning came, and Bateman stepped out of the Porter's Office and unlocked the gates at St. Gregory's. He stooped to pick up the morning papers, carrying them into his private rooms. As he waited for the kettle to come to a boil he leafed leisurely past the front pages. World events held little interest for Bateman. Football scores were more like it, football and page three of some of the racier tabloids. It was a matter of some consternation to him that no one at St. Gregory's subscribed to the tabloids.

Bateman was halfway through his first cup of tea when a smallish headline caught his eye. He put down the steaming mug and peered at the newspaper more closely:

LOCAL ACADEMIC FOUND DEAD

A Fellow of St. Gregory's College of the University of London
was found dead late Saturday evening. The man, identified as
Mr. Hugh Fraser Campbell, a graduate of the University of
Glasgow, was discovered slumped over his desk.

Mr. Campbell had been a Lecturer in Politics at St. Gregory's
for the past six years. He was unmarried, and is survived by
his parents, who live in Berwick-upon-Tweed, and by a sister
in Peebles.

No cause of death was given, though suicide has not been ruled out. The police are treating the death as suspicious.

Bateman read the article over twice, then folded the paper carefully and put it with the post, to be delivered to the common room later. Almost unconsciously he patted the watch pocket of his waistcoat: the cheque from the newspaper was still there. He would deposit it on his lunch break.

IN THE SENIOR COMMON ROOM the same notice, and those in other papers, was the centre of conversation.

'Disgraceful, that's what I call it. They make us sound like a Soho strip club.' The speaker was Sidney Westgate.

'I wouldn't know about that," retorted Clarissa Soames dryly, 'but it's certainly playing havoc with classes. The students are so busy nattering amongst themselves that they haven't absorbed a word I've said.'

'I know exactly what you mean,' Westgate replied. 'First period this morning I was drawing a comparison between the Vedic and non-Vedic Indian religions. Crucial to Christmas Exams. I doubt even a third of them were paying attention.' Westgate warmed to his topic. 'It's merely a symptom of a more basic problem, lack of self-discipline. Not tolerated in our day. And look what we've got for it: perfectly able-bodied young people on the dole, rioting and having babies when they don't even have a job. It's no wonder we have to join the EU in order to compete.'

Westgate's dissection of the nation's social ills was interrupted when the door opened and J. MacAuley Trewilliger entered the room. His clothing, if not immaculate, was at least respectable, and he seemed conspicuously sober.

Soames's eyebrows shot up. 'Hullo, Tree. Bit early for you, isn't it?'

'I suppose it is, rather,' he replied blandly. 'After the singular events of the weekend I thought the quality of conversation today might make the effort worthwhile.'

Both Soames and Westgate were silenced by his retort. In the corner, however, someone stirred whose existence had so far gone unnoticed. 'I don't think it's anything to make light of,' Griffith-Jones complained. 'After all, it was my medication that Campbell used to do away with himself. Suppose the police charge me with criminal negligence, or something like that?'

'You *will* equip your rooms like a veritable pharmacopœia and then leave them unlocked, Ewart,' Westgate snorted. 'I never leave my rooms without locking up. Too many young felons about ready to crib an exam. In any case, Campbell was an adult—legally speaking. I don't see how his killing himself can be put down to you.'

'It's not my fault I have a delicate constitution. Anyway, this is supposed to be a civilised place, with certain standards of conduct.'

'Quite so,' Soames replied, uncharacteristically acting as peacemaker. 'Westgate's right. If the man was determined to do away with himself, he'd have found a way, whether it was your pills or something else. Why don't you have a cup of tea?' she asked, rising. 'Earl Grey?'

THE COLLEGE PORTER stood at attention. He was undergoing a proper bollocking from Anscombe, and all things considered it vied with having a root canal without the benefit of an anesthetic. 'What do you mean, you know nothing about this?' Anscombe fairly shouted. The man facing him had never seen him so angry.

'Nay, sir, I know nowt about how them papers got hold of it.' Although he tried to appear calm, his trembling hands gave him away.

The Principal leaned across the desk and stared into the man's face. 'You don't? Read the papers, man! They've got all the details here. Where Campbell was found. What he taught. Where he took his degrees.'

'Meybe they got hold of one 'o college brochures. We're always given 'em out,' he said defensively.

'Oh really? And that's how they knew his parents lived in Berwick-on-bloody-Tweed, is it? Or that he had a sister in Peebles?' Anscombe's face was beet red. 'Damn and blast!'

It was the first time Bateman had heard the Principal curse. 'I'm sure I couldn't say, sir.' He looked down at his shoes. The cheque in his pocket now seemed small compensation for the ragging he'd endured for the past ten minutes.

'Well, let me speak plainly. You may find the events of recent days amusing, but I don't. And it'll be more than your job is worth if I see any more revelations in the gutter press. Do I make myself clear?'

Bateman assured the Principal that he had indeed made himself clear. With an injured look on his face, he left Anscombe's study, running the gauntlet of an equally disapproving Mrs. Coates and an amused Jeremy Asquith in the outer office as he did so.

BACK IN MCDERMOTT'S FLAT, the alarm on his mobile went off, and with it came the realisation that Sally Beck's funeral was scheduled for one hour's time. McDermott shaved and put on a dark suit and tie, walked to the lockup and pulled out the Morgan, and made his way toward St. John's Church in Clapham. With its red tile roof and its Norman bell tower it stood out as a beacon of hope for those in the rather cheerless borough.

As he pulled up to the kerb McDermott was pleased he had decided to come. A pathetically small group of mourners was in attendance. Only one elderly couple stood on the church steps, next to the Becks. Neighbours, he decided, or perhaps relatives from the North. Further away, two young women in their late teens or early twenties stood self-consciously, both smoking cigarettes, waiting for things to get underway. One he recognized from the inquest as Sally's ex-flatmate, Beryl Potter; the other was unknown to him, perhaps another co-worker at the clothing factory. McDermott considered having a word with them if he could get them off to one side. Even though the circumstances were far from ideal, the exigencies of police work sometimes required turning a blind eye to social etiquette.

As he closed his car door McDermott caught Albert Beck's eye. For a moment the old man squinted against the sun, but then came the flash of recognition. He whispered something in his wife's ear, and she turned and smiled wanly. McDermott climbed the steps.

The husband spoke first. 'Hullo, sir. Good of you to come. We didn't expect it.'

'Good morning, Mr. Beck.' McDermott turned to his wife. 'Mrs. Beck. How are you getting on?'

'Better, sir,' she replied, pulling the collar up on her coat against the wind. 'Bert and I thought she—Sally, that is—would be as happy here as up North. She allus seemed to take t' London.'

And it saves the cost of transporting the body, McDermott thought, and then chastised himself. 'It's a pleasant little church,' he observed. 'Did she—that is, do you—come here regularly?'

'Not really. Me and Bert stopped comin' regular-like when Sally left home. The young folk today...' Her eyes began to well up and she looked to her husband for strength.

'So what will you do?' McDermott asked, more to make conversation than anything else.

'Well, the missus and me have been talkin' it over. Not much to keep us here now, so we reckon we'll go back home—to Yorkshire, that is. Should never have come South.'

McDermott's interest was piqued. 'What did bring you—or Sally—to London? It's not an obvious choice.'

The old man paused, looking for the right words. 'Suppose it started with her gran's legacy. Sally always were a bright girl. Everyone could see that. When my dad died me mum had a bit o' money put by, and paid for our Sally to go to a posh boarding school, Caxton, it were, not far away. She did champion there for a bit, then gran died. After that Sally's work slipped, and we could see she were unhappy. When she turned sixteen there was no chance of her takin'—what do they call 'em—A level exams—for university. She came home, but there was nothing in the Dales for her, and when she turned seventeen she told us she wanted to move to London and find a job. She were always a strong lass—no chance o' talkin' her out of it, so we let her go. After a bit she wrote and said she'd found a job as seamstress, and afore the year went by we packed up and came South to be near her. Reckon it were the worst choice she ever made.'

McDermott took it all in, thinking of his own wife's sudden death, ironically, on a London bus not far from where Sally had died. *We make plans under the illusion that we're in control of our lives, then fate takes a hand and we have to start over.*

A few minutes later, in a chill wind on a bleak day, an anonymous vicar delivered a generic eulogy over the remains of a person he had never met, in a small chapel made to seem larger by the paucity of mourners in attendance. After wishing the Becks well, McDermott returned to his car. The two young women had already disappeared. For perhaps five minutes he sat there in silence, the rolled-up windows insulating him from the urban sounds around him. He had offered the Becks a lift, but they had declined, preferring, he supposed, to walk off one small bit of their grief.

BY THE TIME HE RETURNED to Charing Cross it was close to eleven, and McDermott realised that he had yet to put in a decent morning's work. His first stop was to brief Galbraith on the weekend's developments. He made his way to the Superintendent's office and paused outside the door, buttoning his suit jacket. When he entered he found the secretary in the midst of typing memoranda for her bosses' signature.

'Hello, Glynis. Is he free?'

'I think so, sir. Just a moment.' She announced him on the telephone, and a moment later he was beckoned inside.

'Morning, sir, 'McDermott said. 'Have a moment?'

'Depends. Are you looking for a salary rise?' he smiled, motioning for McDermott to sit down. Apparently their earlier exchange had been forgotten.

'Not these days,' McDermott smiled, dropping into the nearest chair.

Galbraith was not one to waste words. 'Sam Loach came to me the other day, asking for additional manpower. I sent him to you.'

'Yes sir. He showed up, all right. Wanted to borrow George. I had to tell him no.'

The Superintendent's expression hardened fractionally. 'Why was that? I was under the impression that your workload was rather light at the moment.'

'Over the weekend there have been some developments in the Beck case. That's the young woman who was run over by the bus. You'll be getting the incident report today, of course, but I thought it better to speak with you directly. In an elliptical way I'm becoming involved personally. I'd like your opinion on whether I should withdraw from the case.'

Now Galbraith was frowning. 'That sounds serious, McDermott. I'm listening.'

McDermott unbuttoned his jacket. 'Well, we traced the woman all right. Apparently she'd been leading a double life as a sex worker in the East End, and just recently had enrolled as a student at St. Gregory's College.'

'Your alma mater, isn't it?'

'Exactly, sir. We interviewed a number of the faculty, on the supposition that one of them might have been involved with her.'

The Superintendent's brows raised slightly. 'In the absence of any evidence? Bit of a long, shot, that.'

'In the normal course of things, I'd agree. But since she died near the college and during the lunch break, we thought it unlikely that someone from her old life—she'd changed her name—had followed her around all morning without being observed.'

'Seems reasonable. Go on.' Galbraith leaned back in his chair.

'Well, the interviews themselves were not particularly helpful: no one admitted to knowing anything—including knowing the victim herself—and no one had anything like an alibi.' McDermott admitted. 'But two facts emerged in the wake of the interviews. One, the Principal is retiring and several of the faculty have applied to succeed him. It provides a possible motive.'

'Interesting. And two?'

'On Saturday evening one of the Fellows—himself a candidate—was found dead in his rooms. A threatening note, perhaps written by the Beck woman, was found under his body.'

'Yes, I read the weekend reports this morning. Murder or suicide?'

'We were obviously supposed to think it was suicide. But it's not in the running. The pathologist's report indicates whisky was poured down his throat after death.'

'So we have a murderer at St. Gregory's who's killed twice in the past week. Bloody hell! The press haven't connected these, but I suppose it's only a matter of time,' he paused for a moment. 'You said you were involved personally. How so?'

McDermott leaned forward. 'The candidate selected to succeed the Principal was one of Sally Beck's teachers, and a former professor of mine, a good mentor, in fact. I'm not sure I am best positioned to lead this inquiry.'

The Super considered the matter for some moments before speaking. 'You know the drill. Ordinarily I'd agree with you. Even if you were objective, the appearance is still there. However, in this case...'

'Sir?'

'You're familiar with St. Gregory's. And I've seen you work before when personal issues were involved,' Galbraith said, thinking of the death of McDermott's wife. 'I'd like you to remain on the case for the moment at least. Your knowledge of the place may very well be useful. What are your own thoughts at this point?'

'Well, sir, the college has its shares of loonies and secrets, like any other closed community, but it's basically sound. I wouldn't like to see it suffer damaging publicity unnecessarily. And I just returned from the Beck woman's funeral. She was the only child of an elderly couple. It would give me immense satisfaction to collar the person responsible.'

'Very well. Stay on the case, then, as long as it can be done without compromising the investigation. And keep me informed.'

'Right, sir.'

'And McDermott?'

'Yes sir?'

You recommended Tinker to Loach? Really?' He smiled.

'Best I could come up with on the spur of the moment, sir.' He smiled back.

'Right.' The Superintendent's expression said he wasn't buying it.

ENTERING THE INCIDENT ROOM McDermott found that both Ridley and Quinn had arrived and were waiting for him. The coffee was cold, so they headed for the Canteen.

'What have we got, Willie?' he asked, as they found a corner table and sat down.

Quinn sighed and consulted her notebook. 'Not much, I'm afraid. I checked the class lists. There were six students who shared more than one class with the victim. Four of those said they didn't even recognise her, what with it being so early in the term, and several of the classes being so large. But'—here she paused meaningfully—'the fifth said she'd seen her with a young man, in the quadrangle, on the morning of her death, having a bit of an argy-bargy.'

McDermott looked up. 'That's interesting. Perhaps we're finally getting somewhere. Did she know the name of this lad?'

'No, but I had her go through the student IDs. She picked him out, all right: he's the sixth student who shared a class with her.' Quinn passed the photo over the desk.

McDermott made a face. 'Not exactly a matinee idol, is he? Says here his name is Simon Short. Have you spoken with him?'

Quinn looked aggrieved. 'Not yet, sir. I only finished getting this information this morning. I'd planned on running him down this afternoon.'

'Good. Well done. What do we have on the Fellows?'

'I spoke with Anscombe. Apparently the committee made their decision late Friday night. He telephoned Boothroyd to give him the news shortly after ten PM.'

'Right. I'm not sure how that helps in any case. If Boothroyd hadn't known the job was his, and Campbell somehow was a threat—though for the life of me I don't see how he could have been—then possibly—*just* possibly he might have murdered Campbell to ensure it was his. But since he already knew he had the job, and if Campbell had something on him, then he still might have killed Campbell, to *keep* the job. Either way he had a motive, but in the absence of more information neither motive is very convincing.'

'So it would seem, sir.'

'Do we have anything else yet?' McDermott asked. 'What about Westgate's missing wife?'

'Nothing so far. She seems to have dropped out of sight. No letters to other faculty wives, and Bateman—the porter—says Westgate himself hasn't received anything from her for years. We could always ask Westgate himself, of course, but do we want to set the cat amongst the pigeons?'

McDermott meditated. 'Not at this stage, at least.' Any promising leads?'

'I understand she has—or had—a sister in Gravesend. I thought I'd get on to her, see if they've kept in touch. As a last resort, there's always Revenue and Customs.'

He winced. 'That's walking on eggs. You know how the public is about the use of confidential tax information by other departments, especially the police. And the opposition party likes nothing better than to get hold of that sort of issue for the Question Period. Lots of grief there. I'm not sure it's worth it, lacking a better reason.'

Quinn nodded in agreement. 'I'll keep plugging, then.'

McDermott pushed back his chair. 'That's ninety per cent of the job, isn't it?' He turned to Ridley. 'What about Burton-Strachey? Anything on your end, George?'

'Yards o' it, Guv, and it's all muck. For starters, our lad's alibi for lass's death doesn't wash.'

McDermott noticed his allusion to Burton-Strachey as a lad. Whenever George did that, McDermott knew, it was because the person had passed, in his mind, from Person of Interest to Suspect. More often than not, he realised, Ridley turned out to be right. 'Give it to us, George. Don't be coy.'

The Sergeant hunched over the table conspiratorially. 'You know that banker feller you told me to go see? Very helpful, he were. Seems Burton-Stracheys are only just gettin' by. Said he 'ad to cover cheque last week so our lad could sell off some stocks and nip in t' bank and make up difference. But them's just the stringy bits.'

McDermott saw that Ridley was clearly savouring the story, and did not move to deny him his pleasure. 'Go on.'

'First, Burton-Strachey were at bank—on Southampton Row—to make good on cheque near noontime last Tuesday. That's t'other direction from where he said he were, and just three streets from where Beck woman were killed.'

McDermott glanced at Quinn. 'Good work, George. It certainly raises some questions, doesn't it? What else?'

'Them's the fat bits, Guv. The banker put me on to his stockbroker. Mind you, not easy pickens there. Man was as silent as a Welsh Sunday at first, but once he sussed there might be criminal actions involved, he came through right enough.'

McDermott's patience was beginning to wear thin. 'And?'

The man sat back in his chair and spread his suit jacket expansively, tucking his thumbs in to each side of his braces and grinning broadly. 'Seems our lad's been taking a bit of a flyer. Playing the stocks, he were—and none too well, neither. Managed to make molehills out of mountains, he has.'

'Lost a lot of money, eh? Well, that's not a crime, or we'd have half the brokers in The City in the nick.'

Ridley cast an arched brow at him. 'Aye, but it wasn't his t' lose. His wife's money, it were—in her name. And I had a look at summat called transfer requests, moving money from stocks to bank account. Unless I'm gone potty some of his wife's signatures—them as are most recent—don't match up with specimen signatures on file at bank.'

McDermott whistled. 'So Burton-Strachey's been moving his wife's money around without her permission. Let's see, that's uttering false documents, conversion of stolen goods, possibly fraud, perhaps abuse of trust...' He looked at Quinn. 'We may have a case for the CPS here.'

'How do you suppose it ties in with the Beck and Campbell deaths, sir?' Quinn asked.

McDermott ruminated. 'Any number of ways. For example, he could have been using some of his wife's money to pay for indulging his sexual fantasies. If Campbell found out about his sex life and tried to blackmail him, and he was already skint, he wouldn't have had the money to pay him. He may have decided it was simpler—and more certain—to kill Campbell rather than to buy his silence.'

'That would explain Campbell's death, but not Sally Beck's—and not the note,' Quinn parried.

'Maybe she was also trying to blackmail Burton-Strachey. She shows up at St. Gregory's, recognises a steady client, and decides she can make more off him standing up than lying down.'

Quinn followed the logic of his argument. 'You mean he might have been blackmailed by two people at the same time? Surely that's a bit much, isn't it?'

McDermott shrugged. 'It's been known to happen. But you're right: there are any number of possibilities.' He looked at his watch. 'Almost lunch time. I think we should visit the good professor and ask him a few questions. And what better place than at home? Do you suppose the missus will be in?'

TWENTY THREE

Leaving Quinn to pursue Simon Short and the elusive Mrs. Westgate, McDermott and Ridley took an unmarked car to see the Burton-Stracheys. As they turned on to Park Crescent the older man commented on the surrounding homes. 'Nobs, I shouldn't wonder. If he done it, it'd be a pleasure to put him in the nick.'

McDermott laughed. 'You're a closet bolshie, George. You think everyone who's got loads of money must have come by it dishonestly.'

'Well now, I never met one who didn't,' Ridley replied darkly.

McDermott's speculation had been correct. The doorbell at number eight Park Crescent was answered almost immediately by a small, smartly dressed woman in her mid-fifties. 'Yes? May I help you?'

'Mrs. Burton-Strachey? My name is Colin McDermott. Is your husband at home?'

The woman looked from one to the other of them a little uncertainly, as if trying to assess whether they were life assurance agents or had come to see about the drains. Deciding they were neither, she asked them to wait in the hall and went to inform her husband.

McDermott glanced at his surroundings. The stairs leading to the first floor were of polished oak, overlaid by a Turkish runner. The entranceway was patterned in alternating squares of black and white marble laid on the diagonal. Against one wall was a small escritoire with several unopened envelopes upon it; McDermott noticed that most were bills. Next to the writing desk was an elegant long case Sheraton clock in burled walnut.

Voices carried from the room beyond. 'Who? I don't know anyone named McDermott. Damned inconvenient, just as we're sitting down to lunch. I'll see to it myself.'

The door opened suddenly and Miles Burton-Strachey emerged. 'I'm afraid that just at the moment—Oh, it's you,' he said, recognising them.

'Good of you to see us, sir. My apologies for calling on you at home, but it's a matter of some importance.'

'Not the best of times. We're just sitting down to eat.'

McDermott was unfazed. 'It won't take long, I'm sure.'

Burton-Strachey's expression became wary. 'I really don't know how I can be any help, Inspector.'

'Inspector?' He had not noticed that his wife had entered the hallway behind him. 'What's it about, then?'

'It's nothing. Just some nonsense about Campbell, I suppose.' He looked at McDermott. 'Or is it about that student who got herself run over?'

'Neither, as it happens. May we step inside?'

Burton-Strachey reluctantly stood aside, and the quartet—or more precisely the two duos—entered the dining room. The midday meal was obviously a matter of some ceremony in the household: a large Regency mahogany table was set with a white damask tablecloth, and napkins in sterling rings. There were two forks and three spoons at each of two place settings, and on the buffet nearby a white wine was chilling in a sterling silver ice bucket alongside some expensive-looking crystal. McDermott wondered how Burton-Strachey managed to make it through afternoon classes. He casually admired a painting on a nearby wall. 'Venetian School. Guardi?'

The professor's expression took on more respect. 'Indeed. Just through here,' he added, indicating the room to one side. 'I hope we can make this brief, before my lunch gets cold.' He led the way into the reception room. In front of an Adam fireplace a sofa and matching chairs were done up in what appeared to be an expensive pale pink and green brocade. McDermott took the nearest available chair before it had been offered him. From the look he received it appeared to be their host's favourite. Burton-Strachey and his wife seated themselves on the sofa. Ridley lingered for a moment, then, deciding that he wouldn't wait for an invitation that obviously was not forthcoming, helped himself to the remaining easy chair nearby.

'Well, then, what's this about?' The man, McDermott reflected, was like a lamb in a rush to its own slaughter.

'It concerns our interview at St. Gregory's on Friday last,' McDermott said casually. 'If I recall correctly'—he made a pretense of consulting his notes—'you indicated that on the day that the young lady was killed—the preceding Tuesday—you had come directly home at lunch time. Is that correct?'

'Of course it is. I said so, didn't I?' Burton-Strachey was the picture of self-confidence.

'And that's still your account of things, sir?'

The man's self-assurance was quickly replaced by a measured, but nonetheless detectable, wariness. 'Didn't we just cover this? If all we're going to do is go over old ground, I fail to see why this couldn't wait—'

'We'll try not to keep you any longer than necessary, sir. It's just that, frankly, we've come into some information that suggests your account may not be entirely accurate. It's our understanding that on the day in question you went to a branch of Barclay's, in Southampton Row, at lunch time.'

The man's expression darkened. 'Really, Inspector, I must say I find this line of questioning extremely—well, impertinent. Perhaps I did get the dates mixed up—or perhaps you did,' he added as an afterthought.

'I'm afraid that's not likely, sir,' McDermott reached into his inside coat pocket and produced a sheet of paper which he unfolded. 'This is a photocopy of a dated deposit slip signed by you. As you were in classes that day until after bank closing hours, I'm sure you'll agree it must have been at noontime.'

Burton-Strachey glanced briefly at his wife, who stared openly at him, awaiting his reaction. 'This is outrageous! Am I to understand that I am suspected of being involved in that young woman's death? I can assure you that I am not.' He sat back, the picture of English upper-class indignation.

'I didn't say you were, sir—at least not at present,' McDermott replied ominously. 'This is an attractive house,' he added, admiring the room. 'In an expensive area, as well. I had no idea that university professors were so well paid.'

The man began to pale as he saw where the discussion was heading. 'Not that it's any of your business, but my wife and I are of independent means.'

'Oh, I know. In fact, in the course of our enquiries we had occasion to look into that. I gather you've been having a slight cash flow problem lately. Nothing to worry about, of course—happens in the best of families.'

Hillary Burton-Strachey was now giving her husband her full attention, while he was becoming increasingly wary. 'Nonsense. Nothing serious at all. Just a matter of transferring some funds from one account to another. And I must say I resent—'

McDermott cut him off. 'From the stock account at your brokers, you mean? Yes, we know all about that.'

'Stocks?' The reference had caught his wife's attention, as McDermott had intended. 'You didn't mention anything about selling stock, Miles.'

'Nothing to bother you about, dear. Simply a matter of liquidating some investments which had proved to be...less promising...in recent months.'

'My money? *Daddy's* money? But surely that would have required my signature, wouldn't it, Miles?'

By now Burton-Strachey was looking positively ashen. 'We can discuss this later, dear. The Inspector is not interested in—'

Again McDermott cut him off. 'Oh, but I assure you, sir, I am. At this point in our enquiries we are treating everything as possibly related.'

'But wasn't Campbell responsible for the woman's death?' he objected. 'Bateman said—that is—I've done nothing wrong.

So Bateman knew what was in the note, and put it about. McDermott turned his attention to the obviously perturbed woman before him. 'I wonder if you can tell us where your husband was last Friday evening?'

'I've already told you—'

'I'm speaking to your wife, sir,' McDermott said quietly. The professor's jaw dropped, but he was silent.

Hillary Burton-Strachey turned her frown from her husband to McDermott. 'Last Friday? Let me think. Oh, yes. That evening I was at a meeting dealing with the Brexit referendum – you know, the vote to withdraw from the European Union. First Brussels did away with pet quarantines, and now we have foreign squirrels decimating our English species. Then we had all those *French* people invading the countryside, and lorries choking our roads. Now it's illegal immigrants sneaking in from Calais and going on the dole, and Greece and Spain nearly going bust and pulling down our economy with them. Mark my words, Inspector, membership in the EU has been the end of Britain as we have known it!'

'Some say that actually withdrawing from the EU might do the same,' McDermott replied dryly, 'although the issue is beyond my remit, I'm afraid.' He brought her back to the matter at hand. 'Do you recall when you left the house that evening?'

'It must have been around half six—no, it was closer to seven. I remember because I arrived late to the meeting. But surely you don't think Miles was involved in Mr. Campbell's death. We hardly knew the man.'

'That remains to be seen, ma'm. In any case, there remains the matter of questionable financial transactions.' McDermott rose. 'We will be looking into this further, sir. In the meantime I suggest you consider taking legal advice. You might also find it useful to put your wife in the picture,' he added. Hillary Burton-Strachey's expression left little doubt that injunction would be carried out.

As they returned to the car, Ridley said, 'That's got the wind up. No doubt about it—he's on the fiddle all right. Why don't we bring him in?'

'So far we've nothing tying him in with either death. I just wanted to give him something to chew on.'

'I don't get it,' Ridley persisted. 'We've got him dead t' rights on the fraud bits.'

'Let's not rush our fences, George. If we'd brought him in for questioning on murder charges he'd have had a solicitor there before we could make coffee, and we'd have had to cut him loose before wringing anything out of him,' McDermott replied. 'As it stands he's facing a much more threatening adversary: his own imagination—not to mention his wife. Mark my words, he'll do something foolish and end up handing himself to us on a platter.'

'Shouldn't we have put a man on the house, then?'

'You must be getting old, George. You didn't notice Noakes in the Vauxhall Corsa near the entrance to Portland Place?'

Ridley rewarded him with a scathing look.

When they returned to the incident room Quinn was nowhere to be found, but McDermott discovered a telephone message waiting for him: It was barely legible, but appeared to say *Prof. True lager telephoned. Please call back.* McDermott picked up his interoffice phone and punched a button.

'Marsh? Did you take this message? Right. Was it 'Trewilliger' by any chance? Right. What time did he call? Any sense that it was urgent? No, I'll get back to him later.' He put the scrap of paper in his pocket.

McDermott surveyed his desk. There was a report from Forensics describing their findings in Campbell's rooms, though it contained nothing especially surprising. Neither the door nor windows had been forced. Prints of several of the faculty were found on the door handle, the light switch, and the desk. The blackmail note itself had been handled by Anscombe and the Brigadier, and, McDermott was not surprised to learn, Bateman. A partial print which had been identified as Sally Beck's was also on the note, along with several of Campbell's. Other prints had been obscured by the extensive handling the note had received. A check of the small phial of pills, the flask of whisky and the tea set had surrendered only Campbell's prints. There were, the report noted, a variety of fibres present—mostly woollen—and a great deal of miscellaneous residue suggesting that Campbell had not been the most conscientious of housekeepers. The fibres were all matched to jackets, trousers and sweaters in the victim's closet, or were sufficiently general as to be untraceable. The one perhaps surprising revelation was the discovery, beneath Campbell's bed, of a box containing a small number of well-thumbed soft-core porn magazines. An examination of the fingerprints on those confirmed they were Campbell's. McDermott was becoming discouraged.

CHISWICK WAS SANDWICHED BETWEEN Brentford and Hammersmith, just below the A4 and not far from the heart of London. Wilhemina Quinn pulled up in front of number Twenty-six Hexham Gardens and surveyed the area. The term 'gardens' was, she reflected, something of a misnomer: there was little greenery evident, and what little there was bore the signs of long-standing neglect. The neighbourhood consisted of a few dozen dated semis surrounded by several tower blocks of anonymous grey concrete. The address she was looking for was in one of these. She sighed. In her experience people in high-rise flats took little interest in their neighbours; if she were to get anything useful it would probably have to come from the Shorts themselves.

She located flat 514, rang the bell and waited, rang again, and yet a third time. Foolish not to call, of course, but she hadn't wanted to put anyone on their guard. She was about to leave when the lift doors opened and a smallish woman wearing a dark woollen coat and scarf and struggling with three plastic carrier bags emerged. When she saw Quinn she looked at her curiously, as if she had been expecting someone else, someone different. Quinn spoke first. 'Mrs. Short?'

The woman looked vaguely perturbed. 'Look, if you've come about the rent, I've already told your boss—'

Quinn reached in her bag and produced her warrant card. 'I'm afraid we're talking at cross purposes, Mrs. Short. My name is Detective Constable Quinn. I'm with the Metropolitan Police, CID. I'd like to speak with your son. Do you expect him soon?'

The effect was immediate. The woman dropped one of her bags, and, as she bent over to pick up the groceries, a second bag disgorged its contents on to the hallway floor. Quinn helped her scoop up the tins and bottles and boxes and produce, and the woman unlocked the door to the flat. Quinn followed her inside and went through to the kitchen, where she set the groceries on the counter. Then she returned to the lounge, where the woman was standing, struggling to regain her composure. 'I'm sorry if my visit has upset you, Mrs. Short. Can you tell me why you seem so alarmed?'

Jane Short removed her coat and scarf. 'I'm sorry. It's just that...that is, I thought you were someone else.'

Wilhemina Quinn sat down beside her. 'I think we both know that's not it, don't we? When do you expect your son home?'

The woman turned on her angrily. 'Why can't you people leave Simon alone? He hasn't done anything. Who is it now? You were wrong three years ago, and Simon's still getting over it. If you question him again—'

Quinn realised she had stumbled on to something, and that a certain amount of tact was called for. 'Mrs. Short, this is just a preliminary enquiry. Simon's not been charged with anything. We are simply in search of some information about one of his mates at school. He's got nothing to fear.'

'That's what your lot said last time! Then he had to go down to the station house, and the newspapers got hold of it, and in the end your people had to admit he had nothing to do with it.'

'With what, Mrs. Short?'

'With the death of that young girl, of course.'

TWENTY FOUR

Wilhemina Quinn finally extracted an outline of the events that had so shaken Jane Short. Simon had been a person of interest in a case three years earlier involving the disappearance of a twelve-year-old neighbourhood girl whom he'd known. Despite prolonged questioning he had maintained his innocence. The girl's body was found near a railway line several weeks later; she'd been sexually assaulted and strangled. Once again Simon had been brought in for questioning. In addition, he'd been required to undergo DNA tests. Shortly after that he was released. No arrest had ever made in the case. Their neighbours, however, had harboured their own suspicions, and Jane Short and her son found themselves living even more solitary lives.

Quinn shuddered at the thought of what Simon and his mother had been through. Jane Short looked very tired and markedly older than when Quinn had first seen her in the hallway, only minutes earlier. 'Do you see now why I can't let Simon go through this again?'

Quinn was conciliatory. 'Of course I see your point, Mrs. Short, and believe me, I don't want to upset your son unless it's absolutely necessary. But you have to see our side, too. A woman has died—someone your son knew. If she mentioned something to him—well, it may help us to identify her killer. If she'd been your daughter, you'd want that, wouldn't you?'

'They said the same thing last time.' When Quinn did not respond, Jane Short continued. 'It was all so different when Robert was alive. He died when Simon was nine.'

Quinn said simply, 'I'm sorry. Robert was your husband?'

The woman nodded. 'He was a sales rep for a German firm which made medical instruments. His job required travelling around to the various hospital authorities in the UK. One morning there was a terrible accident on the M25. There was dense fog—several lorries were involved. He had just left for an appointment in Guildford. They shouldn't allow those huge lorries on the same roads with cars.' She still sounded bitter.

'After Robert died, we had to move. His life insurance wasn't enough to enable us to stay in the same house. We moved to a flat east of the docklands, near the Isle of Dogs. But then the developers moved in and rents went up, and we had to move again. Simon seemed to blame me...' Her voice trailed off.

A key rattling in the lock told them that Simon had arrived. His mother started as the door opened and Simon came into the room. One look at his mother's face told him something was wrong.

'What's going on here, then? Who are you?' There was no mistaking the menace in his voice.

'Simon? My name is Wilhemina Quinn. I'd like to speak with you, if I may.'

He stared at her, a look of contempt spreading over his face. 'You're a copper, aren't you? Never mind, I can see it. What's it about, then?' He loomed over her, his anger barely under control. Quinn was regretting having come alone.

'We merely want to ask you some questions about a classmate.'

Simon's defiance eased somewhat. 'From St. G's?'

'That's right, Simon. I understand you knew her. Sheila Bannerman.'

At the mention of her name Simon's body stiffened, and his mother noticed it. 'Oh, Simon, tell her you're not involved!'

Simon looked from one to the other. 'Involved in what? What do you mean, *knew* her?'

'I'm afraid she's been killed, Simon,' Quinn said quietly.

He stared at her blankly. 'And you think I did it? Oh, fuck, just like—'

'As I've said, we've no reason to think you're involved, Simon, but we know very little about her. You could help us to fill in the blanks.'

He spat out the words. 'Not fucking likely.'

'What do you mean, Simon?'

'Just that she didn't want anything to do with me. We had...words.'

'About what?' she asked, when nothing further was forthcoming.

He spat the words out. 'I wanted to ask her out. Just to see a bloody film—not even a proper date, really. She told me to sod off, in front of people. It was fucking humiliating!'

Simon looked to his mother, ignoring Quinn. 'I've had nothing to do with her,' he shouted, tears welling up in his eyes. 'You hear? Nothing.' He turned and ran out of the tiny flat, slamming the door after him. In the distance Quinn could hear the echo of the stairwell door closing behind him. She turned to his mother, whose expression revealed all too clearly her apprehension. 'You see? Just like before,' she moaned, searching in her coat pocket for a tissue. Then her tears turned to anger. 'Now leave us alone. Just bloody well clear off!'

MCDERMOTT OPENED A BOTTLE OF OATMEAL STOUT, slipped off his shoes, and rested his feet on the coffee table. Scanning his CD covers, he still harboured bad memories from his encounter with Victoria at the concert a couple of days earlier. He decided a change of pace was called for, and selected a remastered version of Art Tatum and Lionel Hampton that he had treasured for years, the original dating from the days of vinyl recordings. He had resisted the trend to download music, preferring instead the collection of compact disks and records that he'd acquired over the years.

McDermott had a sense that things might be coming to a head. If Burton-Strachey behaved as expected...

Just as the music began to wash over him the telephone interrupted his reveries. He was irritated by the intrusion. 'Yes?' he snapped.

'Sir? It's DC Quinn.'

'Sorry, Willie. You have something, I take it?'

'Yes sir. I thought you'd like to be brought up to date on certain developments. I traced the boy who was apparently involved with the Beck woman at

St. Gregory's. It seems it's not the first time he's been implicated in the death of a young woman, sir.'

McDermott muted the CD. 'I'm all ears.'

Quinn summarised the earlier case, ending with the fact that no arrest in the case had ever been made.

When she had finished McDermott asked, 'Do you know why not?'

'Not yet, sir,' Quinn replied. 'I only learned of the incident from the mother. Apparently it caused quite a stir in the district. Even after he was released the family was ostracized by their neighbors. They had to move, and then move again, for different reasons. She says he's still feeling the effects.'

'I see. Did you get a chance to interview the boy?'

'Only briefly, sir. He seemed quite torn up about Sally Beck's death—insisted he'd nothing to do with it. Said they'd had a bit of a set-to on Tuesday morning, and he'd not seen her since. Then he ran out of the flat before either his mother or I could stop him.'

McDermott's eyebrows shot up. 'Did you put out an All Stations on him?'

'Not yet, sir. I'm afraid that would only make matters worse, and as yet we've very little to tie him in with the Beck woman.'

'It's your call, Quinn. What do you propose doing about it?'

There was a pause. 'Well, sir, I'd like to have a go at the records—see what that earlier case was all about, and why no charges were ever laid. Whether there was insufficient evidence to proceed, or whether the evidence actually eliminated him as a suspect.'

'I agree,' McDermott concurred. 'In the meantime, it mightn't hurt to keep in touch with the mother. Find out if—or when—he returns.'

'Right, sir. I've told her to phone me tomorrow, either way. Despite the fact that she doesn't trust the Police, she doesn't want more misunderstandings; I think she'll be straight with us, if only because it's the lesser of the evils.' She rang off.

TWENTY FIVE

When McDermott arrived at the station the next morning Quinn had more information for him. 'I've located Maureen Westgate,' she said, obviously pleased with herself.

McDermott had already relegated Sidney Westgate to a minor compartment of his brain. The man was a bully and a bore, but probably not a murderer. He tried unsuccessfully to rally some enthusiasm. 'Oh yes?'

'I think I mentioned a sister in Gravesend? I ran her to earth last evening, after we spoke. She didn't want to help at first—insisted her sister had "suffered enough at the hands of that miserable sod." Said her sister had put it all behind her. But when I told her there was a possibility that Westgate was mixed up in a murder investigation, I think she saw the opportunity for some revenge.'

'And?'

'She offered to ring her sister and see if she was willing to talk to us. Not ten minutes later she called back and said her sister didn't want to know.'

'A dead end, then?'

Quinn could not conceal her pride. 'Not quite. I got on to British Telecom, got the telephone number she dialed, and ran her to earth.'

McDermott's respect for the new DC was growing by the moment. 'Nice work. Where is she?'

'Eastbourne, sir. Runs a small book shop there. Shall I go down and see her?'

He considered their options. 'At this point Burton-Strachey seems our best bet. Still, best not to put all our eggs in one basket. Go down and find out whether Westgate has any skeletons in his closet—anything that might drive him to commit murder.'

AS SHE DROVE DOWN THE A23 Quinn considered how best to approach Maureen Westgate. Since the woman had already said that she wanted nothing to do with her former husband, even if it meant evening the score, a different tack was called for. Quinn wondered if she could play on the woman's sympathies for a victimised woman—Sally Beck. She stopped briefly in a lay-by to collect her thoughts, before continuing on.

Nearing the outskirts of Eastbourne, Quinn stopped and searched her mobile for a street map of the city. She made her way to Marine Parade, which fronted onto the sea. It was a bleak day: a chill wind swept in off the leaden waters, and the few tourists about had donned anoraks or carried umbrellas or were simply huddled together in shop doorways, looking for something of interest to occupy their time. On the shingle below one hardy soul anchored a canvas chair against the wind. The amusement pier was deserted at that hour. Most shops had closed for the season. The only one still open sold salt-water taffy and Brighton Rock. The seaside resort had changed little since she had vacationed there occasionally as a child: it had often rained then, too, she recalled, and she and her parents had sought the shelter of a small cafe on the pier, where a boy near her age had openly stared at her, to her simultaneous embarrassment and delight. She could still see his face, and wondered briefly what had become of him in the intervening years.

Quinn drove past a bandstand, dreary in its isolation, and proceeded to Blackwater Road. *Buy the Book* was a modest concern, its bins of secondhand books and publisher's remainders speaking eloquently of the marginal existence afforded the proprietors of such enterprises in the age of big bookstore chains and the internet. The trim around the windows and door was fading, and where the water collected, was peeling as well. Quinn noticed a sign, *Eastbourne College*, just down the street; it was likely the sale of used texts that kept the place going. The sign over the door read *M. Wells, Prop.* She was using her maiden name, then.

Emerging from her car Quinn crossed the road and entered the shop. A rather plain-looking woman with wheat-coloured hair flecked with grey was wiping the spines of a row of books with a damp rag, in a vain attempt to purge them of the musty smell that permeated the premises.

The woman turned to greet her. 'Good morning—or perhaps I should say not a very good morning! In any case, please feel free to look around. Are you looking for something specific? We do special orders.'

Quinn produced her warrant card. 'Mrs. Westgate? I'm afraid it's a different sort of business, actually. I'm Detective Constable Wilhemina Quinn.' She produced her warrant card.

The woman's face fell. 'Oh, Christ. What do you want? I told my sister I didn't want to talk to you.' She looked at Quinn sharply. 'How did you get my address, anyway? I'm bloody sure Joan didn't give it to you.'

Quinn ignored the question. 'I understand your feelings, Mrs. Westgate. Really I do. But you may be able to help us in a rather important matter.'

'I'm not Mrs. Westgate any longer, she snapped. 'If you'd done your homework you'd know that. My name is Wells—that's the name I was born with. Anyway, why should I help you? I've spent the last several years getting the memories of that man out of my mind, and it's only just beginning to take.'

Quinn said, 'Of course, I know how you feel. But your ex-husband may be involved in the death of a young woman, and possibly in that of one of his colleagues as well. We can't be certain at this stage, but if he's responsible, you wouldn't want him to get away with it, would you?'

Maureen Westgate looked shocked. 'Sidney a murderer? You're grasping at straws.' When Quinn did not reply she sighed and looked at her watch. 'Oh hell, why not? It's not as if I'm overwhelmed with custom, is it? Tell you what: buy me lunch and I'm yours for an hour.'

One hour, a cheese and tomato sandwich, and three cups of coffee later, Quinn was on her way back to London. As she wove her way amongst the lorries on the A22, she reflected that in a happier context Maureen Wells would be an interesting person to get to know.

SITTING DOWN TO A PUB LUNCH, McDermott and Ridley discussed the events to date. 'Call this a Ploughman's, do they?' the older man asked in disgust. 'The pickle's gone soft, the bread is stale, and just look at the cheese: I've seen mice turn up their noses at bigger bits than this.' He popped a pickled onion into his mouth and took his plate back to the bar. McDermott smiled and dug into his Lancashire Hot Pot. Ridley returned shortly, his plate piled high with cheese and onions, and surmounted by three huge slabs of fresh bread. 'Now, then—*that's* a proper ploughman's,' he beamed.

'So it is,' McDermott agreed, wondering where George would put it all. 'Any progress this morning?'

'Oh aye. Have I ever let you down?'

'Let's not go there. So what have you got?'

'"You asked me t' look into that feller Askew's alibi?'

'Asquith,' McDermott corrected him.

'Aye—that's the one,' Ridley agreed, unperturbed. 'Well, I checked, all right. British Rail does 'ave train runnin' through Lake District. Mainline from Glasgow, it is. Comes into Euston, just as 'e said.' He paused for effect.

'And? Obviously you've got something else, George,' McDermott persisted, his fork poised in mid air.

'Only it were delayed Tuesday last. Derailment of goods train near Crewe. Had to backtrack all the way to Stockport and get on t'other line. Even with time made up, it were over two hours late gettin' into station—well after two PM, it were. Short of it is that Askew couldna' been on it and arrived when 'e did.' He flashed a big grin, marred somewhat by the fact that a piece of cheese had lodged itself between his teeth.

'Well done, George! A bit of a dark horse, our Mr. Asquith. I had him pegged as merely a *poseur*. I wonder what he's doing that needs hiding?'

'I dunno, Guv. Want me to bring 'im in for questioning?' Ridley clearly relished the prospect.

'No, not just yet, George. But it would be interesting to know what he's up to.'

'Best keep an eye on him, then?'

'Not you personally. He's seen you twice, remember. No, we'll put someone else on it.'

They turned to their food. A few minutes later George Ridley took a last swallow of ale and belched. 'Reckon I fair pushed boat out,' he gloated, looking at his empty plate. McDermott just shook his head.

As they returned to the station from lunch Marsh looked up apprehensively, and McDermott knew something had happened.

'What's up?' he asked.

'It's St. Gregory's, sir. We got a call from the Principal there not twenty minutes ago. It seems Professor Burton-Strachey's gone missing.'

'What? Has DC Noakes checked in?'

'Yessir. He's waiting in your office.'

McDermott nearly blew the door in, with Ridley trailing close behind. A man sitting in a chair near the window jumped up, obviously ill at ease. 'What happened, man?' McDermott demanded.

Alan Noakes was in his late twenties, and had only recently been promoted to the CID. His duties had been minimal to date, and mostly supervised. Now, in his first task of any responsibility, he had, in a word, blown it. He could invisage, all too clearly, being sent back to the ranks. He stammered. 'W-Well, sir, I'm not exactly sure. That is, I watched the house, just as you asked. There was a terrible row just after you left. Him and his wife went at it hammer and tongs. You could hear it from the street.'

'Go on'

'Well, n-nothing happened yesterday afternoon. Shortly after ten the lights went out. I was relieved at eleven. At seven this morning I returned, and was told no one had entered or left.' He seemed to calm down as he consulted his notes. 'At around eight AM the light in an upstairs bedroom went on, then the bathroom, and a few minutes later the kitchen light went on. The row started over again.' He noted meticulously, as if recording these facts somehow compensated for the lapse that McDermott knew was coming.

McDermott patience was being tested. 'Jesus wept, man. Get on with it!'

Again Noakes struggled to regain his composure. 'At eight forty-five the front door opened, and our man came out. He was wearing a dark grey suit and topcoat, and carrying a brown briefcase and a black umbrella. He walked right past me, down Portland Place, until he caught a bus. I got on right behind him. It turned on to Mortimer Street—which becomes Goodge—and he got off at Tottenham Court Road. From there he walked to St. Gregory's.'

'So far it doesn't sound as if you've lost him, Constable. Go on.'

'Well, sir, after stopping at the porter's room and his own office, he went into one of the classrooms. I couldn't very well follow him in there, could I? Not without being noticed,' Noakes said defensively. 'So I waited at the far end of the hall, in an alcove, figuring to pick him up when he came out.'

McDermott could contain himself no longer. 'Bloody hell, man, get on with it!'

The DC looked at his shoes. 'Well, sir, that's when he gave me the slip. When the bell sounded at the end of the class the door opened and the students came streaming out. When the professor didn't follow after a couple of minutes I finally had a look. There was another door leading to a rear stairwell. I caught up with one of the students, who told me Burton-Strachey had given them a surprise exam, telling them to take the full period— not to leave the room under any circumstances until the class was scheduled to end—and to leave the completed papers on the desk. Then he left by the rear door.' The man looked miserable.

'I take it you put out an All Stations immediately?'

'Oh yes sir,' Noakes replied. 'Full description. But it was the better part of an hour before the alert went out, I'm afraid.'

'Crikey,' Ridley interjected. 'He could be on his way t' Melbourne by now.'

McDermott remained calm. 'Don't panic. If he's decided to leave the country Borders will have him in their computers. And it's doubtful he's somehow already managed to leave by private means. No, my guess is he's either still in the country, perhaps planning to take the channel train or ferry as a foot passenger. He turned to the officer. 'Right. No use crying over spilled milk. When you caught on you acted correctly. Have you taken any other steps?'

The man looked blank. 'No sir—I mean, what else was there? As the Sergeant said, he could be anywhere by now.'

McDermott ushered him from the room. 'All right. We'll take it from here. Apparently the man's no fool. It could have happened to anyone. Go to the Canteen, have a cuppa and calm down. Report back here in ten minutes, though.'

As the door closed he turned to Ridley, whose disgust was evident. 'Don't worry, George. He won't let that happen again soon. Now to work. Telephone

Burton-Strachey's wife. See if she has any idea where he might have got to. Ask her if she knows where he keeps his passport, and to check if it's still there. Then get on to the taxi firms. See if any of them picked up a fare at St. Gregory's after nine this morning—or if anyone recalls picking someone up in the area answering his description. If you draw a blank get on to the car hire firms. Get .to help you on the phones if you need it' He picked up the telephone. 'I'll get hold of Anscombe: maybe he has some ideas.' As an afterthought he asked, 'Have you got the number of Burton-Strachey's bank manager?'

McDermott telephoned Anscombe, then the bank manager. From the former he learned that the professor had missed his last two morning classes. 'No surprise there,' he said after ringing off. 'He was none too pleased, though, when I told him the man had probably done a bunk—he asked how he was going to replace his Fellows when they'd either got themselves killed or disappeared. That will be the least of his worries if the press get on to this—and we might have to bring them into it if the good professor doesn't surface soon.'

From the bank manager McDermott learned that Burton-Strachey had been in that morning, just after opening, and had closed out his joint chequing account. McDermott asked how much that had been. There was a brief pause while the manager checked, and then he came on the line again to reveal that there had been just under £400 in the account.

'Christ, how far does he think that's going to get him?' McDermott muttered.

'I beg your pardon?' the voice on the other end enquired.

'Nothing. Tell me, does Burton-Strachey have a credit card with the bank?'

'Of course, sir,' the voice replied, then, after a pause, somewhat apprehensively, 'Should we cancel it?'

'Not just yet. But put a caution on it: if any new charges come in, notify me immediately.' McDermott gave the manager his name and extension. If the man was fool enough to use a credit card to finance his escape, it would provide a convenient electronic trail.

A few minutes later, George Ridley put down the telephone at a desk in the far corner. 'That were his wife. Beside herself, she were. Said they'd argued after we left last night, all right—and again this morning. Accused him of bein' involved with the lass who'd been killed. Asked him how long it'd been goin' on. He denied everything—even usin' her brass. She went right 'round bend when I told her he'd emptied out their account. Insisted I arrest him for theft. Told her we couldn't do that seein' as it were a joint account. She had no idea where he might be headed. Asked what she should do. I told 'er to see a solicitor specialisin' in divorces,' he grinned.

The DC returned, bearing two mugs of tea, and peered around the door cautiously.

'Any news, sir?'

'Some. He's scarpered, all right.'

'Then he's dropped out of sight, sir?' Noakes asked miserably.

'Only for the moment. Sit down and get a grip. Is that for me?' McDermott asked, taking one of the mugs from the man's hand. Noakes moved to hand the other to Ridley, who had returned to the telephone, but he waved him off. 'We already know where he went when he gave you the slip,' McDermott continued. Ordinarily he would have been more tactful, but he wanted the lesson to sink in. 'He made straight for his bank and withdrew everything from a joint chequing account—less than four hundred quid as it turns out. It won't get him far.'

Noakes looked repentant, and eager to make up for his blunder. 'What do you want me to do, sir?'

'Nothing for the moment. When George gets off the blower see how far he's progressed down that list of taxi company numbers, and split the remainder in half. I'll be back shortly. The Super will have to be told.' McDermott was responsible for those under his command, and he knew Galbraith would not be pleased.

The officer contemplated the task before him, and sighed. It was a mistake he wouldn't soon forget.

A LONG TWENTY MINUTES LATER McDermott returned. 'Where's Noakes?' he enquired.

'Gone t' loo, Guv.' Ridley managed to convey the sentiment that that was exactly where he belonged.

McDermott had an idea. 'George, have you put anyone on Asquith yet?'

The Sergeant shook his head. 'What with all the confusion I clean forgot,' he admitted.

'No problem. Put Noakes on it. It'll give him a chance to redeem himself.'

'Oh, aye,' Ridley replied darkly. Clearly in his books the man was beyond redemption.

THE AFTERNOON PASSED without any new revelations. Ridley had already left for the day, and McDermott was pulling on his coat, when Wilhemina Quinn entered the incident room.

'What happened?' she asked, reading his expression.

'Apparently Burton-Strachey decided the South of France would be nice this time of year,' McDermott said.

'You're joking! When did this happen?'

'This morning. No word yet, of course, but I'm optimistic. For one thing, he hasn't enough of the ready to get far.'

'Small mercies,' she responded. 'I suppose that means Westgate is out of the running?'

'It certainly looks that way. But I've an open mind,' he smiled grimly. 'What have you got on Westgate?'

Quinn removed her own coat and pulled up a chair. 'Nothing that we can take to the bank, I'm afraid—especially since Burton-Strachey's taken French Leave. The ex Mrs. Westgate—her maiden name is Wells—married young, while she was naive and he could have been perceived as a catch. Apparently he soon disabused her of that notion. Became a petty tyrant, first with his students and then with her.'

'Over what?' McDermott asked. 'Wasn't compliant in the bedroom, was she?'

'Get your mind out of the gutter, sir. Apparently everything but. As she tells it he hadn't shown much interest since their wedding night. Men!'

McDermott frowned. 'That could mean he was getting it elsewhere.'

'Possibly. But you can't have it both ways, sir. If he'd been a sex fiend you'd have jumped on that as evidence he's our man.'

'Fair enough. It's just that he gets up my nose. I'd like him to be guilty, I guess. What about the dust-up over the ABH?'

Quinn nodded. 'It seems that over time he'd become more and more contemptuous of her social position—or rather lack of it. Put her down, always found fault with whatever she did, or wanted to do—that sort of thing. One day when he came home he found her entertaining a friend—an old school chum. They'd run into one another and spent the day shopping and reminiscing over lunch, and doing all the things old school chums do, when he walked in. Found his dinner wasn't on and his slippers and pipe not laid out, so to speak. He called her friend a silly bitch, and when Maureen protested he struck her across the face. Broke her nose. It was her friend—who was a nurse at St. Guy's—who persuaded her to have him charged with ABH. Later she thought better of it, and had it reduced to Breach of the Peace—against the advice of the Public Prosecutor.'

McDermott leaned back in his chair. 'Interesting. Wouldn't happen today. She'd have had no choice. And hardly acceptable behaviour for someone who so conspicuously fancies himself one of society's elites. Came to her on bended knee, did he? I'd like to have been a fly on the wall.'

'Unfortunately, it didn't take. Oh, he was remorseful at first. Very apologetic. No doubt concerned about his position at the college. For several months he behaved himself. But gradually he reverted to his old ways. Started by making cutting remarks about her housekeeping, then became sarcastic at parties, running her down in front of others, that sort of thing.'

'I gather the reconciliation didn't take. What happened then?'

'Nothing in particular,' Quinn replied. 'One day she simply looked at herself in the mirror, decided it wasn't going to get any better, and packed her things. Would you believe it? Actually left him a note on the bloody fridge: *Get your own dinner. In fact, get your own life.*'

'You're saying they haven't been in touch since? What about her divorce, alimony, her share of the property?'

'She didn't bother,' Quinn replied. 'Said she never wanted to lay eyes on him again.'

'Surprising.'

'Not once you get to know her, sir. What's surprising is that they got together in the first place. As different as chalk and cheese: she's caring and open and not at all pretentious, and underneath it all, rather bright. He's cruel and autocratic and arrogant—as we well know. And if you want my opinion, beneath that massive ego breathes a rather ordinary intellect.'

McDermott smiled. 'You may be right. Did you ask her whether she thought Westgate could have been involved in the goings on at St. Gregory's?'

'I didn't *just* graduate from the Staff College, sir!' Quinn said. 'She doubted that he could have been involved—said he might hit someone if he was provoked, or even if he wasn't, but that it wasn't in him to plan a crime. "It would require too much foresight" were the words she used.'

'I wonder if she allowed her own prejudices to get the best of her,' McDermott mused. 'Still, it doesn't make him the odds-on favourite, does it? By the way, I've had some news on the lad you interviewed.' He pulled a manila file folder from the top of an untidy pile on his desk.

'Simon Short?'

'The very same. Seems the DNA samples positively eliminated him in the rape-and-murder case three years ago. Of course, that doesn't mean he's not involved this time. By the way, his mother called this morning. He came home looking rather the worse for wear. Seems a couple of yobboes happened on to him in a local park. Some bruised ribs and a few cuts about the face, but he'll live. I've asked the Chiswick station to take his statement. What do you make of him?'

Quinn considered her words carefully. 'He's certainly not your all-around captain of the eleven,' she said. 'More your basic, run-of-the-mill geek. If he made advances to the Bannerman—sorry—the Beck woman, then my guess is she'd have wasted no time pouring cold water on him. Depending on the circumstances it could have been quite traumatic to someone as intro-verted as he obviously is. Suffering that kind of public humiliation can fester and grow.'

'If it did, it grew quickly,' McDermott reflected. 'We know he chatted her up the morning of her death—and was rebuffed; the girl you spoke to said as much. You saw him. Do you think he's capable of violence?'

'Isn't everyone, if the circumstances are right—or rather, wrong?'

McDermott contemplated her remark. 'It still doesn't add up, though. We've been assuming all along that whoever killed Sally Beck also killed Fraser Campbell, since her note was found underneath his body. This Simon lad might have killed Sally, but putting aside for the moment the question of whether he has an alibi for Campbell's death, I don't see him as having the opportunity, and it certainly doesn't sound like his style. He'd have more likely coshed Campbell over the head. No, it just doesn't fit—not by a long chalk.'

For some moments the room was quiet, then Quinn broke the silence. 'As I see it, sir, there are two possibilities: the first is that one person committed both murders—the second presumably to cover up the first. The second is that we're dealing with two separate crimes.'

'There's a third possibility: that the central crime in this affair is Fraser Campbell's death, and that the Beck woman was killed to cover his death.'

'But she was killed first, sir.'

'Perhaps she stumbled on to something, and had to be put out of the way before the rest of the plan could proceed.'

Quinn looked at him skeptically. 'I suppose anything is possible, sir. That doesn't explain the note, though.'

'No, it doesn't, does it?' McDermott rubbed the back of his neck and opened his top drawer, looking for some aspirin. Not finding any he stood up and began to put on his raincoat. 'Let's call it quits,' he said, the fatigue showing on his face.

As he reached for the light switch the telephone rang. 'What now?' he muttered as he crossed the room and reached over his desk. 'McDermott. Yes. What? You don't say! When? No, keep him there overnight. Don't question him; I want him to develop a whole new set of worry lines. Right. No, I'll send a car in the morning. Oh, and thanks. Well done. I'll mention your lads in dispatches.'

When he turned around McDermott was beaming, his headache forgotten. 'We've got Burton-Strachey. He turned up at Harwich trying to board a ferry. Bless this tight little isle!'

TWENTY SIX

McDermott fixed himself a whisky and was contemplating the evening before him. He scanned the theatre listings, wondering which play Victoria had in mind, trying in vain to recall whether she'd mentioned the theatre. He stiffened his drink and looked forward to an enjoyable evening.

It was barely half six when he pulled into Victoria's driveway. She answered the bell promptly. 'You're early,' she said, mascara in hand.

'And you're radiant,' he replied, nearly believing it.

'The difference is that I'm always radiant,' she teased, tossing her makeup brush into her bag and picking up her wrap. She handed him the tickets. 'Would you like a drink first?'

'Better not,' McDermott replied. 'I had one after work.'

'That bad, was it?'

'Actually, it ended on a happy note. I just hope the play is half as satisfying. By the way, what is it?' he asked.

'You'll see. Actually, I think you'll enjoy it. A contemporary play with a classical theme. It's called *An Unbecoming Women*. It's about Boadicea, and the struggle for women's rights. You know—sort of a history of feminism. Didn't I tell you? It's a fringe production.'

McDermott's heart sank. *Was it too late for that drink?*

JEREMY ASQUITH EMERGED FROM THE SHOWER and, after towelling off, reviewed his sartorial options for the evening. Deciding that fawn-coloured linen slacks with an ecru silk shirt and matching socks over tan loafers were acceptable, he dressed, took a last look at himself, and left his rooms, being careful to lock his door. Not ten minutes later he was comfortably ensconced at a corner table at the Museum Tavern, holding court amongst several earnest acolytes who were quite certain there was no one quite like him in the whole of London. It was an opinion with which Asquith wholly concurred. Fully immersed in the drama of his own small circle, he failed to notice the unassuming, plainly-dressed man who arrived shortly after he did, and who stood at the bar sipping a lager, occasionally regarding him in the mirror.

AS THEY LEFT THE THEATRE, Victoria asked McDermott what he had thought of the play.

'Honestly?'

'Of course!' *Men,* she thought. *Why would I want to hear anything else?*

'Well then, I'm afraid I found it all rather tedious. I mean, do we really need to be reminded of the history of womankind from Lysistrata to the Suffragettes? We all know women can be the equal of men—just look at Maggie Thatcher.'

'But that's just the point,' Victoria said. 'Look at the way you men regarded her: the 'Iron Maiden'—just one of the *boys*—in drag. Keep in mind she's long gone from the scene; how many women have you seen taking her place?' She warmed to her subject. 'Besides, too many women *don't* get it yet. And some men have to be periodically reminded. Why, just today in court—'

McDermott interrupted. 'I take your point, Victoria, really I do. But isn't all this sabre rattling counterproductive? You have to admit, it can be off-putting. Now, take yourself, for instance—'

'Myself?' Now it was her turn to interrupt. 'Are you suggesting I put you off?' She rummaged in her bag for her cigarettes. In the time she took to find them McDermott reconsidered his choice of words.

'Of course not. That's my point. You just go about your job, quietly and competently. Nothing flashy, but every day you show that a woman can do—'

'Quietly and competently? Nothing flashy? In other words I just soldier on—*the little engine that could?*' She lit a cigarette and inhaled deeply, her dark eyes flashing by now. Neither her temper nor her smoking were pluses in his book.

McDermott noticed with alarm that her anger was rising fast. 'Don't put words in my mouth, Vic. You're very good at your job—just look at where you are. But you didn't get there by cutting off the privates of your male counterparts.'

'A lot you know,' she retorted as she exhaled angrily.

He glanced at the dashboard clock. It was shaping up as a long night.

Although they'd planned a late dinner after the theatre, by unspoken mutual consent he headed directly back to Victoria's house. The journey was conducted in stony silence, the frost inside the car a stark contrast to the unseasonably warm evening. When they arrived McDermott turned into the drive and drew up to the door. When Victoria put her hand on the door handle she said, 'Please don't bother. I can see myself in.'

But before she could get out of the car McDermott summoned up the courage to say what was on his mind, and had been for some time. 'You know, Vicky, perhaps we should stop seeing each other for awhile. I think we both need time to reflect on our relationship.' It had always been an open affair from the outset; each had been seeing other people, and neither, it seemed, had been ready to take it further. Now, it was clear, it was a time for stepping back.

After a noticeable pause Victoria opened the door and got out of the car. 'Well, you've obviously given it some thought, Colin. You may be right. In fact, I rather think you are. Good night, then.'

But as McDermott drove off he felt a great burden had been lifted from his shoulders.

THE NEXT MORNING QUINN WAS ALREADY IN THE INCIDENT ROOM and had done a good forty minutes' work when McDermott made an appearance shortly before nine. 'Morning, sir,' she said cheerfully. 'Have a good evening, then?'

'Don't ask!' McDermott scowled, removing his coat. 'Bloody avante-garde pseudo-intellectual crap. Whatever happened to simple good old-fashioned entertainment?' He surveyed the room. 'Any chance of getting a coffee around here?'

Quinn decided that absence was the better part of valour. 'I'll pop up to the canteen.' She bumped into Ridley going out. 'Morning, George. Got your brass knickers on?' she asked, *sotto voce*. She motioned toward McDermott and made her exit.

But Ridley was not one to be intimidated easily. 'What's up, Guv?'

McDermott looked up, his mind already immersed in his work. 'You haven't heard, then? Burton-Strachey turned up late yesterday. Harwich. I'm sending a car for him this morning.'

Now it was the Sergeant's turn to be annoyed. 'And how would I know that, seein' as it's you who's supposed to tell me?'

McDermott blanched. 'Sorry, George. What with one thing and another— Oh hell, Galbraith doesn't know either.' He reached for the telephone, stabbing at the buttons. 'Yes, Glynis. It's McDermott. Is the Super in yet? Thanks. Hello, sir. Thought you'd like to know we picked up Burton-Strachey late yesterday. No, we'll question him here. Right, I'll keep you posted.'

He hung up just as Quinn returned with three mugs of tea. 'This won't happen on a regular basis, you understand,' she said.

'Wouldn't think of it. Sorry for the diatribe, Willie.'

'Apology accepted, sir. The play wasn't up to expectations, I gather?'

'Two hours of pedantic tedium followed by another half hour of squabbling, if you must know.' He accepted the tea gratefully. I don't suppose there's any news, then?'

'That's where you'd be wrong, sir. While you were enjoying yourself last evening I was working the phone, pestering mobile service providers.'

McDermott was in no mood for games. 'And?'

'And I finally got a result. A small provider had an account registered to a Sheila Bannerman. Pretty clear that it's our victim. The phone hasn't been used since the morning she died.'

McDermott's day was taking a turn for the better. 'Finally a break. What else did you find out?'

'Well, sir, for starters the account was billed to a postal box. The calls were all brief—one to two minutes each, and always came in the afternoon or evening. Most numbers were blocked, but one wasn't. I called it last night and spooked a middle-aged perv by the sound of it. He didn't want to talk— said his wife was at home, but I convinced him to meet me at a local he named. No question it was the Beck woman. He identified Sally's mortuary photo, although he knew her as Sheila. No last name. Seems she had a flat near Canary Wharf where they'd get together once a week or so. I have the address, but no warrant yet. I'm assuming we want to visit the flat and talk to the landlord, then have Forensics turn it over for prints and trace evidence.'

'Too true,' McDermott beamed, his earlier funk forgotten. 'Get over there and suss out the landlord. While you're doing that I'll get on to a magistrate for a warrant. Once we have it we'll contact Forensics and join them there.'

As McDermott lifted the cup to his mouth the phone rang, and Ridley picked it up. 'Aye. Oh, aye. Hang on.' He turned to McDermott. 'It's that Anscombe feller from college,' he whispered conspiratorially.

McDermott put down his cup. 'Good morning, Principal. What can I do for you? Is that a fact? No, I haven't seen the morning papers.' McDermott swivelled toward the window. 'Actually that's old news. We have Burton-Strachey in hand. No, last night. I'm afraid I can't be any more specific at the moment. I'll tell you what, I'll put the Press Office here on it. Yes, you'll be amongst the first to know. Quite all right—no trouble. Good bye.'

He turned to face Ridley and Quinn. 'Either of you seen this morning's papers?'

They shook their heads.

'Apparently they've run a story on Burton-Strachey's disappearance. Anscombe's in a flap,' he said, punching the telephone again. 'George, what's the name of that chap in Media Relations—you know, the sandy-haired chap.'

'You mean Hewitt?' Ridley replied.

'The very one—yes, hello. Is Gordon Hewitt in yet? DI McDermott calling. Thanks. Gordon? McDermott here. Fine, thanks. Look, can you do us a favour? There was a death at St. Gregory's College over the weekend— yes, that's the one. A colleague of his is getting play in the press for it. The morning papers have him as missing. Yes, playing havoc with the college, I gather. Got hold of his wife, I expect. Could you put out a routine report that he's *not* missing? That's right. We have him, so he's not missing, right? No, he's not been charged with anything—yet. Just say you don't have any further information at this time. That's right. No, I know it's not much. Thanks.' He rang off.

'That should calm Anscombe down,' McDermott said, turning to Ridley. 'George, would you see about arranging a car to pick up Burton-Strachey? Tell them no talking on the way back: I want him to stew in his own juice. When he arrives have him taken directly to an interview room and notify me. I want to rattle his cage.'

TWENTY SEVEN

It was going on eleven when the custody sergeant called to say that Burton-Strachey had arrived. McDermott took Ridley and Quinn in tow and headed for the interview rooms. A uniformed PC stood just inside the door watching the professor, who managed to look both humiliated and defiant at the same time. The room was almost bare, except for four chairs and a table on which sat a tape recorder. One chair was occupied by Burton-Strachey; the others were vacant.

McDermott entered the room with a flourish. 'Mr. Burton-Strachey. Good to see you again. Of course you remember DS Ridley and DC Quinn.' The man nodded perfunctorily. McDermott sat down at the other side of the table and switched on the recorder, identifying the people in the room. Ridley joined him at the table. Quinn took the remaining chair, but placed it against the far wall, facing the group. 'You know, when I suggested you might want to seek legal advice I meant a *British* solicitor.'

Burton-Strachey was not amused. 'I've the right to go anywhere I want. You've not charged me with anything. How dare you have me detained and thrown into a cell, and brought here like—'

'Like a common criminal?' McDermott suggested. 'You're quite right when you say you haven't been formally charged—yet. But you were told that there appear to be certain irregularities in the handling of your wife's accounts. Before we go any further, I must caution you that you do not have to say anything, but it may harm your defense if you omit something which you later rely on in court. Do you want the services of a solicitor?'

'I don't need one. I haven't done anything.' Burton-Strachey protested. 'I didn't kill that girl—nor did I kill Campbell.'

'Interesting that you should mention that, sir, since I never said Campbell had been murdered. But suppose we start with what you have done.' McDermott turned on the recorder and said, 'The date is October eleven. The time is—'he consulted his watch—'eleven oh five AM. DI Colin McDermott conducting a preliminary interview in connection with the deaths of Sally Beck and Fraser Campbell. In attendance are DS George Ridley, DC Willie—sorry—Wilhemina Quinn, and—' he looked to the officer. 'PC Innes, sir,' he supplied. He turned to the man facing him across the table.

'State your full name and address, please.'

'My name is Miles Alexander Burton-Strachey. I live at number eight Park Crescent, Regent's Park.'

'Your occupation and employer?'

'I am Wycombe Professor of History at St. Gregory's College, of the University of London.'

'Please describe your actions on October third, commencing at eleven AM.'

Burton-Strachey stared at the man for a moment, as if he hadn't heard the question; then he began in a tired voice: 'I gave a class in Contemporary European History from eleven until eleven-fifty. Then I excused the class and returned to my study, where I dropped off my notes and collected my coat.' He paused.

'Go on.'

'I had to go to my—that is, my wife's and my—brokers, and then to our bank. I did so, and returned to the college just after one. At half past one I gave a lecture on Late Medieval History. At two thirty—'

'Just a moment, sir,' McDermott interrupted. 'You are aware that the statement you just made contradicts, in some important particulars, an earlier statement you made at St. Gregory's on Friday last?'

The man shrank in his chair. 'Yes, I suppose it does.'

McDermott pressed him. 'Which, if either, is a true account of your actions?'

Burton-Strachey glared. 'The statement I have just given you.'

'Why did you lie to us earlier? What were you trying to conceal?' Quinn looked as if she disagreed with McDermott's confrontational tactics, but his expression counselled patience.

'I-I simply felt that my financial affairs were none of your business,' he said. 'I still do,' he added defiantly.

'You are referring to your banking transactions of recent months, involving your wife's money, about which Sergeant Ridley and I spoke with you at your home, in the presence of your wife?'

'You know the answer to that,' Burton-Strachey snapped.

'Please answer the question directly.'

'Yes, it concerned my wife's investments.'

'Your bank is Barclay's, I believe? In Southampton Row?'

'That's correct.'

'Just a few streets, in fact, from where the Beck girl was killed—killed at almost the same time as you say you were making your way to the bank.'

'I've already told you I didn't do it. I didn't even know the girl.'

'So you've said.' McDermott changed direction. 'You received a note that morning in the Porter's Office, didn't you? What was in it?'

'None of your business,' Burton-Strachey replied, by now glowering at everyone in the room.

'Isn't it true it was a blackmail note sent by the Beck woman—the same note, in fact, found on Fraser Campbell's desk, under his body?'

'That's not so,' he protested. 'It had nothing to do with the girl, nothing at all.'

'We've only your word for that, haven't we?' McDermott probed.

Burton-Strachey slumped forward. He put his face in his hands, rubbing his temples. When he looked up he spoke softly, as if all the life had been drained from him. 'It was from my banker, indicating that our account was overdrawn in excess of my line of credit. I knew I would have to sell some securities immediately, in order to cover the deficit. That's why I left the college suddenly at noon.'

McDermott glanced at Ridley, who nodded. He would check it out. 'Why did you lie about it in the Senior Common Room?'

Burton-Strachey glared at him. 'As you well know, Inspector, St.Gregory's is a small college. My wife was unaware of our financial situation. I'd hoped to keep it that way—to somehow cover the losses. Perhaps if you had questioned me privately, instead of in front of everyone...' His voice trailed off.

Another chicken coming home to roost. McDermott leaned back in his chair and, for a moment, stared up at the ceiling. The harsh fluorescent lighting bathed the room in a clinical light, intentionally dehumanising its occupants and taking from them any illusion of having control over their lives. He looked down to stare at Burton-Strachey. Whatever his sins, the man wasn't an accomplished liar. McDermott was almost convinced he was telling the truth. If he was, McDermott was way off base.

He looked at the clock. It wouldn't do any harm to let the man stew in his own juices, McDermott reflected. He switched off the recorder. 'I'm feeling peckish. We'll break until two. Constable, take the professor back to his holding cell and see that he is given lunch. I'm afraid it won't be grilled sole today, Mr. Burton-Strachey.'

The man ignored his sarcasm. 'Am I under arrest, then?' he asked miserably.

'You have obstructed our investigation, professor. But not at this point—so long as you cooperate.' McDermott replied ominously. Turning to Quinn he said, 'Notify his wife that he's here. She can see him this afternoon if she wishes. You might suggest that she bring along a solicitor.'

'I told you I didn't kill that girl!'

McDermott looked down at the man. 'For the moment you are under suspicion of uttering false documents and abuse of trust.' He left the room with Ridley and Quinn in tow, leaving Burton-Strachey to contemplate his fate. Walking down the hallway McDermott said 'Get ahold of the duty solicitor, George. We'll need magistrate's warrants for his bank and stock brokerage records. I think we have enough to charge him, but we'll need documentation for the DPP.'

'What, right now? I reckon they've all buggered off for lunch,' the Sergeant said, dismayed. Geroge's meals were a matter of some importance to him.

'Just set the wheels in motion, George. Plenty of time to pick them up after lunch. I'll see you both back here at quarter to two.'

MCDERMOTT DECIDED TO PAY A VISIT to Norman Anscombe. Arriving at St. Gregory's College just after noon, he passed under the arch and into the forecourt. During his first visit, following Sally Beck's death, he had been preoccupied by the case. But now he paused to take in the scene, and in the full glare of daylight the memories came flooding back. It was here that he'd arrived, full of high hopes and equally high spirits, many years ago; here that he'd been exposed to worlds as yet unknown to him, increasing at the same time his self-confidence and his sense of humility; here also that he'd taken, almost on a whim, a course in art history, the same course that introduced him to a then-young lecturer named Boothroyd, who, through the force of his personality, had shaped McDermott's decision to specialise in art, which ultimately led to his meeting the woman he would marry and the daughter they would have.

So much had happened since then. But the buildings seemed largely unchanged. The students lounged on the grass or conversed in small groups, or cycled past him on their solitary ways, oblivious to his mission and its possible portent for St. Gregory's. McDermott made his way to the Principal's Office, and was redirected to the Dining Hall. When he arrived, Anscombe looked up and invited him to join him for lunch.

McDermott noticed that the fare had not improved since his days as a student, but decided Anscombe might open up over the meal. While the Principal picked at glazed ham and broad beans, he mentioned McDermott's actions to contain the scandal that threatened to overtake St. Gregory's.

'I'm grateful for your efforts, Inspector,' Anscombe said between mouthfuls. 'It's been all I can do to fend off the reporters since they learned of Campbell's death and Burton-Strachey's disappearance. Thank God they haven't connected that young woman's death to us yet.'

'They have their work to do, I suppose,' McDermott observed. 'But St. Gregory's does seem to have its share of eccentrics. Perhaps it's selective recall, but I don't remember quite as many in my day.'

'How do you mean?' Anscombe asked warily.

'Well, for starters there's your resident peacock, Asquith.' He glanced at a nearby table where the subject of his remarks was holding court amongst admiring undergraduates. 'I can't make up my mind whether he's really as fey as he lets on, or merely doing it for effect. Then there's a dipsomaniac, a wife abuser, a hypochondriac, and an embezzler and forger who tries to disappear altogether.'

Anscombe regarded him carefully. 'Really, Inspector. As an Old Boy you do seem to be rather harsh on us. We've no more 'eccentrics,' as you put it, than any comparable institution. And times have changed: these days a man's sexual preferences are his own business—'

'So long as no minors are involved?' McDermott interrupted.

'Just so,' Anscombe conceded. And as for the 'dipsomaniac' as you so indelicately put it, MacAuley Trewilliger remains one of the leading authorities in his field. His research and publications helped put St. Gregory's on the academic map during its formative years *and* he remains an exceptional teacher. The college owes him something, I think. It's only a wonder to me that we don't have more of them here.' McDermott wondered whether he was referring to exceptional teachers or dipsomaniacs.

'And the others?' asked McDermott.

'The incident involving Doctor Westgate happened some years ago. As you are no doubt aware his wife left him shortly afterwards, and although he cannot be regarded as one of the more amiable of the Fellows, to my knowledge his conduct within the College has always been within the bounds of academic probity. As for the reference to an embezzler,' Anscombe continued, 'I must confess I am at a loss. Perhaps you would enlighten me?'

McDermott brought the Principal up to date. He looked pained. 'Really, I'd no idea. I suppose that means I should be looking for more than a temporary replacement, then?'

McDermott was amused by the man's priorities. Still, he had his job to do. 'It's early days yet, but even if he is not sentenced to a prison term, which I think unlikely, he will be tied up in legal proceedings for some time.'

A server brought coffee and raspberry flan, which Anscombe regarded with obvious distaste. He picked at his food in silence for some minutes, then spoke. 'You seem to be focusing on this young woman's rather brief time with us, Inspector. I'm no policeman, but I would have thought that investigating her previous life would be more productive.'

'And we are looking into that, of course. But you do seem to have an inordinately high number of deaths here, Principal.'

Anscombe picked at a spot on his tie. 'As I said earlier, no more than any comparable institution. You mustn't allow your professional imagination to run away with you.'

'So I've been told,' McDermott replied. 'Well, thank you for your time, sir. I'll leave you to your work. I'm sure we'll speak again.' Anscombe half rose from his chair, his lack of enthusiasm apparent.

As he returned by the corridor linking the Principal's study to the dining room, McDermott fingered a piece of paper in his coat pocket, and recalled Trewilliger's call on Monday afternoon. He'd let almost two days go by without answering it, so he set out for the man's rooms. When there was no response to his knocking, McDermott tried the door, and finding it unlocked, pushed it partially open. He called out softly. The only answer was the rhythmic ticking of a carriage clock on the mantelpiece. For a moment he thought the room was empty. Then he spotted a figure slumped over, the hand draped over the arm of the chair. The skin was pale in the overcast autumn light coming from the window; at the foot of the chair an ugly red stain had disfigured the carpet.

Oh, God. Not another one! he thought to himself. He closed the door softly behind him and approached the front of the chair, being careful not to touch anything. He put two fingers on the man's neck in an effort to find a pulse, and peered into the waxen face intently.

One eye languidly opened. 'Hullo. I must have dropped off. Did you knock?' Trewilliger asked, stirring with great difficulty into a more upright sitting position.

McDermott breathed a sigh of relief. 'For a moment I thought—well, never mind.' He picked up a crystal wine goblet from the carpet and placed it on the small table next to the chair. When the man looked at him quizzically, he said 'Detective Inspector McDermott, professor. I believe you telephoned me the other day.'

To McDermott's dismay, Trewilliger looked no less confused. Had he left it too long?

'I did? Oh yes, I remember now. It was about that fellow Campbell— the one who died,' he replied distractedly. 'I gather there is some question whether he killed himself.'

'Yes, sir,' McDermott equivocated. 'Do you have any information that might shed light on the matter?'

'Well, to be truthful, I'm not entirely sure,' the professor said, beckoning McDermott to an adjacent chair and reaching for the remains of the bottle of wine. 'It's just that I may have—that is, I think I heard voices coming from Mr. Campbell's rooms the day before he died.'

'That would be Thursday, sir?' McDermott's expression masked his disappointment. A visitor to Campbell's rooms a full day before his death could, he realised, have been anyone.

'No, Friday—at least I think it was. His body was discovered Saturday evening, if I remember correctly. So he died sometime Saturday?'

'Not exactly, sir. Although his body was discovered Saturday, it appears he died late Friday, from a substance either he or someone else administered earlier that evening.'

Trewilliger's mind set to work. 'Then it could be relevant—the conversation, I mean.'

'It certainly could be, sir,' McDermott agreed, noting with alarm that Trewilliger had drained his glass and was reaching once more for the bottle on the table. 'Would you like me to ring for a coffee, sir, or perhaps a tea?'

The man regarded him for some moments, and then smiled. 'You needn't be concerned about my drinking, young man. The Lord knows I haven't done, for some time now. Like any other analgesic,' he said, rising from his chair, 'its effects become less pronounced with time.' He shuffled toward the fireplace. 'You see this clock? A gift from my students one year—a gentle reminder, I think, to be punctual for my lectures.' He paused, and McDermott wondered if he had lost the thread of the discussion.

'You said you'd heard something?' he prompted hopefully.

'That's right. It must have been sometime around eight or so—I remember it was getting quite dark out...' he paused again.

'Yes?' McDermott was coming to appreciate, not for the first time, the exquisite subtleties involved in the art of torture.

'Well, as I say, it must have been around eight o'clock. Someone knocked at his door—I recall because for a moment I thought it might have been my door. After a moment I heard Mr. Campbell reply, and someone entered his rooms.'

McDermott felt his heart sink. 'Then you didn't recognise the voice?'

'Oh no, I'm afraid not. They spoke softly, you see—well, not softly, exactly—not as if they were whispering. More like you and I now—in ordinary tones, I should say.'

McDermott was growing desperate. 'Could you tell if it was a man or a woman—one person or more?'

Trewilliger considered the matter. 'One person—I'm certain of that—but as to gender, I couldn't be sure—a man I think.'

'I see. And could you make out what they were saying?'

The professor looked sheepish. 'Oh no. I could tell *that* someone was there, not *what* they were talking about. I'm sorry. Have I been wasting your time?'

'Not necessarily, sir,' McDermott replied, rising from his chair and moving toward the door. 'Tell me, how long was this visitor there?'

Again Trewilliger looked embarrassed. 'I really can't say with certainty, Inspector. Perhaps half an hour—certainly not more than an hour.'

McDermott paused. 'Excuse my asking, but how can you be certain, sir?'

'Because I remember looking at my watch. I was peckish, you see, and I wondered whether the kitchen would still be open. It closes at nine.'

'I see. One more thing, if you don't mind, sir. Was it a civil conversation, carried on in ordinary tones? Or were they arguing?'

'I should have thought it an amicable meeting. They had tea, I know.'

McDermott turned halfway through the door. 'If you couldn't hear their conversation—?'

'I heard the kettle on the boil.' He replied.

As he left Trewilliger, McDermott passed by Campbell's rooms and noticed the adjoining door ajar. There was no sound from within, but on impulse he knocked. Almost immediately the door swung open, and a voice said 'Yes? Oh, it's you.' McDermott was used to the response; it went with the job.

'Good afternoon, Professor Soames. Do you have a moment?'

'I suppose so.' She spoke as if she were granting him a royal favour. She stepped to one side and McDermott entered her rooms.

He scanned the room with interest. The desk was piled high with books and examination papers arranged in tidy stacks, the only free space being accorded to a small table lamp and a computer. The walls were lined with volumes of texts and academic journals dealing with economics, but Clarissa Soames was not a slave to her profession: a particularly handsome edition of Quiller-Couch's *Oxford Book of English Verse* vied for attention with Chamberlain's biography of the first Elizabeth. A slim volume titled *The Leap*

From Leucadian Heights: In Defence of the Mitylene Poets (McDermott tried in vain to recall just who the Mitylene poets were, and why they needed defending) took pride of place alongside a study of the Bloomsbury circle rather sensationally titled *Ardent Victorians: the private lives of the Bloomsbury Group*. A copy of Simone de Beauvoir's *The Second Sex* rested somewhat incongruously alongside much-thumbed editions of Burckhardt's *The Greeks and Greek Civilisation* and Thomas Martin's *Ancient Greece: From Prehistoric to Hellenistic Times*. Without doubt the professor was a person of formidable intellect.

'You have a question, I believe?' Her expression suggested that her time was valuable.

McDermott sank easily into an ancient, though comfortable-looking, armchair. It threatened to swallow him whole, and it was with some difficulty that he arranged himself so as to maintain some semblance of authority. She elected to remain standing near the door. The implication of a master-pupil relationship, or perhaps merely that of an unwelcome visitor, was difficult to ignore.

'Actually, it's nothing important,' McDermott said. 'Just some loose ends, really. The Principal and I were discussing your colleagues over lunch, in particular Mr. Burton-Strachey and Mr. Westgate.'

'Indeed. And did you come to any conclusions?'

'Not really,' McDermott admitted. 'The Principal made the point that the Beck girl was here so briefly it's hard to credit that she could have had time to become involved in something serious enough for her to be killed.'

Clarissa Soames' eyes widened fractionally. 'I thought her death was an accident?'

She looked at him with the practised eye of someone used to ferreting out the relevant bits of an undergraduate's verbal wanderings. 'But if she was murdered,' she added, 'I suppose it might have been a result of finding herself out of her depth. After all, London isn't Yorkshire, is it? Too many temptations for the young here. Too many ways to go wrong.'

Soames walked to the window and gazed for several moments at the quadrangle beyond. When she turned she spoke with a quietness—and McDermott thought, a sadness—that was all the more eloquent because it seemed so uncharacteristic. 'Tell me, Inspector, do you enjoy poking about in the recesses of people's lives, exposing their darkest secrets? I shouldn't like to have your job.'

'There are days I agree with you, Professor Soames. But until human nature undergoes a fundamental change, I'm afraid it goes with the job.' McDermott rose and went to the door, then paused. 'Just one last question, if I may. Do you recall hearing anyone knock at Mr. Campbell's door sometime between seven and nine Friday evening?'

She regarded him for a moment before answering. 'If you recall, I was out that evening. Dinner and the theatre.'

'Of course—I'd forgotten. Well, I won't take up any more of your time.'

'I'm sorry I can't be of more help, Inspector, but there you are.'

Leaving McDermott to wonder just where, indeed, he was.

TWENTY EIGHT

By the time McDermott returned to Charing Cross station it was just past two, and Ridley and Quinn were waiting for him. 'Must be nice havin' a two hour lunch, Guv,' the Sergeant chided him. 'Any chance of takin' us along next time?'

'Trust me—you wouldn't have enjoyed it, George. The Stilton wasn't ripe. Actually, I looked up Mr. Trewilliger. A shade—but only just—more sober than Saturday night. He said he'd heard someone talking to Campbell in his rooms on Friday night.'

Quinn looked up. 'Just the break we've been wanting, sir.'

'Don't go getting your hopes up, Willie. Although he's fairly certain about the date and time, I'm afraid he couldn't make out who it was, or what they were saying.'

'Bloody great help that is,' Ridley said.

'Sir, what about Burton-Strachey? We're set to resume questioning him at two,' Quinn reminded him.

'Yes—I'd not forgotten,' McDermott replied. 'Let's pay the good professor a visit, shall we? Let me have your opinions on the way down.'

As they walked down the corridor Quinn said, 'There's not much doubt that he's been fiddling his wife's accounts. But I don't see him as a murderer. For one thing, although he might have killed Campbell, to kill the Beck woman he would have had to do so and then get to *both* his stockbrokers and his bank, and sit down and deal calmly with a manager about an overdrawn account, having just committed murder, all in less than what?—discounting travel time, perhaps forty-five minutes in total. I just don't see him having that sort of *sang-froid.*'

McDermott considered her reasoning. 'Couldn't it have happened the other way round? Perhaps he dealt with the bank manager first and then killed the Beck woman.'

'Frankly, sir, that's doubtful. He would have had to go to the bank, do his business, and return to the campus where he picked her up and followed her to High Holborn—either that or he ran into her by chance on the way back to campus. No, it just doesn't make sense.'

McDermott was forced to agree.

When they entered the interview room they found that Burton-Strachey had a visitor, a middle-aged man in a pale grey bespoke suit that reflected well on The Inns of Court. Burton-Strachey seemed a good deal more confident than when they had last spoken. 'This is my solicitor, Mr. Mayhew.'

'Indeed. Then you decided to take my advice. Glad to hear it,' McDermott said, not entirely untruthfully. In his opinion formally charging Burton-Strachey was fast becoming inevitable, and the presence of his solicitor might serve to expedite the process.

'I understand you have been interrogating my client without benefit of counsel, Inspector. Really *most* injudicious. The courts are becoming quite sensitive to that sort of things *these days.*' He made it sound as if McDermott had been policing the Australian outback for the past several years.

McDermott was unperturbed. 'Mr. Mayhew, did your client mention that on not one, but two separate occasions—including the beginning of our formal interview today—I actually *advised* him to seek counsel? Did he suggest that he was a poor ivory-tower academic who had been unjustly accused of murder, or did he tell you that he's been fiddling his wife's brokerage accounts without her knowledge to the tune of tens of thousands of pounds? Did your client mention that in order to cover his losses he's been signing her name to the transfer certificates? Did he inform you that after we questioned him at home he promptly went to the bank the next day and withdrew the balance, and then tried to leave the country? Did he say that, despite the impressive town house in Park Crescent, he is overdrawn at his bank and in all likelihood would be unable to pay your fees?' Mayhew's expression told him this last shot had particularly hit home.

The solicitor glared at Burton-Strachey, but only for a moment; then it was on to business as usual. 'What my client told me,' he said imperturbably, 'is, of course, privileged. The point is, what exactly did my client tell you?'

'He said he hadn't done anything. A veritable paragon of virtue, your client. I'll get you a transcript of our earlier interview in due course. McDermott placed his hand on the man's shoulder and adopted a less adversarial tone. Look, we're not out to hang your client; but he's got to be more forthcoming with us. So far he's told us a pack of half-truths that my dead aunt Agnes wouldn't have swallowed whole. My DC thinks he's not guilty of anything more serious than financial incompetence; my Sergeant wants him on toast for the whole lot. Me, I'm as open-minded as the next man; but he needs to tell us what he knows.'

Mayhew asked to speak with his client alone, and when he emerged several minutes later, said, 'My client is prepared to make a full statement, Inspector.'

'Excellent,' McDermott replied. They returned to the interview room. After the solicitor and Burton-Strachey had seated themselves, McDermott turned on the tape machine and spoke into the microphone. 'Resuming the interview of Professor Miles Burton-Strachey, in connection with the deaths of Sally Beck and Fraser Campbell. The date is October eleven, and the time is two-twenty-three PM. In attendance are Mr. Burton-Strachey's solicitor, Mr. Mayhew, DC Quinn and DS Ridley.' He turned to Burton-Strachey. 'Professor, you wish to make a statement, I believe?'

'Yes,' he answered churlishly.

'It is my duty to remind you that you do not have to say anything when questioned, but it may harm your defense if you omit something which you later rely upon in court. Following your oral statement a transcript of your remarks will be prepared, and you will be asked to read it over and make any necessary corrections, and then to sign it. Do you understand?'

'Yes.'

'Very well, then. When you're ready.'

They emerged from the interview room as Burton-Strachey was being led away to the Charge Room to be photographed and fingerprinted and arraigned for a preliminary hearing. McDermott shook hands with the solicitor and they parted amiably. 'Mayhew's a nice enough chap,' he smiled, 'once you cut through the professional veneer.'

Quinn and Ridley looked at McDermott as if he'd just lost his mind. 'I never met one of them blokes that weren't cold as a widder's heart,' he muttered darkly.

The Sergeant made for the gent's, and McDermott and Quinn returned to the office just in time to field a phone call from downstairs. 'Yes?' he answered. 'Certainly. Show her up.'

A few moments later there was a knock on his office door and Hillary Burton-Strachey entered. 'Inspector McDermott? I wonder if I might have a word.' She glanced uncertainly at Wilhemina Quinn.

'Of course. Do have a chair. This is DC Quinn. She's working on the case—the deaths at St. Gregory's, I mean.'

She seated herself on the edge of the chair. 'So you think my husband is involved?'

'That's not clear at this point,' McDermott said. 'Have you been down to see him yet?'

'I'm going there shortly. I really can't believe Miles is a murderer.'

'We have to look at all the possibilities, Mrs. Burton-Strachey. The facts are that he misled us about where he was at the time of the young woman's death, and that he did receive a note which apparently caused him some distress on the morning of her death.'

'Yes, I know about the note—he said it was from our bank. Surely you can check on that?'

'We'll look into it of course—although even if it should prove to be true it doesn't mean your husband didn't also receive a blackmail note,' he added. 'As I said, he has no firm alibi for the time of either death.'

Hillary Burton-Strachey stared at him. '*Either* death? You mean you suspect him of killing Mr. Campbell as well?'

McDermott glanced at Quinn. 'They do seem to be related.'

'Inspector, my husband couldn't have been involved. I know him. Look, I realise that he's not perfect, but it's simply not in him to set about deliberately murdering someone. It's—it's so *uncivilised!*'

'Your husband found himself in a desperate situation, ma'm,' McDermott replied quietly. 'It's been my experience that given the right circumstances people are capable of almost anything.'

Her eyes flitted around the room, settling briefly on Quinn, then on the papers on his desk, before returning to his steady gaze. 'I suppose we've nothing more to discuss, then.' She stood up.

'Please try to understand, Mrs. Burton-Strachey. I'm only trying to prepare you for what you may have to face later.' She did not reply, and he closed the door behind her, shaking his head.

As she left, McDermott remarked to no one in particular. 'Amazing. He steals—or at least manages to lose—the bulk of her inheritance, then does a bunk with what little cash she has left, and not two days later she marches in here prepared to defend the bugger to her death.'

'Perhaps he's all she's got,' Quinn remarked quietly.

McDermott was interrupted again by his mobile. He smiled and leaned back in his chair. 'Hello, Dierdre. This is an unexpected pleas—What?' He pulled himself upright suddenly. 'I'm so sorry. How is Phillip bearing up? Tell him he mustn't blame himself. Is there anything I can do?' He paused. 'That's difficult. She's an adult, legally speaking, and you have no reason to think she went against her will, right? Yes, of course, I'll see if she knows anything. No, I'll talk to her in person. Right. Take care. My best to Phillip—I'll be in touch.'

When McDermott replaced the telephone Quinn broke the silence. 'What happened, sir? You look dreadful.'

McDermott spoke slowly, trying to make sense of what he had just heard. 'Pamela Townsend, my daughter's best friend—and my Goddaughter—has apparently just disappeared.'

The drive to Oxford cut into his case work, but McDermott knew he had to go. He had to speak to Megan himself, see whether she knew anything – above all, where Pam might have gone. The obvious possibility, of course, was that she'd gone to her lover. But the Townsends had never met the woman, didn't even know her last name, and had no contact information for her. And as he had told Dierdre, legally speaking Pam was an adult; he couldn't even launch a missing persons enquiry without leaving himself open to charges of abusing his powers.

He reflected on the personal crises Meg had experienced in her life: they were few, but significant. *First her mother is killed, then her best friend disappears.* At least when her mother had died Megan had been too young to comprehend fully the enormity of her loss. This time it was different, because Meg and Pamela had known each other virtually their entire lifetimes. He recalled laughing off Meg's concern for her friend, and thought how callous his words seemed in retrospect. He wondered if Meg would hold them against him, though in one respect it was irrelevant: he blamed himself.

WHILE MCDERMOTT WAS CONTENDING WITH TRAFFIC on the M40, Alan Noakes sipped the latest in a succession of low-alcohol lagers in his fourth public house, all within the past twenty-four hours. He was beginning to develop a new respect for the internal constitutions of academics when something he saw caused him to pay closer attention. He watched events at a nearby table unfold with keen interest, and weighed the alternatives of keeping his man under surveillance versus phoning in to report what he had seen and asking for instructions. Another debacle like the last one was simply not in the cards; one more slip-up and he'd be patrolling the streets, issuing parking tickets. He pulled his mobile from his jacket and feigned making a call, all the while recording the scene playing out before him.

DURING THE DRIVE BACK TO LONDON McDermott replayed his talk with Megan over and over in his mind. He had arrived in the late afternoon. Meg had not yet returned from classes, but the porter had let him into her rooms once he flashed his warrant card. Half an hour later her roommate had appeared, surprised to find him there. When he told her there was a "family situation" she had offered to stay with a friend across the hall until called. McDermott had been grateful for her understanding.

Megan was a different story. He watched with relief as she returned *sans* boyfriend; that would have been an additional complication. At first delighted to see her father unexpectedly, she read in his face immediately that something was terribly wrong. When McDermott explained that Pam had disappeared his daughter had gone into denial, then had begun to sob. She rummaged through her bag and came up with a bottle of benzodiazepine, taking two tablets and waving off McDermott's concern. Then they'd quarrelled over the pills, Megan saying she needed them to deal with the stress of her classes and the news. That set off alarm bells with McDermott, who argued that she was on a dangerous path. In the end Megan relented and agreed to talk with the college physician about alternatives.

When they finally returned to Pam's situation, another forty minutes was spent fruitlessly, trying to discover where she might have gone. But it turned out Megan knew little more than Pam's parents. No last name, no address for her lover. She had Pam's mobile number, of course, but so did Dierdre, and she wasn't answering. Of course, that didn't mean that Pam wouldn't try to contact Meg, who would be more sympathetic than her parents. She agreed to plead with Pam to contact her parents – that is, if she called at all. McDermott had offered to stay the night in Oxford, but Meg had insisted that she was fine, that what she needed most was time to come to terms with what had happened. McDermott wound up by calling her roommate over and giving her his personal mobile number. He waved off Meg's suggestion that they visit Pam's parents on the weekend, arguing that it would be better once they knew more. Before he left he spoke with the Principal of Meg's college and explained things. Her manner indicated that she was experienced in these matters, and McDermott left Oxford feeling as good as he might have under the circumstances.

QUINN HAD NOT BEEN IDLE while McDermott was away. Armed with the address of the flat the Beck woman had used for her clients, she tracked down the landlord. The Canary Wharf area was an inspired location, what with all the investment bankers located there. But when she located the landlord she was in for shock and a disappointment. The shock was that the rent for the one-bedroom flat was nearly three times what Quinn earned in a month. She reflected, not for the first time, that her job was woefully underpaid.

The disappointment stemmed from the fact that Sally Beck had terminated her leasehold a month earlier, when it expired. Flats in the area were in demand, and the property management company hadn't wasted any time thoroughly cleaning and repainting the flat. By now new tenants had already moved in. Worthless, then, for gathering forensic evidence.

TWENTY NINE

The formal charging of Burton-Strachey meant that McDermott could no longer keep the press at bay. By Wednesday several of the morning papers carried the story, but on the inside pages, a small mercy for which Norman Anscombe was quietly grateful. With little information to work with, most simply reported that a Fellow of St. Gregory's College had been arraigned in connection with undisclosed charges that were apparently unrelated to the recent and sudden death of a colleague several days previously. The cause of that death, it was reported, had yet to be determined. The entire item, Anscombe noted with satisfaction, took somewhat less than three column inches. The more sensational tabloids, however, gave their usual full play to their readers' imaginations: a full column on the front page of *The Sun* was devoted to the recent events at St. Gregory's, suitably (or unsuitably, depending on one's point of view) headlined by a banner in bold print that read *College for Crime! Death and Dishonour Stalks Dons* above a photo of St. Gregory's outer quad. Anscombe opened his desk drawer and extracted a large bottle of antacid tablets.

Arriving at Charing Cross station uncharacteristically late, McDermott entered the lift, and was surprised to find Derek Galbraith with the Assistant Chief Commissioner responsible for Territorial Policing, meaning the day-to-day policing of Greater London. 'Morning, sir,' McDermott said as the ACC pointedly checked his watch.

'Morning, McDermott,' Galbraith replied. 'Any developments in the St. Gregory's case since we spoke last?'

'The dailies should be on your desk by now. We charged one of the Fellows yesterday with crimes apparently unrelated to the deaths.'

'And the murderer of—what was the name—Cameron?' the ACC asked.

'Campbell, sir. We have a staff meeting on that in a few minutes. 'This is my floor, I think. I'll keep you posted,' he said, grateful for the escape. The pair watched him disappear down the hallway.

When McDermott entered the incident room he found Quinn charting their progress on a large whiteboard. Across the top was a timeline of events, beginning with Sally Beck's renting the bedsit on Carburton Street, then being killed by the bus, and extending to the discovery of Fraser Campbell's body on Saturday night. Below that was a grid with columns headed by the words 'Suspect' and 'Opportunity.' A third column labelled 'Motive' was conspicuously empty. Along the left-hand side of the grid Quinn had written, in large capital letters, the names of each of the Fellows of St. Gregory's in a further vertical column. At the points where the columns and rows intersected, she was entering the alibis given by each suspect. Those that had been verified had a check mark next to them; those she apparently doubted had been followed by a query mark.

'Morning. What's all this? Nothing on Channel Four last night, then?' he asked, winking at Ridley.

'Very droll, sir,' Quinn replied. 'I thought we could do with some order. As the information adds up we're in danger of losing sight of the details.'

McDermott settled into his desk chair, and regarded the board. 'I see you've omitted some of the faculty and staff at St. Gregory's. Any particular reason?'

'Well, for starters, there's the matter of motive. The Principal—Anscombe—has the strongest alibi of any of them. During the first death he was having lunch in the dining hall, in full view of several Fellows and the serving staff, not to mention hundreds of students. And during the time that Campbell was killed he was in a meeting with the other members of the Selection Committee. To assume Anscombe was our killer would involve assuming that two members of the board and his secretary—not to mention hoards of students—are prepared to perjure themselves on his behalf.'

'Not the Brigadier, certainly. He'd do what he saw as his duty though the heavens should fall. The others?'

Quinn looked at the board. 'Well, there's Soames. Her alibi for the Beck girl's death is shaky—remember she said she was in her rooms working on lecture notes? But her alibi for Campbell's death is partly confirmed.'

'Partly?' McDermott looked at her skeptically, as though the notion of an alibi partly confirmed made about as much sense as someone being partly pregnant.

'Yes sir. I checked with the restaurant she mentioned—Poon's, just off Russell Square. They remember her, all right. It seems she had some rather pointed observations about the quality of the food.'

'No surprises there. But you said her alibi was only partly confirmed?'

'Yes sir. I checked with the Garrick, where she said she went following dinner. An usher thought she remembered the face, but couldn't be sure that it was Saturday she'd seen her. Since the ticket was a gift there was no record as to which night she'd been there.'

'I see.' McDermott paused. 'Who else have you eliminated?'

'Well sir, there's Mr. Trewilliger. To be frank, I don't see him doing it. For one thing—if you'll pardon my saying so, sir—most of the time he seems to be in too much of a fog. For another, if we assume blackmail was the motive for the first death, and that frequenting a prostitute was the cause—well, it's a bit much to credit him as having that type of inclination, sir.'

'Be careful not to judge a book by its cover, Willie. But I take your point. Anyone else out of the running?'

Quinn turned things over in her mind. 'Yes sir. There's Mr. Griffith-Jones. He has no alibi for the Beck woman's death, but you recall he claimed he was on the telephone to his sister in Wales during Campbell's death. British Telecom and the college records confirm a call was placed from his extension to his sister's number, at around half seven. Theoretically that would have given him sufficient time, either before—if he was a cool customer—or after the call, to nip in and dispatch Mr. Campbell.'

'*Theoretically?*' Ridley interjected. 'Alf o' London could've done it, *theoretically*.' He enunciated the final word as if it was part of some vile foreign tongue.

'Good theories are a bit thin on the ground right now, George; we have to consider all possibilities,' McDermott reminded him. 'Though I agree he wouldn't have been my first choice either.' He glanced at the board. 'Very well, then, who does that leave us with?'

Quinn approached the board. 'Well, sir, assuming that it was a member of faculty, and not simply persons unknown, that leaves us with Mr. Asquith, Dr. Westgate, Professor Burton-Strachey, and—'

'Professor Boothroyd,' McDermott finished the sentence for her. 'How do you rank them?'

She hesitated. 'In ascending order of probability I would place Mr. Burton-Strachey last, for the reasons I mentioned yesterday. Although he has no alibi for Campbell's death, I don't see him having enough time to visit both his broker and his banker, and then push Sally Beck under a bus. And if he didn't do the one—'

'—I know,' interjected McDermott, 'then he didn't do the other. Have you considered that his motive might have nothing—at least in the strict sense—to do with the Beck woman's death?'

'What do you mean? We've always assumed—'

'—that whoever killed Sally Beck killed Fraser Campbell; and we did so because the probability of two unrelated killers striking at St. Gregory's during a single week was too remote to be considered. Right?'

Quinn was becoming exasperated. 'Your assumption, if you recall, sir.'

'Just so. But let's keep an open mind. Perhaps Sally Beck was attempting to blackmail Campbell, and someone got on to that, and used it to kill Campbell to cover their own tracks for quite another purpose. Remember that Burton-Strachey told us in the Senior Common Room he'd gone directly home for lunch the day that she was killed. Later, when that was shown to be false, he said he'd lied to keep the information that he'd been to his broker from his colleagues at the college—and thereby from his wife.' McDermott gestured wildly to make his point, and a pencil he'd been holding went sailing through the air, bouncing off a corner of the desk, and rolling toward the corner of the room.

McDermott stooped to pick up the errant pencil and resumed fingering it. 'Suppose it wasn't only Burton-Strachey's wife that it was vital to keep the information from?'

'Sir?' Quinn asked, not grasping his point.

'We know that he had applied to succeed Anscombe as Principal. Unlike the larger colleges, at St. Gregory's the Principal's job involves a great many financial duties: there's establishing faculty and staff salaries, overseeing departmental budgets, forecasting annual needs for the Ministry—even having a say at the Board in managing the investment funds that form the core of their long-term resources. If word got around that he couldn't even manage his own household investments his candidacy to succeed Anscombe would have been dead in the water. Remember, Campbell said he'd spent the noon hour in Russell Square—directly between the college and Southampton Row, where Burton-Strachey's bank is located. He might have seen something.' McDermott spread his hands on the desk before him.

'But what about the Beck woman's death?' Quinn persisted. 'Who killed her, then?'

'Tha's dead easy,' Ridley broke in, unable to contain himself any longer. 'No one. The Beck lass slipped and fell under wheels o' bus. But her death set off chain of events that threatened to expose our lad, who sussed that Campbell could put paid to his alibi, and did him in 'afore that could happen. By gaw, that's champion!'

'Not exactly, George. It's still only a theory,' McDermott reminded him.

It makes sense, though. We need to have 'nother go at Burton-Strachey.'

'My thoughts exactly. What about the other suspects, Willie?'

'Well, sir, based on my interview of his wife, I would think Westgate is next likely to have done it. Although he said he was out walking when Campbell was killed, he can't prove it. But there again, he was seen in the dining hall during Sally Beck's death. Dammit—I want him to have done it,' she exclaimed.

There was an awkward silence, which McDermott moved to fill. 'I know what you mean: simply in terms of personality he seems the most likely. But it baffles me how he could have done the deed, given the fact that half a dozen people—none of whom are overly fond of him—are prepared to swear he was in the Dining Room when the Beck woman died. Unless, as George said, her death was merely accidental, a catalyst for other events. I've lost track. Who does that leave us?'

Quinn consulted the board. 'Mr. Asquith and Professor Boothroyd, sir. At this point I would be hard put to choose between them.'

I wouldn't. McDermott thought to himself. Aloud he said 'Run out your reasoning, Willie.'

'Asquith has to be regarded as a starter since we know he lied to us about being on the train from Carlisle when Sally Beck was killed. And the claim that he spent the evening of Campbell's death with a male friend has, I think, to be put in the same category as an alibi provided by a spouse.'

'Agreed. Motive?'

Quinn shifted uneasily. 'That's more difficult, sir. One possibility is that, as you've suggested, he's not what he seems. The revelation of that would certainly threaten the image he's sought to cultivate.'

'Possible, but thin, as a motive for murder,' McDermott argued. 'Convince me.'

'Well, we're assuming the motive was sexual—a liaison with Sally Beck herself. But a person in her position gets to see a great many things. If Asquith had anything else to hide—well, he's rather theatrical, isn't he? And sort of dishy in his own way. Suppose, for example, he'd acted in a porno movie, or even been a rent boy? The blackmail note was ambiguous, wasn't it? It doesn't actually *say* he was a client.'

'That's possible, Willie. Stupid of us to have missed it. It certainly merits our having a deeper look into Mr. Asquith's background. What do you think, George? Check our man out for form. The Vice Unit can give you a hand.'

Ridley frowned, but had to admit it was possible. By now his already-bleak view of academics was descending to new, uncharted depths.

McDermott decided that the question that had been nagging him could be put off no longer. He looked at the Constable. 'There's just one suspect left to deal with, then. What's your take on Boothroyd?'

Quinn took a deep breath and resumed. 'I've given it a lot of thought, sir. To be frank I would have thought Professor Boothroyd is also past it as far as sexual peccadilloes go. But we're talking about something that could go back some years. And in terms of alibi, he's the least well off of any of them. On both occasions he claimed he was home. On both occasions his only alibi is his wife. He neither made nor received any calls during the times in question, and no one came to the house. Moreover, he had a far stronger motive than any of them for Campbell's death: by then he had been told by Anscombe that he'd been tapped to succeed him as Principal. If Boothroyd had been involved with the Beck woman, even years ago, and somehow Campbell knew—or even suspected—it, he simply could not afford to allow Campbell to live.'

McDermott had to admire the undeniable logic of her argument; he could hear the same words being uttered by a Public Prosecutor to devastating effect. Since the case was traced back to St. Gregory's he had resisted taking seriously the possibility that his friend and former mentor was possibly a murderer. He swiveled his chair to face Quinn directly. 'You're right, of course. The possibility can't be ruled out. Get on to Anscombe. Tell him you want to review Boothroyd's personnel file.' McDermott was interrupted by the landline telephone. 'Yes? Put him on.' He covered the mouthpiece with his hand and whispered 'Noakes.' Ridley sat forward in his chair, and Quinn relaxed slightly, grateful for the diversion.

McDermott removed his hand from the mouthpiece. 'McDermott here. *What?* You're absolutely certain? When did this happen? Why didn't you telephone earlier? Right. Where is he now? And you? No—stay put. We'll be there directly.'

As they made their way toward St. Gregory's, Ridley and Quinn badgered McDermott with questions. He remained cryptically silent for most of the journey. He was also, Quinn thought, curiously satisfied. It seemed that matters had come to a head. He resisted all entreaties, however, simply stating the obvious— 'Let's get to it, then'—as their car pulled into the outer quadrangle, closely followed by a marked Panda unit. DC Noakes appeared from the Porter's Office on a slow trot.

'He's still in there, sir. Shall I lead the way?'

'Not just yet,' McDermott replied. He turned to the two uniformed PCs who had emerged from the car behind them. Pointing to a large oaken door at the far side of the quad he said, 'You take that entrance. Go all the way through the dining hall: you'll find a second door leading to a corridor on the left. Don't let a tall, suntanned man with long fair hair in his late twenties leave. Any questions?'

'No sir,' the senior of the two replied, and they went off clutching their hand radios.

'Now we go.' McDermott set off across the quad for the door nearest the faculty wing. Noakes scurried through, and Quinn had to hurry to catch the door before it closed, holding it for the older man, who was bringing up the rear.

Once inside it took only a moment for their eyes to adjust from the bright sunlight to the subdued electric lighting of the oak-panelled hallway. McDermott marched almost soundlessly down the corridor until he came to the last two or three doors, pausing briefly to read the names, then moving on. He stopped at the final door on the right-hand side of the hallway and knocked heavily.

'Asquith? Open up. Come on—We haven't got all day.'

After a brief delay the door swung open. 'Keep your hair on!' Then 'Oh, it's you. What do you mean, making a ruckus like that?'

McDermott brushed past the man and moved into the centre of the room, his eyes taking in everything at once. The others followed, leaving Asquith standing at the door. 'Here, now—what do you mean by bursting in like this?' Asquith's voice had taken on a guarded tone.

'Oh, I'm sorry. You haven't been introduced to everyone here, have you?' McDermott turned to his colleagues. 'You've met Sergeant Ridley and DC Quinn, of course. But I don't believe you know Detective Constable Noakes. You know Mr. Asquith here, though, don't you, Noakes?'

Taking his cue from McDermott, Noakes chimed in with an air of self-assurance he hadn't show before. 'Oh yes, sir. I've seen a great deal of Mr. Asquith over the past two days.'

'You have? I've never seen you before. Why are you spying on me?' Asquith was trying to keep up the pretense, but without much success; even his public-school accent was fast abandoning him.

'You told us you came down to London Tuesday a week ago by train from Carlisle. That's not true.'

Asquith was caught off guard. 'It isn't? Of course it is—I've said so.'

'There you go again, lad,' McDermott said, borrowing a page from Ridley's book. 'If you're going to tell a porkie, you'd better make a proper job of it.'

'I'm afraid I don't know what you mean.'

'All rather simple, really. You see, the train from Carlisle was re-routed due to a derailment Tuesday last. It arrived at Euston Station over two hours late. You're dead clever, you are: you arrived at the college over an hour before the train did, and well in time to have killed Sally Beck.'

Jeremy Asquith visibly paled as he struggled to regain his composure. 'Who? I guess it's true what they say: anything not worth doing is not worth doing well. So what if I did mislead you? I fail to see how it can possibly be significant. Suppose I did decide to drop in on a friend, and lost track of the time? It's not a crime—an indiscretion, at best. What business is it of yours?' He waved his hand dismissively.

'Ah, but that's the rub, lad. It is a crime to tell a lie to a policeman, and when you led us up the garden path we decided you'd bear watching. Noakes, would you be so good as to bring Mr. Asquith here up to speed on his recent activities?'

The officer stepped forward and made a great show of producing his note-book. 'At approximately seven thirty-four on October eleventh—that's last evening, sir, I observed Mr. Asquith leaving St. Gregory's College. He walked toward Tavistock Square, but before he got there he picked up a taxi. I did the same and followed him to St. Martin's Lane, where he entered a public house'—he consulted his notes— 'the Lord Palmerston. I followed him in and seated myself so I could observe him unobtrusively.' Noakes was trying a bit too hard to get back into McDermott's good graces.

By now Asquith suspected he was in serious trouble, but he tried to put the best face on it. 'Look here,' he said, some of the plumminess returning to his voice, 'if simply imbibing alcohol was an offence, I should think you'd have most of my senile colleagues in Dartmoor by now.' He dropped into the nearest chair and fumbled for a cigarette in an unconvincing attempt to appear calm.

McDermott moved around the room as he spoke. 'Don't disparage your elders, lad. Remember you'll be old yourself, one day. Hello, what's this?' He picked up a vicuna coat from where it had been tossed in a chair and began to rummage through the pockets.

By now Asquith was straining to regain his calm. 'See here, Inspector. You've no right to just burst in and search my personal belongings. This isn't bloody Russia, you know!'

'Welcome to the Twenty-First Century, Mr. Asquith. The distinction between Russia and the West is growing smaller every day. In any case I don't need a warrant. DC Noakes here saw you committing a felony.'

Asquith blanched. 'A what?' The public-school intonation had returned, but his voice had acquired a ridiculously high pitch.

'A felony, lad—you know, one of those things that carries with it an extended visit to one of Her Majesty's prisons.'

'I—I don't know what you're talking about. You're really not making yourself very clear.'

'Oh, I forgot. Noakes neglected to mention just what he saw at the Lord Palmerston last evening. Constable?'

The young man had his notebook at hand. 'At quarter past eight Mr. Asquith made a call on his mobile. Not ten minutes later he was joined by another, younger man, who went directly to Mr. Asquith's table, as though he knew he'd be there.'

'This whole scene is entirely unnecessary, Inspector. I've already told you that I was meeting a friend.'

McDermott ignored him. 'Go on, Constable.'

Noakes resumed his narrative. 'At eight-seventeen the younger man produced a small fold of bank notes from his pocket and passed them to Mr. Asquith, who placed them in the inside pocket of his jacket. Then he passed a small polythene bag under the table to the younger man. The latter left the premises almost immediately. The same scene, with variations, was repeated twice more that evening, until Mr. Asquith returned to his rooms at approximately eleven-twenty-eight PM.' Noakes closed his notebook with a flourish.

McDermott gazed down at Asquith, who by now presented a most unprepossessing sight. 'You've been a busy lad. For starters, there's possession of a controlled substance for purposes of trafficking. That's a felony, and no amount of limp-wristed hankie waving is going to get you out of the cow dung. Then there's suspicion of murder. Of course, if you really are innocent of any wrongdoing, simply showing us your mobile should help to clear things up.'

By now Asquith had had an opportunity to conjure up a position, and he decided to brazen it out. 'Oh dear,' he said. 'I'm afraid I misplaced it. Likely put it down in a pub, and simply forgot about it. Bit of a nuisance, actually. Dreadfully sorry,' he smirked. Then, as his confidence grew, he added, 'See here. All this is rubbish, Inspector. You have nothing but your man's word for it that anything he alleges took place. I will not be treated like a criminal. Now please leave.'

McDermott simply smiled. 'Oh, did I forget to mention that Noakes here recorded the entire event—and several others, I gather—on his mobile? Constable, can you share your information with Mr. Asquith here?' He turned to face the Sergeant.

But before Noakes could take out his phone, McDermott heard a dull thud behind him. As he turned around Quinn said, 'I'm sorry, sir, but Mr. Asquith seems to have fainted.'

A few minutes later Jeremy Asquith had regained consciousness and had been taken away by Noakes, vehemently protesting his innocence. McDermott turned to the troops. 'George, you, Willie and I will give this place a proper going over. You two start on his room. I'll give Anscombe the bad news.'

'YOU MEAN TO SAY THE MAN WAS DISTRIBUTING DRUGS to our own students?' Anscombe was incredulous.

McDermott, however, was blandly matter-of-fact. 'As far as the students go we have no information on their identity, though I've no doubt Asquith will supply us with names soon enough. My guess is that he used the Lord Palmerston—and probably a number of other pubs—precisely because he didn't want to risk being recognised. In that case he'll hardly have sold to students here at St. Gregory's.'

The Principal sighed and removed his glasses and began polishing them meticulously. He looked at McDermott. 'You think he's your man, then?'

'It certainly looks that way.' He ran through the reasoning Willie Quinn had laid out earlier that morning.

'Well, at least that's out of the way, then.' Anscombe seemed pleased with the prospect that St. Gregory's would soon return to some semblance of normality. Then another thought struck him. 'Do the press have to be informed?'

McDermott rose from his chair. 'As with Burton-Strachey, once Asquith's been charged, it's a matter of public record. All the papers keep someone at the Old Bailey, for just this sort of information.'

At times like these Anscombe's academic tendency to defend freedom of expression gave way before more pressing considerations. He smiled wanly. 'I don't suppose we could invoke national security, could we?'

THIRTY

By the time McDermott returned, Ridley and Quinn had searched most of Asquith's belongings. Surprisingly, they had failed to turn up his mobile. Either the man had been telling the truth or he was more cunning than they had given him credit for. McDermott was considering calling in experts from the Drug Squad when he noticed a large black sports bag stuffed to the rear of Asquith's closet. He pulled it out and opened it up. Inside he found a worn baseball cap, a tan leather jacket, a pair of denim pants, a black tee shirt, and a grey hoodie. There was also a pair of scuffed workman's boots. But perhaps most intriguing were two sheets of temporary tattoos. 'Have a look at this,' he said, dumping the lot on the bed. Not exactly our man's usual attire, is it?'

Quinn looked at the labels. 'All this gear is from Europe,' she pointed out. 'Unless Asquith is remarkably loyal to specific brands, it suggests he picked it up over there.'

'Why the tattoos, though?' Ridley asked. 'E doesn't seem the type.'

'A good question, George. My guess is that he wanted to change his appearance. You have to admit, he'd be easy to miss in this getup.' He thought a moment. 'When we return to the station we'll have the bag and its contents checked for traces of drugs. We might just get lucky.'

She nodded and returned to her own work, and a few moments later emerged from a dresser drawer with something in her hand.

'What's that? Don't suppose he's kept a record of his dealings, has he?'

Quinn shot him a skeptical look. 'No such luck, sir, but maybe as good. Some travel receipts.'

McDermott's ears pricked up. 'Let's have a look.' He thumbed through them quickly. Presently he looked up. 'A bit of a pack rat, mister Asquith. He's been busy—and once again, not entirely truthful. When he said he was in the Lake District recently he was in France and Italy, according to this regional Eurail Pass. In fact, he seems to have taken quite a number of trips to the Continent—including most of the school holidays and long vacs for the past couple of years. My guess is that Asquith was well on his way to becoming the Sainsbury's of the local drug trade. Let's keep looking, shall we?'

Forty minutes later it was getting on lunch time, and they had nothing more to show for their efforts. Ridley surveyed the clutter. 'By gaw, I've seen summat the sort 'afore, Guv, but it were a rubbish tip.'

Quinn was equally pessimistic. 'I'm afraid I agree, sir. There must be another way of going about this.'

McDermott had returned the clothing to the sports bag and set it aside. He said, 'Collect everything paper and dump it on the bed. Everything—Oyster cards, dry-cleaning tags, sales receipts, bills—the whole lot.'

The Sergeant snorted. 'Take the rest o' day to sort through it all.'

Ridley and Quinn sat on the edge of the bed, separated by the small mountain of detritus documenting Asquith's daily activities. McDermott paced the room, irritated by his inability to latch on to anything of significance. 'Let's see what we know so far about the mysterious Mr. Asquith,' he said. 'First of all, he shops for most of his clothes at Marks and Sparks and John Lewis, except for this rather curious cache of workman's gear. Secondly, according to these receipts he has his British togs cleaned regularly by the Gower Street outlet of the Nice-N-Brite chain. George, if we come up with nothing else, you might check with them to see if he's ever had the rough clothing cleaned by them, or had his clothes picked up from or delivered to another address.'

Ridley nodded without enthusiasm.

'Considering Asquith's rather exotic sartorial taste,' McDermott continued, 'his preference in foodstuffs is surprisingly middle class. Orange Pekoe tea, Tesco biscuits, instant soup mixes and cheap wines—whatever else he is, our Mr. Asquith is no gastronome.'

He stared out the window for some moments, apparently lost in thought, then turned and faced his colleagues. 'His personal toiletries are equally unimpressive—the sort of things one can find at any Boots outlet. It's my guess that he did very little, if any, entertaining here, which makes it all the more likely that he considered his rooms to be a safe haven. Let's make one more sweep, shall we?'

Another twenty minutes passed with little result until George Ridley emerged from the bathroom holding a key in his hand. 'Now then,' he said, beaming, 'Suppose this is of any use?'

'Let's have a look.' McDermott turned the key over in his hand. It was silver in colour, just over two inches long, and smooth except for four numerals stamped into the shank on one side. 'Fits a safety deposit box, I'll wager. Where did you find it?'

Ridley coloured. 'Well now, I had t' spend a penny. As I were rollin' tissue down, I heard a funny clickin' sort o' noise. I took paper off and opened roller. Key were inside.'

'Well done, George. Now, where do you suppose it belongs?'

Ridley made a sour face. 'No bank book in pile o'er there,' he said, looking at the bed. 'Could be any number o' places. Even if it were in London—and we've no reason to think it is—we could turn over 'alf o' city and 'ave nowt to show for it. Canna' make bricks w'out straw,' he snorted.

'George, I suppose it would be asking too much to expect a Yorkshireman to be anything but a pessimist. It must be the weather. Now, how about some constructive suggestions?'

Quinn coughed discreetly. 'Perhaps the College has a record of Asquith's account, sir. He may have his salary deposited directly.'

'Brilliant, Willie. George, you keep looking. I'll check with Anscombe. Willie, come with me.'

Quinn struggled to keep up as she followed McDermott through the hallway. 'Where are we going, sir?'

'To see Anscombe, hopefully to kill two birds.' He replied.

It was well past his lunch hour, and for much of the morning Norman Anscombe had been occupied deflecting queries from Fellows and students alike regarding the rather conspicuous departure of Mr. Asquith in the company of two uniformed officers. Losing no time, he had already set in motion the complex arrangements involved in permanently replacing the man. Among other things, those arrangements included informing the Chancellor about the vacancy and, inevitably, the reason for it. The brigadier had not been best pleased. Anscombe found himself faced with the prospect of ending his term of office less on a single sour note than on a veritable symphony of dissonance. It was not a prospect he much fancied.

In desperation Anscombe had instructed his secretary, Mrs. Coates, to take all calls and to tell anyone who asked that he was unavailable for the day. It was therefore with some asperity that he picked up the telephone. 'Yes?' he enquired brusquely.

'I know you asked not to be disturbed, Principal,' Mrs. Coates said, 'but Detective Inspector McDermott and Constable Quinn are here, and would like a word with you. He is quite insistent.'

'Oh, very well—show them in,' he snorted, the small civilities that usually marked his relationship with his secretary now gone by the wayside.

A moment later the door opened and McDermott and Quinn entered the room. 'Hello again, sir. Sorry to bother you, but we are in need of some information which we think you may be able to provide.'

'Indeed. It seems to me that every time I assist you with your enquiries the college finds itself with yet another black mark.'

McDermott smiled. 'It is rather beginning to resemble Pandora's box, isn't it? However, I think you'll agree it's better to cut out all the cancer at once, so to speak, and get it over with.'

'I'll overlook the mixed metaphor, Inspector, if you will come to the point,' Anscombe said wearily.

'We merely need to review two personnel files, if you don't mind.'

Anscombe raised a skeptical brow. 'Indeed. May I ask why?'

'Simply a matter of procedure, Principal. We need to eliminate certain individuals from our enquiries.'

His expression indicated that Anscombe wasn't buying it. 'Whose files do you require?'

'Mr. Asquith's and Professor Boothroyd's. DC Quinn will look them over and return them to you.'

Anscombe's expression changed from skeptical to alarmed. 'Really? Ansquith I might have expected. But Professor Boothroyd?'

McDermott wasn't giving anything away. 'As I said, merely a matter of form.' The Principal resigned himself to the inevitable and picked up his phone.

By the time Quinn finished reviewing the personnel files it was getting on one-thirty, and she returned to Asquith's rooms. The expressions on McDermott's and Ridley's faces told her they had found nothing more, and Quinn managed to suggest that her efforts had been equally fruitless. McDermott was unconcerned. 'A good morning's work, all things considered,' he said. 'Let's get back to the canteen and have a nosh. They're doing roast lamb with mint jelly.'

As they climbed into the car McDermott said, 'Any joy with the files, Willie?'

Quinn's face managed to suggest that her efforts had been equally fruitless. 'Nothing conclusive, sir. I do plan to speak with Professor Boothroyd, however, just to clear up one or two points.'

McDermott gave her a penetrating gaze, as though he suspected her of holding something back. But he said nothing.

THEY COMPLETED THE TRIP IN SILENCE, a case of history repeating itself. Dropping off their coats in the office they took the lift to the canteen, which was almost deserted, most of the staff having eaten lunch some hours ago. McDermott took a tray from the stack, collected his utensils, glanced up at the menu, and approached the hot food counter. 'Good afternoon. I'll have the roast lamb, please.'

'It's not on. Sorry,' the server said nonchalantly.

McDermott's face fell. 'Really? Well, let me see.' He looked again at the menu board. 'How about a Cornish pastie, then?'

'None left, I'm afraid,' the server replied in equally detached tones.

Again McDermott consulted the wall. 'The plaice?' he asked hopefully.

She shook her head. Behind him, Ridley and Quinn smirked at one another.

By now, McDermott's temper was getting the better of him. 'Well, perhaps it would save time if you told us what you *do* have!'

'No need to get shirty,' replied the server, glaring.

'I'm sorry. It's just that we've put in rather a long morning. Can you tell us what you have left?'

'Macaroni and Beef' she replied, '—and mushy peas.'

'Mushy peas? Good God.'

The server's eyebrows shot up. Apparently McDermott had offended her again. 'Perhaps I'll just have a pudding. You do have some left, don't you?'

'Oh yes, sir,' she replied brightly. 'Raspberry flan. Very nice it is, too.'

McDermott sighed, and moved on to the coffee urn, his tray empty.

When Ridley and Quinn joined him at a table a few moments later, he surveyed their plates with obvious disdain.

'What's the matter, sir? Don't you like mushy peas?' Quinn asked straight-faced.

'Expect 'e allus had 'em as child,' George chimed in. 'Bound t' put you off, that.'

'Very funny. Look at that disgusting colour. Food isn't mean to be...*chartreuse!*' he declared, and added, 'So what did you find out, Willie?'

Quinn sipped at her coffee. 'Asquith didn't have his salary deposited directly. He collected his cheques directly at the Porter's Office every two weeks.'

'He doesn't make it easy, does he?' The disappointment showed in his face.

'However,' she continued, his mood brightening visibly, 'at my request the Principal exhumed a stack of old payroll cheques from the files. I examined the endorsements on the backs. They'd been cashed at a variety of places— including hotels and Tesco's, and not a few at pubs and wine bars, would you believe it?'

McDermott sensed Quinn was holding back. 'And?'

'And three—just three—had been cashed at the same branch of the same bank—the Merchants Trust, in Gower Street.'

'Near the dry cleaners.' McDermott said.

'Got it in one, sir. I called them myself. Seems he opened a safety deposit box there two years ago. It's the little things, isn't it, that trip people up?'

McDermott smiled, reached across the table and took a forkful of Ridley's flan. 'Get in touch with the on-call magistrate, Willie. Explain what we've got so far, including Noakes' video of Asquith's dealing. We'll need a warrant to examine his bank account and his safety deposit box.'

Quinn's expression darkened. 'That reminds me, sir. We were going to process Sally Beck's flat near Canary Wharf.'

'Right. Once you got onto the property management people there. Are we ready to call Forensics?'

'That's just it, sir. I'm afraid we came up empty. It seems she cancelled her leasehold at the end of the month, just before she registered at St. Gregory's. Since then the flat's been cleaned and repainted, and new tenants have moved in. I'm afraid it's a dead end.'

McDermott looked like a dark cloud had passed over his grave. 'Well, no one said it would be easy. Any thoughts?'

Quinn frowned. 'Well, it's not what we have, but what we don't have, that's been bothering me, sir.'

McDermott was puzzled. 'I'm listening.'

'Well, sir, it's like that Sherlock Holmes story—you know, the one about the dog that didn't bark?'

'Yes, I know the one. What about it?'

'Would someun' mind lettin' me in on things?' George Ridley asked.

'It's simple, really George—or as Conan Doyle would have said, 'elementary:' following a crime at an isolated farmhouse, Sherlock Holmes alludes to 'the curious affair of the barking dog.' Someone—Watson, as I recall—asks, 'what barking dog? No dog barked.' and Holmes replies 'That's what is curious.' The point is, if the person who entered the house was a stranger the dog would surely have barked; the fact that it didn't meant the intruder was someone known to the household—a family member or frequent visitor.'

'Never!' Ridley snorted. 'That's too clever by half. But what's it got t' do with Askew bein' a murderer?'

McDermott looked at Quinn. 'I'm sure the constable is about to tell us, George.'

Quinn took her cue. 'Well, sir, if you recall the forensic report for Campbell's death, no unusual fibres were found in Campbell's rooms. There were various types of wool—tweeds, mostly—and cotton, and a few nylon fibres that matched an anorak in his closet.'

'Yes?'

'But there was no linen, sir, nor silk fibres found at the scene. And if you recall Mr. Asquith's wardrobe—'

'Yes, I know, Willie. With the exception of the bag we found in his closet, all of his clothes consist of linen trousers, combed cotton and silk shirts, and cashmere sweaters. He had one leather and two suede jackets, along with the mandatory British topcoat. All in hues that should have stuck out like a cat burglar at a Policeman's Ball. None of it matched the forensics from Campbell's room. In short, you're saying that if Asquith murdered Campbell he did so in his birthday suit.'

They walked back to the incident room in silence. As they passed though the outer office, Quinn said, 'Sorry to rain on your parade, sir.'

'Not at all, Willie,' McDermott replied. 'We don't want to put our foot in it. Well, it simplifies our questioning of Asquith. We'll focus on the drugs issue for the moment and see where it leads us from there. George, Anscombe gave me the name of Asquith's previous employer. I want you to get on to them this afternoon: find out as much as you can about what our Mr. Asquith was like, who his friends were, and why he left. And George, I'd also like you to get on to Borders and check when Asquith last entered the UK. In fact, have them send a list of all of his exits and entrances for the past couple of years. Got it?'

'Now, then, I hope my hearin' hasn't gone in past hour,' Ridley said.

As they went their separate ways, Quinn's expression darkened. She'd forgotten to mention what else she'd found in the files, and not about Asquith.

After instructing Forensics to go over Asquith's rooms for any minute traces of drugs that could prove useful in court, McDermott called downstairs and arranged for Asquith to be taken to an interview room, and told Noakes to meet them there. Quinn said she'd join them once she'd paid a visit to Asquith's bank and taken care of another matter that was nagging her.

IT WASN'T LONG BEFORE QUINN FOUND HERSELF in front of Boothroyd's home. She was ushered in without ceremony, and apparently, without concern. After the mandatory offer of tea, which she declined, Quinn got down to cases.

'Professor Boothroyd, you've been at St. Gregory's quite a while.'

His wife was perched on the edge of his armchair. 'Donkey's years, I'm afraid. And not over yet. I suppose you should know that I've been asked to replace the Principal when he retires at the end of the year.'

'So I understand, which brings me to the purpose of my visit. Some years ago I believe you authenticated a valuable work of art for the college, which subsequently turned out to be a fake.'

Boothroyd stiffened. 'A painting, yes. Unsigned, and erroniously attributed to Rembrandt. But not a fake, as you put it. Several centuries old, and unsigned. As you might be aware, Rembrandt ran an *atelier*, a workshop, in which his pupils routinely did preliminary work, or in some cases finished details, in many of his paintings. Not unusual for the day, but it makes things difficult under the best of circumstances.' He spread his fingers as if in supplication. 'But yes, the simple fact is, I erred.'

'And the college wound up paying far more for the painting than was warranted.'

He looked pained. 'That is so, I'm afraid. The work—an oil painting on wood—was clearly presented to us as *attributed* to Rembrandt, and its provenance was unclear. After examining it I judged it to be an original. Some months later it was determined to be by one of his followers. It's value was rather less, as you say, than the College paid for it.'

'I'm surprised the news didn't make the newspapers of the day. I've checked.'

'Quite right. The terms of the original sale had been quite specific, as I've said. No claim had ever been made by the seller, a collector on the Continent, or his dealer, that it was an original Rembrandt. If it had been signed, of course, it would be worth in the millions, if not more. Lacking a signature it was offered for a fraction of that, and an enticing acquisition.'

'I don't understand. How could you be sure it was a Rembrandt, then?'

Boothroyd looked down at his hands. 'There are tests, of course. We x-rayed the work and found evidence of another, incomplete work, underneath. A finished version of that painting was known to have come out of Rembrandt's studio. Then there were the pigments themselves: all colours and materials Rembrandt had been known to have worked with. But most of all there was the brushwork. Rembrandt was famous for his ability to render texture and light in a manner that was unique. It all seemed to be there.'

'So what happened? What led to the work being classified as a fake?'

Boothroyd let out a sigh. 'As I have said, it was not a fake, and no one has ever claimed it was. It was unsigned, and was only ever described as *in the style* of Rembrandt. It's provenance had become unclear as a result of the war—World War Two, I mean—when many works of art had gone missing, either hidden away by their owners or stolen by the Nazis. When the College considered purchasing it for our collection the former Principal approached me on behalf of the Governors and asked my advice. I studied the work, and was able to place it as of the period, and having a compositional structure known to have been used by Rembrandt.' He looked up from his hands, directly at Quinn. 'There was never any suggestion that I'd misled the Board, or had profited by the College's decision to purchase the work. I simply made an error in judgment.' Boothroyd's wife placed a comforting hand on his shoulder.

Quinn gathered her thoughts. 'Excuse me for asking, Professor Boothroyd, but how much of this was public information? It must have been rather embarrassing for you.'

'It would have been embarrassing, of course, if it had come out. But the College was in an awkward position as well. In the end it was decided to retain the work, but in storage. At a later date it will be reoffered for sale—but strictly as an unattributed work "in the style of," you understand.'

'Still, the damage has been done,' Quinn replied. 'The College paid more for the painting than it needed to. Some might say that your reputation, in fact your judgment, is now open to question. Put bluntly, if you can make an error in your own field of expertise, how can you be relied upon to preside over an entire college and what must be a sizeable budget? As I see it, if the error had been revealed during the search for Anscombe's successor, your chances might have been seriously harmed. You realise this is pertinent to our enquiries sir,' Quinn said. 'I have no choice but to pass it on to DI McDermott.'

The man looked at her closely for several moments. 'You must do what you must do, of course. But don't expect him to thank you for it.'

She knew he was right, and did not relish the prospect.

THIRTY ONE

At **Charing Cross** the interview began according to form. McDermott was not surprised to learn that immediately upon having been charged, Asquith had availed himself of the services of a solicitor. When he was brought to the interview room, she was already at his side, smartly but not elegantly dressed in a dark blue suit, and with a small notepad and an air of quiet competence about her. McDermott placed her in her late thirties. She was not unattractive. It crossed his mind that she probably knew Victoria. He decided to begin on a cordial note.

'Good afternoon. I take it you are representing Mr. Asquith. I'm DI McDermott. This is DS Ridley, Detective Constable Noakes, and PC Innes.' He indicated each person in turn.

'How do you do,' she said politely but without warmth. 'I am Deborah Manning. Before we begin, can you give me the particulars leading up to Mr. Asquith's arrest?'

McDermott and Ridley sat down at the interview table opposite Asquith and his solicitor, the others standing near the door. Then McDermott filled her in.

When he had concluded, the solicitor said, 'I see. And that's it, then?' managing to convey, in the time-honoured manner of her profession, the implication that her client had been detained upon the flimsiest of pretenses.

'That's it for the moment. We are collecting additional evidence. You will appreciate that the information leading to Mr. Asquith's arrest only came into our hands this morning.'

'Ah, yes. That would be the allegations of young DC Noakes here.'

McDermott recognised the defence counsellor's tactics for what they were, and move to head them off. 'The 'allegations,' as you refer to them, are the eyewitness observations of a veteran CID officer, conducted over a period of some hours, inside a well-lit public house, and supported by photographs taken at the time. I should hardly place them in the same category as the imaginative ramblings of an elderly lady without her spectacles on a dark night.'

Miss Manning was unfazed. 'No offense implied, Inspector. I only meant that well, if you'll pardon me saying so, it seems curious that, to use your own words, your man here observed these alleged transactions over a period of hours without making an arrest or calling for assistance. Rather curious procedure, don't you find?'

'No, I don't. Asquith was under observation as part of a larger investigation concerning the murder of one of his colleagues. Noakes was under orders to observe, but not to intercede without first checking with me. That is precisely what he did. But he also recorded the events on his mobile, and that evidence will be made available to you in the fullness of time.'

Manning's expression told him that this was news to her. But she recovered her composure quickly. 'Do you mind telling me where all this is going, then?'

'As I said, all in good time, Miss Manning. At the moment we're here to question your client. If you don't mind, we'll get down to it.' He walked over to the audio recorder and switched it on, adding the particulars regarding date and time, and the names of those present. Then he turned to Asquith. 'For the record, you are advised that anything you say will be taken down and may be used in evidence against you. Would you state your name and address, sir?'

'I am Jeremy Asquith, and I reside at St. Gregory's College, London.' Clearly, with the arrival of his lawyer his self-confidence had returned.

'Your occupation, sir?'

'When not being persecuted by the police, I am a Lecturer in Romance Languages at St. Gregory's College.'

'Just answer the questions, please,' McDermott said. 'Tell us where you were on October eleven, between the hours of seven and midnight.'

Asquith looked at his solicitor for direction, and she nodded. 'I returned to my rooms from the dining hall—it must have been around half six. Then I showered and changed and went out. I suppose it was well after seven by then.' He paused as if he expected that meagre amount of information would satisfy them.

'Out where, sir?'

'Out walking, at first. It was an unusually warm evening for this time of year. I decided to take advantage of it.'

'I see, sir. And what happened next?'

'I began to walk up Tavistock, when I remembered that a chap I'd run into a few days earlier had said he'd been in town until mid-week, and that if I was free I should join him for drinks at the Lord Palmerston that evening.'

McDermott smiled disarmingly. 'Go on, sir.'

Asquith removed an imaginary piece of lint from his trousers, and continued. 'I decided it was too far to walk, so I plumped for a taxi. I must have arrived there shortly before eight. I ordered a sherry and found myself a nook. When my friend appeared we had another drink or two. We chatted for a while and he left. I stayed for a bit longer, nursing my drink. During that time two or three other chaps whom I know slightly dropped by the table. I left shortly after eleven, picking up a taxi in Charing Cross Road—I remember because I was anxious to beat the theatre crowds. I went directly back to St. Gregory's. I didn't look at my watch, but it must have been well before midnight.'

'And then you went straight to bed and slept the sleep of the just?'

'That's uncalled for, Inspector,' Deborah Manning intervened. 'My client—'

'Your client has been leading us up the proverbial garden path, Miss Manning, *and* wasting police time. He turned back to Asquith. 'What was the name of this person you'd arranged to have drinks with?'

'I—I'm not sure. Raymond something. He was a casual acquaintance. I'm not good at last names.'

'Where did you know him from, then?'

'We met in a wine bar as I recall, some weeks back.'

'This wine bar—you wouldn't by any chance recall its name, would you?'

'No. Why should I? One identifies these places as much by their location as by their names.'

'But it is in London?'

'Of course,' Asquith answered confidently, apparently sensing the battle was going his way.

'I see. While out for a stroll you just happened to recall the plans made several weeks previously? And on the strength of that casual acquaintance you took a taxi halfway across London on the off chance he might have remembered as well? Sounds like something out of Noel-bloody-Coward.'

'Of course it sounds foolish if you put it like that. But if he hadn't shown, it would have made little difference—I'd just have had a drink or two and left.' Asquith looked up at McDermott as if daring him to disprove the reasonableness of the explanation he had just given.

This time McDermott decided to take the challenge. 'As it was, you stayed put and half of London unexpectedly came tripping over themselves to pay homage to you. These two or three other lads—by the way, which was it? Two or three?'

Asquith was wary. 'I'm not sure. It could have been either. I'd had several drinks by the end of the evening. I simply don't recall.'

'Very well, their names, then. Who were they?'

Asquith stared at McDermott defiantly. 'As I've said, I can't tell you.'

'You mean you *won't* tell us.'

Deborah Manning interrupted. 'Inspector, I really must object to my client being badgered in this manner. If you don't stop being abusive, I shall file a complaint with Standards and Practices.'

McDermott leaned across the table until he had her full attention, and then spoke softly. 'Miss Manning, I recognise that we both have our jobs to do. But so far your client here has been spinning tales that wouldn't make it past a kindergarten class. I suggest you remind him that this is a formal proceeding, and that making false statements to the police is a serious offense.' He turned back to Asquith. 'Now, then. You've just told us that you first met this gentleman in a wine bar in London, several weeks ago. Is that right?'

Asquith was more cautious, now, his voice more subdued as he sensed a trap. 'Yes.'

'Could you be more specific about the date? Would it have been as long as two months ago? Did you and this other gentleman both recall that you had agreed, as long as two months ago, to meet for drinks that particular evening?'

Asquith looked at McDermott defiantly. 'Of course not.'

'One month, then? Could it have been as long as four weeks ago?'

Asquith went sullen. 'No, I suppose not,'

'So it must have been in the past three weeks, is that right?'

'I suppose so. What bloody difference does it make—'

'Just this. According to travel receipts found in your rooms you were out of the country during that time. Can you tell us how you managed to be in London when your Eurail Pass indicates you were in France?'

Asquith went pale, and McDermott moved in for the kill. 'By the way, we turned up a sports bag in your rooms. Stuffed with clothing one wouldn't normally associate with you—rough trade, one might say. Care to comment?'

'Oh that. It was for a fancy dress party. Been so long ago I'd forgotten about it.'

'And you went all the way to the Continent to purchase it? You must really take your dressing-up seriously.'

Asquith managed a glare.

'I should mention that we're having the clothing and the sports bag tested for traces of drugs. It's funny how sometimes things simply fall into place.' When Asquith set his jaw in defiance McDermott spoke quietly and reassuringly. 'Look, lad, no one's going to bring out the thumbscrews—Miss Manning here will see to that. But we know you're hiding something, and we're fairly certain we know what it is. It will go a lot easier on you if you made a voluntary statement at this time.'

Asquith looked at his solicitor, who shook her head. 'I have nothing to say.'

'Very well,' McDermott sighed. He knew that time was often more effective than persistent questioning, and that a break in questioning sometimes resulted in a contradiction, or even a confession, when the interview resumed. 'Take him back to his cell. We will resume tomorrow at two.'

Deborah Manning looked mildly skeptical. 'Why the long break?'

'Because by then I expect to have the evidence I need to formally charge your client with at least one felony,' he replied.

WHEN SHE RETURNED TO CHARING CROSS POLICE STATION Quinn pealed off for the ladies' room. She had a lot to think about before confronting McDermott with the information she'd gleaned from visiting Boothroyd. It was obvious that her boss still harboured a strong affection for his former mentor, and she didn't relish being the one to break the news to him. Still, needs must, she told herself, and joined him in his office.

She found McDermott and Ridley in a confident mood. 'Unless I miss my guess, our Mr. Asquith will be in a more cooperative mood tomorrow,' McDermott said. He was sitting at his desk and scanning his email for messages.

Ridley was sitting nearby, glancing with distaste at an unappetizing layer of film in his coffee cup. Unsure of himself, Noakes had remained standing. He waited for some moments while McDermott massaged his eyes with the palms of his hands, then cleared his throat.

McDermott looked in his direction. 'Sorry. Did you want something, Noakes?'

'No sir. That is, will you be wanting me for anything else?'

'I don't think so. Good job this afternoon—you had him on the run, all right. Is your report on last night—'

'In your inbox, sir,' Noakes replied.

'In that case call it a day. What with last evening's work you've put in donkey's hours. But be here for half past one tomorrow—I want you on hand in case Asquith comes up with any other porkies.'

'Right, sir. I understand. See you tomorrow, sir.'

McDermott didn't bother replying. Noakes' obsequiousness was beginning to grate.

'Reckon if he keeps at it he'll make Commissioner?' Ridley asked as the door closed.

'I shouldn't be surprised, George. Why? Do you want the job?'

Ridley snorted derisively. 'Not half!'

Quinn decided her opportunity wasn't going to improve. 'sir, I have some new information for you.'

McDermott turned his gaze to face her directly. 'That's what we live on, Willie, information. What have you got for us?'

For the next twenty minutes she laid out what she had found in the College files, and the interview with Boothroyd and his wife. She watched as McDermott's enthusiasm turned to dismay, and then to something very much like despair. When she had finished he reflected on what he'd just heard.

'It could be nothing—or everything,' he said. 'It gives him a motive, of course, and his alibi for both deaths—his wife's claim that he was at home with her—is hardly worth taking into account.' He looked up from his reflections, first at Ridley and then at Quinn. 'But thank you, Willie, for going the extra mile. I'd rather get it right, even if Boots is involved. It can't have been easy, putting it to him like that, and then coming to me. But you did the right thing. Give me some time to mull things over, and we'll meet tomorrow to determine our next steps.'

AS HE BATTLED THE RUSH-HOUR TRAFFIC McDermott realised that despite the information they had collected, key questions remained unanswered. It was still possible, of course, that Burton-Strachey was their man—though the more he saw of him the less inclined he was to believe it. Then there was Jeremy Asquith. Was he the prime mover, the common denominator in all this? Had Sally Beck somehow known about his trafficking in drugs, and tried to blackmail him? Was that what had set the chain of events in motion? McDermott knew it was within the realm of possibility, and he wanted desperately to believe it—because if Asquith hadn't committed the murders, and Burton-Strachey hadn't, that left only Boots—the one person he'd hoped wasn't involved.

McDermott was interrupted in his reflections by a courier on a motor-cycle suddenly cutting in front of him from the wrong side. He gave the driver a two-fingered salute and concentrated on the road until he reached the comparative tranquility of his flat.

Twenty minutes later McDermott was enjoying a steaming hot bath with Ellis Marsalis playing in the background. His mind was wandering somewhere among the distant days of his youth in Ireland when a discordant note sounded, and he became aware that the telephone was ringing. He muttered as he rose from the tub and wrapped himself in an oversized towel. Still dripping wet, he entered the bedroom, feeling a draught and noticing with dismay that he had left the window ajar. 'Bloody Hell!' he said to no one in particular, and picked up the telephone. 'Yes. Hello? Oh, sorry, Dierdre—I was a million miles away. Any word from Pam? Did she—that is—was she open to meeting with you? Great! When? That's brilliant. No, that makes sense. Neutral ground. Yes, I drove up last evening—Meg was in shock, of course. How are you and Phillip holding up? I'll call her with the news. Yes, she'll be over the moon. Look, if you are up to company, I can drop by on the weekend. Right. Until then.'

McDermott replaced the telephone and sat on the bed, weighing his friends' grief against the many joys he had known with Megan. In his job he had witnessed no small amount of heartbreak, and he knew that but for a very few there was someone somewhere who would suffer, someone who would feel a loss, an emptiness that could not be filled, someone for whom the nights would always be a little longer. All things considered, the Townsends had been fortunate.

McDermott was still sitting on the side of the bed when the telephone rang a second time. The CD player had stopped, but he hadn't noticed. He picked up the receiver. 'McDermott. Oh, hi Meg. Yes, Dierdre just called a few minutes ago. Apparently Pam's contacted them. She wants to meet with them. No, a café, apparently. Yes, she just showed up at her partner's flat, nothing prearranged. Seems her partner was the voice of reason. Told Pam that was no way to leave things with her family. Yes, sounds pretty level-headed to me. Maybe there's hope. How about you? You're sure? Yes, I promised her I'd stop by this weekend. Apparently Phillip's blaming himself for what happened. The devil of it is he may be right. Look, this is costing you a small fortune. Right, then, I'll keep you posted. I love you too, Meg.'

Lost in thought, McDermott did not replace the receiver immediately. The recent developments at St. Gregory's had distracted him, mercifully, from the tragedy that had occurred closer to home; but Dierdre's call, followed by Meg's, had brought it all back to him. The happy moments, he reflected, were soon forgotten; the tragedies required years to work themselves out.

He was interrupted by the telephone once more. This time it emitted an irritating siren sound. He replaced the receiver on the hook.

For the rest of the evening McDermott went through the motions of fending for himself. He opened a tin of prepared soup and heated it, sliced off two thick pieces of bread to give it some substance. Then he went into the living room and washed down his meal, poor as it was, with a bottle of bitter. He tried watching television, but his mind wandered as he turned again to the Townsend's crisis, and then to the deaths of Sally Beck and Fraser Campbell.

And before long he fell asleep in his chair.

THIRTY TWO

T **he next morning** McDermott was jarred awake by the strains of *God Save the Queen* and the announcement that BBC Three was beginning its broadcast day. He sat there wool-gathering for several moments, the morning sunlight assaulting his eyes. When at last he tried to stir he was greeted by a sharp pain in his shoulder. As comfortable as his overstuffed chair was, he had remained for some time in an unaccustomed position, his head thrown back, his mouth agape, one arm over the side of the chair. Now, as he tried to move, it seemed to him that every fibre of his being was asserting its existence. His neck was stiff, and his entire right arm was numb to his fingertips. His mouth and throat were dry, his tongue was fuzzy, and as he tried to turn his head his temples throbbed insistently.

McDermott remained where he was for several moments, slowly moving each part of his body in turn, testing it, and gently restoring the circulation. It was, he reflected, a little like Tai Chi for the elderly.

When at last he rose from the chair McDermott discovered that his lower back and legs apparently had elected to remain where they were. He made his way gingerly to the bathroom, where he half-filled a tumbler with water and rummaged through the medicine cabinet for an analgesic. Not being a great believer in drugs, the only thing he could find was a nearly empty box of paracetamol tablets that, according to the label, had expired several months earlier. Mindful of Megan's recourse to painkillers he swallowed the two remaining pills anyway and contemplated whether it was wise to attempt shaving just yet. Deciding that it wasn't, he turned on the shower, and while the bathroom was heating from the steam he rummaged through his wardrobe to select some clothes. Today even that simple task seemed intimidating.

Emerging from the shower McDermott dressed with some difficulty. His fingers had decided that they had never seen a necktie before, and as he bent over to do up his shoelaces the throbbing in his head returned. He considered breakfast, but his stomach sent a clear message that such a move was ill advised. He settled for a peppermint tea.

Deciding that he could put off work no longer, McDermott realised that he was in no condition to contend with the Tube. He headed out to the street and flagged down a taxi.

WHEN MCDERMOTT ENTERED THE INCIDENT ROOM George Ridley looked up from his morning paper. 'Crikey, Guv. You look like summat cat dragged in.'

'Good morning to you too,' McDermott replied, tossing his coat on the back of a nearby chair, where it promptly slid on to the floor.

'Have a cuppa?' the older man asked, as McDermott retrieved the errant coat.

'Why not? It can't hurt—can it?' McDermott managed a smile.

'I'd a thought you'd nowhere to go but up, by the look o' things,' Ridley grinned, handing him a steaming mug. Had a bit of a knees up, last night, did we?

'As a matter of fact, I spent the night at home in front of the telly,' McDermott admitted testily. 'That's just the problem, if you must know.'

'Ah, well,' the Sergeant nodded sagaciously, obviously deriving great enjoyment from McDermott's condition, 'I've allus' said that nowt good comes o' watchin' telly.'

McDermott's sense of humour was rapidly ebbing in the face of George's apparent *bonhomie*. 'Anything new since last night?'

'Bit o' surprise there, Guv. I got on t' blower this mornin'. Principal of Askew's former school, in Bristol. Seems he left under a cloud after gettin' some wee lass up the spout.'

'Did he just? A man of many talents, our Mr. Asquith. Anything else?'

'Just that,' Ridley replied, pointing to a buff-coloured envelope on the corner of his desk.

McDermott put down the mug and reached for it, frowning as he did so. 'The Magistrate's Warrant. That's quick work—when did it come in?'

'Not five minutes 'afore you did. The Super brought it down. Asked for you personal-like—wanted t' know how things were comin' along.'

McDermott groaned. 'And you told him I was having a bit of a lie-in, I shouldn't wonder.'

Now it was the sergeant's turn to look martyred. 'I never did no such thing. Said you'd been up burnin' midnight oil on this 'un.'

'My apologies, George. This puts rather a new light on things. Do you think you can get this over to the bank and be back by eleven?'

Ridley looked mortally offended. 'Does a dog 'ave fleas?'

McDermott laughed. 'Sorry for doubting you. I'll move up the interview.' He looked around. 'Where's Quinn?'

'I've not seen hide nor hair of her.'

'Very well. You get over to the bank. I'll get on to Asquith's brief to let her know we've changed the time for our little chat.'

Deborah Manning was not best pleased when McDermott told her he was moving up the questioning of her client. She pointed out that she had other clients as well, and hinted darkly that unpleasant things would drop on McDermott from a great height if he began questioning Asquith before she arrived.

McDermott had just put down the telephone muttering to himself about women solicitors when Quinn burst in, hair askew and grease all over the front of her coat. 'Sorry, sir. I had a puncture on the way in this morning. Would you believe it? No one offered to stop and help. There must have been two dozen Beemers and Mercs, and even a Bentley passed by, and all without a by-your-bloody-leave. I ask you, what are British manners coming to?' She opened her bag and rummaged inside it for several moments. Apparently not finding what she was looking for, she took a paper napkin from where George had left it on the table and, wetting it with her mouth, tried in vain to remove some grease from her sleeve.

McDermott opened a desk drawer and extracted a small bottle of cleaning fluid. 'Here, try this.'

After several minutes of scrubbing, she sat down and sighed. 'It's no good—it's stuck fast. I only hope the cleaners can do something with it.'

'They can work miracles sometimes. I remember I spilled wine on a cricket sweater once—' He paused, lost in thought.

Quinn looked up. 'sir?'

'I've just had an idea. Nip over to Asquith's dry cleaners. See if they can recall ever having cleaned anything out of the ordinary for him. Out of *his* ordinary, that is—in the past three days. Be back for eleven. That's when we're questioning him. You can drop off your coat at the same time,' he added as an afterthought.

An hour later neither Ridley nor Quinn had reappeared. After the ragging he had taken from Deborah Manning, McDermott had no wish to compound the felony by rescheduling Asquith's interview a second time. Finally he decided he could delay no longer, and DC Noakes in tow he took the lift down to the detention cells.

When he emerged from the lift McDermott saw Deborah Manning in the corridor, talking with her client. He spoke to the custody officer, who directed him to a nearby interview room. As Manning and Asquith passed ahead of him through the doorway, McDermott glanced surreptitiously at his watch. It was quarter past eleven.

The room was somewhat larger than the one they'd used the previous afternoon, but furnished with CCTV cameras in opposite corners of the ceiling and the ubiquitous audio recorder on the table. Jeremy Asquith took one of the chairs on the side nearest the door. Deborah Manning sat down next to him. She proceeded to remove a file folder and a notebook from her attaché case. The officer who had escorted Asquith from his holding cell remained next to the door; Noakes elected to remain standing, and positioned himself behind McDermott.

After the necessary preliminaries Deborah Manning spoke first. 'Well, Inspector? Have you anything new for us today?'

McDermott took a chair facing Asquith and settled in. 'Yes, by all means. Did you have a good night's rest, Mr. Asquith?'

'Any chance of a fag?' he asked.

McDermott smiled in spite of himself. 'Actually, that raises an interesting point, Mr. Asquith. Unless I miss my guess, you've been running with the hares and hunting with the hounds. So why the clothes and mannerisms?'

Deborah Manning interrupted. 'What are you playing at, Inspector? Surely my client's personal preferences are not at issue. Unless I'm very much mistaken, one's personal...proclivities...are not at issue under the law.'

'No, that's all right—I'll answer the question,' Asquith replied laconically. 'Very adroit of you, Inspector. As it happens you're quite right about my behaviour being something of a pose. If you check into my background you'll find that I left my previous post after a student of mine had the bad sense to become pregnant. She miscarried, thank God, but in the wake of events it was considered—what's the phrase?—mutually beneficial that I seek a position elsewhere.'

'I don't understand, Mr. Asquith. Why the charade?'

Asquith's expression took on an uncharacteristic lassitude. 'Strictly speaking, Inspector, I am not gay, at least not exclusively. You might say that like the proverbial garden gate, I swing both ways. That is not, these days, a crime.'

McDermott was perplexed. 'So I repeat: why the charade?'

Asquith sighed, and McDermott thought it was perhaps the first time he'd seen the man express a genuine emotion. 'I am what is known in academic circles as a gypsy scholar,' he said cynically. 'During the past several years I have held four different positions—filling in for faculty on sabbatical, or being declared redundant due to budgetary restraints, or simply let go because my research did not show sufficient promise. I am under no illusions, Inspector. If I do not hold on to my present position I am unlikely to succeed in obtaining another post in the near future; and a degree in Romance Literature is hardly in demand in the outside world. It is much more difficult for the college to dismiss me if doing so appears to be a case of bias against someone with an unpopular sexual orientation.'

'So let me get this right. You *pretend* to be gay to make it more difficult for Anscombe to fire you?' he asked incredulously.

'Not pretend—I merely do not conceal my true sexual orientation. As I've explained, I am not gay, Inspector. I am "bi." Now, may we get on with things?'

McDermott studied the man for several moments. 'Very well, Mr. Asquith. Yesterday during formal questioning you were asked about your activities at the Lord Palmerston public house on Tuesday last. This morning I want to begin by asking you about your movements on the previous Tuesday—that would be October third. Do you recall that day?'

'More or less,' Asquith answered, the sullen glare returning.

'Well you might do, Mr. Asquith, for it was only the second day of term at St. Gregory's. Does that help?'

'I recall the day vividly, Inspector. It was a high point in my life—a moment that will live forever in my memory. Now will you get on with it?'

'All in good time, Mr. Asquith.' *Where the devil were Ridley and Quinn?* 'Would you please describe your movements on that day, beginning at, eleven in the morning?'

Asquith glanced at his solicitor. The tone of his voice, when he finally answered, was suddenly more subdued. 'I was...out of town.'

'Out of town. Could you be more specific, please?

Asquith stirred uneasily in his chair, and looked to his solicitor, who nodded. 'I was in France.'

Progress at last. 'Where, exactly?'

'Paris—and Marseilles.' The latter, McDermott knew, was well known as a major transit-point for drug trafficking.

McDermott pressed the point. 'Previously you told us that you were returning from the Lake District by rail.'

'I was supposed to be doing so. I had finished my research early, and decided to take a few days off before the start of term. Since the college had funded my research, I knew the Principal wouldn't have approved using the time for personal reasons, so I simply omitted mentioning it.'

'I see. And how long were you abroad?'

'I told you—a few days,' he replied guardedly.

'Have relatives there, do you?'

Asquith looked to his solicitor, who took her cue. 'Unless the law has changed without my noticing it, it is not a crime for a British subject to go abroad. You seem to be wasting both my client's time and my own. If your questioning has a point we'd all be very grateful if you would come to it.'

'Certainly, Miss Manning. In fact, I was just about to do so.' He turned toward Asquith again. 'In your statement given at St. Gregory's College on, let me see, October sixth, you indicated that you were on the train from Carlisle during the morning of the third.'

'I have already explained that, Inspector. As you yourself have shown, I was on my way back from France. What possible difference does it make where I was returning *from?*' he asked, exasperated.

'Just that if you'd been on the train, your alibi for the death of Sally Beck would have been unshakeable, since she died slightly before one PM and the train did not arrive at Euston Station until well after two. But the ferries begin arriving at Dover at around quarter to five each morning. So you must be considered a suspect in the death of Sally Beck.'

'You're mad! I didn't even know the bloody woman, much less kill her. This is really too much.' He turned to his solicitor. 'Do I have to sit here and listen to this rubbish?'

Deborah Manning spoke calmly. 'I trust you have more to base your accusation on than merely my client's being in London, along with perhaps eight million other people, at the time of the Beck woman's death?'

'I will be coming to that directly, Miss Manning. At the moment I want to focus—' His words were cut short as Wilhemina Quinn burst into the room.

'Sorry, sir. Am I interrupting?'

'Not at all,' McDermott said. 'Miss Manning, I believe you know DC Quinn?'

'We've met,' she said perfunctorily. 'You were about to tell us why my client is suspected in the death of the Beck woman, I believe?'

'All in good time, Miss Manning. However just at the moment I want to speak privately with Quinn here. 'Interview suspended at'—he consulted his watch—'11:36. We will return shortly.' Taking her by the arm, McDermott made his exit, ignoring Manning's glare.

In the corridor, McDermott expressed his relief. 'Thank God. I was beginning to wonder—' Something about her expression warned him that all was not well. 'You did get to the cleaners?'

'Yes, sir, Nice-N-Brite in Gower Street, just as you asked.'

'Well? What did you find?'

'Nothing helpful, I'm afraid, sir. He's always had his clothes picked up and returned to the college, and no one can remember ever seeing anything out of the ordinary from him—nothing like the gear in the sports bag. Everything was linen or silk or leather. I showed them a list of the fibre samples from Campbell's rooms. They're certain he's never brought in anything like them.'

'That's torn it, then. The best we can hope for is something on the drugs charge, and George has dis—' He stopped in mid-sentence as he recognised the sergeant lumbering down the passageway. *Not before time.* 'George, you're a sight for sore eyes. Tell me you have something. I could use some joy about now,' he said, lowering his voice to a whisper.

'Oh, aye. Summat middlin' fair, I reckon,' Ridley replied enigmatically.

'What is this—a conspiracy? Spit it out, man.'

'Just this.' He produced several large brown manila envelopes he had been carrying by his side. He tore the end off of one and tilted it toward his other hand. Out poured half a dozen banded packets of fifty-pound notes, one spilling onto the floor. He bent over and picked it up. 'Now, then, I reckon tha's what yer lookin' for?'

McDermott whistled softly. 'There must be a small fortune here. Taking the opened envelope from George's grasp and handing her the others he said, 'Willie, take these to Forensics immediately; if it's drug money—and I'm betting it is—there'll be traces on it. I want a full report—this afternoon if possible. George, come with me.' As he turned McDermott totally missed the fury on Quinn's face.

McDermott entered the room a moment later, Ridley following close behind.

Deborah Manning was incensed. 'Look here, Inspector: my time is extremely valuable. I demand that you charge my client here and now or release him.'

'As you wish, Miss Manning.' Reaching across the table he switched on the recorder. 'Resuming the interview of Jeremy Asquith, at 11:45. DS Ridley is present, DC Quinn has left the room.'

In the moment it took him to turn and face Asquith his expression became grim and his voice stern. He reached into an envelope and tossed a packet of bank notes on to the table. 'Mr. Asquith, these is from your safety-deposit box in the Gower Street branch of the Merchants Trust—one of many such packets, I might add. Can you tell us how you came to be in possession of such a substantial sum of money?'

Asquith had gone a deathly pale, and his solicitor intervened. 'I assume you have a warrant.'

'Quite right, Miss Manning. And I should imagine that the amount of currency we found rather exceeds your client's earnings as a junior lecturer.' He turned to face the man directly. 'I'm betting that the records of your access to your safety deposit box correspond closely with your visits abroad, Mr. Asquith. A matter of some interest, I should think, to Her Majesty's Revenue and Customs. Who knows? Perhaps they'll decide that an audit is in order. Oh, and you should know that the money found in your box is, as we speak, being tested for traces of illicit drugs.'

The expression on Deborah Manning's face spoke far more eloquently than anything Asquith might have said. 'It would seem my client has not been entirely forthcoming with me, Inspector. If you'll allow us to speak privately for a moment, perhaps we can come to a mutually acceptable arrangement.'

McDermott snorted. 'That's between you and the Crown Prosecutor's Office, Miss Manning.' He turned again to face Asquith, whose expression spoke volumes.

'Jeremy Asquith, I am charging you with suspicion of smuggling, suspicion of possession of a type A substance for the purpose of trafficking, and obstructing the police in the course of their enquiries. Tomorrow you will be brought before a magistrate and remanded for trial. The Court will consider an application for bail, but given the nature of the charges the Public Prosecutor will probably oppose it. Do you have anything further to say at this time?'

'Get knotted!' Asquith glowered vehemently, summoning up the last measure of defiance at his disposal.

THIRTY THREE

Back in the incident room McDermott sat down at his desk and pondered the situation.

'Took a bit o' chance back there, I reckon,' Ridley observed.

'Not so much as you might think,' McDermott replied. 'If you have legitimate money you put it into a building society, or some other account where it will earn interest. That means bank records, with copies to HMRC. No, when that much money, over an extended period, is involved, odds are that it's queer.' He smiled at the unintentional pun. 'No, mark my words: Asquith will cough in time. The question is, how does all this tie in with the Beck girl's death?'

'Maybe it don't,' the older man ventured.

'That's your Yorkshire optimism coming to the fore again, George. No, it must do. The question is how. Of course it's possible that—' he stopped as the door opened and Quinn returned.

'*Sir*,' she said tersely, taking a chair and glaring at him.

McDermott could not ignore her anger. 'Something bothering you, Quinn?'

'Yes, sir, now that you ask. I asked to be assigned to you to learn the ropes. Any green PC—or for that matter a filing clerk—could have delivered that evidence to the lab. As it was I missed the opportunity to observe a crucial interview.'

McDermott blanched. 'Of course. Stupid of me. I'm sorry, Willie. I was distracted in there. Anyway, it was entirely my fault. I apologise. Next time you'll be front and centre.'

Quinn had steeled herself for a denial, or even a dismissal of her concerns. She was not prepared for McDermott's acquiescence. She lowered her voice. 'Of course, sir. I'm sorry I made such an issue of it. It's just that—'

'No, you were right to do so. Consider the matter closed.'

Quinn turned away, torn between contrition and outrage at the apparent ease with which he had apologised. She had nurtured a seething anger, only to have the cause of that anger dissolve almost immediately before her eyes. Unable to decide whether she had been vindicated or merely fobbed off, she turned to the issue at hand. 'Oh, I almost forgot. The lab did a quick preliminary check of the bank notes while I waited. Traces of cocaine, all right, diluted for street use. The full results should be on your desk by this afternoon.'

McDermott sat up in his chair. 'Now that is good news. It seems our Mr. Asquith is rapidly becoming the odds-on favourite for the Campbell and Beck murders.'

'Excuse me, sir, but how do we have him for the murders?' Quinn asked.

During the next several minutes McDermott laid out his scenario to Ridley and Quinn. It was, he explained, likely that Asquith had dealings with many Londoners. In the course of her life on the edge of the underworld, Sally Beck might have come to learn of those dealings. She would have recognised Asquith on arriving at St. Gregory's, and perhaps tried to blackmail him with that knowledge. Asquith would have realised her presence at St. Gregory's could not be tolerated: she had attempted to blackmail him. So when he found an opportunity he pushed her into the path of the bus. When Campbell had cottoned on to his involvement—McDermott wasn't yet certain how this occurred—he killed Campbell and planted the note on his body, hoping the police would read it as a suicide and end the investigation there.

Although Ridley accepted this explanation, McDermott noticed that Quinn was skeptical. 'Something's still bothering you, Willie. What is it?'

'I'm not certain, sir. Is what we've got enough to convince a jury?'

'That's for the DPP to worry about. I'm certain he's our man.'

'It's just that we don't have anything really linking them. That is, neither Asquith and the Beck woman nor Asquith and Campbell.'

'Well, we certainly have to tie up the loose ends,' McDermott conceded. 'But that's foot-slogging stuff—checking out Sally Beck's mates, showing them Asquith's photo—mark my words, someone will recognise him.'

But even as he uttered the words, the seeds of doubt had already been sown in McDermott's mind.

THE REST OF THE DAY passed uneventfully. George Ridley laboured at a computer, preparing his statement of how the safety deposit box key was found and the subsequent discovery of the money, and naming the bank manager as a witness. McDermott waited until he received the lab report and then informed Galbraith of Asquith's arrest on drugs charges. The Superintendent was pleased with the progress he had made, and promised to pass the information on to Interpol for followup on the Continent.

Burton-Strachey had posted bail and was released pending arraignment on the charges of breach of trust; he returned home to his wife, who took full advantage of the fact that she now held the upper hand. Not far away, Norman Anscombe uttered a small prayer of thanksgiving that life finally appeared to be returning to normal at St. Gregory's. By late afternoon Ridley was ready to call it quits, and everyone agreed that, all in all, it had been, in his words, 'a right champion day's work.'

As McDermott entered the parking garage he recalled with dismay that he'd left his car at home. He was walking up the ramp to find a taxi when a horn sounded behind him. He turned, prepared to give the driver a scowl, and recognized Willie Quinn behind the wheel of a red Mini Cooper. 'Want a lift, sir?'

He recalled he still had some fence-mending to do there. 'Thanks,' he replied gratefully. 'It looks as though it might rain.'

McDermott guided her up the A400 into Camden Town, into the warren of streets that comprised Little Venice. As they turned on to Warrington Crescent he gestured with his hand. 'That's it halfway down—next to the letter box.' A delivery van parked in front pulled away from the kerb as they neared the address and Quinn executed a neat u-turn into the vacant space.

'Very posh, sir,' Quinn said as she took in the white Portland stone and portico graced by Doric columns on either side.

'It's conveniently located.' McDermott looked at his watch. 'It's early yet, and the traffic will take a while to thin out. We have time for a drink.'

Quinn hesitated, torn between her desire to avoid sending the wrong signals and wanting to get to know her boss better. She was still feeling a bit guilty about her earlier outburst, even though she reckoned she'd been in the right. McDermott read her thoughts. 'Come on, Willie. What's past is past. If we're to work together we should get to know one another better. I promise not to bite.'

Inside the flat McDermott took her coat and pointed to the sitting room, then offered her a drink.

'Thanks. I'll have a single malt, if it's on offer.'

'Great minds.' McDermott removed a bottle of Glenrothes and two glasses from the teak drinks cabinet.

Quinn surveyed the room and took an easy chair next to what seemed to be a functional fireplace. 'You have a lovely place here, sir, if you don't mind my saying so. I'd no idea Inspectors were so flash.'

'Please, it's 'Colin' off the job. Yes, it is nice. I've been fortunate, in many ways. My wife and I stumbled on the leasehold just as it was coming on the market. The previous tenant was a banker. He'd just been transferred to Kuwait, and was anxious to move.' He handed her a drink, and poured one for himself.

Quinn sipped at her drink and looked about the room, her eye finally resting on the table beside her where a framed photograph of a woman and child was displayed. 'Is that your wife?'

McDermott paused, and took a deep breath. 'Was. She was killed in 2005. The terrorist bus bombing in Tavistock Square.' Although his tone was casual, his expression suggested it had happened yesterday.

She turned scarlett. 'Oh, how horrible! I'm sorry!'

'It sounds terrible to say so, but it's getting better with time. We had— have—a lovely daughter,' he said, pointing to a more recent photograph.

'She's beautiful. Is she still at home, then?'

'She's at Oxford, reading politics.' His pride was evident.

Quinn experienced a brief pang of envy. Coming from a family of modest means it had been all her parents could do to send her to a grammar school of moderate reputation. She had made the most of it, reading eagerly and absorbing quickly the best of what her teachers had to offer. But there had been no question of going on to university, even with a partial scholarship. She'd been angry at first, frustrated that she could not indulge her natural curiosity and sharpen her obvious skills; but over the years her anger had given way to mere regret. Her own experience, she reflected, had given her an insight into what motivated the Sally Becks of the world to take desperate measures to escape their circumstances. Britain was still a long way from a classless society.

McDermott settled into a matching chair on the other side of the fireplace. 'What about you? Don't tell me you're married to the job already?'

She laughed. 'Not quite sir—Colin!' She paused before continuing. 'Actually, I'm a single mum, divorced. My son, Jason recently turned four. You know the age: into absolutely everything and always asking "why." A neighbour lady looks after him during the day, and we try to spend time with his grandparents on the weekends. Things will be simpler next year, when he begins school.'

'It can't be easy,' McDermott reflected. 'Ignore me if I'm being nosy, but what about the father? Does he help?'

Again Quinn coloured briefly, obviously ill at ease. McDermott was just about to change the topic when she spoke. 'Mick and I parted ways because he always seemed to have his an eye on the main chance. When he became involved in something I was uncomfortable with, I told him it was either his dodgy friends or me. He chose his friends. I should have known better,' she said, unable to keep the bitterness out of her voice.

McDermott shifted in his chair. 'I'm sorry. Don't be too hard on yourself. Our job carries its share of burdens. But it sounds as though you made the right choice.'

Quinn reflected on his words. It hadn't been a choice, not really: given her work, it would have been only a matter of time before Mick ran afoul of the law, and then her life would have been even more difficult. The wrong choice and her career would have been in jeopardy—perhaps even at an end. And then there was the matter of Mick's influence on their son. Only a matter of time before a boy begins to emulate his father. It had been a turning point, certainly, but one she had ceased to regret.

Bringing herself back to the present, Quinn was drawn to the bookshelves on either side of the fireplace. Scanning the titles, she was impressed by the breadth of McDermott's interests. There were books on Eastern religions and Western art, ancient philosophy and contemporary physics, Irish poetry and Scottish history. Her eye rested on a small paperback titled *Boundaries of the Mind: cartography and the way we think, by Colin McDermott*. She picked it up and read the flyleaf. 'But this is you!' she said.

He laughed. 'Don't be so surprised, Willie. It's one of the small perks accorded authors that they can display their vanity in their own homes.'

Quinn reddened. 'I didn't mean it like that, sir. I only meant—well, it seems rather an improbable subject, doesn't it?'

'Not so improbable as one might think,' he replied, settling back in his chair. 'For most people maps are simply a guide for getting from one place to another. But they're also interesting for what they reveal about how people view their world, and they contain a wealth of information about the way people think about themselves. For example, an egocentric empire—think f the Romans— will unfailingly place itself at the centre of its maps, relegating other nations—even those more developed—to the hinterlands. And the myriad of little beasties that decorate the edges of early maps—in part they're a reflection of peoples' fear of the unknown, of *terre incognitæ*.'

'That's very interesting,' Quinn said, in an abortive attempt to stifle a yawn.

'Sorry. It's a passion of mine, as you can see. I sometimes forget it's not everyone's idea of a riveting subject.'

'That's all right. My mum collects salt and pepper sets.'

He laughed. 'Right, Willie, you put me in my place. So what about you? Your parents are still alive, I take it.'

'My folks live in Torquay. Dad's retired. He worked on the docks at Southampton for forty years. My mum has always been a homebody. Since he took his pension he drives her batty around the house.'

McDermott looked at her through his glass. 'Any brothers or sisters?'

Quinn coloured. 'Just one brother. Three years my junior. He was a bit wild as a kid. Nothing serious, really, but it almost kept me off the force. We haven't heard from him in years.'

McDermott frowned. 'That's a shame. Family is important.'

'And you? Any siblings lurking in the cupboard?'

He grinned. 'Two, actually. Older sister, younger brother. Both in Ireland, where we lived when I was a lad. Niamh is a crofter and a vet. She's got two strapping children and a husband who designs bespoke computer software and sells it to clients around the world, if you can believe it.'

Quinn noticed that he'd made only passing mention of his brother. His own black sheep? She decided the question could wait for another time.

McDermott drained his glass and rose to refresh it. Quinn's, he noticed, was still nearly half full. 'So how are things working out with George?'

The question took her by surprise. 'Well, I suppose. He takes a bit of getting used to, but I don't think he has it in for me.'

McDermott shook his head. 'Not a malevolent bone in George's body—not that I've seen, anyway. Despite appearances, he's not a misogynist. He's simply rather uncomfortable when he's around the fairer sex.'

'Is that a misogynist term, Inspector?' she asked, her eyes laughing.

McDermott found himself staring at those eyes. They were clear and pale blue, and full of intelligence as well as humour. A face far too easy to like. He pulled himself back to reality and looked at her glass, which was by now down a quarter. 'Shall I freshen that for you?'

'No thanks,' she said, rising. 'Remember, I'm driving. I should be off.'

As he collected her coat and saw her to the door she looked once more around the flat. 'I must say, it's very well kept for a single man. Do you have someone come in and do for you?'

He laughed. 'I wish. My daughter's always after me to get a housekeeper, but I've never got round to it. When it gets too bad I call in a neighbour woman who can use the money.'

'Well, then, you do very well—for a man, I mean,' she teased.

A few moments later Quinn slipped behind the wheel of her car. 'See you Monday.' He waved as she pulled away from the kerb. *Not bad*, she reflected. *Actually, rather dishy.* But relationships with senior officers, she knew, could end a career, and it was always the woman who got the short end. She focussed on her driving; it wouldn't do to get pulled over.

THIRTY FOUR

Sunday morning came, and after a light breakfast McDermott set out for the Townsends.

Dierdre answered the door when he arrived. Her face wore the care of recent events, though she brightened when she saw who it was. 'McDermott, good of you to come. Come on through, we're just having our morning coffee. Can I get you one?'

'Sounds good.' He passed along the hallway and into the kitchen where, he knew, much of their domestic life took place.

Phillip was at the breakfast table, still in his pajamas and bathrobe. 'Hullo, McDermott,' he said, glancing up from the newspaper. Although he hadn't yet shaved, he seemed marginally more, what? —*collected*, maybe that was it—than on McDermott's previous visit.

She placed a cup of coffee on the table. 'There you are, Colin. Have a seat. Are you up for breakfast?'

'Thanks, but I've already eaten,' he said.' He decided to wade in directly. 'Is Pam here?'

Dierdre joined them at the table. 'You just missed her, I'm afraid. She's out at the chemist's. Woke up with a migraine. Said she needed some painkillers for the stress of the past few weeks. Under the circumstances we agreed.'

McDermott was reminded of Megan's recourse to tranquilizers, and held his tongue. It was a quick fix, to be sure, but perhaps under the circumstances, the lesser of the evils. Nonetheless, they'd have to talk again.

He turned to her husband. 'And how are you, Phillip? Need I ask?'

'I've had better weeks, obviously. We both have.' He looked up. 'This is my doing, of course. I see that now.' The man's misery—the grief and the guilt—were unmistakable.

'Hindsight is 20/20, isn't it? I don't know what I'd have done in your position. Perhaps the same; maybe not. Likely no better.'

'Cold comfort, if you don't mind my saying so. I've made a real meal of it, haven't I?'

'No more so than many parents would have done in your place. That's the rub, isn't it? We can't live our kid's lives for them. They have to make their own way, themselves.'

'God knows I'm not yet an old man, not one of those pathetic blokes who sits on park benches all day and who have given up on making sense of things and are content just to watch the world go by. But I swear I don't understand all the changes in young people's lifestyles: tattoos, piercings, drugs, riots...'

'Come on, Phillip. Sure, young people's behaviour may be changing, but you and I—everyone—is a product of their upbringing. Things were different, simpler, when you and I were growing up. Our kids live in a different world, one of mobiles and texting and social media and clubs, and yes, what not so long ago would have been termed deviant behaviour. You reacted as most of our generation would have done. The important thing is what you do from here on in. You've got a chance to set things right.' He paused. 'Not everyone gets that opportunity.'

Townsend shuddered, then took a sip of the steaming liquid. 'So what do I do now?'

'I think you know the answer to that, Phillip. You take her back on her own terms. This isn't about winning and losing; it's about family, and caring. Who was it said love must be unconditional?'

Philip snorted. 'Some bloody Hollywood screenwriter, I'll wager.'

McDermott shifted his gaze to Dierdre. She smiled. The stress was unmistakable, but he thought he detected some small measure of relief. 'You know, when we went to the cafe Pam's partner was there. Did I mention that she's training as a doctor? It was actually reassuring to meet her. She's an intelligent and caring person. Isn't that right, Philip?'

Townsend's expression softened. 'Actually, she seemed nice enough. Not what I'd imagined. We've invited her—them—over for dinner tonight.'

Small steps, thought McDermott. But necessary all the same.

Dierdre interrupted his thoughts. 'How is Megan doing? Did you give her the news?'

'As you might expect, she was devastated at first. She wanted to visit Pam right away. I urged her to wait a bit, and she saw the sense in that. But once things have settled down I'm sure wild horses won't keep her away. Just let me know when.'

Philip glanced out the kitchen window, his eyes lingering on McDermott's Morgan. 'I see you still have the old banger. How is she treating you?'

McDermott smiled. 'Better than you are, you old git. I don't take her out much these days, although I did have occasion a few nights ago, when I took Daphne to the Albert Hall.'

'Daphne?' Pam raided an interrogative eyebrow. 'I thought you were seeing a woman named Victoria?'

'"Was" is the operative word, 'McDermott said, spreading his hands. 'We decided to part company for awhile.'

Pam sipped at her cup pensively. 'And this Daphne. How did you meet her?'

McDermott looked away. 'Actually, we're colleagues of a sort. She's a Home Office pathologist.'

Pam laughed. 'Good god, Colin! Can't you ever leave your work at the office?'

He looked over to Philip for help, but he was clearly enjoying himself. Mustering what passed for mild indignation he said 'And what makes you think we discuss work – all the time, I mean?'

'If you say so.' But she looked unconvinced.

Later, as he drove home, McDermott considered their conversation. Had he been too hard on Philip? He decided he hadn't. With some people it took plain talk to make an impression. Didn't mean that they were thick, or uncaring, just that you had to get past whatever was dominating their thoughts and influencing their judgments. It seemed to him that Philip was coming around.

WHEN MCDERMOTT ARRIVED AT THE STATION the next morning he outlined to Ridley and Quinn his plan to link Asquith to Sally Beck. Conducting a house-to-house enquiry in the area of Sally Beck's flat in the East End would, he knew, be a formidable task, involving dozens of officers interviewing hundreds of shopkeepers and neighbourhood residents. George offered to contact Vice to see if Asquith's face was known to them. McDermott agreed, and suggested asking them to use their contacts on the street as well. It was getting on noon, and they were just finalising their plans when the telephone rang. Ridley, who was closest, picked up.

'Aye? Aye—nowt strange about that. Never. Go on—pull the other 'un. Right, I'll tell the Guv. Ta. Cheers, mate.'

He turned to face McDermott and Quinn. 'That were Noakes. Seems our lad's lawyer's been right busy. She spent two hours wi' Askew after we left. The short of it is our lad Askew's remembered a bloke who'll swear he came over on the *noon* ferry with him. No way he could'a made it t'city by time Beck girl died.'

McDermott was frustrated. Could he have got it wrong? He felt like a five year old who'd just been told Father Christmas didn't exist. 'That tears it. We'll have to vet the fellow, of course, but if his alibi stands up then our— *my*—theory isn't worth bugger all.'

For several moments the group resembled less an assembly of CID officers than it did a wake. Finally Quinn spoke up. 'Look, sir, we knew it was just a theory at this point—one amongst others. What was it you told me yesterday? "Interpretation is a matter of perspective." If this witness is telling the truth—and I say *if*—then we'll simply have to go back and take a harder look at the others.'

'You're right, of course. I'll put everything on hold. George, I want you to check out this so-called witness. Run his name through the CRO; maybe we have something on him. Then get on to the Passport Office—and SeaLink if necessary—to confirm he was on that ferry. While you're at it, check his own passport for suspicious trips abroad. We can't rule out the possibility that one of Asquith's trafficking friends is going to bat for him.'

'And me, sir?' Quinn asked.

'Willie, you get the brass ring. If Asquith's alibi checks out, I want you to focus on Boothroyd. Your objective will be to establish a connection between him and the Beck woman, or to break down his alibi for either death. And for good measure check out his personnel file. Given my former relationship with him, there must be no room at all for any appearance of favouritism.'

Quinn looked distinctly uncomfortable. Although she had known it could come to this, she didn't relish the task of telling McDermott that his former mentor and friend might be a cold-blooded killer.

In the silence that followed Ridley asked, 'How 'bout you, Guv?'

'Me? I'm going for a walk. By tonight either we'll be ready to move on or I'll ask Galbraith to give this case to someone else.' He stood up and reached for his coat.

As he closed the door behind him, Quinn and Ridley looked at each other in shock and dismay. 'Have you ever seen him like this, George?' she asked.

'Only every time we worked a case.'

MCDERMOTT WAS DEPRESSED. He was acutely aware that all of his theories had come up blank. He realised that he'd been fighting this case all along, refusing to follow the most obvious line of enquiry, one that anyone else in his position would not have hesitated to pursue. It made him angry and ashamed. He considered talking with Derek Galbraith, but to go to him at this point in the investigation would be to admit defeat.

He punched the button for the lift impatiently, and before it arrived decided to take the stairs. Exiting at the ground floor he crossed the lobby, oblivious to the greetings of his colleagues, and turned toward the Strand.

It had rained earlier that morning, and the pavement was still damp as tiny droplets of mist hung in the air. McDermott pulled on his coat and followed the labyrinth of back streets that led to the Victoria Embankment Gardens. He entered by the nearest path, and as he walked, he began slowly and painfully to sort out his thoughts.

As he passed by the statue of Robert Burns McDermott noticed the many species of small birds and waterfowl that comingled peacefully. A family of sparrows jostled amicably with several wood ducks and some finches for some grain that an unknown benefactor had sprinkled along the path. In the centre of the melee a pair of elegant Canada Geese surveyed this unseemly chaos with evident disdain. Above the trees McDermott could just make out the London Eye against an ominous sky.

He walked by an elderly lady sharing some crusts of bread with some avaricious pigeons, gave way to a pair of joggers, and continued on past a man who sat on a bench muttering to himself, haranguing passersby for no apparent reason. The sight of two young men walking hand in hand brought McDermott's thoughts back to the Townsends. The irony of their family crisis had not escaped him: the fact that Pamela had chosen to go public with her lifestyle—a very contemporary approach—played against her father's rather Victorian sense of embarrassment, and had resulted in a conflict that had overtaken them all. His mind was drawn back to the play he had attended with Victoria: the Greeks had not balked at attributing masculine traits to their heroines, nor feminine traits to their heroes. The Mitylene poets, he recalled from somewhere, had even idealised love within the gender. Was this a mark of progress, he wondered, that we have lost sight of the deeper relations that two people, regardless of gender, can experience? What was so unthinkable about her choice of a partner that had split the Townsends apart? Who was it had said recently, *More things in heaven and earth?*

McDermott forced himself to focus on the matter at hand. It was the loose ends in this case that bothered him: the handbag that had proved so elusive, the fact that several suspects had no really firm alibis. Of them all, Asquith, he knew, was the most likely suspect—the person with the most to lose were the truth to come out. What was it Soames had called him? *The poor man's Oscar Wilde.* But Burton-Strachey could have killed Sally Beck, even in the limited time allotted him—indeed, Griffith-Jones, as implausible as he was, might have engineered the telephone call to his sister precisely to supply himself with an alibi. They only had his word for it that his medication had been stolen. Most vexing of all, McDermott realised, were the doubts he had shoved to the back of his mind concerning Boothroyd; for he knew he hadn't given his old friend the close scrutiny he would have accorded any other suspect in similar circumstances.

McDermott thought back to his conversation with Wilhemina Quinn the previous evening, and their discussion about maps and conceptual frameworks. This case was just a matter of looking at the facts from a fresh perspective: given the correct point of view the pieces would fall into place and everything would make sense.

As he sauntered along the glistening pavement an idea struck him, and he wondered how he'd failed to notice it before.

McDermott stopped in the middle of the path, working out the implications of his thoughts. Sometime during his ruminations the skies had opened up. What had begun as a gentle rain had gradually increased to a steady downpour; but McDermott was oblivious to its effects as he grappled with the germ of an idea. The few persons who still remained in the park were scurrying for cover, and gave little thought to this solitary individual who had neither hat nor umbrella, and who was apparently unconcerned about becoming soaked to the skin. Already the rain had taken the crease out of his trousers, and his hair had been blown askew by the wind. To anyone used to judging by appearances, McDermott was looking somewhere between disreputable and suspicious.

As luck would have it, two Parks Officers who had been patrolling on foot and had taken shelter under the eaves of a nearby café had been watching him with interest. 'What do you think?' asked one.

'Hard to say. He doesn't look a vagrant.'

'Maybe he's mental. He doesn't seem to notice the rain.'

'I don't much fancy leaving cover to find out,' said the first man.

'Well, if we're going, let's hop it, before we get even more soaked.'

The sight of two uniformed officers running toward him in the rain brought McDermott out of his castle-building. He looked up just as they arrived. 'I've been a fool. It was right in front of me all the time!'

'Now then, what's that, sir?' one of the constables asked.

'The answer, of course. Right there—all the time.'

The officer was torn between humouring the man and getting on with it. One thing was certain: policy directives about being polite to the public notwithstanding, he didn't take kindly to standing in the rain with a raving lunatic. 'Now then, sir. Can you tell us where you live? We'll see that you get home.'

McDermott brushed his arm off impatiently. 'Do I look like I'm gaga?'

'Not for me to say, sir. Now if you'll just tell us your name—'

'My name?' McDermott temper rose at the apparent obtuseness of the man facing him. 'I'll tell you my bloody name!'

The officers' attitudes changed dramatically when McDermott produced his warrant card, and they attempted to minimise the damage by apologizing profusely and retreating as hastily as possible. McDermott reached into his jacket pocket and withdrew his mobile, punching the buttons like a man possessed.

'Is that you, Quinn?' McDermott yelled, one hand over his free ear, the rain almost drowning him out. 'Yes, it's me. Is George back yet? No, we haven't time—I've been a bloody fool. Listen, here's what I want you to do...'

A few minutes later the officers watched from underneath a tree in disbelief as an unmarked area car going against the traffic with two PCs in front and a woman in plainclothes in the rear seat pulled up sharply at the kerb on Villiers Street. McDermott had by then calmed down considerably, although in the judgment of the constables he was still highly agitated. He entered the car, which executed a three-point turn and sped off in the direction of the Strand. The two officers watched the car disappear in the rain, and looked at each other. 'If that's what it's like in the CID, I'll stick to patrolling the parks, thank you,' one said, shaking his head.

'Too bloody right,' echoed the other.

WHEN THEY ARRIVED AT ST. GREGORY's McDermott ordered the uniformed officers to remain in the car and made directly for one of the faculty offices. Finding it locked he checked his watch, and deciding that the Principal and Fellows were still at lunch, proceeded toward the Dining Hall. Then, thinking better of it, he changed direction and headed for the Principal's office. As he expected, Mrs. Coates was at her desk, and upon McDermott's urging was persuaded to call the kitchen and have a message conveyed to Anscombe that his presence was required. She did so reluctantly, making little effort to conceal her view that things had come to a fine state when the tail was wagging the dog. The Principal arrived shortly, and not a little put out. 'What's the meaning of this, Inspector? I hope you have good and sufficient reasons for throwing the college into disarray,' his look implying that the state of his stomach and the welfare of St. Gregory's were intimately related.

'The very best, sir,' McDermott reassured him. 'I would like to examine the personnel files of several of the faculty, please.'

Anscombe's face fell. 'Are you telling me that you're about to arrest yet another of the Fellows? Good God, man. What do you think we're running here – Murder Incorporated?'

'Nothing so dramatic, Principal. I merely need to confirm one or two facts before I proceed further.'

Anscombe sighed. 'Very well. I can arrange for you to examine their file, if you'll just let me know who it is.'

McDermott shook his head. 'I'm afraid that's not possible at this time, sir.'

'Not possible? Why ever not?'

'I'm afraid not, Principal. First, it's only a suspicion. And if I were to give you a name, and there was something to it, and you encountered that person before I did—well, I'm sure you see how it is. The best thing would be to bring us the files of all of the Fellows that Sheila Bannerman had classes with.'

By now Norman Anscombe only wanted to be rid of the man whose sole mission in life apparently was to bring about the destruction of his very own *alma mater*. 'Very well. I'll have Mrs. Coates bring you the files. But I must insist they do not leave this office. You can look at them over there.' He motioned perfunctorily to a nearby table. 'These are confidential files. If you need to take them away, I insist that you get a court order,' he added in a transparent attempt to reassert his authority.

When Mrs. Coates arrived with the pile of documents, her expression spoke volumes. She looked at Anscombe pleadingly, as if hoping that he would at the last moment withdraw his permission to examine the records that she clearly regarded as her own special domain. But he said nothing.

As Anscombe and the secretary left the room they sat down with the files. Quinn asked, 'What exactly are we looking for, sir?'

'There must be something in one of the Fellow's background that will connect them with the Beck woman,' he answered, engrossed in his own efforts. 'I should have pursued this earlier. Organise them by date of engagement. I'm interested in anyone who's come to St. Gregory's during the past fifteen years.'

It didn't take long to narrow the list to just five persons. They set the other files aside. 'That's it, then. Asquith, Burton-Strachey, Campbell, Soames, and Westgate. Where do we go next?'

McDermott was thumbing through each of the files as she spoke. 'Something someone said recently reminded me that—hello, what's this when it's at home?' He pulled out a letter of recommendation in support of one of the Fellows for a teaching position at St. Gregory's.

Quinn looked at the document and for a moment was baffled. Then she spotted the return address. She looked at McDermott as though he'd just discovered the holy grail. 'Sir, that's it! How did you know?'

'I'll tell you later,' he replied, packing up the other files. Ignoring Ancombe's stipulation he folded the document and put it in his jacket pocket. 'Tell the constables to move the car round the corner and wait for instructions. I don't want anyone getting the wind up when they see a couple of uniforms hanging about.' When Quinn returned McDermott had obtained Anscombe's master key to the college, over the Principal's deep misgivings.

Twenty minutes later McDermott and Quinn were carefully examining the contents of one of the offices, meticulously replacing each object in turn. Quinn paused in the midst of sorting through the contents of a desk drawer. 'What exactly are we looking for, sir?'

'I can't be sure—I only know that we'll recognise it if—make that *when*—we find it,' he answered, apparently engrossed in his own efforts. 'It's a hundred to one shot that—hello, what's this when it's at home?' he asked, withdrawing his arm from behind a row of books on an upper shelf. In his hand was a small pearl-coloured leather handbag. Placing the bag on the desk he gently prodded the flap open with his pen and tipped the contents onto the desktop. Inside were a change purse, a ring with three keys on it, some tissues, an assortment of loose coins and lip gloss, a small mirror and a comb. There was also a London Transport Oyster Card and a student identification card issued by St. Gregory's College. McDermott extracted it carefully, using his pocket handkerchief to handle it by the edges. The name on the card was Sheila Bannerman. The photo was unquestionably that of Sally Beck.

Quinn's voice was barely a whisper. 'What do we do now, sir?'

'We wait, I suppose. I hadn't counted on half the faculty skiving off for the afternoon.'

Her mobile rang, and Quinn turned away and listened for a moment, mumbled something, then rang off. Then she turned back to McDermott. 'Sir, I've just had a call from George. He tried to reach you, but apparently your phone is dead. He says we should return to the station immediately. Something to do with Asquith.'

McDermott was stunned. Had he been proved wrong yet again? He tried his phone, but realized he'd left it on in the Park, and the battery had given out. After considering his options he carefully wrapped the bag in his handkerchief and, placing it inside his coat, walked to the door. He looked around the room, and motioned Quinn out, locking the door behind him. He glanced up and down the passageway, and walked quickly toward the administrative wing at the front of the building. He left by the nearest door and walked through the entranceway and down the street to where the area car was parked. Once there he instructed one officer to return to the College and position himself outside the door in question. McDermott described his quarry in detail, and told him to detain anyone answering that description. The constable indicated that he understood and started off toward the college entrance.

THE TRAFFIC WAS HEAVY, and another twenty minutes passed before McDermott and Quinn arrived at the station. McDermott burst into his office, startling Ridley, who was on the telephone. He motioned to McDermott that he'd be off shortly. When he put down the telephone he said, 'That were Askew's brief. Seems he's ready to make a full statement.'

'Why? What's going on?' asked McDermott uncomprehendingly.

Ridley flashed a wide grin. 'Tox Lab came back with results on his clothes and those bank notes. You were right about traces of drugs. But it weren't merely street drugs. It were nearly pure heroin. Seems Askew's connected to a major supplier here. 'Spect he's lookin' at a long stretch inside. Reckon once he talks to his lawyer he'll ready to cough—dealers, suppliers, the lot. He'll want to know what we can do for 'im in return.'

'Well done, George. We'll call his brief and arrange for another interview. Sounds as though we're making progress at last.' He paused to assess the implications of these latest developments. McDermott was certain he knew who had killed Sally Beck. But was it possible that he was dealing with two unrelated murders? He still had a problem accepting that there were two killers at St. Gregory's, and that each had struck within the space of a single week.

THIRTY FIVE

At St. Gregory's College most people were preparing for the weekend. News of Boothroyd's appointment as Principal had by now made the rounds, and the Burton-Stracheys, attempting to put the best face on things, prepared to throw a small celebratory dinner party for him, mindful of the fact that he would soon be in a position to influence Miles' fate. Burton-Strachey rationalised that the only real expense involved was the food, since he had laid down the wine cellar over the past decade, and it had long since been paid for. Ever the sour loser, Sidney Westgate had declined his invitation, electing instead to remain in his rooms, where he considered his own options. He and Boothroyd had never been close, and that was unlikely to change. Bateman, required by his duties to remain on call, settled down in his quarters to indulge his secret passion, watching *Eastenders* with a can of bitter. Griffith-Jones was packing for a brief personal leave, arguing he was feeling poorly. He checked his pockets to confirm that he had his train ticket to visit his sister in Wales, and then, taking two Gravol tablets for the journey, carefully closed and locked his door, returning a few moments later to retrieve his travel bag.

Clarissa Soames passed Griffith-Jones on his way out. 'I'll see you in a few days,' he said cheerfully. 'I'm off to visit my sister.'

'You're off,' she replied ambiguously.

Soames continued on her way, crossing the quadrangle and passing through the dining hall. As she opened the door connecting the dining hall to the fellows' lodgings she came to a dead stop: there was a uniformed officer pacing in the corridor beyond. At the moment he was facing the other way, distracted by a noise from the quad. She closed the door silently, and made her way back into the dining room, where she pondered the significance of what she'd seen.

A moment later, considerably put out at having his television viewing interrupted, Bateman lumbered out of the Porter's Office and made his way, at an unhurried pace, across the quad and toward the wing which housed the Principal and most of the faculty rooms.

AFTER RINGING ASQUITH'S BRIEF to let her know the most recent developments, McDermott followed up on the document he'd discovered in the college personnel files. He placed a call to Yorkshire, and, after a few minutes of being transferred from one person to another, had the information he needed.

He had just rung off when the telephone rang again. He picked it up immediately. 'McDermott here. Really? Yes, put him on.' After a moment he straightened in his chair. 'What? When? Where are you now? Well, get in there, man. No—break it down if you must. And stay on the line.' There was a long silence and then McDermott went pale. 'Jesus wept! Is she still breathing? No, I'll get an ambulance from this end—you try to get some coffee into her. There's a dining hall at the far end of the corridor. We'll be there directly.'

McDermott slammed down the telephone, leapt from his chair and grabbed for his coat in one motion, heading for the door and gesturing for Ridley and Quinn to join him. 'It's Soames,' he said grimly. 'She spotted our man without him noticing. Worse luck, she managed to get him off the door and get into her rooms. She's tried to top herself using the same medication that did Campbell in!' He paused briefly in the outer office. 'Marsh, get an ambulance over to St. Gregory's right away—attempted suicide. And have a car and driver standing by downstairs immediately. Full drill—blues and twos.'

In contrast to the drive earlier that afternoon, the trip to St. Gregory's took less than six minutes. By then the ambulance had already arrived. As they pulled into the quadrangle, two paramedics emerged from the building with a stretcher bearing Clarissa Soames. McDermott was out of the car before it came to a full stop. 'How is she?' he hollered to the attendants.

'I've seen better, sir. At her age...' He left the sentence unfinished.

'Well, do your best,' he urged, and made for the door.

'Bloody hell!' one of the men said as he opened the rear door of the ambulance. 'What does he think we do, anyway?'

While the uniformed Sergeant positioned one constable at the gate and another on the door to the building to deter onlookers, McDermott marched down the corridor to where a small knot of people had already gathered. Anscombe was there, as was Westgate, Trewilliger, and Bateman and Mrs. Coates, along with several members of the kitchen staff. The Principal looked decidedly ill.

He pushed his way past them, ignoring their questions. If Anscombe looked pale, the young officer was positively green.

'I'm sorry, sir. I had no idea—' Ridley and Quinn had caught up to McDermott, and closed the door behind them.

'What happened?' McDermott snapped.

'I got this call—'

'What call?'

'I'm trying to tell you, sir. Not ten minutes after you left the porter came over and said there was this telephone call for me, from you—insisted it was urgent.'

McDermott saw at once. 'And you left your post to answer it?' he asked incredulously. 'What did you think this thing is for?' he asked, jabbing at the portable radio attached to the constable's chest.

'Yes sir. I mean, I know I shouldn't, but I thought—I guess I didn't think.' The officer looked miserable.

'You got that right,' McDermott ranted, then brought his anger down a notch. 'Ok. What happened next?'

'Well, sir, when I picked up the telephone there was no one on the line. I debated calling in, but decided if it was you you'd try to get me again. After a minute or so, when you didn't ring back, I returned to my post.'

'And realised you'd been had.'

'Well, yessir. After a few minutes,' the constable admitted. 'I tried the door, and it was locked, just like before. Then I got to thinking. I radioed the duty Sergeant, and when he heard I'd left my post he put me straight through to you.'

McDermott was wrestling with his anger, telling himself that he'd committed his own share of blunders in this case. 'All right, get a grip on—what's your name, anyway?'

'Wells, sir. And I wish I was at the bottom of one now.'

McDermott smiled in spite of himself. 'All right, Wells. It was a damned foolish thing to do, but you were up against a clever woman.' He looked around the room. 'I don't suppose she left a note?'

'Oh, yessir.' Wells rummaged in the upper vest pocket of his tunic. 'I knew you'd want it kept safe.'

'God help us.' McDermott snatched the paper out of the man's hand and unfolded it carefully, trying not to damage any prints that might still be there. He scanned it briefly, then passed it to Quinn, who'd put on latex gloves by then. She read it with George looking over her shoulder:

Inspector McDermott:

So it's come to this. I feared it would.

When I saw the officer on my door that you had puzzled it out I knew my options were quickly disappearing.

It was almost like a game, wasn't it? But you must believe me that I was not merely playing with you. You proved to be a most formidable adversary. When you questioned Asquith's pose that evening at the Principal's dinner I knew that the wheels had been set in motion. I realised too late that using the Gertrude Stein play as an alibi had been, shall I say, 'inopportune.'

You must be wondering why I found it necessary to go to such brutal lengths. I assure you, it was not done lightly. I do not make a practice of resorting to violence, nor do I condone its use. That I have come to use it myself I find almost as humiliating as having my private life exposed.

About ten years ago in Yorkshire, Sally Beck—at least that was how I knew her—had been assigned to my care as her housemistress at The Caxton School, my previous post. Following her grandmother's death we were both in need of comfort, for quite different reasons, and found our solace in mutual intimacy. But our relationship as teacher and pupil had been poisoned; I could see it in her eyes. It wasn't long afterwards that her work began to slip, and then she started missing classes. I lived in dread that she would reveal our relationship. When she told the Headmistress she was leaving school, I was actually relieved.

I didn't hear from her again until recently. Not long after Sally left I moved to London and came to St. Gregory's. I thought I was beginning a new life. I had no idea she would turn up here as well.

I suppose you have learned of Eunice Finch's death. Not long after I arrived at Caxton I met Eunice, who taught mathematics there, and she and I became lovers. I flatter myself that we were not unlike Stein and Toklas, save one difference: each of us treated the other as an equal. But she learned she had cancer, and less than ten months later she went into palliative care. She put on a brave face, but we both knew she'd never leave alive. She asked me to help her.

One day the pain became unbearable. I could see it in her eyes. She was on a morphine drip. She looked at me pleadingly, and I could not bear to see her suffer further.

It was not difficult to increase her morphine drip until she became unconscious. When her heart monitor alarm went off, I simply reset the machine before the nurse responded. It proved to be enough. There was one terrible moment when her physician looked like he knew what I had done, but he didn't say anything. He knew it was only a matter of time. Though I miss her terribly, I don't regret what I did.

And now I find myself in a similar position, facing a lifetime punishment myself, but for actions for which I am quite clearly responsible. How the Greeks would have approved!

Sally and I were from different worlds; I never imagined she would turn up here. She did not attempt to blackmail me, but she blamed me for her changed circumstances, and was determined that I should suffer as she had done. When she threatened to expose me I knew I would have to silence her. I followed her, not knowing what I would do, and when I saw the bus approaching as she stepped into the street it all became so clear, so easy. I took her handbag afterwards, fearing there might be something in it that would incriminate me. That part was actually quite easy: I simply retrieved it from the street during the confusion, and swept it into my own bag, which was quite large. Later I smashed her mobile and threw both in the Thames. At the inquest, when there was no mention of St. Gregory's, I really thought I had got away with it. In retrospect I suppose you wanted it to appear that way.

I regret having killed Fraser Campbell. At our first meeting in the common room you asked where we all were when Sally had died. I said I was in my study, preparing my lecture notes. When Campbell told me that he'd been in Russell Square at lunchtime I suspected he'd seen me returning from High Holborn, and thus was in a position to expose me.

I knew I had to act quickly. I went to Campbell's rooms that evening, ostensibly to borrow a book. The man behaved like a cat amongst the pigeons smug in his conviction that he somehow had the Principalship, as he put it, 'all wrapped up'. When he claimed you had been lied to that afternoon in the SCR, the man virtually sealed his own fate.

I offered to make tea. I remember that I actually said 'Shall I be mother?' You have no idea how that grated. Anyway, I slipped Griffith-Joneses' medication—half of it, actually—into his cup. I'd tasted it earlier that afternoon and found it quite bland, but just to

be certain I used Lapsang Souchong to mask the taste. Quite odious,
really. Tell Griffith-Jones he really must be more careful with his
medications. After twenty minutes or so of conversation Campbell
became drowsy and lost consciousness. I poured more whisky down
his throat, just to be certain, and put the note on the desk, hoping
you'd take it for what it seemed. You can imagine my chagrin later
when I learned that it was Burton-Strachey he had seen, and not
me. The gods must have enjoyed their little joke.

I must end this here. I hear your man returning, and sooner or
later he will put two and two together and investigate. I saved the
remaining capsules for just this contingency. You will understand
that I do not wish to suffer the indignities of a public trial, nor the
humiliation of seeing my colleagues make vulgar jokes at my expense.
Although I cannot stop them making their remarks, I can at least
avoid having to listen to them, and the prospect of prison is equally
repugnant. Well done, Inspector. How many other criminals-who-
are-also-victims do you number amongst your successes?

Clarissa Soames

'My God,' Quinn whispered.

'Yes, it does rather take the gilt off the gingerbread, doesn't it? A young woman who only wanted to put the past behind her; the Short's lives turned upside down, if only briefly; Campbell murdered unnecessarily; Burton-Strachey's financial misdeeds brought to light; Asquith's drug-dealing unearthed; and an entire institution's reputation jeopardised—all due to a moment of weakness in a grieving woman. What was it Soames asked me in her rooms? *'Do policemen enjoy poking about in the recesses of the human soul, exposing its dark corners?'* Perhaps she was right: maybe when all is said and done we're just licensed voyeurs. It doesn't bear thinking about.' McDermott's mind turned to the Townsends: their crisis, he recognised, also had been instrumental in solving this case. *More than enough suffering to go around.*

WORKING ON THEIR REPORTS back at Charing Cross station Ridley said, 'I still don't get it, Guv. How'd you know Soames was behind it all?'

'There were simply too many anomalies, George. First there was the matter of the handbag. Remember, several people who witnessed the accident said they thought they'd seen one. And yet, despite a thorough search of the area, it never turned up.'

'But we explained that—remember? We decided someone—a kid most likely—'ad seen it lying there in the street and made off with it.'

'Yes, but think about it, George. If a kid nicked it, he'd have been taking a risk. He might stick it under his jacket for a bit—long enough to find an isolated alleyway—but he'd hardly keep it with him longer than absolutely necessary. Odds are he'd have pocketed the contents—cash and bank cards—and then tossed it in the first rubbish bin he came to, where it would have turned up. No, that was the first thing that bothered me. And then I asked myself who would be inconspicuous if she was seen with a handbag? And the answer was: only another woman.'

'But that'd be takin' a big chance. What if someun' saw her pick it up?'

'Then she'd only to say that she saw the accident and was retrieving the girl's bag for her. It was a calculated risk, of course, but not nearly so risky as pushing her into the street in the first place. She must have thanked her lucky stars when the Beck girl decided to cross the street between the two lorries— it gave her just the cover she needed. Then there was the matter of alibis.'

Quinn looked up. 'Sir?'

'Virtually everyone else had an alibi for one death or the other. Anscombe was best off: he had an alibi for both: he was in the dining hall when Sally Beck was killed, and in a meeting with two Members of the Board when Campbell was murdered. Westgate had no alibi for Campbell's death, but was in the dining hall when the Beck woman died. You agree that both Griffith-Jones and Trewilliger were non-starters?'

She nodded.

'Well then, that left Asquith, Boothroyd, and Soames. For a while it certainly looked as if Asquith was our man: he had no good alibi for either death, and, as we discovered, plenty of motive. In fact, if I'd not taken that walk in the Gardens at noon, I'd probably be charging him now.'

'I don't understand. What did the park have to do with anything?'

McDermott leaned back in his chair and sipped at a coffee long since grown cold. 'Everything. As I was walking, trying to think things through,

I saw a pair of young men holding hands. That set me to thinking about homosexuality—you recall that my Godchild, who is a lesbian, tried to kill herself just two days ago. Well, that set me to thinking about why it has to be like that—why in this day and age people are still persecuted for their sexual orientation. I remembered that the Greeks accepted gay relations fairly openly. I recalled seeing several books in Soames' rooms that dealt indirectly with repressed sexuality. She complained about men who always had to reduce everything to sex. That was a clever move on her part: instead of denying it outright and putting me on the alert, she tried to shame me into changing the subject myself—and it almost worked. Finally, there was the business about Sally Beck's being from Yorkshire.'

'Excuse me?' Quinn looked confused.

'When I visited Soames in her rooms she attempted to pass off the Beck girl's death as a case of a naïve young woman from Yorkshire coming south and somehow getting in over her head.'

'A plausible explanation, sir,' Quinn said. 'She wouldn't be the first one.'

'Quite right, Willie. Except, if you recall, I never mentioned that Sally Beck was from Yorkshire. Not in our initial interview with the faculty in the Senior Common Room, nor later. And classes had only begun two days earlier. If Sally was just another faceless student, as Soames alleged, she couldn't possibly have known that much about her background.'

Ridley broke out in a broad smile. 'Hoist on 'er own petard, then.'

McDermott was surprised at George's allusion, but before he could manage a suitable reply the telephone rang. He picked it up. 'McDermott. Yes? Really? When? I see. No, none that I'm aware of, but I'll look into it. Thanks for giving it your best.'

He replaced the receiver and reached for his coffee. 'That was the hospital. It seems Soames had a weak heart. She died in the ambulance before it arrived.'

Quinn sighed. 'Another victim.'

'In a way, certainly,' McDermott admitted. 'But she murdered three people, if you include her lover, and I've no doubt she'd have killed again if she thought it necessary. At least this way the college—and the Becks—are spared the publicity of a trial.'

Quinn had a thought. 'Are you going to tell the Becks about their daughter's life here in London?'

'I don't see why I should. It will only give them heartache.' He paused. 'You know, all this began with her gran's legacy, which enabled her to go to the Caxton School in Whitby, where she met Soames. That's when her life started to come apart. Once she arrived at St. Gregory's and recognized Soames, it was a given that more trouble would follow. Ironic, isn't it? Her gran couldn't possibly have known that her good wishes for Sally would set in motion a chain of events that would lead to three people's deaths, including her granddaughter's. A bittersweet legacy.' What was it Quinn had said earlier? *Small mercies.*

McDermott drained his cup, making a face at the bitter residue that had settled in the bottom. 'One small ray of sunshine in all this, though. Sally Beck's bank balance can be given over to the Becks. We can explain it as the residue of her gran's legacy and her savings from work, which in a sense is true enough. They can use the money, and they'll be pleased to think of their daughter as living frugally and planning for her studies.'

He looked at his watch. 'I should tell Galbraith before he leaves for the day. Take any calls, will you? I can't imagine anything else happening today.'

AS HE ENTERED THE SUPERINTENDENT'S OUTER OFFICE McDermott almost collided with the Assistant Chief Commissioner, who was just on his way out. Both he and Galbraith wore smug expressions; Galbraith's promotion must be just a matter of time, then. He couldn't help drawing a comparison with the machinations that had occurred over Anscombe's vacancy. 'McDermott,' the ACC asked, 'Any progress on those deaths at St. What's-its-name?'

'Yes sir. We've got a result. We collared our man - in this case, a woman, actually.'

The commissioner's jaw dropped momentarily. 'You don't say! Well done. Always knew you had it in you, my boy. Galbraith, you take good care of this young man. He's a comer.' He closed the outer door behind him.

The Superintendent gave him a hard look. 'I hope you weren't having him on, McDermott. The ACC doesn't take kindly to having his leg pulled.'

'Never more serious, sir. Can we talk?'

Twenty minutes later McDermott emerged from Galbraith's office, having briefed Galbraith on the case. He'd also stressed Ridley's contribution to solving it, and noted that he seemed to be well on his way to forging a good working relationship with Wilhelmina Quinn. Galbraith seemed pleased, their earlier differences over Ridley's retirement forgotten.

McDermott made a mental note to drop in on the Boothroyds on the way home and give them the news. The college had been riven by scandal, and there would be a lot of rebuilding needed; but he'd done more than his share, he reflected, in rooting out the deadwood. Boots could begin with a clean slate.

MCDERMOTT'S CONVERSATION WITH GALBRAITH had taken longer than expected, and it was dusk when he made his way back to his office. It was his turn to be smug, having learned that DCI Loach would not be replacing Galbraith after all. He knew it was petty, but he couldn't help thinking that he'd like to be a fly on the wall when Loach got the news.

As he passed through the incident room McDermott stopped and stared at Ridley and Quinn, who were working on their computers writing up the case reports. They both looked as though they could do with a rest. 'Come on, you two, let's pack it in. There's nothing that won't still be here tomorrow.' As they made their way down the stairs, McDermott added, 'Treat yourselves to a drink. Have a good evening. We've done well, all things considered.'

The older man beamed and made for the Gent's on the ground floor. Pulling on her coat, Quinn caught up with McDermott as they made their way down to the parking garage. 'And you, sir?' she asked. 'Treating yourself as well?'

'As a matter of fact, I am. Daphne Fielding has tickets for the Barbican.'

'Really? What's playing?'

'It's her treat,' McDermott said. 'A Celtic band out of Glasgow, kitted out in tartans and leather, I understand. I think they're called *Filthy Habits*.'

Wilhemina Quinn was still laughing when she left the building.

Acknowledgements

In writing this book I had the great fortune of having access to many experienced crime writers, including Peter James, Louise Penny, Cath Staincliffe, Eric Brown, Peter Kirby, Michael E. Rose, Phyllis Smallman, Mike Ripley, and Maureen Jennings. As well, several officers and detectives at the Met, either retired or on active service, have contributed valuable information and saved me more than once from committing embarrassing errors. They include DS Claire Hutcheon of the Art & Antiques Unit, Inspector Andrew Gorzynski of the Metropolitan Police (retired), Carol Sullivan of the Royal Parks Operational Command Unit, and Met officer PC Atkinson of New Scotland Yard. PC Matt Parnell of the Holborn Police Station also unwittingly provided nuggets of colour whilst processing my own case file when I had my pocket picked in London! Finally, Bruce Redwine, James Wilson, Roya Abouzia, and the skilled folks at FriesenPress have each helped turn a rough stone into a much more polished work. Any errors remaining, as well as deliberate inventions in the service of the plot are, of course, mine alone.

Ridley's War

At a military reunion in a rural village in Yorkshire, two generations of families from dramatically different circumstances come together in a compelling mystery of guilt, greed, fear, and war:

Gordon Baker-Simms and his spoiled son Julian: both born into a life of privilege, would they kill to preserve it?

Ben Richards and his troubled son Jason: does a father's duty extend to concealing his son's crimes?

Samuel Hearn and his son Noah; used to being feared and suspected, it came with the territory when you were gypsies.

Bert and George Ridley: one a veteran of WW II, the other a CID detective. Both would suffer; one was destined to die.

Ridley's War is scheduled to be released in 2018.

ABOUT THE AUTHOR

After a successful academic career that included teaching crime fiction and creative writing, Jim Napier turned to writing full time. Since then he has published nearly five hundred reviews, interviews, and articles about crime writers, both in print and on multiple Internet sites, and has participated in writing workshops in Britain and Canada. He has chaired or participated in panels on crime fiction at Montreal's Bleu Metropolis literary festival and at the Canadian crime writing festival, Bloody Words. He has twice served on juries for the Arthur Ellis Awards for Canadian crime writing, and in 2010 he chaired the Arthur Ellis Awards. Along with such notable crime writers as Louise Penny, Peter James, Sophie Hannah, Simon Brett, Marcia Talley and Rhys Bowen he contributed to an anthology on the craft of crime writing titled *Now Write! Mysteries*, published by Tarcher/Penguin. In 2012 he was commissioned to write biographies for several Canadian crime writers for the Canadian Encyclopedia, and also joined Louise Penny in co-chairing a fiction writing workshop at the Knowlton LitFest. *Legacy* is his first crime novel in the Colin McDermott Mysteries; the second, *Ridley's War*, is nearing completion.

Legacy is published by Friesen Press and distributed by Ingram, and is available at over 35,000 online booksellers worldwide including Amazon, Barnes & Noble, and Chapters. eBooks are distributed through the Apple iBookstore, Amazon Kindle store, Google Play Bookstore, Nook Store and the Kobo Store.

If you enjoyed this book, please consider posting a review on Amazon.com. It needn't be long or detailed, simply your honest reaction. It's quite easy to do so: simply go to Amazon.com/books/Jim Napier/Legacy– and thank you for your time!

Further:

For more on the *Colin McDermott series*, or to contact the author, go to http://JimNapierMysteries.com

Also on Facebook at Facebook/Jim Napier Mysteries

For reviews, interviews, and more, see http://deadlydiversions.com

Printed in Canada